# WILD BASEBALL ROMANCE

# MARI LOYAL

*For everyone who has been
caged in their minds.
You can be free.*

# HEAT LEVEL AND CONTENT WARNINGS

Before starting this novel, I encourage you to first read this section to determine whether it's the right fit for your personal circumstances.

This book is closed door romance, which means there is innuendo, kisses are descriptive, and characters don't shy away from their attraction.

There is mild to moderate use of cuss words, particularly in emotional moments. However, there is no use of f-bombs, religious blasphemies, or known ableist terms.

The heroine is cheated on by her ex at the start of the book. The hero's family was emotionally abusive and have caused him trauma. There are depictions of near- and one full panic attack. Adult characters may consume alcohol on the page.

Visit my website mariloyal.com for general content warnings that apply to my books.

# CHAPTER 1
# ROSE

## LAST SUMMER

Not to be a baseball nerd, but sometimes in life you have to make a risky play. Especially when you're trying to make things official with the star pitcher of a professional baseball team.

I make one last check in front of the mirror and nod to myself. My outfit is just in the range of librarian chic and playful, a red sundress with white polka dots that shows a hint of skin, under a light white cardigan that is cropped at my waist, paired with cute Mary Janes. Two simple pearl earrings poke from under my abundant curls. No one who sees me walk out to the parking lot would ever assume that I have a heart attack-inducing little number under this cute outfit.

But that's because nobody in this building has any idea that I'm about to mount one final, hopefully fulminating attack on Ben Williams.

"Tú puedes," I tell my reflection, closing one fist and pumping it.

Oh, hold on. My makeup's a bit smudged.

I rummage inside my small but mighty makeup case, retrieving some essentials to fix up the whole area around my lips.

In all fairness, it's way too hot to wear cardigans and I'm sweating. But the sundress is girlier than anything else I typically wear to hang out around a bunch of baseball players brimming with testosterone. I just put it on to see if it got any reaction from Ben.

The plan is flawless. There was no game today and we're home, so typically what the guys do is just train and watch film. I was sure we'd run into each other in the corridors, at the cafeteria, or maybe while recording clips for social media… but we haven't. Not even once.

It's fine, though. That was just phase one of the big play that I've dubbed Operation Catch a Boyfriend. Now I'm ready for phase two.

After smacking my lips to test the tint, I return all my knickknacks back into my purse and zip it up. I finished my video edits early and scheduled a delivery of food and flowers at Ben's, timed for my ETA. I know for a fact that he and the rest of the team have a meeting with the coaching staff to debrief for tomorrow's series, so he'll get home late. I estimate that I'll have around an hour to set up and freshen up.

There's some foot traffic on the corridor when I make my way out of the women's restroom. What appears to be half of the team is being herded by part of the training staff.

That includes my roommate Hope Garcia, who waves her arms up and down from the rear. "Chop chop, we don't have all day," she says with clear annoyance. Nearby, her boss does the same.

One of the players notices me standing by the restroom door. "Hey, Mena. No videos this time?" he asks, almost disappointed.

"I'm off duty," I respond in a far too serious voice as if I was a policewoman or something like that.

"Bummer, that would be way more fun than this," he grouches and his buddies around all agree.

"What's the deal?" I whisper at Hope when she pauses beside me.

Shaking her head, she explains, "Beau says we're going to study yesterday's game loss in detail, so you can imagine how excited these bunch of toddlers are about that."

My mind whirs with time estimates. It's not like they're going to take seven hours deconstructing a three hour long game, but it does tell me that Ben may be delayed. I'm going to have to adjust my plans accordingly.

"How long does that typically take?" I inquire in what I hope is a casual tone.

"At this rate, it could be—"

Someone wolf whistles and I don't need two guesses to know it can be no one but Lucky Rivera, even before his voice reaches us. "Please, ladies. You can't stand together like this. It's way too dazzling."

"Move along, Rivera." Hope waves her hands without acknowledging him further.

The team's most notorious flirt chuckles and finally appears in my field of vision, his arm slung around the shoulders of his taller buddy, Cade Starr. The latter is a relatively normal guy—relatively because he has the cowboy good looks that belong more in Hollywood than here, and also because he and Lucky often engage in silly prank wars that give me tons of social media content.

I shake my head to myself, glad that I don't have private dealings with either of those two.

Not just because they're unserious clowns, but also because they're among the top of the team's lookers. The amount of requests that the PR, marketing, and media teams get to do more features of Lucky Rivera and Cade Starr has become kind of a running joke. I can't imagine how stressful it must be for their current or future partners to keep them interested.

Not me, I gravitate toward more normal guys that won't bring out my myriad insecurities. That's what attracted me to Ben in the first place. Yes, he's an elite athlete boasting of a lovely musculature, but he has a boy next door face. He doesn't get confused for an actor or a model, and the mustache he's sporting lately makes him look like the average Midwestern man that he otherwise is.

Average looks, good upbringing, hardworking, and interested in me? Sign me up, baby.

I really thought that was all it would take to make me happy. Ben checks all those things and when he started to take notice of me, I thought I was set—that I had finally found the man of my dreams with whom I could start my own family.

Except there's been one major obstacle: we work together. Ish.

I'm the social media manager for the team, which is fancyspeak for I create content, edit it, and post it on social media. It's nowhere near as simple as it sounds because there's a hierarchy of command I have to follow that includes my boss, the rest of the marketing team, along with the company guidelines, and it's precisely the last ones that throw a wrench in here.

It's not like I'm banned from dating withon the team, but it's true that there aren't many women in the organization and there are exactly zero public couples. Whoever goes first is probably going to get an amount of scrutiny that neither Ben nor I are interested in.

Thus, we've been dating in secret for almost a year.

And I repeat that: *a year*.

But I'm in this to build a life together—not to store a few titillating encounters in hidden corners in the back of my mind, to look back on them fondly from the rocking chair in a retirement home.

Based on the fight we had last week, I'm not sure that Ben is on the same page.

"See you at home?" Hope's voice snaps me out of it.

I jerk my face up to offer her a smile, and she's so busy herding the last of the guys that she doesn't notice anything amiss about it.

How I wish I could tell anyone about what I'm going through with Ben. My roommates and I aren't on pajama-party-every-night level, but I'm sure they'd have really good advice considering that both of them also work for the team.

And more than everyone, I wish I could tell my mom. She's my best friend and confidante, my rock, the one person on this earth who sincerely cares about me.

I'm pretty sure none of them would have approved of a relationship where I'm kept a secret from the beginning, though. Which is why I think my only move left is to brave this with Ben, come as it may.

From there the plan was born: go to Ben's fancy apartment downtown, set up a feast on the table complete with candles and rose petals, toss more petals on the beautifully made bed, lie on said bed and petals in my most show stopping lingerie set and…

Tell him that if he wants this to continue, it *has* to be official. No more being afraid. No more keeping us like a dirty secret.

Speaking of. There's Ben rounding the corner behind everyone else.

My heartbeat flutters higher and higher at the sight of him, like a butterfly lifting into the sky. He hasn't noticed me yet because he's chatting with someone but it's okay, he'll definitely notice me when he finds me on his bed later.

Something gets my attention in the corner of my eye and

my heart stops. I'm momentarily stunned by the contrast of feelings before my brain kicks in.

It's Logan Kim, the main catcher of the team, and inarguably the top looker. He's the one that Ben is chatting with as they walk over. Unlike Ben, though, Logan's eyes are on me. Or rather, they shift from me to Ben, and back to me. It's quick, almost imperceptible, but he fixes a cocked eyebrow my way that speaks volumes.

I don't know what expression I had on my face that gave me away, and I try to wipe it. But I know it's too late and Logan Kim literally just realized I have a thing with the team's star pitcher.

I'm supposed to head the opposite direction and now that the corridor is clear, I pick myself up to do precisely that. As I approach, Ben's words drift to my ears at last and he's so into his tale of how one type of pitch felt compared to another one during practice, that he doesn't even notice when I walk by.

The farther I get from them, the harder my heart beats. I place a hand on my chest, willing it to calm down. I'm not sure if it's because I just gave myself away to the unofficial captain, who happens to be the most shrewd guy on the team—or if it's because my plan is officially a go.

I hop in my blue Toyota Corolla and do a few breathing exercises I've seen Hope do after her intense workouts. Turning the vehicle on, I figure that I still have to go to Ben's to receive the catering order. Maybe I can watch a show to unwind as I wait.

See? The Logan Kims of the world are the reason why it's imperative that Ben and I become public.

I don't think he's a blabbermouth like Lucky Rivera, but Logan is pretty by the books. It's that quality what has made him the leader of the team, and I have no doubt he'll pay more attention to Ben and I from now on. The second he catches us in one of those hidden corners that Ben likes, we're toast.

I brave downtown traffic at rush hour while listening to my dad's favorite salsa singer, Oscar D'León. I didn't get to meet Dad, but Mom passed along enough of his idiosyncrasies that I can still feel him in my life. This is one—apparently Oscar calmed him down, and now he does the same for me.

The catering bags await outside Ben's apartment door when I arrive, which is slightly annoying because they're early. I take a deep breath and start humming Llorarás, one of Oscar's most famous songs, and gather all the bags to bring them inside. The food and I are going to wait who knows how long, so I end up putting it in the fridge.

That only burns me ten minutes at most. Whipping around, I take in the dark of the apartment and flutter about turning lights on, fluffing pillows, lowering the thermostat five degrees so I'm not sweating through my makeup anymore. I finally chuck the cardigan off and flop on the couch, grabbing a couple of cushions to I make myself at home.

I palm around searching for the remote, but maybe being so comfortable finally makes my adrenaline crash because my body slacks, I become one with the soft velvet, and close my eyes without ever turning the TV on.

*

The darkness is pierced by a giggle.

My brain latches onto that anomaly and starts to focus. I remember having turned on all the lights, so it shouldn't be so dark. With a little groan, I turn my face and find myself breathing better. It's because I had buried my face into a cushion. I open an eye by a slit and shut it quickly. The overhead lights almost gave me a headache.

That's when I notice the giggle again. Did I leave the TV on?

I crack the other eye open and it falls on the black TV

screen. Yeah, that checks out. Pretty sure I faded away before even finding the remote.

"Oh, Ben."

Wait a second. That's not my voice.

I spring to a seat, opening and closing my eyes to catch my bearings. Another sound comes next, this one different. The same one that people make when they eat really delicious food, or when…

My head whips in its direction.

There, up against the door, are Ben and a woman tangled together. All I can see is his back from here and for some reason, I latch onto the fact that he's wearing one of his favorite date outfits. Fancy jeans and an expensive polo that makes him look like a frat boy. He's wearing the woman's legs around his waist like a belt, using his hands to keep her in place while he devours her mouth.

For a moment, all I manage is to swallow the cotton in my mouth.

Trembling, I reach for the coffee table where I left my phone. It's a few minutes past nine, which means I was out like a light for three hours. But as the screen lights up, I notice a text that Ben sent me around two hours ago.

**James Bond BF**

Hey babe, we're finishing up pretty late here and I need some rest. See you in tomorrow's flight?

*Rest?*

I glance back up and the woman's hands are now working his polo up, while he buries his head against her neck.

My hands are still unsteady as I center my phone's camera and take a quick video of the action, and snap a few pictures.

Occupational hazard, maybe, but I'll need proof that this happened so that I never consider being a guy's secret ever again.

They're so involved in each other that they don't even hear

me get up from the couch and grab my things. It's only when I'm a few steps away from them that I clear my throat, say, "Excuse me," and they stop.

By this point, Ben is shirtless and his jeans are unfastened. The woman's legs slide down until she stands behind him and before the door I need to exit. Slowly, my ex turns over his shoulder. His eyes widen.

"B-Babe?"

"No," I snap through gritted teeth. "Miss Mena to you."

"Er, I can explain it. This—"

"Excuse me," I repeat even louder, leaning to the side until I find the woman.

There's only marginal relief that she's someone I don't know at all, but the confusion on her face tells me she literally didn't expect another woman to be here. Which tells me this asshole obviously didn't tell her he had a girlfriend.

Is this why he really never wanted to make us official?

Heat rushes to my eyes and I have to steel every muscle in my body against the visceral need to break down. Instead, I set my attention on her in her date dress, similar to mine—tight, short and pretty. "Can you please step aside? I need to leave."

"I—I—" Her jaw slackens. She looks up at Ben Williams and back at me. "Did you just call her babe?"

"No, I…" He grunts. "Rose, wait a moment."

He dares put his hand on me and I jerk free right away. I cast a withering glare at him that works—he does, in fact, shrink a little. "I guess I should thank you."

"What?" He scrunches up his face.

"You just saved me from humiliating myself for you." I shrug as if none of this was important. As if my heart wasn't breaking into a million pieces. "We're over, Ben Williams. Don't you talk to me or touch me ever again."

"But—" he splutters.

"FYI," I tell the other woman. "He dated me in secret for

almost a year. I don't know if it's because you're his official girl-friend or if it's because he has a dozen of us, but you should dump his ass too." With that, I turn to the door and open it.

He makes a grab for me but it's almost comical. His jeans choose that moment to slide down, which is right when an elderly couple walk by out in the corridor.

"Honey, isn't that Ben Williams, the Orlando Wild pitch-er?" the woman asks.

The old man shakes his head. "Nah, that's clearly some sleaze."

Spurred by the comment, the other woman leans down to grab her heels and purse. Without dallying, she follows me out of Ben's apartment in her bare feet.

That's the moment I decide that I'm done chasing the happily ever after that my parents enjoyed briefly.

I'm done with dating and men—period.

# CHAPTER 2
# LOGAN

## END OF MARCH

Yeah, yeah. I get that winning the first game of the season feels nice, especially when it's against the Denver Riders that Ben Williams left our team for. Revenge and all that. But this is just game one of the first series. There's a whole season ahead of us and you'd think we just won the World Series with how everyone's celebrating.

I rub my ear under the shower spray, but it doesn't dull their hollering and laughing that the wall tiles amplify. Someone—I'm gonna take an educated guesstimate that it's Lucky Rivera—grabs a bottle of shampoo and sprays it all around like it's champagne, and soon the rest of the stooges are doing the same. If someone slips and ends their season early they're gonna deserve it.

Perhaps I should be thankful that they're saving me the effort of soaping myself. But I do turn around because I have no interest in eating shampoo.

"Did you see that?"

"That was amazing, bro!"

"We got this! We *so* got this!"

"Our battery's sick. I bet Williams is eating his words."

Williams's words refers to a little interview he partook in yesterday. A *SPORTY* News reporter caught him after practice and asked what his feelings were about opening the season against the team that nurtured him as a star pitcher.

"I don't feel very much, to be honest with you," he said with that shit eating face I've never been able to stand. "I'm just glad to have left an organization where growth is impossible, and eager to show them just how much I have developed as a Rider."

Puh-lease. Who does he think he is? Pedro Martinez?

Meanwhile the bunch of clowns I call my teammates are chanting Cade Starr's name, and even I have to admit it's funny. Starr was a decent relief pitcher last year—good, even—just not as remarkable as Williams. But dude has had stratospheric growth over Spring Training, and I don't know if the guys are chanting his name because they recognize Starr as the example of the growth Williams claimed is impossible here, or simply because the cowboy pitched a perfect game tonight.

I wipe a smirk off my face and finish washing myself. Ever since Hope Garcia started working for the team, it became convention to at least put on our underwear by the lockers behind the shower stalls. Not that we really think anything would shock her at this point—especially not now that she's publicly dating one of us—but it's a respect thing.

Since I have perfected the art of do-not-screw-with-me though, the clowns allow me safe passage to the lockers. It's a combination of the mean glare I was born with, plus the tattoos. The many tattoos.

After making quick work of toweling and putting on the first layers, I'm about to taste freedom from the noise when someone all but tackles me from the side.

"Look at you, all quiet in your little corner," Rivera shouts in my ear, his arm hooking around my neck and forcing me to bend down.

Something like a growl comes out of me. "Take your butt away from me, Rivera, before I punch you wherever I can reach."

The threat is credible enough that he steps away. I slice a glare at him, wishing I could wash the patches of me that were in contact with the little pest again.

He folds his arms, his face dripping with amusement and water. "I know you won't want to talk about this, but I do want to acknowledge that I know you're the one who's raising that cub into a full blown tiger." He jerks his head somewhere behind him, and I don't have to ask who he's referring to. We both know this is about Starr.

"Whatever," I grunt as I towel my hair. "And if you're going to make an allegory, at least make it with the proper mascot."

"What are baby alligators even called?" He scratches his head through wet curls.

"Shoo." I wave my hand, uninterested in the rest of this conversation.

With one last chuckle, the guy peels himself off the lockers and goes find someone else to bother.

If I was annoyed before he dropped by, I'm even more so after he leaves. I wasn't expecting to hear that from the most happy go lucky—pun intended—guy on the team. His boundless energy, the pranks, the terrible jokes that range from Dad-level to racy, make it easy to forget that he does have a sharp brain in his skull socket. Rivera noticing that I'm the puppeteer behind Starr's progress should make my chest swell, maybe even make me join in the revelry.

Not when I'm in conversations to get traded somewhere else.

I hang the towel around my neck to rummage through my

backpack until I find my phone. The screen lights up with some texts from Pete Kaplan, my agent.

> **KAPLAN**
>
> That was wild—ha!
>
> I could see your price tag going up with every inning

That makes my eye twitch and I stuff the device back in the backpack before any of these hawks can read the texts. I haven't given Beau or the rest of the staff a heads up about my plans because, well, there are no official plans yet. Kaplan and I are in the very early exploration phase of seeing which teams are looking for a catcher, and the fact that I won't accept demotions will no doubt complicate the process.

For all intents and purposes, I'm committed to this team and that's how it's going to remain until the very last second.

I'm one of the first ones out of the facility. We play in our turf for this series and the next, which is why I'm interested in getting as much rest at home away from the stooges, as I possibly can. Fortunately I have a short drive ahead of me, which is great because I'm hungry.

What's not great is that there are two people in the way between me and my Paningale V4 R. I'm about to side step them when I pay more attention.

What the hell are Ben Williams and our social media girl discussing about?

I don't even know if discussing is the right word either. At first I think she's got her arms folded in annoyance, but as I stare a second longer I realize that's not the case. Her arms are wrapped around her torso like she's protecting herself, and Williams is the one who is gesturing around. Angry.

I'm familiar with these body languages. Everyone in my

family has adopted both roles a million times against each other.

Sighing, I look down at the helmet in my hands. A comfortable sofa and a nutritionally balanced meal await at home, and all the sounds I'll listen there are me chewing if that's what I want. Maybe I can listen to an audiobook. Relax. Disconnect from the world and from my own brain.

Nope. My feet make the call and take me directly to the melee.

Clearing my throat, I stop a few paces from them. It's enough to get Williams's attention.

It's obvious how red his face is even under the streetlights. He's breathing hard like he was running at full throttle, and not screaming at a woman.

Meanwhile, her eyebrows are drawn and she glares at the former starting pitcher of our team. A curl has escaped to fall over her face and she huffs hard enough to send it back. I was expecting a sign of fear on her expression but I don't find it. Maybe I could've just kept going to my bike and peeled out of here.

But just to make sure, I ask, "What's going on here?"

"Stay out of this, Kim," Williams barks.

I click my tongue. We formed a battery for two years. He should know by now that the only one I obey is myself.

"Are you harassing our social media girl?" I ask, going for the nuclear option right away because I'm not one to waste time with pleasantries.

"No!"

"Yes." I zero in on Rosalina Mena's response. Slowly, she unfurls her arms from around herself and turns her big brown eyes to me. "You see, Ben and I dated in secret for like a year until I caught him cheating on me. I dumped his ass and moved on. He hasn't, and apparently he thinks that it's my fault he's not getting any action again." She slides a vicious glare at him.

"It is. I know you took pictures—my security camera caught them! Did you put them on the internet?" he hisses and takes one step closer. "Did you—"

I don't even know what in the actual hell I just heard. What I do know is that I'm not going to let this piece of shit get physical. The second he raises a pointy finger at her, I slide in between.

Williams freezes and gradually lifts his face to meet my eyes. It does help that I have tall genes. My father was basically a giant in his day in South Korea, and my mother is a whole runway model from Sweden. This is the one contribution I'll thank them for.

"Whatever it is that you were going to do or say," I mutter very low, hoping she doesn't hear from behind me, "I advise you to shove it up your ass, and I also remind you that there are cameras here."

"You damn—"

"Nuh uh." I shake an index. "Don't say something I'll be forced to make you regret. Turn around and go."

He grits his teeth, which somehow intensifies the red in his face. "This is none of your damn business, Kim."

"You're right." I take a step closer and lower my eyes to his. "But you're going to make it my damn business if you keep bothering Mena. Go. *Now*."

For a moment, Williams continues to breathe like a truck, his eyes blazing with all the hatred that was always living inside of him and he no longer has to hide.

Yeah, I know this guy hated my guts all two years we formed a battery—which I always found interesting when he was the one reaping the fame and the glory from my hard work —but I'm not the petty little shit that he is.

He tries to catch a glimpse of Mena behind me and I make

a point of blocking his view, even though I don't know if she's still behind me or if she took the chance to high tail it out of here. But finally he gets the hint that nothing further is coming from this and he swivels on his heels.

Pretty rude of him to make his team bus wait for his tantrum, and I kindly hope they left his ass behind.

"Thank you, but I had it under control."

I straighten. So she's still here, huh?

Glancing over my shoulder reveals her annoyance. Like she genuinely thinks she didn't need help.

I snort. "Sure, and your body language didn't scream *help*." At last, I put on my helmet and since no further comment comes, I hop on my bike and turn it on.

It's only when the roar subsides to a resting state that I realize she's talking. I turn back to her and she says, "Um, I didn't really mean to spill all the beans like that—I was just so mad and uh…" I take one look at her wringing hands and the way she bites her lower lip, and it's enough to deduce what she wants.

I flip my visor open. "Let's put it this way," I say in a flat tone of voice. "I already guessed some of this and never told a soul, why would I start now?"

Her pretty eyes widen to an impossible extent.

"You two weren't as discreet as you maybe thought." I check my watch. I'd have loved to be lounging at home a half hour ago. "Now, can I go?"

"Y—Yeah."

She's still rooted to the spot, so I have no choice but to walk the bike back out of the parking spot until I'm able to drive away. Her figure's still in the same place when I check the rearview mirror.

# CHAPTER 3
# ROSE

The marketing and broadcasting department of the Orlando Wild team has twenty one people, including me, and we meet every Friday morning in plenum. There's nothing remarkable about this because, unlike the players, we don't have off season down time.

But there's something different today, and it's not just because it's my first department meeting after serving my very short suspension.

I half wonder if someone spiked the coffee with something stronger. Yet, I know it's not because of that. The team won its first series against the Denver Riders, who are a World Series contender. Tonight is game three of the second series against a weaker team, and so far we've won all games.

It's too early to get excited about what this means, but anyone who has worked for this organization for more than a year knows that we've never had as strong a season start before.

Like, ever.

And if anyone should be capitalizing on this, it should be this department.

"—Ramp down the mic'ed up interviews?" one of the

producers is asking. "Polls from fans say they're not very popular in the middle of the broadcast because it distracts players."

My boss, Dave Rogers, director of social media, chimes in, "And this is what we have social media for, ladies and gentlemen." He turns to put me on the spot. "Rosalina, what do our followers say?"

I collect myself while clearing my throat. "Posts on TikTok and Instagram that prominently feature the players are the most viewed, liked, shared, and commented on by far. Unfortunately, much more than replays or team advertising."

"What kind of posts?" one of the marketing managers asks.

"Interviews, Q&As… just anything that shows their personalities," I explain.

"Hmm." She leans back in her chair. "That's great but we need to make sure that whatever we do is to grow the Orlando Wild brand, not the individual players."

"And yet it's the players who are popular," says one of the promotions folks, speaking truth to power. He makes a very indiscreet *ahem*. "Especially the lookers."

I freeze in the middle of a smile. I was just about to agree when that reminded me of something. Or rather someone.

The lookers. This is the designated name that the marketing team has for the most handsome players in the Orlando Wild. And boy, is this team blessed with some outstanding specimens.

Sure, we historically we haven't been the best team but no one, not even the most spiteful internet troll, can deny that we pack the top hotties of the league. And at the very top of them is…

Logan Kim.

The guy I spilled all my embarrassing secrets to in a moment of anger.

Thus, the guy I'd love to avoid for the rest of my life if I could. Except he's the most popular player across all our social media.

In fact, this one time I posted a five second clip of Logan removing his mask after tagging out a runner, and I don't know if it was the sweat dripping from his skin or the fact that he had some hair plastered on his face, but he ran his tongue across his lips as he smirked down at the runner.

That was last year's most viral video on our TikTok account, and it was only surpassed this year by Cade Starr's interview about his ideal woman.

Dave places his elbows on the table and leans forward. "And that's why my proposal is to use the lookers to increase the value of the Orlando Wild brand. We need to create a lot more content centering them."

"Thirst traps?" a woman from the digital content team asks with a sly smile.

"Yes," Dave hisses in a dramatic voice. "Thirst traps with the Wild logo everywhere. That's how we cement the brand."

I choke in the middle of taking a coffee sip, which brings a lot of attention to me. One of the managers points at me with her pen. "Rosalina, can we trust you with the thirst traps?" She seems to be as on the verge of laughter as half of the other people around the conference table.

The other half appear to be annoyed that this is really part of our jobs.

"I—uh. Yes." I set my cup of coffee down so I don't spill it on myself.

"Just make sure they're approved first, okay?"

That's a clear dig at me going a bit rogue last week to help Hope.

Yeah, it set me back professionally. I didn't need Dave's approval for anything before this but now I'm on probation. So, would I do it again?

Abso freaking lutely.

As a broadcast journalism major turned social media manager, I know the power that media holds.

As a huge baseball fan who is a woman and now works for a professional baseball team, I also know how little power women have in this world.

If power is a bit like video games where certain activities drain it and others replenish it, my actions basically depleted my reserves. I have to build them back up, and that means running absolutely every thought by my boss from now on.

I'm more than willing to play that game because I'm here for the long haul, until one day I'm the face of the team during live broadcasts. Me, a mixed Afro Latina.

Go big or go home and all that.

"Trust us, we know that." My boss slices the air with his hand to drive the finality of the point home. "Now, can we talk about Mexico?"

I stand corrected. I thought that everyone was buzzing about how well the team's been performing this week, but everyone turns from interested to electrified at the mention of Mexico.

"Thank you, Dave," says Tom Waterman, the head of marketing and effectively everyone's boss here. "Do we have all the preparations completed?"

The director of broadcasting, Julien Chen, joins in for the first time since the meeting started. "Everything's confirmed on our end. I personally flew out earlier this week to make sure the contractors know what they're doing, and I'm pretty satisfied with the quality of their equipment."

"Excellent." Tom nods before addressing everyone. "I trust you all know how significant it is that the league selected our team for the World Tour Mexico City series, right?"

I sit a little straighter after that, and I'm not the only one.

It's a pretty big deal. Usually the teams that are selected tend to be popular abroad and—

"It's because of the lookers," one of my coworkers murmurs, setting off a wave of giggles and coughs.

Tom breaks into a grin that takes him from a sixty-something-year-old man to fifty for a few seconds. "That's right folks, make sure to get a lot of thirst traps in Mexico."

After the wave of laughter ebbs away, the conversation moves to a new product sponsor we have to place. Aside from the ad board spaces they purchased, we have to make sure to incorporate it into media snippets. It shouldn't be hard because it's a sports drink—we can just have players drink from it during social media clips and fulfill the contractual requirements that way.

I take some notes on my iPad about how we can do this, while in my mind making a mental note about excluding Logan Kim. I'm sure followers would love to see more of Cade's pretty face even if he's now taken.

Some forty minutes later, we spill out of the meeting room to head back to our respective cubicles. My head's buzzing with ideas for content when Dave catches up to me.

"Ready for Mexico?"

"I think so." I slow down for him to catch up because I'm a tall girlie and my boss is a short king. "I got a bunch of cool facts from the team historian that I'm using for a series of videos to hype the match against the Miami Hurricanes."

"They frankly couldn't have chosen a more fun matchup, huh? Two regional rivals with history." Dave chuckles and instead of stopping at his cubicle, he follows me to mine.

"Totally," I agree with a smile. "I'll send you the first three clips this afternoon."

"Looking forward to it." He leans back to glance up and down like he's trying to ascertain that the coast is clear. Then he leans forward again and lowers his voice. "I need to ask you for a big favor, though."

"Okay?"

He rubs the back of his head, his face scrunching into something that looks like embarrassment. Which is totally uncharacteristic. We're talking about a guy who went so viral on Vine—RIP—that it basically landed him this job.

"I need you to cover for me and go to Mexico."

I do a double take. "Dave, may I remind you that I'm on probation? I'm not even allowed to fly with the team right now."

"I know, but it's either you or I hire a freelancer who won't know squat about the team, and may screw up even worse than you."

"Geez, thanks for the vote of confidence." I shake my head.

He lowers his voice even more. "The thing is, I need to have a little procedure done and it can only be next week."

"Oh my gosh." I also lower my voice after the initial spike of surprise. "Are you okay?"

"I think so but this is a better safe than sorry type of thing." I don't detect whiffs of fear, which makes me think this isn't about something that could turn tragic any time. Going by his embarrassment a minute ago, I deduce we're talking about something NSFW so I don't prod.

"Well, I would love to sub in. But the fact is that I can't."

"I already talked with Tom." He shrugs. "Listen, the reason we put you on probation was more about sending a message than it was about you. I personally enjoyed having another viral moment for our KPIs."

Amused, I mumble, "Thanks?"

"The point is that he agreed to let you fly with the team and create content while keeping you on probation."

My eyebrows rise. "How does that even work?"

"I take away your posting rights and do the posting myself up until my surgery, which is scheduled for the day the team flies back. And then Tom takes over."

"Tom," I repeat. "You mean the head of the whole department?"

"That's right."

"And he already agreed to this?"

"Yep."

Sighing, I take a seat and my shoulders sag. For the first time since I mounted what is basically a little social media coup, I feel some shame at having done it. I wouldn't be inconveniencing my boss or my boss's boss if I had just…

But no. Who knows what would've happened to Hope if I hadn't put pressure on the organization with that video.

I'm sick and tired of seeing women be at the whims of the powers that be. I did the right thing and now I have to deal with the consequences, and that includes my chagrin right now.

"Of course I will sub in for you in Mexico," I say at last.

"Great, thank you." Dave straightens up and breathes out in obvious relief. "This is going to count positively toward your record, by the way."

Well, that's good to know, and certainly softens the blow. I had found the silver lining of my probation in that, unable to travel with the team again, this would've halved the amount of time I could spend with the team throughout the season. And that would've meant less sightings of a certain catcher.

After Dave leaves, I drop my face in my hands. Things just never go my way, do they?

# CHAPTER 4
# LOGAN

A lot of people think I sit by myself during team travel because I'm antisocial—and yes, that's true, but it's not the main reason.

It's because I'm claustrophobic as shit.

It's one of the reasons why I took to playing baseball as a kid. From the home plate, all a catcher can see is an expanse of green opening up to the sky. With the ad boards and stands behind me, I can pretend like the world is fully open to me.

Can't do that when I'm caged in a metal death trap along with a bunch of people.

Squirming, I lower myself on my seat to put my face at level with the open window. It's so tiny that I can't even pretend like all I'm looking at is the blue sky, lit by the relentless morning sun, tufts of white clouds floating along.

This is why my preferred transportation method is my Ducati bike. Yeah, I know it's also a metal death trap, smaller than this airplane too, but at least I can feel the wind. It gives more of an illusion of control.

Which is the absolute last thing I have here.

"It's not like that," Miller says from the front, opening his hands until someone tosses a football back at him. He grabs it, placing his fingers in specific places along the seams. "Like this. This is how you put the proper spin into it."

Behind me, the worst stooges of the whole bunch are in the middle of what sounds like a marital fight.

"I told you the rook moves like this." Rivera grunts, followed by dull thuds. Probably him moving the piece.

"Well that's not what the manual says," Starr argues back. Some pages flip and he speaks again. "Look, you're confusing it for the horse."

Rivera huffs. "This game is way too complicated. Can't we go back to playing Uno?"

"We need one more person and"—Starr interrupts himself to raise his voice—"Captain McGrumpy Pants in front of us is trying extra hard to ignore us today."

I start box breathing. Usually I'd also pass the time with some games or reading a book, or making notes on my pocket notepad—but I'm not in the mood today. Today I want to punish myself.

The thing is, when you're in the middle of a professional baseball season, there isn't much opportunity to slow down and take things easy. This is why Kaplan and I called Rob Beau, the Orlando Wild manager, for a meeting as soon as we land in Mexico City. My agent will join remotely, but I'll be there in person to deliver the news to Beau that we want to work on a trade. And it's not like I'm scared of Beau or of having to put on my big boy pants for this chat—I'm a grown ass man who faced much worse in his childhood alone—but it is making me feel some type of way.

Like… guilty.

I know that Beau is counting on me to build up this team to something worth writing home about, especially the pitching staff. That's the reason why he deserves to know my intentions before everyone else. But it's almost like his expectations are what gives me some minuscule pause. None of my previous teams trusted me this much.

Yet, I want to go.

For all the trust Beau has put on me, I haven't done much to show for it. Nothing ties me to the team, or Orlando, or literally anywhere. I don't know what I'm even searching for, but I can viscerally feel that it's not here and that's disappointing. I'm tired of that feeling, and I need something different until I find it.

The plane lurches, almost as if to say *oh yeah? Here, have some nausea, you little shit.*

I press my lips tighter and try to swallow. My throat feels like it's clogged because the saliva isn't going down. Maybe it's too late to take the handy dandy pill I was prescribed to keep anxiety attacks at bay. But the literal last damn thing I need is to have an attack on this plane and—

"Kim?"

The familiar voice cuts through my mounting panic. I crack an eye open and it takes some processing to understand what's happening. First, my eyes fall on Rosalina Mena standing on the hallway, looking down at me with a pinch between her eyebrows. Concern? Annoyance? Who the hell knows what the expression really means.

Her arm is linked to Hope Garcia who stands closer to me, and she does show some clear worry on her face. "Here you go, big guy. This will set you to rights." She offers me a can of ginger ale that is so cold, the tiny condensation beads dull the brand colors.

Oh, yes. This might actually help. If anything so the gas helps me open my throat back up.

But relief after drinking this will show that I have a problem.

I clear my throat. "I'm all—"

The seat beside me shakes as an insufferable pitcher uses it to prop himself up.

"Who are you calling a big guy?" Starr interrupts in mock outrage before I'm able to finish my sentence. "Oh. This thing? He's not a guy—he's Sasquatch."

On the other hand, trading to another more professional team might be just the remedy I need.

"Not my fault that you can barely grow a mustache," I mumble in return while working the tab to open the can with a fizzy hiss.

"Burn," Rivera teases his buddy.

"As if you too could grow a mustache," I grumble and take a swig. A sigh escapes my mouth as the bubbles hit.

Rivera blows a raspberry that turns into full cackling.

Fortunately, Garcia is a bit more mature. She rolls her eyes at them and says to her friend, "Sometimes it's hard to remember that these are grown men and not middle schoolers."

"They make great content, though." Mena grins. As I drink, I notice over the rim of the can that she has dimples in her cheeks. "Maybe I'll do a series on who grows the best mustache on the team."

Before I realize what I'm doing, I'm running my hand down my face, feeling the soft bristle of my facial hair. I keep it trimmed and tidy so that I don't look precisely like Sasquatch, and I'm kind of proud about it.

Mena's eyes return to me for a second, zeroing in on my face. I drop my hand, not really meaning to get her attention or turn this into a competition, and turn back to the window.

Well, this has effectively distracted me for a few minutes.

The women continue chatting with the two clowns behind me for a while more, until the seatbelt lights come on and everyone has to return to their seats. Ironically, the closer the plane gets to the ground and to the prospect of me exiting, the easier I can breathe. I tuck the now empty can of ginger ale into my hand luggage to toss it later, and close my eyes for the landing.

The good news is that the Alfredo Harp Helú stadium is a normal, fully open one, unlike the one in Tampa for example —which I can't stand. Even better, we're headed straight to it from the airport without stopping at a hotel.

Fresh air, here I come.

*

I underestimated traffic as I tend to do every time I've come to Mexico City. By the time we get to the stadium, I'm drenched in sweat from the effort it takes to keep the claws of panic at bay.

I sit near the front of the bus, and I'm just the third person to get out. My lungs can't grab gulps of air quick enough as my teammates file out.

"Dude," O'Brian says to me as he passes by, "It's kinda hot today, but not *that* hot."

Grunting, I march over to the luggage compartment to find mine, doing my best to pretend like my team polo and joggers aren't sticking to my skin with all the sweat.

Stadium staff lead us along to the team entrance and through the maze of corridors inside. My limited Spanish knowledge is enough for me to know that when they say aquí it means that I should follow them *that* way, not the other. Our designated clubhouse is spacious enough, and just as I'm trawling through the mass of forty men trying to pick a locker, I make eye contact with Beau. He motions at me to follow, and so I pivot with suitcase and everything.

"We'll have to be quick, Son, since we're running behind schedule," he says with a low voice once I join him.

"That's fine." Perfect, even. Less time for me to sit in

Beau's disappointment in yet another tiny space. "This shouldn't take long," I add.

We commandeer the empty staff meeting room and I abandon my suitcase and carryon by the door, freeing my hands to fish my cellphone from my pocket to dial my agent.

"Hey, man. I was about to get worried that something happened," he says in his usual tone that people confuse for friendly, but hides his ruthless business nature that made me select him as my agent.

"Traffic," is all I say to that before shifting gears. "I'm with Beau and have you on loudspeaker."

"Perfect," he chimes. "Thank you for meeting us at short notice, Mr. Beau. I'm Pete Kaplan, Logan's agent."

Beau nods. "Of course, I remember you, Mr. Kaplan."

"Then I'll get straight to the point," Kaplan says, but I'm the one who braces. "Logan has expressed a keen interest in trading to a different team."

Even though Kaplan doesn't stop, I inspect Beau for any signs of how this is landing, but the guy's not a baseball manager for no reason. He's a vault and continues listening to my agent with the exact same expression he carried five minutes ago.

"Don't get us wrong, you're shaping up the Wild to be an excellent team this season, but we think the timing is right for Logan to make a move that will take his career to the next level."

Beau finally lifts his eyes from the phone in my hand to my face. Unfortunately for him, I also have a superb poker face. I give away nothing—whether I'm eager about this, doing it just because, in a hurry, or plainly to drive up my salary.

"Far be it from me to prevent a player's growth." Beau utters the words carefully, deliberately packing the biggest punch.

And they land just like that.

My mind takes me back to the interview Ben Williams gave last week before facing us in the opening game, saying that he traded out to the Riders because he wasn't growing enough in the Wild. When in fact, the two men present in this room were solely responsible for any of the improvement that led Williams to a higher pay in Denver.

Shit. Am I acting like Williams?

No. We're not the same at all. This is just how I operate. I've done all I can here.

"But," Beau continues, sharp eyes watching my face. "I would also be remiss if I don't try to keep my best player on the roster."

I blink. I know I'm the best player. It's just my first time hearing it from his mouth.

"That's great to hear. I agree that Logan isn't just a run-of-the-mill player." Kaplan gives out what I can only define as a business laugh. It means that Beau's comment just drew my price tag higher and Kaplan personally enjoys that. "Well, that's all we had for today—just a heads up. I'll stay in touch with you as the conversations progress."

"I will thank you for that," Beau says with a boulder-size of tact. Kaplan can probably read the meaning between the lines: we better not go around this old man's back or else.

After one last round of pleasantries, I end the call and wait for the hammer of Beau's disappointment.

It doesn't come. Instead, he puts his hands in his pants and sweeps an up and down glance at me. "You should get changed before you catch a cold."

"That's what you're concerned about?" I raise my eyebrows.

"Yes, player safety comes first no matter what." He turns to the door and before leaving, says, "Remember that."

"Shit," I mutter in the quiet of the meeting room, the only other sound coming from a whirring fan.

Somehow, Beau's parting words are making me sweat even harder than the barely contained anxiety attack from earlier. I run a hand through my hair, pushing it back so it's no longer sticking to my face.

Past managers have had big reactions to this same conversation, usually manifested as anger.

No one blew up harder than the manager of the New York Eagles, my second team. His top concern had been how my departure would affect my older brother Lewis, who is still their starting pitcher, when I was the other half of the battery.

And not for why I wanted to leave in the first place.

Meanwhile, Beau's worried about my health?

Taking a deep breath, I resolve to store this in a neat little box in my mind and analyze it later. Beau's right in that I have to go change—not because I'm weak enough to get sick from a little A/C on wet clothes, but because I have to warm up for the game.

Then after that I will dissect every minutia of this topic until it starts making sense.

# CHAPTER 5
## ROSE

s it bad if what I'm most excited for about this trip is the food?

My favorite restaurant in Mills Avenue back home is a taqueria that people say sells the most legit Mexican tacos in all Orlando. I can only assume that tacos here will hit it out of the park.

But first, I have work to do around the literal park where balls are hit out of.

My personal preference is to use the Canon that belongs to the team for the wide angles and the faraway takes, but my phone for the up close and personal interviews. The former looks more professional that way, and the latter more genuine to a social media audience that is used to consuming content that comes from other phones on their own phones.

It's why I hang out with two cameras at the same time. One is strapped to my neck and I hold it on my right hand. The other one is strapped to my left hand, ready to rock and roll the second the next unsuspecting player joins me for a water break.

For I am standing right next to the coolers in the shade, while the players warm up across the field.

That's the privilege I get from being part of the team's organization. Meanwhile, the press has no choice but to camp out at their designated area in the stands, which happens to be somewhere behind me where they can stare me down in jealousy.

We have maybe half an hour left before switching back to the gym so that the Miami Hurricanes can use the field, and then a meal before the game. I'm so excited about that. I don't care if it's healthy food for athletes. I have no doubt it'll be delicious.

"Okay, that's enough," a voice breaks through my taco fantasies.

I search for the source and find Logan Kim rising to his feet and lifting his mask. "No more pitching until the game."

From a distance, Cade Starr groans. "But I was just getting the hang of it."

"Finish getting it during the game," Logan fires back with clear annoyance. "Let's get you hydrated, c'mon."

"Yes, Mom."

"I'm too young to be your mother, Starr."

"You're also too hairy." The latter laughs.

I gasp a little. Crap, where do I go?

But I'm too far from the dugout to make a retreat appear natural. I'm definitely not hiding under the table. And the rest of the players are strewn across the field—some running, some stretching, some throwing and catching—and I can't just sidle up to them without interfering.

I resign myself to staying in the path of Logan Kim. As they approach, still having their intellectual conversation, both guys note my presence and give different reactions to it. The catcher—nothing. The pitcher—a grin.

"If it isn't my favorite social media professional," Cade says, stopping at the table to grab a bottle of water and squirt it in his mouth.

"If it isn't my favorite starting pitcher in franchise history," I return with amusement. After framing him in my phone camera, I ask, "What is it like to be starting pitcher for tonight's game?"

From the corner of my eye, I catch Logan stop by the table smack between Cade and I, but staying out of reach from the camera. It also means that we're not letting him grab a bottle.

Maybe Cade notices this because he gives a very brief answer. "As a Texan, it truly is an honor to visit the land of actual tacos not butchered by Texans. Oh, and I'm excited about the game too."

I burst out laughing. What talent he has of charmingly insulting everyone, from himself, to his home state, and to the opponent.

I shift my phone toward Logan as he finally grabs a water bottle. Unlike Cade, though, he squeezes it on his face, spraying water to refresh himself rather than quench his thirst.

And I got it on camera, which is great because this is the definition of a thirst trap.

Droplets trickle down his cheeks and nose even as he finally drinks water, oblivious or uncaring that I'm recording all the action for the thirsty people of the internet.

Before this gets weirder, I ask, "And what's your take, Logan?"

Anyone who finds themselves the recipient to the attention of an extremely good looking guy would feel a little something, right? Butterflies in the belly. A little more heat in the face. Some lack of air in the lungs.

Not me.

His eyes turn to me even as he's still drinking water, and all I want to do is run and hide. It's the only real course of action, because it's not like I can turn back time and undo the fight with my ex. It's all I think about when I'm near Logan Kim, and I have no doubt that scene comes to his mind when he looks at me now. Freaking Ben and his—

"Watch out!"

I do. It's what you're supposed to when you're in a ballpark.

The warning comes from nearby enough to lend it urgency. And sure enough, a round projectile flies at me at Mach speed.

All I can do is yelp and shrink. I don't know if it's terror—like maybe my personal reflex is freezing. But my eyes stay open, waiting for the moment of impact.

That's not what happens, though.

I'm pretty sure what happens is a miracle.

Logan Kim goes from staring at me, to dropping his water bottle wherever it lands. He pivots blindly and reacts like lightning. It's like his hand has a built-in magnet for baseballs. He reaches out and the ball hits his palm with violence—maybe an inch from my face. I yell some gibberish, almost dropping my phone from the shock.

And then there's quiet.

"Mena," the catcher says, dropping the ball and rushing to me. Next thing, his hands cinch my arms and I realize it's to keep me upright when I was about to crumble. My wide eyes focus on his face—on something I've never seen on it. Fear. "Are you okay?" he breathes out the question like it took a great effort to make it.

"I—I—" I fumble with my phone in my hands and nod. And keep nodding. "Yes, I—Thank you. Fine. I am. I'm fine."

His eyebrows twitch and his gaze turns darker as he runs it up and down my body. That's when I become aware that all of it is shaking.

My helpful brain supplies images of what could've happened if he hadn't been two steps from me. I could've died. No, I *would* have died. There would've been no more tacos for me—ever. Audrey and Hope would've had to get a new roommate. I'd have joined my dad and left Mom all alone.

Oh no. Oh shit. I can feel heat traveling up my chest, throat, and into my eyes.

"You don't look fine," Logan murmurs, not releasing me at all.

Steps approach. "Is everyone okay?" one of the players asks. "Rivera batted that one with a bit more strength than necessary. We didn't think it'd go that far but…"

A muscle jumps in Logan's jaw and he tears his eyes away from me. "I will murder him."

"How about instead we take the princess here back to the clubhouse?" Cade asks with something weird in his voice that I can't discern.

"Fine," Logan rasps out. Then he nods at me. "You're coming with."

Distantly, as if the real Rosalina was locked away in a room, I feel a vestige of annoyance at the command. But then he shifts his hold on me, bringing an arm around my shoulders, his other hand still holding my arm just below the point where my sleeve cuts off, his calloused and hot hand wrapped around my clammy skin.

Cade falls in step on my other sound, whistling. "You're lucky that you had this grouch around to save you. I can play catch as well as the next pro, but that was next level."

"Lucky?" I echo numbly.

"I will murder him," Logan repeats in a sinister tone of voice as, coincidentally, Lucky Rivera comes running at shocking speed.

"¡Mala mía!" he shouts still from a distance. "Ay bendito, casi te mato."

Something about this is so ridiculous, it makes a hiccup bubble in my throat.

And it turns into laughter.

Both Logan and Cade glance at me.

"Did you let her get hit?" Cade whispers at the catcher.

"Of course not," Logan grouches.

"Oh. How's your hand by the way?"

"Fine."

I stop laughing abruptly and gasp. "You didn't get hurt, did you?"

But Logan Kim doesn't respond, because that's when Lucky Rivera finally reaches us and he's not even winded by the wild sprint. "Rose, please tell me you're okay and that these two are carting you off out of an abundance of caution and not because I really hurt you or—"

"I'm okay, Lucky." I offer a watery smile. "I should've been paying more attention."

Logan truly lacks any filter, because he says to Lucky, "Wait until I drop her off at the clubhouse, then I'm coming for your ass."

"No murder on my behalf, please," I say, which unfortunately makes the catcher frown down at me, and I notice how his lips curve downward when he does so. They're too full to be considered cute, and yet that's how the gesture lands.

"Fine," he agrees.

We're now stepping down into the dugout toward the clubhouse tunnel and Cade asks, "Which hand did you use?"

"What?" Lucky asks. "I bat right but what does that—"

"Not you." Cade jerks his head toward Logan. "Him. Did you catch with your throwing or your catching hand?"

"I'm fine," Logan repeats in a deadpan.

I become aware of the brush of his chest pads against my elbow, the overwhelming heat radiating off him as he navigates us into the tunnel. It almost makes me feel cold when he finally releases me to take a seat at a plush leather chair in the clubhouse.

Finally, he brings up both hands for Cade's inspection, palms facing up and opening and closing his fingers. "See? Fine."

I think Cade knew which hand Logan used for the catch all along, because he latches onto Logan's right hand and presses his thumb into the palm hard enough that Logan frowns. "Throwing hand, then? Interesting."

Logan tries to snatch his hand free but it's not like Cade's a weakling.

"Hey, Lucky. Wanna know how you can fix the snafu you created?" he asks his friend.

Lucky salutes like a soldier. "How?"

"Find my girl, the love of my life, and ask her to ice this man's hand, the bane of my existence."

At last, Logan tugs himself free. "I don't need icing, especially not before a game."

"Hmm, maybe I should tell Beau that you might've hurt your hand instead?" Cade rubs his chin in an exaggerated pensive way.

Logan balls up said hand's fist. "Or how about I show you how healthy my hand is?"

"If I may..." I raise one of my own shaky hands. Of course, Logan notices right away so I lower the appendage and press it between my thigh and the seat. "I'm with Cade. You need to get your hand looked at."

"I'm—"

"Fine, yes," I finish for him. "You keep saying that. But Lucky and I would feel too guilty if it turns out that you're not okay, especially if it becomes obvious in the middle of the game." I lean forward and offer my best puppy eyes to none other than Logan Kim. "Please."

Both Lucky and Cade turn to the stoic man.

Logan's eye twitches and I'm almost sure that he's going to tell me to screw off, until finally he breaks. "Starr, let's go find your woman."

"That's a good boy." Cade drops a hand on Logan's shoulder, who shrugs it off right away.

Lucky gives me one last look—serious, for a change— inspecting me for any damage. But I'm unscathed except for my nerves, so he finally follows his teammates back out to the field and I'm left alone.

Then I melt on the chair.

My heart is still hammering against my ribcage from the fright, and as my hands drop on my lap, my phone lays face up and I realize that I'm still recording. I scramble to stop it.

"Wait a second," I mumble with a shaky voice. "How far back does it go?"

I tap at my phone to find the last video. It starts as Logan and Cade jog over to the water coolers and I watch transfixed as it morphs from just another cute video, to my almost death.

The way Logan moved is even more shocking when seen on camera—because other than the random *watch out*, there was no other warning of where the ball was coming from. It's like the dude had eyes in the back of his head and knew exactly where the ball would land. Impossible. But I guess it's why he's routinely labeled the best catcher in the league right now.

And he just saved my life.

The camera shakes wildly during the microseconds between him reacting, catching the ball, and dropping it to make sure I'm okay. I jump in my skin as the camera inverts all of a sudden and captures my shellshocked expression.

A groan tears out of my throat. Why did I have to sound drunk instead of straight up saying I was okay? Ugh.

I make duplicates of the video to splice Cade's little inter- view and Logan's thirst trap out of it. There's no way I'm sending the whole thing to my boss, when what I need to do is bury this moment in the back of my mind, along with every other embarrassing thing I've ever done in my life. Right up there with dating Ben Williams in secret, and getting pantsed in the seventh grade.

# CHAPTER 6
# LOGAN

Freaking Beau and freaking Starr and freaking everyone, especially she of the puppy dog eyes. Out of the abundance of caution that Rivera cited offhand, Beau decided to sit me out of game one of the series, even though my hand is in perfect condition.

Now it's the morning before game two, and I'm making a point of showing the trainers that nothing is amiss by lifting some weights. I admit to my status of little shit because I make eye contact with Garcia, and then pointedly glance at the sixty pounds I'm curling my right bicep with, supported by the hand I used to catch the fly ball.

Because that's all it was. It wasn't the kind of rocket that smashes through the window of a car at the parking lot behind the stadium.

Garcia snorts at me and keeps going on her round. We're getting some early morning training before the press junket to talk about last night's game, the expectations of today's, and also how gracious the hosts have been.

And they have been. The food has been so outstanding that

I kinda don't want to go back home. Maybe I should get Kaplan to trade me to a Mexican team.

"Attention, boys," someone calls out from the middle of the floor.

I see the movement through the corner of my eye and set the weight down to watch what the deal is. To my surprise, the top dog of broadcasting for the team stands before us. His name is Julien Chen, I remember once bonding with him about being in the select club of Asians or half Asians—like me—in the organization. What's he doing here?

"The following individuals have been selected for a special event." As he lifts up an iPad, movement behind him reveals our social media manager, who at least doesn't look shaken this morning. "O'Brian, Rivera, Starr…"

I put two and two. This is some marketing shenanigan I have no interest in, which they surely know about since I never volunteer.

Dismissing them, I bend my knees to grab the weight again and—

"And Kim."

I snap my face up. "What?"

My question goes unanswered.

Nearby, Miller comments, "Oh to be popular and get saved from training."

"You still have eight reps left," says Franklin, the head of the personal trainers.

"Ugh."

That's what I should be saying.

"You have fifteen minutes to shower and change into your uniforms," Chen instructs with more authority than I expect out of anyone who isn't a coach. "See you at the charter bus."

Great, whatever this is will be offsite too. Fantastic. Not exhausting at all.

I grumble my way through the gym and even during the

shower. It truly is a curse brought upon me when, on the way to the parking lot, Rivera hangs himself from my shoulders and Starr's.

"I bet this is going to be fun," he yaps in my ear.

Across from him, Starr muses, "Dude, are your feet even touching the floor?"

"I'll have you know I'm six-one. Not my fault you two are giants," the Boricua returns in outrage.

"Get off me," I warn with a glacial tone, rooted firmly on my spot and not moving a single step.

"Aye, captain." Slowly, he slides all the way to the floor and I'm able to keep going.

I park myself at the seat right behind the driver, ready to bounce the second the bus stops. I don't use the middle school logic of the cool kids sitting all the way at the back. People can think whatever the hell they want about me. All I need is to have immediate access to the exit.

Unfortunately, the two stooges sit right behind me. Rivera asks, "Dude, why so close to the front when we have the whole bus to ourselves?"

"I bet it's because he wants to tell the driver how to do his job," Starr responds.

O'Brian and Mena hop in together, and both of them do a double take at finding us so close to the front.

She's first, and as she sweeps her eyes down the expansive corridor all the way to the back, I can almost see her brain calculating what her next move will be. Then she takes the seat across the aisle from me, also at the front. Sighing, O'Brian takes the spot behind her.

Last is Chen, who stands by the driver for a second to say, "Thank you for your collaboration, gentlemen. We're now headed for downtown Mexico City to take a tour bus. The plan is very simple, Rosalina and I will record your impressions about major monuments around the city, hopefully meet some fans along the way, and then we'll come right back for warmups. Traffic permitting, this should take no more than two hours."

"Oh…" Rivera elongates the word in his excitement. "Do we get any food?"

Chen nods. "I believe the trainers packed us some snacks."

"Boo," Rivera grouches, and I admit even I was looking forward to street food.

"All right, kids," Mena says in a much more informal way compared to Chen. "Brace yourselves, for I will record every detail."

"Then stop picking your nose, Cade," Rivera jokes.

"Pff. I was doing no such thing." The offense in Starr's voice makes O'Brian explode in laughter.

I stifle a groan. These are going to be a long two hours.

And of course, Mena is capturing the annoyance in my face with her cellphone camera. "Today's challenge is to see if we manage to get a smile out of the ultimate grump."

I turn away only to find the curtain drawn. I push it open and settle in to watch the scenery as we roll away from the sports city, merging into traffic.

The drive to the drop off point is quite short, and all throughout Mena takes advantage of the close confines to do Q&As with the other guys. Mercifully she spares me. I have no doubt that it's because she feels indebted after yesterday, but I also know it won't go far enough to spare me the rest of the day.

Sure enough, as we do the swap from the charter bus to the tourist one, she trains her cellphone back on me. "Have you been to Mexico before?"

I may be a grump as she said, but I'm a professional one. The sooner I answer her questions, the sooner she moves on to the other guys.

"Yes, a few times."

"Really? What did you come to Mexico for those times?"

Shit. I should've left it at yes only. Now I've stoked her journalistic curiosity.

She's walking backward into the bus, angling for the stairs that Rivera already took to the open top of the bus. I react before I can stop myself, grabbing her waist to stop her. Mena gasps.

I explain, "You're not going up the stairs backwards."

"Oh." She glances over her shoulder. "Good point, thanks. Let's finish this upstairs."

I wrinkle my nose but nod.

"Beep beep," an obnoxious voice says from behind me. "You're blocking traffic."

"Sorry, Cade!" Grinning, Mena twirls around to take the stairs.

"Well?" Starr asks behind me. "Aren't you moving?"

I sigh in the most exaggerated way I can manage, but follow up the narrow stairs. I have to twist myself so that I'm basically climbing sideways, because this contraption wasn't made for me in any sense.

I lift my eyes, trying to convince myself that I'm not willingly walking into a straitjacket—and come face to face with something worse.

Mena's butt.

She has stopped near the top of the stairs, one foot much lower than the other. This is a cruel angle—for me, not for her —because I can now see that she has very shapely thighs. Not small at all, thick enough that I could wrap my hands around them and still have left over, just the way I like them.

I swallow hard and try to look away, but all that's left to see is the metal walls enclosed around me with their chipped trims and edges from many bodies brushing against them over the years.

"Get out of the way, man," her muffled voice is saying to Rivera, who as far as I know is the only one at the top so far.

My eyes rise again, hoping that Mena is finally clearing the obstacle. But she's still planted in front of me.

My throat works with a heavy swallow because my traitorous eyes have now fallen on her butt again. Of freaking course it's perfectly thick too, two round mounds that I could—

Nope! Not going there. Not going there *at all*.

I close my eyes. My teeth are gritted so tight that my voice sounds animalistic as I say, "Mena, tell Rivera that I will toss him into oncoming traffic if he doesn't move away in thirty seconds."

She dutifully repeats my words verbatim, and sure enough she finally emerges into the open air.

I gasp a lungful of it and claw my way the rest of the way up, making a point to look at anything but she of the perfect behind and thighs. Maybe I'm the one I should toss onto oncoming traffic.

This time I take a seat near the middle, which is the closest to the straitjacket stairs. The rest of them pile onto the front, except for Chen who scoots all the way to the back so that he can't appear in Mena's videos.

I'm glad I had enough presence of mind to bring sunglasses to this expedition. I pluck them from the pocket of my uniform pants and slide them on. And you know what? The day isn't unbearably sunny and being early April, it's still relatively cool and breezy. I should've brought a hair tie but I don't mind it too bad that my hair whips around with the changes in the wind. I lean back and fold my arms, legs spread wide enough to fit between the seats and preventing anyone else from joining. This isn't so bad after all.

At the front, the three stooges and camerawoman take in all the sights. Rivera makes big expressions that delight our social media manager. I don't know if it's because she has a particular affinity to the guy or purely from a professional perspective. She did forgive him quite easily after he nearly took her out yesterday.

Meanwhile, Starr is a notch or two more subdued, but just as excited to be here. And O'Brian is chatting up a storm, providing hours of content in a matter of seconds.

I wedge my elbow between the window and the seat in front of me, bending it so I can prop my chin against my hand. The bus rounds a plaza with a massive monument of an angel sprouting from it, and it paints some impressive perspective on a shockingly straight avenue flanked by buildings that look three hundred years old, with even older trees.

"So, what did you do in Mexico before?"

I lift my eyes from the street to the woman now sitting in front of me, her cellphone pointed at my face.

One of my eyebrows rises, debating what to say. I came once as a kid for one of my mother's fashion events, and spent the whole stay at the hotel room. Another time, when Lewis and I were teens, we came to Acapulco to be seen in public as a happy and joyful family. That was right after my parents had such a huge fight, I thought they'd really divorce at last. I spent the whole time at the beach sitting under a shade with my clothes on, hiding the bandages that their fight left me with, after my mother threw a crystal vase on the ground and shards wedged in my skin.

But then there's the time I came in the off season with someone I was dating. That one was supposed to be for fun, including things I wouldn't share on social media, but also ended up in some kind of drama that resulted in a breakup.

Food was excellent each time, though.

With that, I straighten out and look right at the camera, "For the food. It truly is even better than everyone raves about."

"Isn't it?" Mena returns with excitement. "What is your favorite dish so far?"

"Uh." I brush my wild hair away from my face. "I'm going to butcher this but the tacos de flor de calabaza."

"That sounds intriguing." But just when I think she's going to ask more questions, she presses a button on her screen and lowers it.

The expression on her face is so unexpected that my whole body grows stiff.

Her eyes narrow like she's trying to read me between lines.

I'm a professional catcher, for goodness's sake. Nothing gets by me that I don't let it. I know for a fact that I kept my expression neutral while those pathetic memories circled my brain. My eyes are even hidden behind shades.

And yet she murmurs, "You don't have fond memories of Mexico, do you?"

I realize my mouth is hanging open when I snap it close. Even then, I admit, "None. Aside from the food."

"Fair." She nods and does as if to stand, but at the very last second changes her mind and turns to me again. "For what it's worth, I also have a lot of things I don't want to talk about. Ever. Especially about a certain ex of mine." Here, she gives me a pointed look.

Amusement creeps through the cracks of my composure, and my lips twitch. "How long were you waiting to throw that heavy handed hint at me?"

Color rises to her cheeks, which is interesting to watch.

Mena clears her throat. "Let's just say I regretted everything the second it spilled out."

"Ah." I return my chin to my hand and turn back to the window. "The good news is that I'm not a talker so…"

"Thank you," she says with more vehemence than necessary, before sliding off the seat and making her way back to the front.

My eyes lower to her behind for a second before I force them back out to the street.

I can definitely see how tangling with a piece of shit like Williams would be embarrassing for someone somewhat normal like her, but I have exactly zero skin in that game. She needn't worry about me babbling. Especially not when, a day later, I learn that everyone and their mom is talking about her and someone else—me.

A video taken from the stands that shows me saving her from a fly ball is going viral on social media.

# CHAPTER 7
# ROSE

The thing about working for a professional baseball team is that the hours are messed up, and no one does anything to un-mess them up.

We return from Mexico in the wee hours of the morning and while the players get a rest day, I don't have that privilege. We take the team bus from MCO straight to the Orlando Wild facilities downtown, and I get right out to head to the office where a long day of editing footage awaits.

The perk is that, since we don't have a game today, I can go home in the evening and basically transform into a full blown potato. My plan is taking a long bath with my favorite lavender bath bomb, read a book from Madeline Berkley latest series of bodice rippers, and wrap myself in my fluffiest robe to rot in my bed the rest of the night.

I sigh as I round the last corner in the corridor. The walls that separate the back office departments are just iced glass that open to the designated areas. Overhead signs indicate whether you're in the operations department, or marketing, strategy, finance, and the rest. The only office in a different—higher—floor is of course the CEO and owner. And we're all thankful for that because dealings with Charlie Cox are usually never pleasant.

A little shudder racks my back as I enter the marketing area, both from thinking about Cox and also because it's cold here. I rush to my cubicle to grab the cardigan I permanently leave here, and to start taking out all the equipment from my carryon bag. Laptop, camera, phone, cables—so many cables. It probably takes about twenty minutes alone just to set up.

By the time I power my laptop, I have a million ideas running through my head for further edits. This week's posts are going to be fire and I'll—

"Huh?"

I lean closer to my screen. There is, in fact, a meeting invitation organized by one Dave Rogers for me and one Tom Waterman, that was supposed to start fifteen minutes ago.

"Mierda." I jump to my feet, poking my head over the cubicle walls like a meerkat until I zero in on Tom's office in the farthest corner.

The executive office walls are clear glass, and he spots me right away. He motions with his hand for me to join and I probably look like a cartoon to anyone watching me scramble out of my cube.

Am I getting fired? Is that it? But I didn't do anything to warrant that this time—no exposés, no protests, and aside from this meeting I've been in time to every appointment. For goodness's sake, I'm not even dating any players in secret anymore.

Crap, when I think about all my transgressions I wouldn't be surprised if this is it for me. I hope they at least let me pack up the things in my cubicle because I really like them. That custom lavender keyboard cost me a pretty penny.

But then where do I go? Who's going to hire me? Sports social media teams tend to be pretty small. Like, it's just Dave and me in here and we just interface with the graphic designers, producers, and so on.

Dave. Who is supposed to be going into surgery any time today. And instead called me in for a meeting with his boss. That I'm late to.

This has to be bad.

I'm about ready to upchuck the breakfast I had on the plane when I barge into Tom's office. Surely that would be the cherry on top.

"I'm so sorry I'm late I didn't realize we had this meeting and we caught all the morning traffic on I-4 and—"

"Breathe, Rosalina," Tom instructs, using his hands in the universal gesture of *calm the heck down, you freaking weirdo.*

I take a deep breath. Then another.

"I'm sorry for being late," I repeat a lot less winded.

Dave's voice comes out from the speakers. "Don't worry about that. I wasn't sure when you arrived but I'm going into surgery soon, so I thought I should YOLO." Someone should tell him that YOLO is a thing of the past, but that someone won't be me today.

"Um, first of all are you okay, calling from the hospital? And second, is this because I'm getting fired?"

"Fired?" Dave exclaims.

Tom blows a raspberry in the most professional way possible, which is to say not a lot. "Where did you get that idea from?"

"The circumstances are kind of scary for any employee, and that's excluding the fact that I'm on probation," I say very clearly, not missing a beat, even though my heart is hammering like a rabbit's.

It's thanks to the broadcasting journalism training I got in college. Maybe I should plaster on my Miss Florida pageant smile too. It might help me get out of trouble.

"Girl, we don't care about your probation, remember?" Dave asks and I can practically hear him roll his eyes.

"Besides, we only put you on it to appease HR." Tom folds

his arms and leans back on his chair. "The post with the players defending Starr and Garcia's romance is one of our most viral in history. It even brought in new sponsors."

"Right. From a marketing perspective it was a success," Dave adds, including a little cough. "Even if the method was unorthodox."

"And that's why we're disappointed in you right now," Tom throws that from left field.

"Whoa," is all I manage to say and collapse on one of the chairs across his desk. "So I *am* getting sacked."

Dave's tone shifts to a deadpan. "For the last time, no. But we're surprised at how your instincts failed this time."

I drop my face in my hands. "Please put me out of my misery and explain it to me like I'm five."

Tom chuckles, which from him is a series of snorts through his nose. "Dave, will you do the honors?"

"Certainly," my boss picks up from there. "So last night while I was in the hospital room bored out of my mind next to a random stranger who doesn't want to socialize with me—"

An unknown voice from his end of the line says, "Whatever."

But Dave continues. "I was scrolling through TikTok and came across a video about you."

"What?" My face snaps up.

In less than a second, my mind flashes through every single possibility. The time I tripped during the swimsuit portion of the Miss Florida pageant. When I was in college and got turned into a meme after I was filmed eating an ice cream cone during a game with my college baseball team.

Or worse, Ben Williams. The worst of my exes. Does he have some incriminating footage?

But no. I'd really get canned then, and Dave and Tom have already reassured me that's not the case.

"I could tell it was you from your hair," my boss keeps

saying without noticing my lapse, "but the one we see the clearest is Logan Kim saving you from a fly ball."

"Oh." I could melt on this chair right here, that's how big my relief is. But then I sit up straighter again. "Wait, there's footage of that?"

"Yes, it was posted by the *SPORTY* press account."

"And our question is"—Tom leans forward—"Why is it not posted from ours?"

"Because a moment like that?" Dave makes a kissing sound. "Priceless. Kim is a hero, an extremely athletic one. That's the kind of stuff that helps build up the public appeal of the Orlando Wild brand. So what gives, Rose?"

I squirm. "Well, in my defense I almost got my head smashed to smithereens. It kinda stopped thinking for a moment after that."

But that's kind of not it. I specifically remember the moment when humiliation washed over me and I decided not to broadcast that moment to the world.

Which is entirely the opposite of what I should've been doing as the team's social media manager.

Like Dave implied just now, that moment wasn't about me and how I was the defenseless damsel in distress. It was about how outstanding Logan Kim looked.

"Rosalina." Oh no, Tom's voice has turned serious. "I checked out your development plan right before the meeting. You want your next career step to be in the broadcasting team with Julien, right?"

"Yes." I give a stronger nod than I feel.

"You need those journalistic instincts to take over even your amygdala," he says all calm and collected. "No freeze, fight, or flight. Only inform, inform, and inform."

Damn it.

He's right. He's one hundred percent right. I didn't fail

when it came to posting about Hope and Cade, but I did fail this time.

No, wait! I can fix this.

"Actually… what if I say I do have footage?"

"Oh?" both men say in unison.

"I'd have to parse through it and edit it really well because that moment was kind of a mess, but I think I did capture something." Now I'm the one leaning forward. "We can still ride the wave of the *SPORTY* video and make ours go viral."

"You do?" Dave shouts in obvious excitement.

"Shut up, man," the voice of a man on his end of the line says. "Some of us are trying to rest here."

"Some of us?" Dave snorts. "We're the only ones in this room, dude."

Tom clears his throat. "Okay, this sounds promising. But the edit has to be even more enticing than the original *SPORTY* post. How do you plan to accomplish that?"

My brain whirs so hard, there's no doubt that Tom can picture the math signs popping around my head like I'm an in-person meme.

And then—ding! I remember my fave pastime: romance books.

"I could edit it to look romantic. Point of view: you're rescued by the hot baseball player." I spread a hand in an arch across the air. "We have a majority female audience so they'll lap it up."

Tom snaps his fingers. "Bam! That's what I'm talking about."

"Okay great, I can die in peace now." Dave sighs in an exaggerated manner.

"No one's freaking dying here, we just have hernias," the other patient says from the other side.

Tom and I exchange a glance. We unanimously decide to pretend like that part of the conversation never happened.

"Anyway, I strongly suggest you prioritize this project over other posts," Tom says with a nod.

"Roger that."

"Rogers?" a new female voice enters the chat with perfect timing. "I'm here to pick you up for your surgery."

"Gotta go, guys," Dave says. "Wish me luck."

"Good luck," his boss and I chorus.

Dave disconnects from the line and I jump to my feet. "Well, I best get started."

"Don't forget to show me the final product before posting," Tom reminds me.

"Ha. Yes, of course." I chuckle my way out of his office and then do a bit of a power walk to my cubicle, cracking my knuckles to brace myself because I'm about to turn Logan Kim into a damn romance novel hero.

# CHAPTER 8
## LOGAN

Cade Starr is freaking me out.

One crumble of attention and the dude is turning into a monster.

I take my sweet time fixing a wedgie and rearranging my mask while I muse about how to bring out an even nastier pitch out of him. This is game one in the series against one of the weaker teams in the league, so it's not like we're going for broke here, but we should definitely display dominance.

And he's certainly doing that, to the point that it makes me want to laugh.

A new batter steps into the plate, already mumbling vile shit under his breath without even having taken the first swing. That's what happens when you're down eight runs and have only managed to score one.

In just the third inning.

The umpire knows exactly what I'm up to and tries to cut me off, announcing, "Play ball!"

As I crouch and get comfy, I notice the batter choking up on the bat like he's going for a hit on one of the pitches that

Starr can place in the strike zone with laser precision. Bold of this guy to try that on pitch one.

It's like he thinks I'll really let the runners on second and third score.

Since Starr doesn't vibe with the PitchCom, I tuck my right hand between my thighs for old school signs. The one thing that's annoying about him—the real one, not the ones I say are annoying just to keep him off my back—is that he tends to put a hundred percent of his trust in my calls. Rare is the occasion where he rejects one.

On the one hand it's great because he recognizes who has the brains in this battery. But on the other hand, he's fully dependent on me. I can't say that his next catcher is going to be as effective in drawing out his full power as I am.

But that's not my problem.

He throws the fastball right where I wanted, on the inside corner. I don't even have to move my glove.

Of course, the batter connects with it on the perfect spot.

We spring to action at the exact same time. Him, to run to first. Me, jumping to my feet to yell at Rivera. "Third!"

Rivera makes an Olympic leap—a real beaut. The ball doesn't fly with explosive power and he catches it in his bare hand. Rolling with the motion, he tosses the ball from behind him to third.

"Out!" the umpire calls behind me.

Yep, that's one.

But the runner on third is advancing toward home. Brown, our third baseman, needs no instructions. He throws the ball at me with so much force that he goes tumbling forward.

Me? I just put a casual foot on the home plate and catch the ball in my glove. Then I fire it like a cannon to first base.

The runner makes it to home another second later. "Out!" the umpire shouts.

My throw lands in Miller's glove with a poetic thud and lo and behold, the batter makes it to base at last.

"Three outs! Change!"

The crowd roars. Loud enough to make the air vibrate.

"Shit, shit," the third base runner moans as he does a U turn to return to his dugout.

"Music to my ears," I mumble, grinning behind the grill of my mask.

"What just happened?" Starr's eyes are as wide as they can go while we jog over to our dugout. "Like seriously, a triple play? Who are you trying to impress? My momma?"

I snort. We all know he doesn't have one.

Behind us, Rivera's voice joins in. "Bro. Bro! What? *What?*"

I rip off my mask and wipe the sweat off my forehead with my arm. "Listen, I can hear the crushes developing in your voices and you need to stop." Because I'm leaving this season, but I don't say that part aloud.

"But you're single." Rivera laughs.

"It's okay, you're safe from me." Starr puts his hand on his chest. "But only because I'm already dating Hope."

Sighing, I leave them behind because I have an at bat coming up and need to get the pads off. Sometimes these two preschoolers wrap me up in their absurdity and I end up saying things that fuel them. I should know better by now.

As I step into the dugout, I'm greeted by more paws than I'm comfortable with—from players and staff. Even Beau joins in.

"That one's going to make the highlight reels," he says.

*Kaplan will enjoy that*, I think to myself sardonically.

"Triple play, you show off!"

"Pff, off the charts."

"Wow, I'm so glad you're on our team, man."

I focus on removing my chest pad, not showing a single hint about how bad that last one hits. I wish I was as cold blooded as I actually want, just so that the glee in their faces didn't land in the pool of acid in my stomach.

But whatever, the game's still going. I put all this in a little box in my mind and shelve it.

McDonald, one of the hitting coaches, grabs me by the shoulder. "Brown's going to get on base before you no matter what. You have to get him in scoring position."

I nod. Brown's a really good hitter. He's not powerful enough to make the coveted rankings or anything, but he's reliable and a decent runner, and his RBI doesn't lie.

"Their second is still shaken from the error in the bottom second," he continues with that special blend of whisper-shouting that happens in matches where the crowd is rowdy. "Crush it right behind him and we're set."

"Got it."

He hands me the helmet, someone else gives me the gloves. I stuff the sliding mitt in my back pocket and grab a bat on the way out. Brown's just reaching the home plate and starting his jinxes—two swings, a sweep of the dirt with his foot, one more swing.

I stand on-deck, tugging my gloves in place and balancing the bat on my shoulder. Brown makes eye contact with me and touches the tip of his nose. I nod.

Yeah, we're not filling up bases. We're going for it.

Instructions given, he makes short work of it and connects on the second pitch. It's a solid hit, landing between the pitcher and second base in a way that gets the whole formation scrambling. And voila, there's Brown in first.

I'm not an old school type of ball player who believes in rituals. My biggest asset is my brain and that's how I approach every single play, and every single inning. My goal is to screw over with the heads of the opposing team whether I'm catching, batting, or running.

A glance at Beau and he gives me the go ahead to do whatever the hell I want. I'll miss that. It always takes a while to get to this level of trust with a new team. But they'd be fools to test me for too long, anyway.

I step onto the batter's box and the catcher steps inward in an almost drastic way. Are they trying to bean me and walk me off?

Bo-o-ring.

In turn, I stand back as far from the home plate as I can and set out to play my own game.

The pitcher shakes his head twice, probably trying to burn as much of the clock as he can. Finally he throws and I don't move a muscle. The ball whiffs me close enough to fan my shirt.

"Ball!"

Our base coach tells Brown not to run at all, fully trusting that I'll hit the next one—not knowing that I have a different plan.

I start humming my walkup song, even though it's not playing on the stadium speakers anymore. Behind me, the catcher mumbles something I can't discern but is surely not PG rated. Dude's a rookie and clearly why this is enough to rattle him.

He crouches real close again, fifty-fifty chance that he'll ask for the same pitch. Even if he does, his pitcher isn't a Cade Starr who can place the ball at any point at will. So either the pitcher will bean me, or he'll end up pitching farther.

He winds up with just a smidge less enthusiasm than before. The ball makes a pink dot and I'd blow a raspberry if I wasn't already in motion. I tilt back just a bit, giving myself a wider range to swing. The impact comes right where I wanted it, and I'm stronger than the blow. I keep swinging until the ball takes off into the distance.

It's gonna be a foul, so I don't go very far.

"Foul!" the umpire calls out and I jog back to the batter's box with one more pitch for the pitcher's count.

And that's what my plan is. I'm going to tire this guy out until the last second.

The next pitch results in the exact same picture. Funny enough, the ball lands near the same spot as before—well, it's not funny. That's where I aimed.

Then I get two balls, and they start making the pitcher grind his teeth because he's finally caught onto my game. Some of the fans are booing, probably thinking this is boring or cowardly. I don't care about that. I'm the kind of asshole who will happily bunt if it means turning the other team into scrambled eggs.

Fortunately for him, it's time to finish this.

The catcher's no longer aiming for a hit by pitch, and now knows I'm annoying enough that I'll get walked if they keep going. The batter waits a long time to accept the sign and throws.

Oh, it's a work of art. A two seamer right where I like it.

*Come to daddy*, I think while I swing.

The clang against my bat is so satisfying, I wish I could replay the recording at night to lull me to sleep. I finish the swing and watch the ball rise into the air in a perfect rendition of the St. Louis arch.

This makes the crowd's tune change. As thousands of voices rise, I trot to first base and toss the bat to the side. The centerfield runs toward the ball, but the wall gets in the way while the ball keeps going—until it hits the display.

I smile. I couldn't possibly have planned this better.

*

We end up winning twelve to two. Our best game so far in my opinion, better than the perfect game last week.

This one… this is the one that will send the bat signal to the whole league that the Orlando Wild isn't picking its nose and scratching its ass this season.

The locker room is a whole jungle right after the game, and I'm trying to tune them out by toweling my face before the post game interview. One of the broadcast producers gave me a heads up during the last inning that my face's services are required.

A yawn escapes as I trawl out of the clubhouse. Eh, I forgot to leave the towel behind so I'll just hang it around my neck.

I find the camera man and Steve Boateng, our broadcast guy, already set up against the screen that prominently features our team logo of a purple gator with yellow accents. I've done this enough times that I know where to stand.

Boateng gets going right away. "We have Logan Kim joining us tonight after the impressive twelve-two win. How do you feel right now, Logan?"

"Hungry," I kid but not. Since I've been told to be a bit less cutting in these things, I add, "It was a really good game, though. I hope the fans had a good time." Here I offer a little smile at the camera, a second before a fat drop of sweat falls from my nose.

"Congratulations on the win. And on another topic," he continues, "What do you think about the video that's running wild on the internet?"

"I—What video?"

"The wild catch you made that saved our social media manager."

*The what, what?* I ask myself. There's a video?

First time I hear about it, so I have no freaking clue what people are saying online. Surely it can't be bad if she came out unscathed.

Tentatively I say, "I have no doubt that it was the most important catch of my career."

Boateng shifts the microphone toward him and says, "According to some, it has made you the biggest catch in the league." He gives out a rehearsed laugh, like that line was. "Thank you for your time, Logan. We'll let you go get some rest."

"Yeah, thank you." With one final nod, I turn back where I came from.

Most of the guys are already hitting the showers, but first I make a bee line to find my cellphone in my locker. It only takes a few taps to find the top video when I search for my name.

"What the—" Even I know these many million views are not normal.

I hit play on the video and it's just me squirting a water bottle into my mouth while Rosalina Mena asks me something behind the screen. And then the video slows down, and some saxophone shit starts playing in the background as I move.

Okay, I have to admit that it was a freaky catch. I was moved on instinct alone. Of course I had a general idea where the batters stood on the field for practice, but there's an infinite ball trajectory possibilities. Mena's guardian angel must've been the one positioning my hand to the precise spot needed to catch the ball and prevent a tragedy.

But then the video changes to my face as I check in on her.

My absolutely terrified face.

I turn my phone away and sit there for a moment, staring at nothing.

Gathering a deep breath, I look at the video again. It has started all over, so I scroll back to that spot.

The hell am I doing biting my lip like that? Yeah, it was scary, but anyone would think that was my wife about to get murdered or something.

No wonder they put this sexy-times music on top. And a brief glance at the comments confirms that yes, this has painted a target on my back for the women of the internet.

That's one, two… sixteen wedding proposals within three scrolls.

There goes my stinking peace and quiet. And if this shit stays up for longer, I may end up with stalkers of the caliber like Starr got during Spring Training.

Standing up, I mumble, "That ball didn't kill you, Mena, but I will." I toss the towel on my seat and stomp out of the clubhouse, headed for the back office.

# CHAPTER 9
# ROSE



That makes my chest twist painfully. My dad died when I was too young to remember him, but he was still a part of the family growing up.

Pictures of him in his youth line our living room, along with snaps of him and Mom dating, their wedding, and from when I was born. My favorite is from one when I was just shy of twelve months. He held me in his arms and was captured right as he gave me what was probably the biggest kiss in the world. My pudgy little face was scrunched up in joy—there might've been a bit of drool dripping down my mouth that Mom says was from the flash.

And he wore an Orlando Wild baseball cap.

Our franchise is pretty new, just a few years older than I

am, but apparently one of Dad's favorite Venezuelan players was drafted to the Wild right as the team started out. It coincided with the timing for Mom and Dad to leave their home country behind and relocate somewhere safer. According to the legend, Dad chose Orlando, Florida, because of the baseball team.

He passed just before my second birthday in a car accident, but so many things about him stayed with us. His music taste, his zest for life, his face in mine… his love of Orlando Wild baseball.

I don't know him, and even I know he would've gone hoarse screaming in the stands during this game. We were just… wild.

I hug my phone to myself and basically skip to my office. The game footage is going to make for some golden posts. By the time I'm done, I'll more than deserve a bonus. I'll put in my name in the hat for a promotion.

"What you got for us?" one of the ladies in the digital content team greets me as I step into the marketing office, complete with rubbing her grubby hands in glee.

"I don't know if to share," I joke, side-stepping her to head to my cubicle. "You might faint when you see it."

"Is it something juicy, then?" She wiggles her eyebrows.

Aside from the accidental closeup of Logan Kim pulling out his bunched up pants from the crack of his bubble butt? Yes.

I plop on my chair and say, "I just so happened to be right behind the home plate for the triple play."

"Whoa."

"Did someone say triple play?" my boss's voice echoes from afar, I figure he's coming into the office.

"It seems like Rosalina got some good stuff for us," the digital content girl says.

"Oh yeah?" That's a new voice coming along.

Next thing I know, four people other than me cram in my cubicle to watch as I plug my phone into the screens, and replay some of the best bits for them. Much oh'ing and ah'ing ensues, punctuating ideas from everyone in a creative team that has probably not seen better fodder than this season.

I'm not the only one buzzing from tonight's game, and yes our opponent hasn't contended for the World Series in twenty years—but neither have we. And this time it feels very different.

"What if you splice this one… with this one?" my boss asks, pointing at the screen in one hand and holding his seating cushion with the other hand. Poor guy has to use it to sit everywhere until he's all healed from the surgery.

"I was thinking about that," I confirm, dragging my mouse to bring a third clip on the screen. "With this one as the finisher. It'd be with some dramatic flares and sombre music up to here, then with the third clip we speed it up and use a more animated song. Something like…"

"We Are The Champions?" another colleague suggests to a round of snickers.

I raise my hand. "No, we'll save that one for when we win the World Series. We don't want to jinx it."

"You're right." Dave nods.

Our other colleague opens her eyes wide. "Wait, you're serious?"

"Sure. Why wouldn't we—"

"Is Rosalina Mena here?"

We all freeze at the question.

Or rather, at the voice. Because it's not one that we hear often around here.

My coworkers are corporate meerkats. They straighten up to look at the interloper from above the walls of my cubicle. But I'm trapped in my seat between them and my chair, so I can't even ascertain that this isn't a mass hallucination event.

Otherwise, I can't fathom why Logan Kim would be here in the marketing office when, er, by my count he should be showering.

But also, I can't tell my colleagues to say that I'm not here. That would arouse too much interest that I'm unwilling to entertain. As much as I don't want to deal with him, I have no choice but to let this play out.

"Oh wow," the digital content creator whispers behind me. "He's even better to look at in the flesh."

"You're starting to drool, Betty," my boss jokes in an equally quiet voice.

Someone else adds, "Aren't you married?"

"Well, yeah. But looking is free."

"It's a free country, a'ight."

A round of snickers.

"She's here," my boss finally responds, pointing at me even though there's no way Logan can see his hand through the cubicle walls. "But shouldn't you be in the showers?"

*Thank you*, I mouth to myself.

"First, I have some business with Mena." Ugh. Why does Logan Kim sound so much closer?

The traitors start scooting out of my space, casually standing to the same side and giving room to the newcomer. Sighing, I swivel in my chair to meet him.

I don't know what I was thinking. I'm just as stunned to see our catcher in the threshold of my cubicle. He's still in his game uniform, smears of red sand down one knee and the opposite hip, so soaking wet that the fabric sticks to his frame like a second skin.

He's not wearing his mask or pads, but his hair is loose and even though he's combed it back with his fingers, a strand still escaped and is stuck to the side of his face. A face that is darkened by a perfectly manicured stubble and—

A glare.

My eyebrows scrunch. What's his deal?

Taking a deep breath, I try to approach this from a standpoint of maturity. "The air conditioning here is too strong and you could get sick. Let's step outside."

He folds his arms, two works of art between tattoos and muscles that bunch beautifully with the motion. I'm not even being a creep—the guy is objectively a perfect male specimen. At least on the outside.

"I wouldn't get sick from this," he grouches, offense obviously taken.

"Then let's go out for my sake then. I'm freezing." I grab my cardigan from the back of my chair and get up. My four colleagues have the same look on their faces, like they wish they could record this and put it on social media.

I motion at them to stay in the office like they're puppies I'm trying to train, before following Logan out.

Then I shrug on my cardigan and take the lead. His steps tag along all the way as I meander us through the corridors and out to the cafeteria. It's still empty safe for the kitchen staff, since the hungry players haven't yet descended upon it. But it's only a matter of time, so I whirl around and mimic his earlier stance.

The fact that his eyes fall on the lavender flowers knitted at the front of my cardigan annoys me. I don't know why. It just does.

"What can I do for you, Logan?"

Huffing, he runs a massive hand through his hair. "Take down the video."

My knee jerk reaction is to say no. Somehow I temper it down to a "what video?"

"The one about me making the catch that kept the integrity of your pretty little head, and makes me look like a complete simp."

I *oh* and *ah* just as my colleagues did earlier, then add, "No."

"Excuse me?"

"You heard me. Are we done here?"

"No, we are not done here." He scoffs. Or maybe chokes a laugh. Then he shakes his head. "Fine, if you don't have the authority to remove that video, I'll go to your boss."

"Absolutely not." I offer him my best pageant smile, the one that almost got me the Miss Florida crown when I was twenty. "It's one of the most viral videos in the account. You can escalate all the way to Cox if you want, and I'm sure not even he would want to stop the momentum our account is getting from it."

Now he's sincerely annoyed, and this is when I learn that there's a difference between normal-grumpy-Logan and about-to-do-violence-Logan.

A muscle in his jaw jumps from how hard he's gnashing his teeth, and red hot sparks fly out of his eyes. "There is a clause in my contract that prevents the team from publishing anything defamatory or that devalues my own personal image."

"Which is why I'm not posting the video I got of you with a wedgie."

"Mena." He all but growls my last name, and something terrible happens—horrible, absolutely traumatizing…

I break into goosebumps all over.

As I rub my arms over my cardigan, I add, "Listen, as your resident social media manager, I have to learn a thing or two about legalities as well. Defamation means lying, and nothing about that video is a—"

"There's a damn saxophone—"

I try really hard not to laugh as I continue, "—Lie. And also, how is your image being devalued when you're getting thousands of proposals from marriage, to modeling, to indecent ones you'd probably enjoy?"

"Saxophone," he repeats through gritted teeth. "I hate wind instruments."

"I'll use some piano next time."

"Next time?" He does an angry double take, his brow darkening by the second.

"My point is that you're now more popular than ever, and so is the team by default."

"Exactly!" Logan throws his hands in the air, probably the biggest gesture I've ever seen on him. "I save your life and this is what I get? Mockery?"

*Mockery?*

Is he implying that my job is a joke?

"Um, excuse me. I didn't ask for it to be *you*," I snap, lava rising up my throat in the form of a barrage of words. "I'd also rather deal with literally any other guy on the team than put up with this crap. And oh by the way, if you're gonna treat saving my life like it's a favor, you're gonna have to wait for me to return it when you're in the same kind of danger. Good. Freaking. Bye."

I don't wait for him to finish blinking. I turn around and head to the other door. Except my shoulder rams into it and the door doesn't open, which means that my only escape is through the door that Logan is blocking with his massive frame.

Ignoring him, I take the long road circling back the tables, conscious of his laser beams trained on me. But if he thinks that a glare will be enough to make me cave to his will, he has something coming to him. And by coming I mean going—back to my office, leaving him behind and his damn arrogance that has officially soured my night.

# CHAPTER 10
# LOGAN

*ow to Win Friends and Influence People* plays on my living room sound system and I have an exercise mat rolled out over the carpet where the coffee table normally sits.

I keep my eyes mostly focused out the floor to ceiling windows that showcase an expansive Orlando downtown view—expansive by the size of the windows, not by the views. I live in the highest residential building and aside from this one, there's just a handful of other tall ones. On a clear night I can catch the fireworks from the parks in the south, though.

Meanwhile, the rest of me is in a plank position over the exercise mat. It's been fifteen minutes according to the counter on my phone that lays face up on the carpet where I can see it, so I'm not even shaking yet. After this, I'll have a protein shake for dinner, get in the tub to listen to the audiobook for a while more, and catch some early Z's. It's an ideal rest day night before getting back on the road tomorrow.

Of course, this is when someone decides to disrupt my quiet by calling me on the phone.

At first I figure it's my manager with news of a trade, but actually my brother's name lights up the screen. I ignore it.

A huff comes out of my throat not because of the plank, but because he's not taking the damn hint and leaving me the hell alone. He keeps calling, which means I keep not listening to my audiobook. And yes, I'd much rather read a ninety year old book than deal with Lewis Kim.

Finally he drops the call and the relief almost makes me drop the plank. I tighten my muscles again, starting by my toes that are holding up my lower body weight, clenching my stomach to not sag, and fisting my hands to motivate my arms to keep steady. It goes well for a couple of minutes until Lewis calls again.

"Shit," I mumble.

I know him. He's a hound with a bone and won't leave me alone until I give him the attention he craves.

Slowly, I ease down to all fours and grab my phone. I do take several deep breaths before answering. "What do you want?"

"Is that really how you should greet your only beloved brother?"

"Only? Yes. Beloved? Absolutely the hell not." Rubbing my forehead, I add, "Don't make me repeat myself."

"Fine, what I want is to know if the rumors are true."

What rumors? Is this something related to Mena's video that she refused to take down even when I asked nicely?

Anyone who hears this conversation would think, first, that I'm an asshole brother. And second, that Lewis is the youngest sibling by how his voice is all jovial and wholesome, whereas mine radiates hostility.

But that's because they don't know him—or what he's capable of.

"I heard that you may be considering a return to the Eagles."

I freeze and say absolutely nothing. Not even a peep.

What I really want to do is roar like a freaking lion. Did Kaplan approach the Eagles? Did my trade intentions leak? Does anyone in the Wild, other than Beau, already know?

Or… this could be my brother's blatant attempt to suss me out.

See, we don't love or support each other in the Kim-Lindberg clan—we don't console, teach, guide or any of the other shit I assume functional families do.

We play mind games. We fight to win, no matter what.

It's not a secret that I've changed teams every two or three years and that my time is coming up. A couple of sports blogs have even commented on it. My keener teammates may be wondering it. Certainly my sociopathic brother would've picked on it.

Since he knows that I know his shtick, and he knows that I won't give him an inch, he carries on all by himself. "Because we would absolutely love to have you back. Water under the bridge and all that. I would even put in a good word for you."

As if he wasn't the reason I left in the first place.

"Are you done fantasizing?" I ask in a flat tone of voice that gives nothing. The last thing I should do is show that anything he says or does can affect me—even if it does. I learned this lesson before I was even ten years old.

"Think about it," he says with a chuckle. "We can go back to being the best battery in modern baseball history. In fact, I think with our current skill we might even become the best *ever*. We're definitely a shoo-in for the All Star game—"

"I'm hanging up—"

"Logan, c'mon. Our parents would love to see us play together again."

We both know that he doesn't give a flying turd about what our parents think.

"Do us both a favor and go watch that documentary they

filmed about your life. Bye." I end the call before he can keep nagging. The jerk calls back right away and I tap over to his contact and mute him.

I sit back on my haunches as the audiobook picks up where it left off, but there's no hiding the rapid heartbeat in my chest from myself.

I'm a twenty eight year old man. I even found a gray hair on my head this morning. I haven't lived with my parents or my brother in ten years. I'm not financially dependent on any of them, and could even cut them out of my life like my therapist has suggested multiple times.

But every time I hear Lewis's voice, I get transported to my seven-year-old self when he locked me up in a closet for an entire weekend.

Mom's voice takes me back to the night she screamed at Dad so much, she decided that smashing a vase would be a more effective way of getting across how pissed off she was, and the shards that sliced into my skin.

Dad's voice reminds me of my right hand's middle finger, crooked because he kept shouting at me to throw forkballs with a *SPORTY* hardball—even though I was just eleven and already knew I wanted to be a catcher—until my finger broke.

Shit, my breathing's getting short.

Fortunately, the league's getting wiser about player mental health and my medication is on the list of allowed substances. I spring to my feet and eat up the floor in a few strides toward the kitchen.

As I'm washing the little pill down the guzzler, my door bell rings and for a wild second, I fear Lewis is behind it. But I shake my head, remembering that he should be in New York right now or maybe somewhere on the road, I don't know. I know for a fact that we don't play them for a while.

The door camera system shows a different familiar face. One that is also annoying, but at least not terrifying.

I open the door and greet him just the same way, though. "What do you want?"

Rivera, who also happens to be my neighbor, sweeps his eyes from my bare chest, to my black sweats, and my toes. "Excuse me, sir. This is a residential building. Families live here. You need to consider their tender eyes."

He's lucky I'm not buck ass naked.

Folding my arms, I fire back, "Is there anything about you that is tender?"

"No." He grins. "Certainly not my eyes. Anyway, can I come in?"

Well, so much for a quiet evening.

"No." I try closing the door, knowing exactly what's going to happen.

Dude wedges himself between the doorframe and the door. "It'll just be a second."

"You said the same last time and parked your ass on my couch until two in the morning watching Teenage Mutant Ninja Turtle reruns."

He opens his eyes wide. "Don't you love feeling like a child again?"

My teeth grit hard enough to catch his notice. There is *nothing* I hate more than feeling like a child again. Nothing. Not even that ridiculous post on the team's social media that makes me look like a sap.

"You have ten seconds before I shove you out the door," I grit out.

"Okay, okay. Cade's in a pickle and needs our help."

That's unexpected enough that it gives me pause. I really thought this was gonna be about more childhood TV show marathons.

Slowly, I ask, "What kind of pickle?"

"A bad one. Only we can help him."

"Any more details so I can make a decision?" I frown.

"No, he just called me all panicky and I sprung to action." He shrugs, hands raised and palms facing up in the universal gesture of what-else-can-you-do.

Deadpan, I ask, "Has he called nine-one-one?"

"Oh, it's not *that* kind of an emergency, trust me."

Which means this is probably a chick emergency. He screwed something up with Hope and now needs our help to get his head out of his ass. We should probably do that before it fries his brain and we have to bench him for more than one series.

"Fine, let's go," I concede.

"Nuh-uh. Not like that." He points up and down at me. "You need to put on some clothes, pendejo."

"You're the pendejo," I shoot back, knowing very well what the word means. "Of course I'm getting dressed first."

This means that I end up letting him into my apartment. I also have to pause my book so Rivera doesn't fall asleep on my couch while I get dressed. The whole thing takes maybe five minutes and in two more, we're down at the parking lot where he gets in his Escalade and I hop on my Ducati. He didn't give me the address but I follow him closely enough that I don't need it. In fact, I can almost hear the reggaeton blaring in his sound system every time we stop at a light.

The sky is doing its show of colors for dusk. The rainy season hasn't started yet, so the sun and the clouds treat us to quite the masterpiece. I barely even register that we enter a posh neighborhood in Winter Park, so distracted I am by the purple, pink, and yellow hues in the sky.

That's when something more important occurs to me. Since Rivera showed up at my door, all the thoughts about my relatives vanished in thin air. My heart rate returned to normal, my breathing evened... I even forgot to keep playing my audiobook.

Rivera parks by a random building that looks like a bunker

in between pretty houses. I sit back on my bike behind his vehicle, watching as he steps out and walks around.

I bet he's one of the few, if not the only one, who has realized I'm due for a trade. Rivera's way smarter than he pretends—something I'll never acknowledge aloud.

Wait, what is he doing?

I unstrap my helmet and remove it, the better to watch him retrieve some shopping bags from the back of his SUV. And they sport the unmistakable logo of Publix.

"What kind of emergency would require you buying groceries for Starr?" I narrow my eyes.

Rivera smirks at me, then presses his finger to the doorbell of a door that looks like something out of prison. The door opens and sounds spill out. The problem is that I can't really discern them.

"Aren't you coming?" the Boricua asks, jerking his head toward the door.

And only because I don't want to go back home to think about my brother, I hop out of my bike and follow him.

# CHAPTER 11
# ROSE

One second I'm happy, humming a tune as I step out of Cade's house with a bowl of salad I just finished tossing, and the next I'm completely annoyed.

What the heck is Logan Kim doing here?

I don't think he's seen me yet. He's just closing the gate's door behind Lucky, casting a first glance around the oddly shaped yard. I duck below the kitchen island by reflex. Curse this architectonic marvel of a house that has no walls, but the thickest panes of glass. It's only a matter of time before Logan sees me in the kitchen.

"And why should that matter?" I ask my salad bowl, covered with cling wrap and safe from my germs. "I was here first. In fact, the idea of this whole BBQ was borne out of my roommates's desire to cheer me up."

And the reason for that need is *him*.

I've been fuming about last night's conversation and look at him—the jerk has the nerve to act all easy breezy with his damn bike jacket that fits a bit too perfectly around his freaking perfect shoulders and arms, and the damn man bun at the top of his head that no one seems to have told him is out of fashion but looks amazing on him. The least he could do would be to sport a few bandages from the burns I gave him last night.

So why, even though he was in the wrong and I'm the one who won the argument, am I the one hiding?

"Hear me out," I say to the salad bowl. "You don't like good looking men and now you've learned that pretentious men aren't really charming, they're just pretentious." I nod to myself. "So go out there and act like he's a zero to the left."

I jump to my feet and pretend like I was just picking something up and putting it in the kitchen sink. But he's not even looking this way, so the act isn't necessary.

Except Lucky *is* watching.

He opens the door as I come out with the salad, and I'm not sure why his eyes look all sparkly and amused, but they do. "Evening, princesa," he says as greeting.

"Princesa?" I cock an eyebrow.

He shrugs. "Cade calls you princess, so it's kinda stuck now. Need any help?"

"I'm good, thanks." I use my lips to point at the grocery bags hanging from his hand. "You?"

"This is what I train for, c'mon." He does some bicep curls with Publix bags, and I bite my lips not to laugh because it's ridiculous.

"Okay, don't hurt yourself there," I joke while shuffling sideways to hold the door open with my body. "After you."

"Chivalry is not dead!" he exclaims in an overly dramatic way, also shuffling sideways as if this door wasn't wider than a normal one. But just as I'm giving him props for being mindful, Lucky gives me a casual little wink that makes me shake my head.

Yeah, maybe I should've crushed on Lucky last year rather than Ben. Lucky's fun, yet polite. Unfortunately, he's too attractive. His Latin American fan club will probably murder the woman who dares to tie the knot with him one day—if he even settles down.

With a deep breath, I turn away from the door and face the main gathering.

"Look who's here," Hope says with a forced grin that only I can see while she keeps her back to the guys. "It's Logan Kim, your savior."

Years of training for the Miss Florida pageant rush back and I let a brilliant smile bloom on my face, one that I know shows all my pearly whites. "Isn't that great? How are you doing, Logan?"

If I think I'm ready for this, I swiftly discover that I am most definitely not when he turns those dark, clever eyes on me. Every muscle in my body locks with all the effort it takes to not launch the salad at his face. That would be extremely unfair to the veggies.

"Mena," he returns with his deep voice and a tip of his chin.

"Why do you still refer to her by her last name?" Cade asks from the grill, pausing from flipping chorizos.

"I refer to everybody by their last name." Logan makes an attempt to fold his arms but his helmet gets in the way.

Hope springs. "Oh, sorry. Let me attempt to be a good hostess and take your helmet and jacket."

"Wait a damn second." Cade turns around and places the back of his hands on his hips, tongs poking out from one side. He glances first at his girlfriend and then at Logan, and back again. "He does call you by your name and you're so polite only to him. Why is that?"

"Are you jealous, Starr?" Audrey asks from a camping chair across the fire pit that we lit up just a few minutes ago.

Cade frowns. "Yes."

For the first time in my life, I witness Logan's hard expression morph into amusement. And I'm not the only one who remarks on it—Audrey's jaw is equally as dropped as mine. In fact, we even exchange a glance that says *are you seeing what I'm seeing?*

He's obnoxiously perfect when he's serious, but just a hint of a smile makes him almost ethereal. Something in my mind shifts and I have the certainty that from now on, his face is the one I'll picture every time I'm reading a romantasy hero.

Ugh.

"There's no need to be jealous, Cowboy. Hope and I just went out on *one* date," Logan says as he hands over his helmet to Hope, and unzips his jacket.

I restart walking over to the serving table by the grill, finally placing the bowl on it. I dust my hands, all proud of my contribution to the party, and turn around.

I choke in my own saliva.

Logan Kim has removed his jacket and he's wearing one of those tank tops where the openings go as low as his waist. And I didn't know his torso was tatted up too. Like, I don't make it my business to glimpse at the players's naked bodies. The one time I did it backfired tragically.

This time, as Hope walks into the house, Lucky's the one who comes out. He takes one look at Logan and asks, "Dude, where's the rest of your clothes?"

"At home, where I wanted to be tonight," the other guy sasses right back.

"Hey, I'm telling you." Cade points at Logan with a big frown on his pretty Texas boy face. "If you want to keep calling my girlfriend by her first name, you'll have to call everyone by their first names too."

"Fine." The big guy in the man bun shrugs powerful shoulders. Copying Cade's gesture, he starts pointing at each person, "Audrey?"

"Yep." She salutes him.

Logan moves on. "Lucas."

"I go by Lucky. I'm the team's lucky charm."

"Lucas it is," Logan confirms to himself. Right then, Hope marches back out to the yard and he points at her. "Still Hope."

She freezes and glances back. "Uh, yeah. Last I checked."

Then Logan's finger veers to the pitcher. We all can tell this one's tough by the way Logan's jaw muscles jump. He grits his teeth and finally, painstakingly, he grumbles, "Cade."

Audrey mutters, "Atta boy."

And that's when Logan's finger turns to the last person. Me.

"Rosalina."

I gasp in Spanish.

And then, in a fraction of a second, I know that I wasn't supposed to show a big reaction to this. After all, the earth has spun exactly twenty six years since people have been calling me by that name, and no one's voice has made me break into goosebumps all over. My damn goosebumps have goosebumps, and I don't get it.

So I mask it by choking and waving my hands, hoping they think it's because of the smoke from the grill next to me.

"She goes by Rose," Audrey adds in a breezy tone.

"Then Rose," he says without inflection, looking around as if searching for other people whose first names he's going to have to get familiar with.

Lucky frowns. "How come she gets her preferred name and not me?"

"That's not the important question here." Cade grunts. "Was using Hope's name so important that you're willing to make these many changes at once?"

That's when I figure out that Logan wasn't looking for other people, but for the cooler full of chilled bottles. He sinks down to a camping chair that looks like a toy beneath him, and I'm satisfied by the disappointment in his face as he opens the cooler and doesn't find beer inside. Hope filled it up with sweet and unsweet iced tea.

"What the hell is this?" the grouch murmurs.

Cade waves the tongs. "I'm talking to you, Kim."

Of course, the latter flashes that transformational smirk. "Now you'll have to call me Logan, though. Equality and all that."

Hope lowers herself to the chair beside Audrey and leans closer to our roomie. "What the hell are these two weirdoes even talking about?"

"I'm not sure, to be honest. The gist of it is that your boyfriend is jealous about you and the catcher."

"Anyway," I cut in, turning to Cade. "Is there anything I can help you with?"

Our starting pitcher gives me an appraising look. "This right here, ladies and gents, is the real MVP."

That causes a chorus of grumbles and mumbles from the rest, and they all get off their behinds to come over and fix themselves a plate. Cade turns into a one-man fast food restaurant, dropping burger patties on one bun after the next, along with pieces of Venezuelan style chorizo that Hope and I bought at a Latino supermarket.

I take a seat next to Audrey since we promised to split an extra chorizo between us. And then someone sits beside me.

Logan.

I check my surroundings, just to make sure there really were no other choices. But Lucky's already parked next to Audrey, and the lovebirds are whispering sweet nothings to each other behind the chairs they intend to take, marking their territory clearly.

Six chairs. Like all along they did plan on inviting Logan. Why did I not notice it before?

"Ugh," my mouth slips.

"Easy there, Mena," Logan says beside me. "People will think I didn't shower."

I lift a glare at him. "Don't worry, that's not what stinks."

This catches him in the middle of taking a swig of unsweet iced tea, but he cocks an eyebrow at me because he's multitalented that way. After a moment, he asks, "Something else of mine stinks?" He cups his hand over his mouth and sniffs. "My breath? I haven't even started eating that spicy chorizo yet."

"No—"

"It's your attitude, you big oaf," Lucky says before sinking a big bite on his heaping burger.

That's when Audrey sets her plate on her lap and clears her throat to call our attention. "Logan, Rose, this is an intervention."

"What the—"

"Excuse—"

As if pulled by a string, I turn to exchange an incredulous glance with the catcher. I feel equally shocked at the outrageous statement I just heard, and also at the fact that he agrees with me—at least going by the expression on his face.

"It's my fault." The pitcher raises his hand. "I happened to overhear you two arguing in the cafeteria last night, and I told my girlfriend…"

"Who told me," Audrey says, "And that's before you arrived home all ragey and told us."

Lucky's done swallowing his mouthful and speaks. "And I had no idea until Cade called me with the plan and asked me to make sure to bring Kim—I mean, Logan."

My face heats up enough to compete with the fire licking at the air in the middle of this awkward circle, especially when I feel the laser beams of the man on my right.

"Ragey?" he asks.

Huffing, but without looking at him, I say, "You really pissed me off, okay?" Damn it, I didn't want him to know that last night caused such a big impression on me. I pin the girls with a look. "Did we really have to hash this out in public?"

Hope offers a sheepish grin. "We all work and travel together. And Cade and Logan are a battery so they're basically joined at the hip these days. I figured it'd be best to clear the air."

"I'm here for the free food," Audrey says placidly.

"Everything would've worked out if you had agreed to delete the video." Silence descends upon the circle and we all turn to Logan. He's casually spearing a whole chorizo with a fork to eat it like that. "What?" He frowns at the attention.

The first one to react is Audrey. "Turns out that you're all brawn and no brains, huh?"

"No, he has brains," Lucky mutters. "He's just being deliberately obtuse right now."

Cade smacks Logan's knee hard enough to cause an eye twitch. "You were supposed to apologize, you clown."

"Apologize?" said clown asks like Cade just created a brand new word.

"You know what? Yes." I set my plate down on the ground and twist in my chair to face him. "That's exactly what you should do. Apologize for giving me shit about doing my job."

Logan hastens the process of chewing a mouthful and swallows it down before shifting to also face me, putting his elbow on the armrest of *my* chair and leaning into my space. "Excuse me, Mena, but you could just as easily do your job by recording the shenanigans of literally anyone else on the team."

"I thought we were all on a first name basis by now," Lucky says, voice dripping with sarcasm.

"Well, excuse me right the hell back, *Kim*," I say in a saccharine tone, "but then it wouldn't go viral and I'd be doing my job *poorly*, which unlike your case, could really jeopardize my livelihood."

"Hey," Lucky protests. "Are you saying that the rest of us are less beloved by social media?"

"Dude, this isn't about you," Audrey tells him and chuckles.

Kim is giving me the same look as last night, like he doesn't know in quite what category to place me.

I realize we've barely interacted one-on-one until the past few weeks, and if anything he's just getting to know me and understand the fact that I'm not the Afro Latina version of a pretty bimbo, whose life revolves around his and the other players's.

I take advantage of his lull. "Imagine if one day you're practicing with the team and I go over to tell you that your catching form isn't balanced enough. Or that you're relying too much on your brain and not enough on your pitchers. Or that maybe you should consider rubbing Megababe on your butt cheeks so you stop getting wedgies. How would you feel about that, huh?"

Someone chokes.

Kim tilts his head. "Megababe?"

"Oh, c'mon. That's not the most important part of my speech."

"No, I'm genuinely interested in knowing what I can do to mitigate in-uniform wedgies."

I can't tell whether he's being sardonic or not. Clearing my throat, I explain, "It's an anti thigh-chafing product that looks like a deodorant stick."

"Ah." Oh, no. That dangerous amusement is back on his face and it makes his eyes glint like they have their own constellation of stars. "And where exactly would I rub it?"

Lucky bursts out laughing with no self restraint. He has one of those contagious laughs and as the others start to join, and the extent of ridiculousness comes to me in waves, I crack.

And something terrible happens. Horrible. The kind of thing one can't come back from.

Logan Kim also joins in my guffaws. It crumbles my annoyance like it's but a soda cracker.

Damn, he has a warm laughter. I didn't even think there was any warmth in this man.

But it starts ebbing away almost as soon as it comes. He coughs into his hand and leans away from me. That same hand travels to the top of his head, but the man bun doesn't let him play with his hair. He ends up massaging the back of his neck.

After clearing his throat twice, he finally recants. "Okay, I get it. I'm sorry for overstepping." He slouches on the chair, which makes the fabric of his tank top crumble awkwardly and I catch a flash of corded muscle. "It's just that I don't enjoy having the attention on me."

"What?" If anything Lucky laughs harder. "*You?* The fully tatted up Asian viking?"

"Asian viking?" Kim shakes his head.

Audrey snorts. "So glad there's no one from HR in here."

"*Ahem.*" Cade calls us to attention indiscreetly. "So, does that mean you're back to being friends?" Then he turns to his girlfriend and asks her, "Did I do well, darlin'?"

She shakes her head slowly. "Cade, they weren't even friends to begin with."

"It depends…" I give the half Korean, half Swedish, all American guy a side eye. "On whether he's going to act up the next time I have to do my job and it involves him."

"That depends…" His eyes bore into mine, no longer amused and more like inquisitive. "On how much saxophone plays in the background."

"No saxophone." I stick my hand out to him. "Deal?"

He dares to cast a dubious glance at my hand, like it could be hiding one of those zapping toys or something. But finally he takes it into a businesslike shake. "Deal."

But instead of doing the same when he tries to pull away, I tighten my hold and keep him in place. "Cutesy Kpop okay?"

"Rose." He utters my name in the same way as one would *are you shitting me.*

"Oh, he used her name," Lucky whispers so loud that even the neighbors must've heard.

"Logan?" I return sweetly.

His lips curl into a smirk and he tugs my hand toward him, closing just tighter enough around mine that I can no longer equate this to a businesslike handshake. "I love Kpop so bring it on."

Bring it on? Every cell in my body's telling me to run away. Except, as I glance at the extremely entertained jerks around me, I have a feeling that I'm in trouble.

# CHAPTER 12
## LOGAN

never thought I'd see the day when I thought this to myself: but this is what we get for not putting Starr as the starting pitcher for this game.

Granted, we can't win every single one, and he also can't play every time.

The Orlando Wild pitching staff is pretty solid—it's one of the reasons why I came to this team in the first place—and they held us off at a score that isn't embarrassing. But this tells me that some moves need to be made. A different training regime for a couple of the guys, maybe consider trading a third… I make a mental note to talk about this with Beau and Socci.

Or maybe not? I mean, I have one foot out of the door. The Wild will become my opponents whenever I go to a different team. So why should I help them?

Sighing, I catch the last strike that ends the game. Thomason looks dejected on the mound—like he truly believes that at his second season in the pros, he should've been able to hold off a stronger lineup to no runs. This at least I can do something about now.

I meet him halfway and remove my mask. "Hey, what's with the wounded puppy face?"

"Ha." He gives a watery smile. "This wouldn't have sucked so bad for the team if only I was better."

"Listen, kid," I say like I'm not just six years older. "You played for three innings. You're only responsible for your performance during those three innings, do you understand?"

"But—"

"No," I cut in. "That's it. The error Brown made in the eighth? Not on you. The runs that Mendez and Smith allowed? Not on you."

"But I let them score two on me."

I grin. "Yeah, those are on you. See what I mean?"

The guy blinks hard at me. "I… I see it. It's both relieving and not."

"You're welcome." I tap my glove against his chest and jerk my head in the direction of the dugout. "Now let's go, I hear the menu for today is fish tacos and I'm starving."

"Tacos?" That adds some extra pep to his step.

My stomach makes a fearsome gurgle that makes him laugh and hey, I may not have half of the charm of a Lucky Rivera, but at least Thomason's head is screwed back on now.

But as I put my hand on my stomach, trying to get it to settle the hell down, something niggles at the back of my mind. Something about Mexico…

I recognize what's happening after my body moves all on its own. Once more, pulled by instinct, my eyes zero in on something. And it moves me to action.

"Kim?" Thomason asks as I veer toward the home plate again. I wave him off and keep going.

There, on the lower stands right behind the home plate, is Rosalina Mena—Rose, I guess—surrounded by a bunch of women in white Orlando Wild jerseys, with the purple and yellow trims. It's the fact that Rose keeps trying to move her phone and camera out of their reach what tells me this isn't some harmless interaction.

"Hey!" I call out as I walk over. "What are you doing?"

The handsiest of the women eases off when she sees me, and her squeal propagates to the other ones. "Oh my goodness, it's Logan! Guys, it's Logan!" Something about the way she stretches out my name tells me she's drunk off her ass.

"Oh wow, it's really him."

"Hey, Logan, can I have your autograph?"

"Better yet, what are you doing tonight?" A hiccup.

"Can I get on the list?" Then a flurry of laughter follows as they congratulate the owner of that zinger.

I shift my attention over to the team's social media manager. She's tucking her cellphone in the back pocket of her jeans, thinking more about the safety of her devices than her own. Or I guess, in protecting her job more than herself, based on what she said the other night at the cowboy's.

"You okay, Rose?"

She's surprised that I ask, openly showing it with wide eyes and parted lips. "I—Yes, thank you. It's not a big deal."

I raise my eyebrows. Not a big deal? She was just being harassed by five drunk women.

Too late do I realize my mistake. In getting Rose to talk to me, it attracts the drunkards's attention again. The apparent ringleader turns to our social media manager again and points an accusatory finger. "Give it to us straight, are the two of you really in a relationship?"

"Huh?" The question slips from my mouth and goes ignored.

Rose sighs. "Ma'am, for the last time. I'm just a staff mem—"

"Tell. Us. The. Truth!" the woman demands now jabbing her finger in Rose's chest.

My muscles lock, primed for action. But it's not like I can

leap over the boards to the stands and then do what? Bodily handle these women and end up getting sued?

I glance all around and spot a few of the players coming over—they must've seen the interaction and put two and two. At the helm is Lucky and I shout at him.

"Lucky, call security—*now!*"

He freezes for a second and then says something in Spanish that I don't understand, but he turns back around firing instructions to our teammates.

I turn my attention back on the women. Rose has her hands up and managed to put some distance while I was distracted, but there's a drunk woman behind her blocking her exit. I have to do something, but what?

"Do you want to know the truth?" I blurt out, which has the desired effect of calling all attention to me. I fold my arms, stalling for crumbles of time where I can, and look at each of the women in the eyes. I have a feeling some of them see five of me. "I take it you're my fans, right?"

"Oh, yes." One of them melts over the barrier to give me what she thinks is a sultry expression that makes her look constipated.

"I'm *the* biggest fan," one at the back of the group yells out.

"No, *I* am the biggest fan," counters the one who propositioned me a minute ago.

"You're all wrong, I'm the future Mrs. Kim," jokes another one.

I've never been gladder for easily distracted people. As even the one blocking her way moves over to fight over who wants to get in my pants the most, I make eye contact with Rose and telepathically tell her to beat it. She gives me one nod and retreats ever so slowly, carefully, until she's close enough to the stairs that she can bolt to the exit.

I wait even a moment longer, putting up with the most inane conversation that's ever filtered to my ears—they're now up to who wants to give me the most babies—when finally an army of security personnel barrel down the stairs.

Right before they arrive, I say, "The truth is that it's none of your business who I'm dating or not. But regardless of my status, you're not entitled to harass anyone on my behalf."

A series of gasps follow after that, a second before the first security guy reaches them. "Ladies, I'm afraid I will have to remove you from the premises."

"But Logan, we love you!"

"We just want to keep you safe from gold diggers."

Rolling my eyes, I turn my back on them and finally resume my walk to the dugout.

This is when I finally notice the rivers of sweat trickling down my forehead, more profuse even than during the game. Like the stress of that little shitshow was somehow worse than losing a game with a five run deficit.

*

Later, my fuel tank is full of tacos and I'm almost content. I pull away the soft covers of my bed to sink into it, groaning in an R-rated way at the softness of the pillows beneath my head. Now I'm fully content.

Which is why my lizard brain needs to ruin it right away.

This is probably why my therapist says I'm addicted to cortisol. But even knowing that, I reach over to my night table and pluck my phone from the charger. I want to know what people are saying about the game we lost tonight, so I hop onto the social media accounts of the main sports news sources.

It takes some scrolling through posts about other baseball teams and even other sports. Pausing, I pull myself up to sit, letting the sheets slide down my bare chest to my hips, and pick up the phone again. My hair gets in the way so I tuck it behind my ears and there it is, the first video about the Orlando Wild loss.

The commentary starts out fine—harsh, but well deserved. One guy says, "For a team that has been showing some serious grit since Spring Training, tonight's loss harkens back to the days of Ben Williams on the mound for the Wild."

"Are you saying that the Wild were a much worse team with Ben Williams as the starter?" A second guy scoffs. "Because Williams is one of the top pitchers in the league right now, so that makes no sense."

The first one responds, "Maybe. It does seem like this roster plays a lot harder when Cade Starr is the starter, which is really interesting when you think about how he was a relief pitcher for Williams last year."

"Isn't it?" I say as if they could hear me. Snorting, I add, "And that's because you haven't seen what happens when we bribe Starr with pizza."

The video continues though, and their conversation shifts to something a lot less professional. "Now, what everyone on social media is talking about isn't the Wild's loss tonight, but an altercation that occurred on the stands once the game concluded."

"Take a look at the footage that a fan captured."

"What?" I bring the phone closer to my face because right on the screen is the group of drunk women bothering Rose. "*Shit.*"

I can feel that sweet, sweet cortisol hitting me everywhere, and yet I don't stop myself from watching.

Sure enough, some random fan in the stands caught the whole thing on camera, complete with peeks at me from below on the field trying to deescalate the situation.

The comments are a ridiculous mixed bag. Some people call me a hero for intervening. Others have made a connection that this is the second time I come to the rescue of the same staff member. The theories are running rampant already—everything from tame, like Rose and I are dating, to some dramedy Kdrama type where I'm Rose's baby daddy and these are all the women I left for her.

But also mixed in between are comments calling Rose all sorts of nasty names, boiling down to how dare she get my attention. Kind of like what those drunks were saying to her.

I run my hands down my face. Have I screwed over her life when I was just trying to help her?

# CHAPTER 13
# ROSE

Normally I'm pretty well put together for work. I'll wear a cute and professional dress, but with some personality. Or I'll pair a fun cardigan with jeans that look way more expensive than they are. I'll do my makeup and ensure that my curls are the bounciest they can be.

But not today.

Today I look like I crawled out of a trash can.

In my defense, the clothes are clean and I did shower. The issue is that all I could muster was wearing my comfiest gym leggings and a too-oversized sweatshirt with the team logo. I didn't take the time to do my hair care routine, so I just gathered the mass of curls into a messy pineapple bun at the top of my head. And there's no makeup, which is the one thing I should've really done after a sleepless night.

The culprit is the video that my boss now proudly projects onto the wall for the entire marketing department to see.

"And now here's the best part," he says with morbid glee as the camera of whoever recorded this zooms into Logan Kim's worried face.

The audio is spotty but the OP picked up his words

perfectly, maybe by reading Logan's lips, and added some helpful captions for the audience. And so everyone in the baseball community knows that Logan Kim, aloof superstar catcher, with a face card that never declines, was worried about me—the poor social manager of the team. And that's just to correct some of the commenters saying that I'm an intern.

Anyway, now everyone thinks we're dating and that apparently I'm pregnant with twins.

It would be hilarious if, first, this was happening to someone else. Second, if I hadn't stayed awake the whole night watching as comments rolled in like an avalanche. Soon the video reached far beyond the baseball community and fell into the deepest corners of Booktok and Bookstagram. As someone who also belongs to that community, I knew exactly what this would turn into.

Chaos.

Let's just say, after the initial fun wore off and the first handful of death threats rolled in, I had to set all my profiles to private. By that point it was almost sunrise so I just came to work early, hoping that my job would distract me from the internet trolls.

Here we are, though. It's not like the marketing team was going to pass up the latest viral moment.

"This is gold, people." Dave folds his arms and stands back to watch the rest of the video, which is somehow a more dramatic rendition of what happened than the real events.

Yes, it was kind of scary to be surrounded by a bunch of drunk strangers who wanted to see if I had naughty pics of my alleged boyfriend—some fans they are, huh?—but also I didn't think it was a big deal until Logan made it one.

I can admit to myself that this also kept me up last night.

It could've gone wrong. I could've been punched or worse. They could've stolen team property and get me fired. Or it could've escalated until I retaliated and—yep, got myself fired.

I couldn't really be the one to initiate a physical altercation either, even if it was to get them away from me. What I needed at that time was exactly what the providence sent me: someone else to intervene.

But why couldn't it have been Hope? Or my boss? Or someone in the coaching staff? Or security?

No, it had to be the same freaking guy I had already gone viral with before.

I stifle a sigh. I want to complain, but I know I won't find any sympathy here.

Tom leans his elbows on the table. "So, what are we doing about it?"

"I say we lean into it," Dave proposes like the shark he is, even if he's generally a pretty good guy who still has to take his hernia cushion with him everywhere. "Play it up until it stops bringing traffic."

"Does this advance the team's brand, though?" asks another manager—finally, a voice of reason.

*Please say no*, I beg in my mind.

"I think positioning our players as the guys both men and women can aspire to definitely does," responds my boss who I don't like very much right now.

"Rosalina, do you have any ideas?" Tom asks.

Ah, shit. Now every pair of eyes is on me and they're expecting me to perform. I clear my throat and repeat his question aloud to buy myself some time.

Meanwhile, my mind whirs as fiercely as it can while running on no sleep and four cups of Café Bustelo. Of course I wish I could tell them all to screw themselves—see how they'd like to be the brunt of online harassment. But that would prob-ably be funky coming from someone whose entire livelihood depends on social media, right? And not just that, but on making sure that social media is thriving. Which it is right now.

I need to grow a thicker skin. Especially if I want to be in front of the camera more often than random viral videos with the team catcher.

"I do think that pivoting back to our usual content will turn away the new warm audience," I start tentatively. Pause for squirming. Longer pause for humming under my throat in fake deep-thought. Then I continue, "But whatever we do, we have to make sure that the higher ups, HR, and Logan himself are on board."

Tom nods at that. "That's a very good point. I will take that action and come back with a verdict. In the meantime, I want everybody to think about how we can use this. No idea is too outrageous—let's just keep it PG, though." That elicits a round of chuckles.

I hide a snort by pretending it's a cough and bringing my fist to my mouth. Everyone here knows that there are layers of codes of conduct we have to adhere to from our own, to those of all the platforms we have a presence in. It's why I was so pissed at Logan's request of me taking down the Mexico video the other time. It's not like I recorded him while he was half naked or something.

That wouldn't just break the internet. It would break the entire grid. Even satellites.

My mind casually replays the moment in Cade's yard when Logan took off his biker jacket and revealed the flimsiest tank top I've ever seen a man wear. I don't know exactly what made it not be PG rated, if it was the ridges of lean muscle or the tattoos—maybe both. I have no doubt that his fans would kill to have seen that.

Fortunately for me, the meeting moves on to the merch line we have available right now and which items are top or low performers. I try to focus but my brain is starting to shut down, and once the meeting ends I realize that nothing went into my head. And that I have no notes to work on for later.

Dave falls into step beside me. "Any brilliant ideas for your boss about what to do with Logan?"

Somehow I don't think he'd appreciate it if I respond with my real idea: launching him into the moon.

"Honestly, none yet," I admit with a sigh. "I spent the whole night reading comments on that video and my brain got fried."

"Understandable." And he does get it, he's probably one of the few people who would. "Take it easy today while the big bosses agree on whether this is a go or not. But if they do, I expect you to bring your A-game."

"In that case…" I narrow my eyes but decide to go for it. "Can I go take a nap in my car?" I motion at my head. "I'm gonna need this pretty thing to be in working condition if that's what's gonna happen."

"Hmm." He shrugs. "Well, the team shouldn't be doing anything too exciting right now, so go ahead. I'll give you two hours to freshen up."

I rush forward and grab both of his hands, offering him bloodshot puppy eyes. "Thank you. You're the bestest boss ever."

Dave grins. "And don't you forget it. Now go before anyone else figures out what's up."

The only detour I take is to grab my car keys from my cubicle, and hide them inside the waistband of my leggings. But I don't feel bad about the fact that I'm going to get paid for napping. I'm sure that the higher ups will find a way to turn this into a campaign, and I'm just about to be busier than I've ever been.

# CHAPTER 14
# LOGAN

Chief among the things I don't wish to do on a rest day before an away series… is leaving my house.

That is, however, what I'm forced to do tonight because Kaplan is in town, and apparently he has news.

"Spill, man," I grouch when we've been sitting at this hibachi restaurant on the east side of town for what feels like hours. In reality, he's only been perusing the menu for ten minutes, but we both know he's going to order the same thing he eats every time. This is one of his favorite joints in town, after all, for reasons that escape me.

"Hmm, someone's impatient—Oh, they have cocktails now." He smiles at the menu.

Clearly I chose the wrong damn agent. I should've gone for someone like me—direct and efficient, respectful of other people's times and desire not to engage in small talk.

At least Kaplan always has the decency of booking a whole table for the two of us. The last thing I want is strangers hearing about sensitive trade business, especially because I've already pinpointed two different groups of people who seem to know me. Or of me. I don't know if they keep glancing my way because they're baseball fans or if it's because I've gone viral on social media.

Judging by the way a blonde two tables to the right looks at me, I take it it's the latter. I double check to make sure that I am, in fact, wearing clothes and am not accidentally spilling some goods somewhere. With the way she stares, you'd think I'm naked.

By my calculations, I'll have to put up with this for an hour to an hour and a half before the dinner is done. But hopefully she and her party will be done sooner.

"Good evening, gentlemen," a waitress materializes next to me and offers us a red lipstick smile. "Do you know what you would like to order or do you need a few more minutes?" To this, she looks at me like she's expecting something.

I'm normally quick on the uptake but it takes me a second to understand that this woman, who is about as old as my mother, has that little glint of interest in her eye, complete with the heightened cheek color and all.

So… another social media fan, I guess.

"We're ready," I respond firmly, before my agent can keep playing his waiting game. "He's gonna get the chicken teriyaki grill, and I'm getting the mixed grill, no rice, extra egg, double the meat portion, please."

Her eyebrows quirk like I just dropped a double entendre on purpose.

Unlike a lot of players—hell, *men*—I've learned the lesson of not looking for what I haven't lost. Between my weird family and a string of bad relationships, I'm officially done. My life has zero room for more drama—I'm closed for the business of dating.

But the problem with that is that the best deterrent would be to already have a girlfriend or wife. Chicken or the egg, I guess.

"Any drinks?" she asks after a second.

"Water for me, please," I kind of mumble, wanting to be done with this whole night already.

"And a beer for me," Kaplan chimes in from behind me.

"Excellent, I'll be right back with those drinks." After a moment of drinking me in like I'm the tall glass of water, she finally goes.

I swivel on my agent. "You better tell me before dessert or else I'm gonna fry your face on that grill up there."

Kaplan just laughed. "Logan, you're by far my funniest client."

Funny? I'll show him funny.

I force myself to put away my fist because this is a family restaurant.

"Very well, I can see that the murder intent on your face is real so I won't dally any longer. We have three offers."

As far as I'm aware, I had no expectations about this moment. Yet it feels like suddenly the floor is tilting, like I'm the shrimp being tossed on the pan by the chef a table over.

Shouldn't I be yippie yah yaying? This is what I wanted. Three offers is decent. One of them will be the change I need —crave, even. So why do I want to barf all over this pristine grill?

"I'm listening," I rasp out.

"One is from—"

"Here are your drinks," the waitress interrupts and places the beer before before Kaplan, before rounding over to lean fairly close to me to set down my glass. Even though there's an entire damn table next to me where she could put it. I fail to even mutter a weak thanks this time.

"Cheers." Kaplan lifts his glass. "To a successful business transaction."

By rote, I grab my glass and clink it with his. I'm more patient now and wait until he gets a good first sip.

"As I was saying," he continues without prompting. "One is in New York, one in California, and one in Colorado."

I blink fast.

The first one I zero in is New York. There are only two options and neither sounds appealing in the least. First, it's the Eagles—the team that drafted me and my brother, where he still plays. I left in not so great terms and have no desire to go back, so I doubt it's them.

Then there's the New York Jets, historically a rival to the Eagles but with less accolades. Doesn't stop the fans from punching each other in the throat in the streets, which is the least I can expect to receive for joining such an overt adversary of my former team.

Meanwhile, California has five whole options. But it means I have a fifth of a chance of playing for my father's former team, which I have in my list of things to never do. Worse, it'd put me in the same state where my parents still live. That's a hell freaking no.

Last, Colorado. There's only one choice there, and I'm not keen to form a battery with Ben Williams again.

"No," I say without further ado.

Kaplan chokes on his beer.

"Good evening," a chef says as he reaches our table right about the same time. "How are you doing tonight?" He gets his answer as Kaplan keeps choking and I just fold my arms, doing my damn best to contain my irritation. The chef pivots. "So, I hear that it's just going to be you two tonight? Any special occasion? Anniversary?"

The anniversary of my agent's death, maybe.

"Business meeting," I respond, giving great thumps to Kaplan's back until he's able to breathe again.

"Right on." The chef smiles, nonplussed by the thunder on my face.

I turn it back on my agent. "None of those options are going to work."

"But you haven't even heard the deals." Kaplan opens his blue eyes and they're as round as the earth. He lowers his voice. "The Eagles are actually offering you a record sum for a catcher."

"The Eagles?" I whisper-scream, fully offended. "Not even the Jets? What the hell, man?"

"Why is this upsetting? You loved your old team."

"I did—until I didn't and I freaking left."

Kaplan straightens his expression, looks around, and covers his mouth with his hands like we're on the mound talking in front of cameras and sharp eyed managers. "Thirty million, Logan. For a catcher. That's huge."

I splutter but not because of the sum. "Why in the actual shit would they want me back?"

"Uh, only because you're the best damn catcher in the league right now?"

"If so, why did I only get offers from the wrong locations?"

"The—What?" He does a double take. "These are the three best teams in the country right now."

"Oh, great." I lean back on my chair, now fully annoyed because with that hint I know which California team the offer is from. "The Eagles, the Riders, and the stinking San Francisco Goldens are the very last teams I want to play for."

"Well, why didn't you say so before I started negotiations?" He throws his hands in the air.

"Fried rice," the chef announces, placing a bowl in front of Kaplan.

"Thank you," my agent and I say in unison, with equal amounts of annoyance.

"You didn't ask," I fire back sounding like a five-year-old.

"Fine, I will ask now. What do you have against those teams?" Kaplan scrunches up his face, also like a five-year-old.

Placing my elbows on the table, I drop my face in my hands and sigh. "Because."

"Just because?"

"Yeah."

"I'm your business partner, Logan. I'm gonna need more than just 'cause."

"Here's why…" I lift my head and pin him with a glare. "I refuse to go back."

"Let's say that rules out the Eagles, but not the other two."

"Oh, but it does." I frown even more. "I refuse to form a battery with that prick Williams again, and I refuse—categorically, I might add—to go back to my hometown."

Kaplan doesn't know the full extent of my family drama, only that I'm not in the best terms with any of them. But I can see him put two and two in real time. "Ah."

"Yeah, *ah*."

"Sautéed vegetables." The chef puts a hefty bowl of broccoli, carrots, onions, mushrooms, baby corn, and water chestnut in front of me. As annoyed as I've been, I hadn't noticed my hunger until this moment. My stomach gives out a great roar and I grab my chopsticks to start working on the bowl.

Kaplan also turns to his rice. "This will set back the timeline. We may not make it in time for the deadline."

"I'm okay with that."

"I thought the idea was to trade ASAP?"

"Not to the wrong, teams, no."

He grunts. I grunt right back. We tuck into our food with surprising gusto for a business meeting that has gone so sour.

"Any other teams you absolutely cannot consider?" he asks after a while.

"No, literally those three."

It's not a lie. It's kind of funny how those teams are even

interested. The Riders and Goldens don't really surprise me, but the Eagles? I distinctly remember the manager spitting on the ground after I left the premises for the last time. It almost smells like Lewis is the one trying to pull strings behind the scenes. He'd love nothing more than to have me in his hands again, especially now that I could make him the best damn pitcher in the league.

I'd rather eat my sweaty jockstrap. Or even keep playing with Cade Starr.

At least the food is decent, but it doesn't compensate for how much of a waste this meeting has been. I make sure to tip both the flirty waitress and the chef exceedingly for putting up with my shit all night.

Unfortunately, the other flirty woman and her party are leaving the restaurant at the same time as Kaplan and I.

"Are you Logan Kim, by any chance?"

Ah, shit. Here we go.

I turn. The blonde woman is with a group of friends, men and women. They look like they're in college or barely out of it.

"Yes, hi," I say in as neutral a tone as I can manage under the circumstances.

"I'm such a huge fan. Do you mind please giving me your autograph on this napkin?"

I reassess. Yes, she definitely does look up at me like I'm candy. But she's keeping a safe distance and her friends aren't hounding me either. This seems like a normal interaction.

I relax a little and even attempt a smile. "Of course."

She offers a clean napkin sporting the logo of the restaurant, and a regular Bic that has seen better days. I use my agent's back as a table and when I'm done, return everything to her.

"Thank you!"

"No, thank you for your support," I manage to say with the

limited PR training after I once pissed off Audrey Winters from the Orlando Wild PR team.

"And also, congratulations on your new girlfriend." The fan giggles while stuffing the signed napkin in her purse. With one last appraising glance, she says, "She's a lucky gal."

Some of her friends laugh too but they pull her away and veer in a different direction.

I'm still mulling about what she even was talking about as Kaplan and I head toward our vehicles. Maybe this girl confused me for someone else in the end.

"Girlfriend, huh?" Kaplan clicks his tongue. "Is this why you're actually less amenable to a trade all of a sudden?"

"Dude." I shake my head. "I don't have a girlfriend."

"What?" Kaplan stops, forcing me to do the same. "But even I thought you did, especially after your team called me about it."

"They did what?" I tilt my face to the side, presenting my ear for better listening.

"They called me to talk about some publicity stunt with your girlfriend but I turned them away." He stuffs his hands in the pockets of his slacks and cocks an eyebrow. "Should I have accepted?"

After buffering for a good moment, I ask, "First of all, who is my alleged girlfriend? And second, what stunt?" I raise my hand. "Actually, third. When did this happen?"

"The social media girl? The one you've gone viral with. Everyone and their mom is shipping you both, apparently including the team. They want you to do some kind of stunt with her—I don't know. I said no because your time here is limited and this kind of thing won't increase your value."

When he adds nothing further, I grit my teeth and ask, "When?"

"Just earlier today, I didn't think this was important." He waves his hand.

"Kaplan."

"Logan?"

"I hope you have a safe trip back. Good night," I mutter, turning on my heels and heading for my bike waiting under a tree.

"So, was it important?" he asks in the distance, vague amusement in his voice.

Over my shoulder I say, "I'll be the one who decides that." I put on my helmet and hop on my bike, peeling out of the parking lot to go home and do what I do best.

Overthink the shit out of every word that was said tonight.

# CHAPTER 15
## ROSE

I spend most of Friday post car nap in a state of alert, and that's excluding the subsequent cups of coffee that I require to stay functional. I put on my lilac noise cancelling headphones that have kitten ears to focus on these edits. I have two videos to post today, one with a highlight play from last night's game, and another one with some fun trivia about the team.

But my eyes keep going to the corner of my screen with the clock. Tom let Dave and I know that he was about to secure an audience with Charlie Cox, the ultimate boss around here, and the heads of operations, communications, PR, and HR to talk about this little bud of an idea. He's treating this potential social media stunt like it's on par with signing a new player onto the team in exchange for a vet and a draft pick, or something.

The thing is, the meeting is at four thirty in the afternoon. Today is a rest day with no games, so I'm supposed to clock out at five. I can definitely stay longer but I'd rather not. I miss my bed. I wish I wasn't part of this mess in the first place. Maybe I can just wait until Monday.

A little square with a DM from my boss appears right above the clock's corner. I click on it.

ROGERS, DAVID [15:58]:

Excited??

Not how I'd describe it, but this is the one time I won't give my boss the unvarnished truth. I also won't lie and tell him that I'm over the moon at the prospect of fake dating the catcher as a publicity stunt. I lay my fingers across the keys like it's a piano and not a purple keyboard, blatantly stalling.

MENA, ROSALINA [15:59]:

A bit nervous

This is true. I am both high- and low-key freaking out.

ROGERS, DAVID [15:59]:

Get excited!!

This is the kind of once in a million opportunity
that you turn into a bigger opportunity

I sit there for a moment, blinking at the screen in confusion. He doesn't elaborate further so I prod him.

MENA, ROSALINA [16:01]:

What do you mean?

Enough time passes without a response that I start considering just relocating my behind to Dave's cubicle. Until finally he responds.

ROGERS, DAVID [16:12]:

C'mon

Do you really think that if you run this campaign
successfully, this won't advance your career?

MENA, ROSALINA [16:13]:

I'm going to need you to stop gatekeeping information and explain it to me like I'm five

ROGERS, DAVID [16:13]:

LOL

What I mean is, your face will become famous to our fans you silly goose

And the broadcasting team will need a new face when Steve Boateng retires soooo

My eyes pop.
Is he…
Is this…

MENA, ROSALINA [16:14]:

ARE YOU FOR REAL??

ROGERS, DAVID [16:15]:

It's a possibility!!!

I push away from my desk so hard that my chair slams into the wall of my cubicle, making the whole thing rattle. Stuffing my fists against my mouth is the only way I can contain the squeal that threatens to explode my colleagues's eardrum.

This changes every freaking thing.

Dave and Tom know my career aspirations, and it's true that it will require me to be on the side of the camera that I'm not used to. Heck, it even makes sense to use this silly campaign to really get me acquainted with the fans.

As for what happens after Logan and I 'break up?'

Who cares—the whole thing won't be real anyway. This isn't on the same terrain as if Ben and I had dated publicly, to then have him drop me like a sack of potatoes by going to another team. There are no feelings involved now, and it won't be a secret from the team.

I'm so on board now. It legit makes time move even slower, but I'll wait as long as it takes. This might be my big chance.

Six in the evening arrives and passes before Tom returns. By this point, Dave and I are hanging out by the entrance to Tom's office, and he motions at us to go in. At least half of the marketing team is already gone for the day, but even so Tom shuts the door before speaking.

"It's a no go."

"*What?*" Dave and I screech at the same time.

Tom lifts his hand to scratch the back of his head. "Cox is definitely in. Anything that attracts attention to the team is a go by him. And to quote him verbatim, this is the kind of shit that would make merchandise sell like hotcakes. He also started pitching ideas like selling heart shaped hotcakes in concessions." He shakes his head.

"Okay but then what happened?" Dave squints.

"So," Tom continues and folds his arms, "communications and PR are also in, they can spin this like a top. Operations is iffy because this might distract Logan from performing at his best, but I reminded them that we're talking about Logan Kim—*the* Logan Kim."

"Right," I mumble. The guy has enough cojones to march up to someone and tell them to stop doing their job because he said so. Nothing fazes him.

Dave snorts. "Remember his sophomore year with the Eagles? He played a whole series with a broken clavicle until someone noticed. This is nothing in comparison."

"Exactly." Tom opens his eyes wide and nods in an exaggerated way.

I fiddle with the hem of my oversize sweatshirt. I had forgotten about that incident. I honestly didn't need further reminders about how remarkable Logan is.

"So then why is it a no go?" I ask.

"HR said no," Tom says and is immediately interrupted by my boss.

"Screw that guy." Dave snorts.

"Unfortunately he gave the reasoning that the situation between Hope Garcia and Cade Starr might've set a precedent that we don't want to normalize."

"He's gonna eat his words when Hope and Cade get married and have five babies, am I right?" Dave imbues copious amounts of sarcasm to the question, but he's not entirely wrong. Those two are so besotted that I wouldn't be surprised if they get hitched by next season.

"Wait." I shake my head to rearrange my thoughts back on track. "So because Michael Watson from HR said no, then Cox changed his mind?"

"Oh, no. Cox still wants this to happen." Tom shrugs, further confusing me until he says, "The issue is that we then called Logan's manager to negotiate and *he* said no."

I suck in air.

"Sorry, who said no? Logan or his agent?" Dave asks.

"His agent," Tom confirms. "So in that case there's nothing really we can do."

"Unless…" This attracts their attention to me. "Well, I'm kind of on friendly terms with Logan—" At least *now*, but I don't say that part aloud. "Since, you know, Cade and Hope basically drag him everywhere, and I'm Hope's roommate after all."

Tom's eyebrows lift. "Is that so?"

Meanwhile, my direct boss smiles in a very memeable way. Kind of amused but evil in equal measures. "Are you saying what I think you're saying?"

"I can't promise anything." I lift my hands in defense. "All I can do is try but I'd really like to do this in person, and the team is traveling tomorrow so…"

"This can wait a few days. But…" Tom pauses to rub his jaw like it hurts. "You'll have to post something on social media in the meantime that reminds people of you two. Keep them reeled in while giving them a hint that there's more to the story."

"I can do that." I don't know how but there's no way I'm backing away now. "I'll re-splice the footage in a new way, and even if Logan really flat out refuses to collaborate, we'll at least get one last viral video out until we find the next focus."

"Sounds excellent."

"We're counting on you, Rosalina."

Welp, no pressure then.

# CHAPTER 16
# LOGAN

There's nothing intrinsically odd about Mena—I mean, Rose, was it?—waiting outside the team bus to greet the players. The thing is that normally she records our descent from the bus on her phone, maybe asks a few silly questions of the get-to-know-the-player variety, and potentially high fives the willing guys who are by far the majority.

This time around there's only some high fives and no camera, and she zeroes in on me like someone who just sighted their suitcase on the conveyor belt at baggage claim.

I check over my shoulders, but there's no one around me that would typically produce such a stubborn look on her pretty face.

She starts striding over as I join the line of players and staff to retrieve my suitcase from the trunk at the bottom. I keep her approach in my field of vision, but pretend like I'm not paying attention in case she actually was sending that hostile look at someone else.

Except that she stops right beside me and says, "Hey, Logan. Can I have a moment with you?"

And of course one of the stooges that calls himself a

professional baseball player hears this and says in a sing-song voice, "A secret lovers rendezvous?"

I close my eyes. Take a deep breath. And pin him with my patented I-collect-teeth-for-fun look. "One more word out of your mouth and I'll make sure you can't eat solids for a month."

The clown makes a zipping motion over his mouth but it's too late, the damage is done. An avalanche of wolf whistles and laughter ensues.

Clapping of the annoyed variety starts behind me, followed by Hope's voice. "C'mon. No need to make your jealousy hold the line. Get your suitcases and go—home or to find a date, I don't care. Chop chop."

My head turns by reflex and I meet Rose's amused eyes like we do this all the time. It sends a jolt down my spine and I clear my throat. "I best get my bag before the scary trainer scolds me."

"You do that," Rose plays along with a serious manner. "She can be terrifying when she wants."

"Hey, I heard that," the alluded tosses over her shoulder as she passes us, fully skipping the line. We all let her because, yeah, Hope Garcia is the strictest trainer. She won't even let her boyfriend eat pizza ever since the season started.

The social media manager camps on the sidewalk for a few minutes while I join the luggage retrieval fray. Meanwhile, I rack my brains trying to figure out what she wants to do with me now. Is she still pissed at me? Because I already admitted that I acted like a jerk. Verbally. With witnesses. So what else is going on?

"Hey, Kim," a familiar voice calls out me while I shrug on my travel backpack. I turn to face Rivera with a cocked eyebrow. "Behave."

"What?" I ask, confused.

But then he uses his lips to point somewhere behind me.

When I turn over my shoulder, I spot Rosalina Mena still watching me. Her arms are folded and she's tapping her sneaker on the concrete impatiently.

Facing the shortstop again, I ask, "What the hell do you mean with *behave*? When do I ever not behave?"

"Hmm." His mouth curves like he's an old man thinking about his bills. "True. Maybe in your case I should tell you to misbehave. But like a gentleman. Know what I mean?"

"Literally I have no idea what you're yapping about. See you in two days."

Huffing, I break apart from the waning mass of players. I don't follow their pattern of beelining from the bus to their respective vehicles. Rather, I walk over to the social media manager waiting for me.

Every step feels weirder. Like the air closest to her is charged and I'm gonna get zapped.

I stop at a safe distance from whatever this storm is and slide my hands into the pockets of my black joggers. "What's going on, Rose?" My voice is raspy but I refuse to clear it because that could be perceived as a sign of nerves. And I'm not nervous. I'm just a little mystified, that's all.

"Well." She leans to the side to look behind me. "There's something kind of private I need to talk with you about. But a bunch of players are taking a surprising amount of time retrieving their suitcases, what with them getting distracted by us every thirty seconds…"

I run my hands through my hair to massage my scalp, just trying to get ahead of the headache my teammates give me often. "I know a good place where we can talk without witness-es." Something about her demeanor changes and I add, "But still public."

"Great."

She relaxes. Another guy would get angry that he was distrusted.

Me? I can't help but seeing her in a different light. Her usual sunny disposition led me to think that she's a happy-go-lucky, slightly ditzy woman with terrible taste—as anyone who goes out with Ben Williams probably is.

But it turns out that Rosalina Mena is smart. I respect that. "Take out your phone so I can give you the address," I mutter. "That way you can confirm that the place is safe first."

Her eyes widen. "Oh, yes. Thanks." She's still blinking at me as she palms her pockets and finds her phone on one at the back. I'm about to tell her the name of the place when she just unlocks her device and hands it over.

All right, I guess this is faster. I find her browser and key in the name. The correct result pops up right away and I pull up the website before returning her phone.

When I lift my head, I find that she's still watching me. Her head is tilted, eyes slightly narrowed like she's trying to categorize me. Good luck with that.

I motion with her phone again until she takes it. As her attention drifts down to the screen, I say, "See you there in fifteen." And with that I set course to find my Paningale V4 R.

*

I leave the Orlando Wild facilities before she does and beat the worst of the rush hour traffic. This little joint is not on a main road, but it's still part of what is considered Mills 50, an area where Asian businesses abound. This place is where I come when I want a really good Korean BBQ like the stuff you find in San Francisco, where there's a pretty big Korean community. I'm not looking for that aspect, but merely for the food. Sometimes I just crave a killer kimchi.

So, even if Rose decides that what she wants to talk about isn't important after all and prefers to head home, I'm still going to feast like a king tonight. And I deserve it after scraping a win in this series.

"Annyeonghaseyo," the owner greets me without further ado. I'm a regular. He knows who I am. He doesn't care to profit off my fame beyond what I can pay for bulgogi servings and endless banchan. It's a perfect arrangement. I nod at him and he nods back, which tells me my usual table is free.

However, I add, "There may be a second person this time."

"Twice the servings then?"

"I don't know. She may want something else."

His eyebrow twitches. I'm always by myself and I know what's going through his mind now that I mentioned that my possible dinner companion is a she. But I shake my head. Rose isn't a date. Or a friend. I guess we're coworkers, except she said that this topic is private, so it can't be work related.

I grunt, forcing myself out of my overthinking. Without further ado, I sort through the tables to find the farthest booth at the back, taking the seat where I can see the front door easily.

I'll give her exactly ten minutes, then I'm ordering enough food for an army. But I'm only checking sports news on my phone for two when some movement at the corner of my eye gets my attention.

It's her. She's talking with the owner at the front, maybe asking about me—or not. Suddenly she's laughing and the old man joins in. This is the first time I even hear his laughter since I've been coming to this restaurant.

Then she spots me, and her amusement ebbs away pretty drastically.

"Geez." I squirm on my seat. Guess I found the one woman who sees right through my objectively handsome face and down to my rotten core.

Finally, she tears herself away from charming the crap out of the owner and makes her way over. Rose takes the seat across the table, dropping her little purse beside her. She folds her arms and leans them on the table, propping herself up to get a better view outside of the booth.

"Wow, this place looks like we're in another country. How did you find it?"

"I'm a regular." I look away from her and wait to make eye contact with a waitress. I never need the menu, but Rose definitely does.

It takes a tense minute for the menu to arrive and another one while I wait for her to acquaint herself with it. I try not to stare at her, but it'd probably be even ruder if I just go back to perusing my phone.

Her hair is something else, a voluminous mass of light brown ringlets that frame her face. She twists her lips as she reads the options and they're surprisingly full—her lips, not the options. But what snags my attention is her button nose.

I can see myself booping it.

I tuck both of my hands under my thighs just in case.

"What's your favorite dish?" she asks with a soft, distracted voice.

"The bulgogi BBQ. It's marinated beef."

"That sounds great." She slams the menu closed and lifts her head. "And also something with alcohol."

I tilt my head. "They only have beer and soju."

"What's soju?"

"Uh, it's liquor. Mostly from rice."

She nods. "Then I'll try that."

Far be it from me to tell her what she should or shouldn't drink.

The waitress returns and I end up placing the two orders of bulgogi, plus water for me and soju for Rose. She waits for me to explain how soju is supposed to be drank—including how I'm the one who should pour it for her—and then tosses two shots straight.

"Whoa, whoa."

"It's okay, I need it for this conversation." Her entire face is still scrunched up, the second shot hitting her harder than the first one. "This is unexpectedly strong."

"It'll get you shitfaced if you're not careful." I fold my arms and lean back against the booth. "What in the actual hell is it that you want to say that you need to get drunk for?"

She exhales a soju-smelling breath, fills her lungs again, and looks up at me. "Logan Kim?"

"Yes?" I drag out the word.

And then she drops a bomb on me. "Would you date me?"

# CHAPTER 17
## ROSE

Soju is more powerful than I thought. What I just said doesn't click until I watch Logan's mouth drop open and out pours all the water he had just drank.

I'm the one who starts choking.

Meanwhile, he calmly looks down at the massive water splotch down his purple and yellow Orlando Wild shirt, as well as his pants. Dude just gave himself a shower from the shock.

In contrast, I'm about to hack up a lung. He slides his water glass my way and I take it, chugging until my throat opens up and I can kind of breathe again.

"I d-didn't—it—"

"Breathe first," he mutters, now also sliding a stack of napkins toward me.

It takes a handful to clean my face, and another handful to blot out the sweat now trickling from the sheer embarrassment. I clear my throat several times and glue my attention to the wall.

"I don't mean for real. I don't actually have any interest in you," I begin to explain.

"Thanks, that's not confusing at all." Logan snorts.

I cave and turn back to meet his eyes. There's more amusement there than offense, and I get it. How would someone like me hurt his self esteem in any way? He's dated gorgeous professional models, for goodness's sake. Women throw themselves at him on a regular basis.

"All right, I'll start from the beginning." I put both hands on the table. "The videos that have gone viral of the two of us have brought unprecedented traffic to our social media accounts, and it's starting to reflect in the ticket and merchandising earnings."

Logan pushes the sleeves of his shirt up his forearms and folds his arms. A second later I realize why that had to be the succession of actions. His forearms, corded with defined muscles and thick ropes of veins, seem to grow in size with his arms folded. I wonder if he's torn his clothes before just from simple movements that no one else has to consider.

A second later, he lifts one eyebrow slowly. "Is that so?"

Somehow I resist the urge to squirm.

"Yes. Spoiler alert, your jersey's the top bestseller right now. The next one is a very distant second." And all of this is true, I did some research in preparation for this conversation.

"And how does this pertain to me dating you?" Why is a corner of his lips rising like that? "Or not."

"That's what I'm getting to." Here I pause to rearrange myself on my seat. Logan must know I'm stalling, because he diverts his attention to turning on the grill on the table and taking utensils from the cup against the wall. He puts two chopsticks on his napkin, and a fork and knife on mine. "Erm…"

"I'm listening." He leans back once more, tilting his head back in a way that makes his eyes half close. When he looks at me like that, my train of thought derails twice more before I figure out that the alcohol is hitting me.

Of course I know that Logan Kim is conventionally *very* attractive. There's just no way *I* am finding him attractive, though, not when I don't care about guys who are out of my league.

I reach for more liquid courage and he stops me—by grabbing my hand with his much larger, hotter, calloused one, and prying mine away from the bottle. I watch as he pours me another shot.

"Drink slower this time."

I don't. I slam that shit like it's my job, and he shakes his head at me.

After wiping my mouth with the back of my hand and finding that the third shot had less kick, I continue. "So anyway, the marketing team would like to make a series of videos with the two of us. We haven't really defined the particulars—we'd prefer to have your okay before we think any further about this. But basically, we'd let the public think that there's something between us to keep them hooked."

"Fake dating?" He blinks hard. "That only happens in books."

I reel back. "How do you know that?"

"What? I read books." Logan frowns, fully offended.

"But… romance books?"

"I read everything. Even picture books." He folds those thick arms again.

A waitress comes bearing an enormous tray packed with tiny round dishes that she starts loading onto our table. Logan helps her make space for more, and I'm distracted from the food by picturing Logan Kim reading a big romance tome with a straight face. Only when the big dishes come—bowls of rice, a pile of lettuce leaves, and a mountain of raw meat—do I finally snap out of it.

Wait, are those scissors? And a tong?

"Wait, wait." I try to take it all in at once. "What do I do? How do I eat this?"

"I'll show you," he responds in that deep, slightly velvety voice of his. "First, we have to grill the meat." Using the tongs, he grabs little mounds of the meat and spreads them evenly over the surface of the grill. He sets the tongs down on the plate with yet more raw meat, and tips his head at me. "So, fake dating."

I shake my head hard. "Right, I guess that's what it is. It would only have to be in front of the camera though, no big deal."

"Is that what you think?" His lips pinch into an expression of pity. "The second a fan catches us being all…" He motions between us. "Like this to each other, that illusion will be shattered and that'll be all social media talks about."

I blow a raspberry. "So what are you suggesting? That we fake date twenty-four-seven?"

"Definitely not on rest days." He picks up the tongs and starts flipping meat.

I open and close my mouth, flabbergasted. Like, I expected outright refusal but that's not it. He's proposing we go above and beyond.

And a potential promotion of my dreams awaits down the line. Doesn't seem like a huge sacrifice to me.

"Fine, go big or go home, right?" I shrug like this is no biggie. "We fake date beyond the camera to be really convincing and get even more viral. Does this mean you're in?"

"No."

"What?" I screech.

The absolute jerk is still as cool as a cucumber as he reaches for a lettuce leaf and starts putting random food on it, finally topping it with a piece of perfectly cooked meat. He makes a bundle with the leaf, keeping everything inside, and reaches over the table to offer it to me.

"This is how you eat all this. Say ah."

"I know how to feed myself," I mumble, eyes wide.

"*Ah.*" He opens his mouth, exemplifying like I'm a baby and not moving an inch. I get the feeling he is willing to stay frozen like this until I comply.

My stomach roars, prompting me forward. I bite big and take the bundle of food off his hand. He nods like he's proud of me, and busies himself with preparing another bite.

Fortunately, that keeps him from noticing how my cheeks are full to bursting. I cover my mouth with a hand, just in case I'm about to embarrass myself. Flavors hit my tastebuds from every direction and it's so good that I moan.

This does get his attention.

His eyebrows make that slow rise again. "You like it?"

I can't speak, so I just nod and keep chewing.

He measures the same amount of sides on a new lettuce leaf, except he adds twice the amount of meat *and* also stuffs a spoonful of rice down his gullet. I can't even get angry that he put less meat on my bite when I can't compete with his appetite.

Once I'm done eating, I get started on assembling a bite for myself and ask, "So why not?"

"How good are you at keeping secrets?" he asks while chewing, not at all concerned with appearing tidy and demure like I have been.

So I stop caring too and start stuffing food in my mouth as I talk. "Decent, unless it's a life or death situation."

Logan swallows down his food and immediately reaches for more. "I'm planning to change to another team this season. It's why my agent already declined this request."

I freeze.

Do a double take.

Open and close my mouth.

Oh my word. The fans will be devastated.

The *team* will be devastated.

My chances of a promotion are ruined.

"Wait, so you already knew? And you made me say all this?" I whine.

"First, I didn't make you." He gives me an annoyed look. "Second, I didn't know that this was the personal thing you wanted to talk about."

"Ugh." I make a grab for the soju bottle but he's faster. Instead of pouring a full shot, he gives me half. "Don't be stingy now, especially not when you're betraying us."

"I don't know what those two things have to do with each other, but you need more food in your belly and less alcohol."

"I'm twenty six, not sixteen," I mumble through a mouthful. He snorts.

"Fine, but don't blame me for your hangover tomorrow." At last, he tops up my shot glass.

I drink it together with the food and—whoa. "Well, shit. This is delicious together."

"I know," he says in a sullen way, and I remember that he's not supposed to drink alcohol in the middle of the season. He can—certainly some of the guys do, like my ex—but it can also really affect performance, and the very disciplined guys like Logan Kim would rather keep making the millions of dollars for longer.

"When are you leaving us?"

"I don't know. Negotiations are under way."

I lean forward. "Couldn't we just pretend to date until you go? Stage a breakup when it's time? That'll also get us engagement."

Logan also leans forward, elbows on the table. "Is that all you're after? Views on social media? You're willing to go this far for that?"

"Well…" His eyes narrow at my little slip. He did share a

humongous secret just now so maybe I should reciprocate. "Actually, there's a chance this could get me a promotion."

His lips curve. "Now we're talking."

"Steve Boateng is retiring soon, and maybe if I get my face recognized by the fans I can apply to take his position." I shrug, like what I'm saying isn't my dream since college, ever since my hopes of becoming Miss USA crumbled to dust.

"And hypothetically," he comments while spreading more meat on the grill, "if I wasn't leaving the team, what would I even get out of this?"

"Uh…" I—shit. I can't think of anything convincing enough, so I start spitballing. "Higher brand recognition? More endorsements? Maybe from beauty brands? Commercials? Cameos?" When nothing seems to land, my mind starts to break. "A fake girlfriend who can beat off your Annies with a stick? Or how about a fake girlfriend who can feed you? Say ah."

"What?" His face scrunches up.

"Say *ah*." I shake the bundle of food I prepared in front of his face.

Still staring at me, he reaches forward to bite the food. I jump a mile when his upper lip brushes against my finger ever so slightly.

But Logan doesn't seem to notice. As he chews, he asks, "What did you say about Annies?"

"You have some pretty, uh, intense fans. Trust me. I've seen their unhinged comments." I spread a hand over my chest. "I can shield you from them."

"Yeah?" He tucks his hair behind his ear and leans back. "And what if they try to manhandle you again?"

"That's what security is for." I offer my sweetest smile, and also lift up my shot glass so he tops it with the last little bit in the bottle. Grunting, he reaches for the bottle and obeys. "Good boy."

He stops. "Am I a dog now?"

"Just practicing for when we're fake dating." I laugh and toss back the last of the soju. A big *hah* comes out of me when I'm done. I can feel the heat of the drink expanding through my ribcage and if it wasn't for the food, I'd be well on my way to slurring my words. So I won't get a second bottle, which is a shame. It really is yummy. Maybe I should just come here again.

After a moment of placid eating where he consumes twice the amount of food I do in the same time, and where the waitress keeps bringing more side dishes and rice, I say, "What about charity? Helping your fellow coworker get the promotion she has dreamed about for years."

"Do I look like I have a heart?" He seems almost offended by the notion.

I tilt my head. "Something is pumping all the blood through your big body, right?"

One of his eyes twitches and he presses his lips tight. "What if I get traded tomorrow?"

"Then it's no big deal. We probably won't have sufficient content to reel people in by tomorrow." I lean forward again, but smiling this time. "What if you don't get traded so fast?"

"I already have three offers." He takes a big sip of his water.

"Well, did you accept any?"

Grudgingly he admits, "No."

"Then I have a chance." I tilt my chin up. "And if I don't convince you tonight, I'll try again tomorrow."

"You'll be too hungover tomorrow to remember most of this conversation."

"I am very stubborn, Logan Kim."

"So I am discovering." He turns to signal to the waitress. "One more, please."

"No, thanks. I actually won't drink more—"

"Of meat," he explains. "And I'm glad—if you have a second bottle we might end up in the hospital. Are you eating that?"

"Go for it, you animal." I slide my half eaten bowl of rice toward him. I'm not even going to ask him where he puts all that food away when his forearm muscles are taunting me like that. Besides, I've seem him sweat. He'll burn all of this at the gym tomorrow before even playing a game.

I switch to water after that and eat more of the veggies and the meat, but by the time we're leaving the restaurant I'm definitely swaying a little. I stumble on a crack on the sidewalk and Logan grabs me by the elbow.

"That's it, you're not driving," he announces.

"But…" I motion toward my car parked at the back. "My car! I can't leave it here."

"Yeah, you will. There's no way in hell I'm letting you drive."

"But—"

"Rose." My name coming out like a growl from his throat paralyzes me. "I'm taking you home and that's final."

I scrunch up my face in a grumpy expression. "Fine."

I don't know what I was expecting, but he steers me to stand under a lamplight. "Wait here."

"Okay." I hold tight to my purse like that alone can stop me from swaying.

Logan disappears into the darkness and I struggle with making out much of the parking lot with the bright white light above me. Crickets sing all around me, competing with the leaves twinkling in the wind. It's starting to sound like summer, and summer is prime baseball season.

I can't believe that Logan Kim will be gone by that point.

A different sound comes on then, like a roar. Something slightly familiar but jarring against the crickets. And then he appears under the light again, and he's offering me something black and kind of shiny.

"Put this on."

"Hmm?" I squint down at it.

"It's my jacket."

Slowly, I glance up. "Why would I need your jacket?"

"Just put it on." He pushes the bundled up fabric against my belly.

I make a big operation of him holding my purse while I put on his blasted jacket—and it takes me two tries to get my left arm in the correct hole. Then Logan takes one step closer and I watch, almost like an out of body experience, as he fits the bottom tabs together and zips the jacket up all the way to my throat.

A waft of some kind of cologne hits my nose. It's pine and man, enough to get me twice as drunk.

My body leans forward as he turns to disappear in the dark again, like I'm trying to follow him. He's back as I'm struggling to keep steady.

"Whoa, there." His hand's on my elbow again. "You're looking slightly worse by the second."

"That's not very kind to say to a girl," I slur, now fully incapable of using my normal voice.

Sighing, he mutters, "Told you to drink more water."

I repeat his words in a mocking way, but then he's pressing something against my head. "What the—" He pushes the thing all the way down and gives it a hearty bump at the top. I blink fast at him through the open visor of the helmet he just put on my head. "Don't tell me…"

"Yeah, I'm on my bike," he says.

"But you can take my car," I whine.

"And then how do I get home?"

I think about this. "My car?"

A smile is threatening to spill on his face. I know it. "And then how do you get to work tomorrow?"

"Uber?" I ask, rolling the r the Spanish way. "Or I could take one now."

"Hell no. I'm not trusting you to a stranger when you're like this."

"But Logan." I say with extra emphasis. "You're also a stranger."

"No, I'm not." He looks for something in his pants and produces it—his wallet? No. His phone. He's dialing someone while keeping his eyes on me. "Hey, Hope. FYI that I'm driving your drunk as shit roommate over to your place—not that one, the tall one with the sharp tongue."

"I don't have a sharp tongue!" I complain, bringing a hand up to my mouth. "It would cut myself, you know?"

"Yes, I did tell her not to drink so much," he deadpans to the phone. "And tell your boyfriend to stop being a jealous prick. Yeah, I'll text you when she's home and you can call her. 'Kay, bye." He ends the call and puts his phone back in his pocket. "Let's go."

Sighing, I force my legs to follow him. His bike is idling just a few steps from us, in the middle of the parking lot. For some reason it looks way bigger than ever.

"How do I even get on this thing?" I mumble, trying to lift a leg over the massively tall seat.

"Hold." Logan leaves my side to easily swing a leg over the bike and settle on his seat. He kicks something and then leans over to point at a small protrusion on the back. "See this peg? Grab my shoulders and put your right foot on it to hoist yourself up."

"Ohh, okay. I can do that, I think." I approach from the side and after a minor hesitation, I splay my hands on his shoulders and pause.

He turns over his shoulder. "What?"

"Hold," I repeat, frowning. "Processing."

That's exactly what I'm doing. His shoulders feel like no other shoulders I've ever touched in my life. They're way harder than I expected, and also larger. In fact, my hands look small on them. I squeeze harder and there's no give. All that accomplishes is searing his contour in my mind forever.

"Foot?" He prompts. "On peg?"

"Right." I'm clumsier than usual but somehow manage to rise on the foot peg, swing my left leg and find the other peg. But now I'm standing awkwardly behind him, bent forward as I grab his shoulders. I speak to the top of his head. "Now what?"

Logan leans his head back and even in my tipsy state, I can tell he's holding back laughter. "Now you sit down, you clown."

"But then it's gonna be awkward."

"What do you mean?" Is it just me, or are his eyes shining?

"Like." I blow an exasperated breath. "My thighs are going to be around your waist. At least buy me dinner first, man."

"Uh." He coughs. "I, in fact, did pay for dinner tonight."

"Oh, true." I lower myself and— "Oof."

This is not my fault. I'm in my cups but not this bad. It's the seat and gravity's fault. This thing is tilted forward and I slide all the way down to crash against Logan's back.

"Oh my gosh, I didn't—"

"Hold tight," he says like I'm not glued to him already. But then he finds my hands, awkwardly smushed against his lower back, and pulls at them. My arms circle his waist and he slides them under his backpack, which he's wearing against his chest. He joins my hands at his stomach and I grab fistfuls of his shirt.

And then we're off.

A squeal tears out of me because at first, it feels like the wind will topple me back and off the bike. But somehow I stay on. Maybe it's because my arms are a barnacle around Logan's unfairly tiny waist. Or because my thighs cinch as tight as they can around him. My head falls against the dip between his shoulder blades and the heat of his back is positively searing. But I know that if I let go of this man for a second, I'll be in serious trouble.

My arms start shaking after a while and he must feel it, because suddenly one of those big hands of his closes around my arm and slides it lower so I'm not fighting so hard against gravity. Except my hands reach the waist of his joggers and that jolts me—there's no way I can relax more than this before making us both crash.

I'm on my best behavior after that, for someone who is drunk and also wrapped up around someone who is a step up from a stranger. I even stay wrapped around him when he finally turns off his bike, deathly afraid of falling.

"And here we are," Logan declares with a raspy voice.

"How do I get off?" I ask directly to his massive back. The world tilts a little and I squeeze him tighter.

Logan coughs and feels around my arms until he finds my hands, then tries to pry them off but I won't budge. "Uh, first you have to let me go."

"But then I'll fall," I explain.

"Not with the kick stand to balance the bike." Oh, that must've been the thingy he kicked earlier. With his other hand, he taps my knee. "C'mon, ease off."

"If I fall, I will hunt you down."

"Rose, you won't die from a fall this low." He really puts some strength into tearing my arms open and it works. Next, he pushes both of my knees to spread and in the blink of an eye he's gone.

I have a quick moment of panic where I don't know where to put my hands and the world starts tilting again, but then a pair of big hands is on my waist from behind, and he lifts me off the bike like I'm not 5 foot 8. I bring my knees up in the air so I don't kick his bike, deep down fearing he would kill me for that.

Finally, I can put my feet on the ground. As he spins me around, I catch sight of his backpack laying on the sidewalk by the spot I usually park at. I sway as I face him.

"Purse," he says, offering a hand palm facing up.

"What, robbing me now?" I joke even as I fumble with the strap of my purse.

My arms are tired from all the effort it took to not blow away into a premature death, and I can't for the life of me figure out this jacket. He's the one who takes my purse and hangs it around his neck, and once again I watch as he unzips his jacket from me.

"Stay still," Logan commands, reaching for the jacket and taking it off me with surprising efficiency, even though for a quick second there I almost eat his shoulder.

As he takes the garment, he returns my purse and I slide the strap over my shoulder. In an exaggeratedly peppy voice, I say, "Thanks for the ride home. Let's not do that again any time soon. But I'm in for food again. Bye, goodnight, bye…" I drag the last word as I stumble around the bike toward the driveway.

"Aren't you forgetting something?"

Serious, I turn over my shoulder and say, "This wasn't actually a date, Logan. I'm not gonna kiss you."

"Not that." He waves a hand like the concept is completely absurd. "My helmet."

"Oh." *Oh.* I wish a black hole could open up and swallow me whole.

I retrace my steps on tippy toes, struggling to pull the thing off my head. Again, it requires his effort to do so. I blow air hard enough to push away a curl that has glued to my face and it doesn't budge.

But then Logan helps me with that too.

He slides the pad of a finger across my cheek, ever so softly, and pushes my hair all the way behind my ear. His eyes are fixed on the motion, and when he's done they focus back on mine.

"I'll do it," he says all of a sudden.

"Do what?" I slur, frowning in confusion.

"I'll fake date you until I get traded."

My jaw drops.

# CHAPTER 18
## LOGAN

don't feel like garbage during this flight, for a change. My mind is busy with enough things that it has no time to latch onto the irrational fear that lives at the back of my mind.

Instead, I'm trying to rehash the key plays we had during the last series, jotting them down on my pocket notepad. I make special emphasis on the plays where we screwed up, so I can think about how we can avoid those mistakes during the upcoming away games.

It's only been maybe ten minutes since being airborne, enjoying some peace and quiet while the seatbelt sign is on, and Starr and Rivera play chess behind me. They'll make a fan of the game out of me because it keeps them quiet like no other. Yet the second I celebrate that in my mind, the seatbelt sign goes off and the place explodes—figuratively, *whew*.

"Okay who wants to check the mole at my back?" someone asks.

"Eww." A pause. "I'm game, take it off."

This is what pisses me off about my flavor of claustrophobia, that headphones exacerbate it. Otherwise I'd be canceling the hell out of these fools with a good pair of Beats.

I try to focus even harder on the play I'm recalling, the one where O'Brian made an error that cost us one run, when someone plops on the seat beside me and places something on my folding table.

It's a can of ginger ale. I look up expecting Hope Garcia, who is the only one to have figured out the drink helps me when flying, even if she doesn't know why.

Instead it's Rosalina Mena. She unfolds the table before her and also places another ginger ale on top.

She turns to me. "Hi, Logan."

"Um, hi?" I ask, raising my eyebrows. I motion at her ginger alc. "Hungover?"

"Tragically," she admits, popping the tab and opening her can with a hiss.

"Isn't this great?" a familiar voice comes from behind and I close my eyes, wondering what happened to their chess game.

Twisting on her seat, her knee bumping against my thigh, Rose asks Rivera, "What's great?"

"You two," he responds and I can practically hear the grin in his voice. "Sitting here together..."

"So is it official?" Starr asks, his voice coming above my head.

Meanwhile, Rose's big brown eyes shift to me, clearly waiting for my response. I guess I'm bestowed with the official task of kicking off this weird fake dating exercise. I snap my pocket notepad shut, tuck the pen inside the spiral, and reach for my unopened can.

"It's not official yet," I mutter, feeling her stiffen. "We're only getting started."

"What?" the two stooges screech at the same time, very much in the fashion I imagine tweens at a pajama party would.

Starr then calls out, "Hey, Hope! Turns out you're winning the bet."

"What bet?" Rose asks sharply.

"Some of us think you two are getting together, and some others don't," explains Rivera in a quiet way, as if he's actually capable of understanding that not everything has to be shouted at the four winds.

Far from getting offended—the way I feel, to be honest—Rose reveals all her pearly whites in a smile that makes her eyes glow from the inside. "Let me guess, you and Hope think we're dating and Audrey and Cade think we're not."

"Damn, you're good." Rivera chuckles.

Sipping from my ginger ale, I narrow my eyes at the woman next to me and she gives me a little shrug. It's not the first time that I get reminded of how shrewd she is, and I don't know what to make of that. I've had enough women try to manipulate me in my life that I'm definitely wary.

Then again, if Rose was trying to play games with me she wouldn't be so damn honest all the time, even when it makes me uncomfortable.

Unfortunately, Hope doesn't modulate her voice when she appears on our hallway. "Wait, are Rose and Logan finally dating?"

In, I would say, less than a second—the whole airplane erupts.

"Aww yeah!"

"Wait, no! I had a crush on Rosie."

"Rosie?" I mouth at her, watching as her cheeks darken.

"Does that mean I can invite you to my wife's party with the other WAGs?" someone asks in the middle of the fray—Brown, I think.

"No—" I start to say.

But Rose slams a hand on my thigh and twists to glance back. "Of course, we would love to be there."

I'm still staring at her hand all snug on my thigh, processing the shock of it. It's close to the knee so it's not like this is scandalous.

Actually, last night was even more so, when her chest was pressed up against my back and her thighs squeezed me tight. And yet…

She removes her hand and before she can see my face, I rearrange it to a mask of indifference. Like that little touch didn't sear my skin through the fabric of my joggers and didn't make me sweat at all. We're adults—*I* am an adult, not a randy teenage boy whose engine gets going by a glance. Why the hell am I acting like one?

Don't tell me… is it because her knee is still pressed against the side of my thigh?

Yeah, Rose is hot, but it usually takes a lot more than this to get my blood pumping.

"Oh wow, so it's official-*official*, huh?" Hope leans against the seat in front of Rose. "When did this happen? How?"

"Like he said, we're just feeling things out for now," Rose responds, smiling. "Now, if y'all don't mind, I actually wanted some alone time with Logan."

"Oh la la," Rivera sings behind us. "Let's go to a different row, Cade. We may not want to hear what happens next."

"Good point, I don't wanna barf my breakfast. Grab the chess."

This is followed by shuffling and some bumps.

Hope shakes her head at them, her mouth twitching with a barely restrained smile. Then she sets her attention back to us, pointing at our faces. "Don't forget, kids. I walked so you could run. Don't get too handsy or you'll get in trouble with the top dogs."

"Roger that." Rose salutes.

And finally, we are alone. I chug more ginger ale.

"That was an interesting show," I mumble once the mini can is empty, placing it back on my folding table.

"You don't say." She snorts through her nose. "But I do have something to talk about with you."

"What now? Should I fake marry you?" I ask in a deadpan.

Her lips press tight. "No, but we do have to discuss terms and conditions." I just stare at her, waiting for more information before I even consider engaging. She checks our surroundings once more, before hunching over to whisper, "It's just that I was thinking—"

"Oh, *shit*," I say in a heartfelt way that earns me a smack.

"I was thinking that couples do things that you and I of course haven't done." After a pause, she adds, "Nor want to."

I feign ignorance. "Oh yeah? Like what."

"Like kissing. Definitely nothing beyond that." Her head tilts forward, eyes skewering mine as if to say *right?*

"Forget the rest, but kissing?" I scrunch up my face. "Who is going to believe you're my girlfriend if we don't kiss?"

"Good point, let's start by not calling me your girlfriend. You were smart in keeping things vague earlier."

"I'm always smart." I fold my arms and like last night, her eyes divert to them for a moment.

"Logan, the point is that this isn't real so we shouldn't be making out just because." She mimics my exact posture down to the incredulous facial expression. "Or are you telling me you're one of those guys who has the emotional intelligence of a gnat, and can only show the bare minimum semblance of connection in the bedroom?"

Like her ex, Ben Williams?

I have enough tact not to ask, but by the stubborn set of her jaws and the hurt flashing in her eyes it's pretty clear that he's who she's thinking of.

I turn away, refusing to witness that any longer. I can't believe that someone as smart as her could've fallen for a douchebag of the category of Williams. But to be viewed from that same lens pisses me off more than I imagined possible.

"Of course not. I don't use women for my own satisfaction." Or anyone, for that matter.

I grit my teeth. I may be the son of two narcissists—and I may also carry some of their manipulative traits—but I'm not trapped in a constant quest to advance myself at the detriment of others, whether that be my career, or my physical needs or whatever.

"I'm glad." Rose actually relaxes against her seat for the first time since she sat down. "That's what I was most afraid of. I'm just... I'm not ready for that level of intimacy again."

Yep. This is all because of her garbage ex.

"You set the tone." I lace my fingers together, watching my forearm muscles jump under my tatted up skin while I grab my own hands tight. "I'm not going to do anything you don't want to, so you take the reins and I follow," I finish.

Silence, except for some clowns on the team who are very loudly discussing who else is available to date from the beauties in staff. Their words, not mine.

Frowning, I lift my eyes to Rose.

She's stunned, that's the only way I can describe it. Mouth agape, eyes wide, eyebrows up—completely frozen in the act of bringing her ginger ale to her lips.

"What?" I grunt.

"I—Uh." She blinks several times. "So if I want to, like... hold your hand or hug you, you'll be fine with that?"

"Sure."

"And also you'll respect my boundaries?"

I pull my eyebrows together even harder. "Of course. What kind of question is that?"

Her breath shakes, but she offers her hand like we're just closing a contract negotiation. "Deal."

"Deal." I twist to grab her hand, so much smaller, softer,

and colder than mine. "Do you need all this in writing or what?"

"No." She shakes her head, eyes still dazed. "I trust you."

And now I'm the one who's reeling.

# CHAPTER 19
# ROSE

"Are you ready, mamacita?" I ask my roommate from the threshold of her bedroom.

"I don't know, I don't think I ever will be." Hope frowns at her reflection in the mirror. "Like, is this girly enough? Does it fit in with the ultra polished WAGs?" She motions at the gray sheath dress that in my opinion is going to put to shame those fancy WAGs. They wish they had a body like Hope's, all lean and strong and beautiful.

I sigh, conscious of the enormous ass that didn't let me become Miss Florida, and forget Miss USA.

"To be honest I don't know, it's also my first time going to a WAGs party." I shrug, hands up in defeat. "But I honestly think you look better than any WAG, so don't worry."

"Save that flirting for your new boyfriend, it is truly lost on me." Hope's expression is deadpanned. She snatches the purse she borrowed from Audrey and follows me out.

"For your information," I say as we walk out into the living room. "Logan's not my boyfriend yet. We're just starting to date."

"And that's the keyword. Yet." She has the nerve to smack

my behind hard enough that I jump. "Trust me, he won't be able to resist all that for long."

"I—" Stopping myself, I just shake my head. It's not like I can explain that the *yet* was a slip up. That he and I won't in fact ever get together. *Ever*.

We are so not each other's types. He's too pretty and notorious for my insecure ass. I'm too opinionated and stubborn for him. I have the feeling he'd fare much better with a woman whose north pole is him, and that's just never gonna be me.

"Oh, yeah. You're absolutely done for. To the slaughterhouse," Audrey says from her armchair in the living room.

"What?" Hope and I ask at the same time.

"I'm agreeing with Hope. You," blondie points at me. "Are the cow. And he… is going to eat you. Wait and see."

I make a face. "I'm not sure I like that allegory. I'd like to think I'm more than just meat."

"You're the whole meal, baby," she says with a nod.

"Erm, thanks." My lips twitch. I put my hands on my hips. "Anyway, are you sure you don't want to join us? We might need your dry humor to oxygenate the overly perfumed air of the WAGs."

"Hard freaking pass." Audrey points at her iPad, at her feet on the ottoman and the cozy blanket wrapped around her. "My life goal is to be a burrito, not a WAG for anyone." She shudders delicately.

"Anyone?" My eyebrows rise. "Like players only or everyone?"

"Everyone. Guys suck." She presses her lips.

Normally I'd agree with my whole chest, but my lips stay glued.

"Unfortunately, we have to go," Hope reminds us. "The guys have been waiting for us for like ten minutes."

I cringe. "Maybe we should've let them in."

"My bad, I wasn't mentally prepared for boy cooties today.

Can I now go back to my cozy game?" Audrey asks, eyes wide and pleading.

"Fine. Don't wait up for us, grandma." I blow a kiss at her and she waves her hand in the universal shoo manner.

Hope is a bit ahead of me so she opens the front door and —there's some hooting and whistling immediately.

"Va va boom! You're gonna set my truck on fire, darlin'," Cade calls out from the driver's seat, the passenger's window rolled down for his shenanigans.

"Oh, shut up you weirdo." But Hope's words lack any bite, especially because she's giggling up a storm as she jogs down the way to the truck.

From the backseat, I can spot Logan running a hand down his face like he's embarrassed to be in the vicinity of the other couple. It makes me want to give him crap.

As I hop on the backseat next to him, I tease, "Do I look so bad that I don't get any sugar?"

Logan Kim, famous mastermind of the Orlando Wild, does a whole double take and mutters, "What? No, you look fine."

Well, ouch.

"Fine?" Cade exclaims, twisting around to look at us. "Dude, that's not how you woo a lady."

"Woo?" Logan scoffs and looks out the opposite window. "Look at you using big words when we all had to help your ass get together with Hope."

Completely not stung by that, Cade bobs his head and says, "That's true, but what you did was give me wings to bring on my flirting A-game. You may not have needed help getting the lady, but clearly you need helping keeping her."

Logan, who has had his arms folded all along, squeezes them hard enough that I'm worried for his circulation. Cade's comment might've hit home, either because Logan's aware that I'm not a real girlfriend to keep around, or because maybe his past relationships haven't been super great.

I rack my brains, trying to remember if I've ever seen him on a long term one and I can't. What's clear though is that I have to change the topic.

I fasten my seatbelt. "Anyway, what else are we waiting for here? Let's go!"

"Yeah, let's. I am so excited that I could barf," Hope comments with sarcasm dripping from her words.

"It's going to be great." Cade keeps his left hand on the steering wheel, his right one traveling over the middle console to—and here I stretch to the side to see—grab Hope's thigh. Quite high, if you ask me. "If the evening sucks, we'll escape and go get pizza."

"No pizza for you," Logan grouches from next to me. "Only when you play a perfect game."

"But—"

"No."

"Hope," Cade whispers in a far too loud tone. "Why did you invite him?"

She answers in kind. "I thought it'd be more fun if it was a double date."

"Ugh."

I snicker for a brief moment until it dies off.

Logan stays in his own world though, like two minutes of bantering were already enough to burn him out for the night—bantering that I kicked off while fishing for a compliment that I didn't really care for and also didn't get.

Biting my lip, I nudge his arm with my fist. The fabric of his white button shirt is surprisingly soft and I'm almost considering touching it again when he turns my way. Clearing my throat, I mumble, "I'm sorry."

Even in the dark at the back of the cabin I can see his brow tighten. "What for?"

"For dragging you along with this and for the teasing." I play with my thumbnails, bummed that I made the extra effort of doing my nails all nice and pretty for tonight. "I'm sure we can still get Cade to drive us back to our homes."

"It's fine." Then he shakes his head hard, muttering, "Why did I say that word again?" Pausing, he clears his throat. "I mean that I have no problem going to this thing with these clowns and you. No need to apologize."

My lips stretch into a whole grin. "Thank you for not lumping me with the clowns."

"You're welcome," he returns in a far too serious way that tells me he's playing around. At last.

Now that he's out of the funk I put him in, I tap his arm again—I need to ask what that shirt is made of—and point at the front with my lips. "Look at that."

Logan leans toward the center, and he's so large that I have to move away or we'll be way too close. "What?" he asks.

"See how they're holding hands?"

He narrows his eyes. "Yeah?"

"Let's try it."

Logan whips his head toward me. The streetlights illuminate his face while he studies mine, trying to find if I'm serious. I offer my left hand, palm facing up and fingers spread wide. I close and open them until he gets the hint.

It feels way more monumental than it should be when he picks up his right paw, and brings it up slowly until it hovers over mine. Then he stops, like he's not sure about this after all. I lift my hand until our palms slap, and veer it slightly to slide my fingers between his.

Okay, I'm a tall girlie. I can't say that I have dainty anything, least of all hands. But his definitely makes mine look tiny. Slowly, I watch as he curls his fingers to close his hand over mine, holding it tight.

The sensation travels all the way down to the toes on my opposite side. I bite my lips not to gasp.

"It's weird," he whispers with a mighty frown.

"Why?" I don't mean it to sound like a whine but it kind of does. It feels unfair that he finds this weird when I'm enjoying it way too much.

"I don't know, just weird." He peeks back at the front. "Not natural, I guess."

"Makes sense." I try to pull my hand away and he won't let me. If he notices me staring at him harder, he ignores me altogether. Instead, he leans back to sit straight, leaving his arm stretched out so as to not pull mine. And I don't know why that tiny, barely significant kindness does something to me.

It is I, actually, the one who spends the rest of the drive propped against my window, staring at the passing streets and cars so I can avoid Logan. Even though my left hand stays firmly engulfed in his.

The logistics of getting out of the truck and shutting the door make our hands break apart. While Logan's rounding the truck, I make sure to wipe any sweat off my hand with my jeans. But then my jeans ride down and he joins me when I'm in the middle of pulling them up. His eyes travel down somewhere to my hips, but I don't have enough time to wonder what interests him there when he's reaching for my hand again.

"Are, uh… Are we gonna do this all night?" I ask for his ears only as we walk behind the lovebirds.

Logan looks down at me for a quick moment. Facing forward again, he answers, "I told you. You're the one who is going to set the tone. If you want something else, you start it."

I draw a deep breath, the responsibility of that finally settling in.

I was the one who initiated the hand holding. Now he's the one not freeing my hand. Does that mean that if I hug him he won't let go?

Hmm. Maybe that wouldn't be so terrible. I wonder if he's a good hugger.

I check him out from the corner of my eye. Even though he's not bulky like a bodybuilder or anything, Logan is still a wall of muscle. Muscle happens to be quite hard and maybe he'd feel like hugging a wall, where I have to be the one to mold to him. The normal guys I dated before Ben were, ahem, far more pliable. Even Ben had a bit of a pouch where this guy has nothing but rock solid firmness. I already know, since drunk-me hugged him from behind on his bike.

I drift away enough that he has to drag me back to his side, which happens right in time before I run into some potted flowers lining the walkway to the front door of this house. It's one of those old money-looking homes that are actually not a decade old, probably boasting a pool and grill the size of the whole townhouse I live in—our unit plus the neighbor's.

The second we walk into the house, we're inundated by players greeting us like we don't see each other basically every day.

"You came! I didn't think you would," Mike Brown says, patting Logan's back.

All the catcher does is grunt at him and glance back at me. I promptly offer a smile. "It's my fault, I'm afraid."

"No, thank you. It's hard to get this guy out of his lair." Mike checks over his shoulder. "I want you to meet my wife, Amber."

A short woman with a pretty brown hair bob appears from behind him. Unfortunately, I can tell right away that her smile is fake. "So nice to meet you. I've seen so much about you online." She offers a hand adorned in many bracelets.

"I hope it's only good things?" I give an awkward laugh when she doesn't grab my hand in full, but only my fingers. Does she think I have germs?

But then she does the exact same thing to Hope and I relax

a little. It seems like this Amber is at least equanimous in her icky treatment of other women. And I say that because she's all gushing and praise for Cade and Logan instead.

"Let's allow the women to get to know each other," Mike says, palming both of his teammates's shoulders to steer them away. "We have some cold ones at the back."

I look up at Logan and find his attention on me. He cocks his eyebrow as if to ask if this arrangement is okay, and I nod at him. I'm a big girl. I was in the pageant circuit in my late teens and early twenties. I know a thing or two about how to sort through mean girls. The last thing I need is for him—or anyone—to fight my battles. Especially not when my roommate may need me to back her up.

And so I link arms with Hope and we walk together into the lion's den.

## CHAPTER 20
# LOGAN

Not to be dramatic but if holding Rose's hand felt weird, it's even weirder when I let go. It's kind of like when I've spent the whole day wearing my mitt and I take it off at the end of the day, and my hand feels too cool and too light.

I flex my hand a few times, trying to get used to normal again.

Sometimes I'm able to engage in conversation with my teammates, or even joke around. But today hasn't been the best day. The elevator in my building malfunctioned this morning while I was riding it. Once I was let out, I abandoned my plan of going grocery shopping and returned right home to put a cart online instead. Even though I was trapped for maybe five minutes in that metal box, it's put me on edge since.

The original plan was that I was going to pick Rose up in my convertible Gran Cabrio Maserati, but I've been so frazzled that I didn't think it'd be safe to drive. That left me with no choice but to call the clown of a pitcher and pack myself in his pickup truck.

Mistake, since I proceeded to make a fool out of myself.

*Fine*. Rose looks more than fine, for shit's sake.

Sighing, I ignore the ribbing of the guys around me, and keep an eye out for Rose. She's in the kitchen, now separated from Hope as a different group of women took the latter to the living room.

So far Rose's body language doesn't scream that she needs rescue. She stands by the kitchen island, chatting with O'Brian's girlfriend. Unfortunately, I've met that girl before and while she's more normal than Brown's wife, she's boring. A clever person like Rose will move on quickly.

"So, you and our social media girl, huh?" The host sets a paw on my shoulder, forcing my attention back to him and the group of guys around us.

"Uh, yeah." I run a hand through my hair, which coincidentally shakes Brown's off me. That's a win.

"How did that happen?" Miller asks with a side eye. "Because I can't see anyone like Rosie giving the time of the day to a grouchy cave troll like you."

"Hear hear," someone else says behind me.

I mumble, "It just happened." Over Korean BBQ and a late night bike ride, but I don't spill those beans.

"It was the power of a wild catch," says Cade Starr, motioning for the kids to gather round. "Listen up, kids"—I scoff at that—"It's not about rescuing the girl so you feel powerful or anything. It's about anticipating her needs and not letting her die from a blow to the head."

I cover my mouth with a hand because I would hate to give him the satisfaction of seeing me smile.

As ridiculous as it sounds, he's kind of right. Yet, what makes him think he's wise enough to advise anyone here? These guys have had WAGs way longer than him, and just because the thing between Rose and I is a farce, it doesn't mean I'm receptive to his yapping either.

Thankfully, one of the guys intervenes—except it's not to

change the topic. "So does that mean that if anyone else had caught that ball, Rose would've fallen for him?"

"She hasn't—" I stop myself. There's no way I can explain this.

But the vultures lean forward.

"Well, well, *well*. Looks like our charismatic catcher hasn't been able to fully charm the girl."

"Do you need some advice?"

"You kiss like this." One of the stooges makes beaks with his hands and touches them together. "Just make sure to get her permission first."

"That's right, my girlfriend says that there's nothing sexier than consent."

"Maybe also rearrange your whole face," Starr says with a grin. "She'll find you more attractive when you don't look like you want to commit murder."

"I only want to murder *you*," I offer acidly.

Funny enough, the person in this whole house who will test my patience the least is my alleged date. I glance back at her and find her in conversation with Brown's wife.

The depth of my visceral reaction knocks the wind out of me. Brown's wife is a narc—short of narcissist. I've known that since I met her. She's all about being the perfect hostess, the center of attention, the perfect wife.

Meanwhile, she makes her husband anguish about pleasing her.

I only know that part because I once overheard a phone conversation by accident, and Brown swore me to secrecy.

That's never been any of my business. *This* is. Rose isn't my anything, but I have to hang out around her now. The last thing I need is for someone around me to catch the attention of the very type of people I want to keep out of my life.

The guys are still talking when I march back inside. A

couple of women in the living room stare at me like they've never seen me before, but I keep going.

"—Would totally love to invite you and Logan for—" Brown's wife is saying.

No stinking way.

Amber Brown stops mid sentence when I appear next to Rose and insert my finger in the belt loop of her jeans, tugging her toward me. "Can I borrow Rose?"

The Mrs. Brown lowers her eyes to the point of contact between my alleged girlfriend and I, and plasters on a brilliant smile that doesn't reach her eyes. It's almost like looking right at my dearest mother. "Of course, we can continue later."

*The hell you will.*

Rose flashes me a look of confusion, but she tags along as I keep pulling her belt loop into the hallway. I check the first door—a storage closet. Then a bathroom. Finally a bedroom. I usher her inside and close the door behind us, locking it. I don't care if people talk, but I won't have anyone barge in for this.

"What the—"

I move away from the door and lean against the adjacent wall, folding my arms. "No, we're not going to wherever the hell Amber Brown was saying."

"But…" Her eyebrows do a whole lot of working for a moment. "She's clearly the head honcho of the WAGs. I need to play nice with her."

"You don't need to do shit." I huff and it deflates my chest. "First of all, you won't have to hang out with them long, remember?"

Once again, she mirrors the exact way I stand, except there's no wall behind her to lean on. "I want to be polite."

"That is the worst thing you can be to a narc."

"A what?"

"A narcissist." I run a hand through my hair. "I'm saying

this for your own sake, Rosalina. Steer clear of people with dead eyes and fake smiles." This comes out a lot harsher than I wish, and I'm sure it'll raise her hackles.

But it doesn't.

Her shoulders droop slightly and she tilts her head, studying me. "You're legitimately worried about this."

"Yes," I admit through gritted teeth.

"Fine," she says with a touch of something. When a sardonic smile takes over her features I figure out why. It's because of me and my inability to compliment her. "I'll figure something out to evade her. Happy?"

"No." My whole body is tense, and I try to alleviate that by running a hand down my face, then my hair, massaging my scalp. "I owe you an apology."

Still with the same half annoyed and half amused air, Rose asks, "For thinking I'm naive enough to not know how to deal with a mean girl?"

"What? No." I motion with my hand as if I could turn back time. "For what I said in the truck."

Her eyes turn up like the scene is replaying in the air and she can't pinpoint what I mean. "Wait, I don't know what you're talking about."

"When I said *fine*," I spit out, and in case that's not clear enough, add, "That you looked fine."

"Oh!" She jumps a little, unaware of what that does for her curves. I force my eyes to stay on her face, but I wouldn't be a professional baseball catcher if I didn't have superb spatial awareness. An awkward laugh comes out of her. "Don't you worry about that. I was just joking around when I was fishing for that compliment. I know you don't find me attractive."

I freeze.

The only part of me that moves is my eyes widening as far as they can go, then blinking hard.

"Who said I don't find you attractive?"

Now her eyebrows rise. "I mean, it's just obvious." I continue to look at her like she grew five heads, and color starts to rise up her throat. Motioning at herself, she says, "I don't look like the models I've seen you date. I'm too… big. And loud, I guess."

Huffing, I tear myself from the wall. She watches me with the same wariness of a lion tamer who isn't sure if her beast is going to pounce.

Our terms don't allow for me to touch her nilly willy, which is fine. I don't need to. I grab the belt loop of her jeans again, my eyes taking a quick peek at how the fabric stretches and exposes the skin of her side just a notch more. Just by pulling her belt loop, I position her in front of the mirror.

I stand behind her and take a step back, stuffing my hands in my pockets. I don't care that she can see me, I allow myself do what I haven't all night—I let my eyes get their fill of her. From the glorious curls that shine like tendrils of honey under the light. Down to the light purple blouse thing that I know must have some type of French name, cinched tight around her chest and flaring out over her waist. To the sliver of skin revealed between the blouse and her jeans. Down to the flare of her hips and lower. My hands tighten involuntarily, and I'm glad I don't dare to reach out. I'm afraid I'd grab handfuls of her ass if she let me.

Slowly, I travel my eyes back up, committing her shape to memory. I'm not even embarrassed when I meet her eyes again. I'm a red blooded guy and she gets my blood pumping furiously.

"I'm not very good with words or with gestures or with much of anything that isn't catching a ball," I say, my breath catching a curl and making it swing. "But I'm really sorry for not telling you how hot you look." I shrug. "Not just tonight. You look hot every day."

Her breath hitches. Color explodes in her face. "Wait, are you for real?"

"Why would I lie?" I cock an eyebrow.

"No, you're right. You're too… too *you* to lie just to make someone else feel better."

"You didn't have to compliment me in return."

Her face scrunches up and she gives out one of those twinkling little laughs that I've never heard tossed my way. It's a lethal combination with the blush still lighting up her cheeks. A blush that I put there.

I force myself to retreat even farther, until the back of my calves hit the end of the bed. I cough into my hand. "Maybe we should go before people start suspecting that I just couldn't wait to have my way with you."

She turns around to face me, hands on her hips. "Right."

Wordlessly, I offer my arm to her. She stares at it for a second and it reminds me of the rule. I'm not supposed to do shit on my own here, so I start to lower it.

But then she links her arm with mine and tugs me the way we came, not minding that this puts us much closer than we've ever been while sober and on firm land. Also not minding that we stay that way the rest of the night.

# CHAPTER 21
# ROSE

'm at my desk editing the wildest video of my career.

I'm sure a third party's opinion would differ—we have actually posted some pretty incredible plays that almost seemed like Hollywood CGI. But none of those videos have attempted to murder me by embarrassment.

Of course, the social media operation started the second I got the green light from Logan. We dropped a couple of videos rehashing the greatest hits—a.k.a. Logan saving the integrity of my head and then from his overeager fans—and I could deal with that well enough.

Dave had a new idea though, and today was the first time we filmed it.

Basically, I went up to a few random players over practice to ask them: *if they had a sister, which teammate would you let her date?* Nothing too spicy. I even got some funny takes. And one of the guys I approached was Logan.

In the meantime, Dave was also recording from afar. The shtick is to show how the other players are all normal and friendly, whereas Logan acts different toward me.

We must be pretty good actors, actually. Even though the

whole thing was orchestrated with everyone's full knowledge, we look like two college kids flirting between classes.

In the video, I walk up to him while he's taking a water break. The sun hits me square in the face and he notices. Grabbing my elbow, he steers me toward the shade from the stands. This part wasn't fake, I recall genuinely thanking him just as I set my phone to record and pointed it at his face. Logan must've figured that was the showtime, because he leaned his arm against the fence, lowering his face so I wouldn't have to raise my phone quite that high.

And I giggled. And tucked my hair behind my ear.

And my boss caught it all on camera.

Groaning, I drop my face on my keyboard and wish I was small enough to run and hide behind my mom.

Okay, I take it back. *He* is the good actor. I thought I was acting natural at the time, but now I can clearly see that I was affected. That the little kindness acts here and there, and the fact that a mouthwatering smell clings to him, were definitely affecting me.

And that's the thing. We've only been doing this fake dating thing for about a week, but he's already treated me so much nicer than Ben did even when we weren't supposed to be fake. That it was revealed to have been a farce later is a different story—my feelings, my hopes and dreams about him, those had been real.

Ben wouldn't even take me out in public, though. Dinner always had to be at his place, or somewhere so secluded that now I wonder if he was embarrassed about me. He never protected me from anything, not even from a crack in the side-walk. And he always hogged the comfy side of his couch, the one with the footrest.

I can't begin to count the amount of times that Logan Kim, a guy who doesn't give a flying turd about me, has looked out for me. It's actually embarrassing.

That's it. I'm just conflating his chivalry and my desire to be treated as a princess—as Cade calls me—when really all Logan is doing is the bare minimum, and I was settling for crumbs with Ben Williams. That's the real source of my embarrassment.

My computer chimes with an incoming instant message and I ignore it, still stewing about my performance in that video.

I have to remember that while Logan is a good actor, I am not, and that none of this is real. I've been burned enough by guys who act all interested at first and then toss me aside, to fall for a guy who is openly faking. I need to get it together.

Then my phone buzzes and since it's close to my face, the vibrations are so strident that I jump in my seat. Audrey's name appears on my screen and while we occasionally contact each other during work hours, it's still kind of rare.

Answering the call, I greet with, "Hey, everything okay?"

"That's my question exactly. I thought you'd jump at the chance right away."

"What chance?" I frown at the blurry reflection of my face over the paused video on my screen.

"You didn't see my message?"

"Uh, no. Hold on." I press my phone between my cheek and shoulder, freeing both hands to use the keyboard shortcuts until I get to the messaging system. Audrey's chat is at the top, unread.

> **WINTERS, AUDREY [11:03]:**
>
> Guess what?? Your best roommate ever just found you an opportunity with SPORTY. Run to my office!

My heart stops.

It kickstarts with a bang.

My voice trembles as I say, "Hope would take offense to that."

Audrey gasps. "The nerve." But I can hear the smile in her words. "So, are you coming or not?"

"Be there in as long as my legs can carry me!" I all but shout, ending the call. I barely have enough presence of mind to lock my computer, survival kicking in even through the excitement after I was pranked *by my boss* when I was in my first year.

He pokes his head out of his cubicle. "Where are you running?"

"PR. Later," I toss over my shoulder, skidding around the corner.

I haven't the foggiest idea what this is about, but I'm sure this is life giving me a lemon—and it will go on my resume and help me make the case for a promotion.

After passing a couple of people in the corridors and excusing myself from chatting as gently as I can, I finally get to the public relations area. I make a beeline for the cubicle that looks like a little garden, with tiny potted plants and flowers hanging from the plastic walls of her mini office. But she's not at her chair. What the heck?

"Looking for Audrey?" one of her coworkers asks from the cubicle across from hers. "She's in the meeting room with Logan Kim."

I turn into a statue.

Logan Kim? Why him?

"Thanks," I say at the same time as my brain clicks into place.

So this isn't an opportunity for *me*, but for the publicity stunt we're doing.

I walk into the meeting room in a more dignified way. Audrey sits across the table, facing the door. She's as elegant as always, with her fancy-looking clothes that she thrifts for a fraction of their original pricing, impeccable makeup, and blonde hair in gentle waves. Opposite to her is Logan in his gym clothes, a sleeveless black shirt that clings to his torso, and blue sweatpants. The guy is too massive for the tiny conference chair, and it squeaks in a terrifying way as he turns to look at my entrance.

He has his hair tied in a bun and it annoys me. The stubble in his face and his hair partially obscuring it often make me forget how ridiculously handsome he is.

I know I'm frowning now but I don't care. "Am I right to understand that this *SPORTY* opportunity is actually for Logan?" I ask.

Audrey motions at me to take the seat next to him and I do. I'm annoyed at his face, not at him.

"Actually, it's for both of you," she starts, lacing her fingers together above the table. "Like we expected, the internet is still buzzing with the two of you and I pitched the concept of a joint feature to *SPORTY* Magazine. The players and the social media managers who turn them into stars."

She makes an arc in the air with her hands as she says the title like she's picturing the byline already. I turn to Logan just as he's doing the same, and we share a smirk.

"Of course," Audrey continues. "This will have the added spin of a budding workplace romance and all that. We'll make it tasteful."

Logan puts a fist against his mouth, elbow on the table. For a second I suspect that he's trying not to laugh, but when I pay closer attention he seems to be thinking about this.

"I assume you first have to call your agent to clear it, right?" I ask, offering him an out.

His eyes shift to me without him moving his head. I can't help but feeling like he's assessing me until finally, he mutters, "I do, actually."

"Great." Audrey pushes away from the table. "I understand

that this is making you waste valuable training time, but if you can call him now and give me a confirmation in the next few minutes, I can get the ball rolling with the magazine before the season gets even deeper."

Also before Logan trades to a different team, which she doesn't know about.

It's the main reason why I figured he needs to discuss this with his agent. It takes a hot second to arrange these promos, no matter how speedy Audrey may want to be, and Logan might be gone before the campaign is scheduled. And then I'll also lose my chance of having a *SPORTY* feature under my belt.

I follow Audrey out of the meeting room, sighing, and she immediately zeroes her emerald eyes on me. "What's up with you?"

"Hmm?" I trudge along with her to her cubicle. While she takes her chair, I lean back against her desk right beside her.

"You look bummed and I thought you'd be excited about this." She tilts her head. "Why's that?"

"It's just…" I shrug, trying to play cool even as I squeeze the edge of her desk harder. "I feel kinda guilty. It would be different if this all wasn't fake and temporary."

"So like, you wish you were dating Logan for real?" One of her eyebrows rises.

"No!" I whisper-shout, then check to see if anyone shows signs of paying attention to this conversation. I lower my voice just in case. "What I mean is that it's weird to be getting this opportunity on something that isn't real. Half of the staff knows the truth but the players don't—heck, even Hope doesn't. It's almost like cheating and… and you know how I feel about cheaters."

"Wow, okay. These two things are nowhere near the same realm. Your work and the way Ben Williams treated you has nothing in common. Because that's what this is: work." Her eyes narrow slightly. "Unless you start to feel something for your performance partner."

I scoff. "Please."

"Or him for you."

I put my paws on her head and feel around. "Did you hurt your head this morning?"

Audrey is what I consider mysterious. She's a great person —she's helped Hope and I out of more than one pickle— funny in her cranky way, and extremely hardworking. Out of the three of us, she's the one who puts the longest hours without even traveling as much as Hope and I do.

But sometimes, like right now, I can tell that there's something brewing behind her eyes that she doesn't want to say. And every time I notice that, she gets one step ahead of me and changes the topic.

She plucks my hands away from her head. "Anyway, don't make *your* pretty head hurt by worrying about things that aren't a big deal. Let's wait to see what Logan's agent says and take it from there, yeah?"

Sighing, I nod, and we settle in to wait.

# CHAPTER 22
# LOGAN

My knee bounces as the line tries to connect to Kaplan.

I'm a grown ass man who can make his own decisions, and actually my decision is already made. But I do need to send a message to the PR and marketing team that I'm not some pushover who is going to say yes to whatever they propose. I have an agent who looks out for my best interests and who needs to be part of the decision.

Ish. I'm still kinda pissed at Kaplan.

"Good morning, Logan," he says in his peppy way.

"Hey," I say in return. "Something came up from the PR team that I thought you should know."

Immediately that makes his tone shift. "Oh, no. Please don't tell me that someone took pictures of you doing something illegal or compromising. I already have enough of that with another client."

"You really think I'm the type of guy to, I don't know, speed on my bike while drunk and naked?" I ask in a deadpan. Like shit, I know I live in Florida but I haven't turned into a Florida Man quite yet.

"Well, no." He settles a bit. "Then what's up?"

"*SPORTY* wants to do a feature with me and… and the social media manager."

After a bout of silence, he says, "The same social media manager who I declined the offer of a publicity stunt with, but you went ahead with all on your own?"

"Uh huh. That one." I lean back on the chair and it emits a terrible squeak like I could break it any second.

"Do you want to do it?"

"Yes," I respond.

"Why?"

Huffing, I sit with the question for a good moment.

There's no real reason. Women don't harass me regularly enough to need the permanent services of a fake girlfriend who can keep them off me. Yes, I feel kind of shitty that the association with me has dealt her so much hate on the internet, but I also could snuff that with a simple statement on my own social media accounts. Or through Kaplan, in fact.

I just… I want to. But that's not a good enough answer for my agent or, frankly, for myself.

Then something clicks. I bend forward to rest my elbows on the table and speak closer to the phone. "Here's the thing. I don't have a firm prospect to trade to. I think it's important that in the meantime I keep playing along with the team and not stirring the pot."

"That's awfully nice for a guy who has cut off other teams cold turkey." He gives out a humorless chuckle. "Are you sure that deep down you don't want to stay?"

"No," I say vehemently. "I don't want to stay. There's nothing here to stay for."

"Call me back when you don't have to convince yourself of that," he says sarcastically.

I snap back. "And you call me back when you have a real deal to consider."

He grunts. I do the same. And we end the call like the mature men we are.

*Asswipe*. I don't know who I'm referring to, if him or myself. Maybe both.

I press my fingers against my scalp and do a little massage, trying to bring me back to zero. I get that all my reasons to not pick any of the teams he's been working with seem irrational, especially when I won't go into the details of why I'd rather retire and become a llama farmer or whatever. From his perspective, I'm probably a more difficult client than the one who is facing a PR nightmare right now.

Yet I can't bring myself to talk.

I've even stopped going to therapy. It gets harder and harder to talk about something that was a big issue but is not really an issue right now, yet is still affecting me. I feel like an immature brat who can't get over himself.

The chair produces another protest as I get up, but manages to stay in one piece. As I step out of the conference room, the first thing I notice is a bunch of curls peeking from over a cubicle wall.

My lips twitch.

I press them tight, killing the smile before it forms.

Tucking my phone in my pocket, I keep tracing the path to the right cubicle and find the two women whispering to each other. Of course they stop the second I show up.

"What's the verdict?" Winters asks.

The verdict is that my agent suspects I've lost the plot. Unlike him, I *know* I have.

"We're game," I answer.

"Awesome. I'll reach out to their team and get this arranged. Thank you both for your support," she says, glancing at her roommate and at me.

"Right." Rose springs to her feet, salutes down at her friend, and squeezes out of the cubicle in front of me. Her eyes lower for a second before returning to my face. "Guess I'll see you around."

I fold my arms and this time her attention glues there. "First of all, we're headed down the same direction. Say that when we really part ways. Second, what are you staring at?"

She coughs. "You do recognize that your tattoos are eye catching, right?"

I look down at the full sleeve tattoos of both of my arms. They're plentiful but the least intimidating art ever.

On my right are vines of Korean roses, their pink petals stark against the red roses that are considered the flower emblem of the US. My left arm is similar but with a mix of small bluebells and red roses, the former being the flower of Sweden.

This tends to attract a whole lot less attention than guys who have skulls or something even more sinister printed on their skin. If anything, it gets me a lot of shit for the girly motif —as if guys also couldn't admire flowers.

That's not even the case here—I just want to pay very obnoxious homage to the heritage both of my parents try to escape. My father likes to pretend that since he's spent all his adult life in the US, he's now more American than Korean. My mother has actually lied to people that she's French, as if her favorite music act wasn't ABBA.

I almost smile again remembering how pissed both of them were when I got my first tattoo, the one on my back.

Returning to the present, I say, "I thought you were used to them already."

"Not really. Most of the times you're wearing long sleeves," she argues back.

"This is fun and all that, but I actually have to take a work call now," Audrey says from her cubicle, shooing us with her hand.

"Sorry, Audrey." While Rose waves at her friend with one hand, she grabs one of my arms. "Let's go, you beefcake."

"Beefcake?" I repeat, letting her drag me out. How dare she call me that way when she has *all that*?

I allow myself one more second of appreciating her tiny waist flaring out to the most amazing behind I've ever witnessed with my own eyes. Her black leggings deserve an award for clinging so perfectly. But then I force my eyes up to her hair and the most curious thing happens.

I don't cool down in the least.

From this close, I'm one hundred per cent sure that her hair is softer than silk, just like the hand that's branding my skin. Everything about Rosalina Mena is soft—except for her tongue. That's the only part that's sharp as a knife.

I bite my lip. Maybe I should break the contact. Her skin on mine is doing things to me that have no business happening in the middle of our workplace.

Gently, I tug my arm free and she lets go. We're alone now, out in a corridor outside of the offices. There's no need for her to keep dragging me.

"Sorry," she mumbles, realizing as much.

"Hmm." I stuff my hands in the pockets of my sweatpants and keep going. She matches my stride without much effort, considering that she's a pretty tall woman. With spectacular legs, if I might add.

Finally, I point to the left where I have to go, sure that she needs to veer right back to marketing. She nods and we stare at each other for a moment. Me, trying not to let my eyes wander below her cropped sweatshirt. Her, studying my face.

Since I'm the king of finesse, I just give her a nod and turn to the left corridor. After a moment, her steps echo behind me, moving away from me. I check over my shoulder as she walks away, hands joined at her back over her butt. I have to make use of my willpower to not keep staring and resume the use of my legs.

Back at the gym, I work out so hard that Franklin, the head trainer, has to order me to go cool down before everyone else.

I grab a towel and sit by my locker, my heart still thumping in my temples. The heavy workout isn't even the reason. "Shit," I whisper to myself. This thing with Rose is starting to go from objective awareness that she's an attractive woman to something different. Something that makes me exert myself at the gym as a coping mechanism.

That's not good.

"Whatcha mumbling there, buddy?" Rivera asks, strutting into the clubhouse along with his best bud and others.

"Buddy my ass," I mumble this time.

"Speaking of asses," he says as he stops way too close for someone whose locker is clear across the room. "I got something for you, my favorite ass."

"Go away, Rivera. I'm brooding."

"This will cheer you up," Starr says, his mouth trembling. "I helped him pick it."

"Then I know I definitely won't like it." I get on my feet and turn to open my locker so I can grab my uniform. But there, where my purple socks should've been, is a different pair. Slowly, I lift my head and turn. "You did not."

The two clowns burst into a fit of giggles, comparable to five-year-olds.

"C'mon, Kim. Show us what you got." Brown grins from beside me.

Maybe I need to really speed up the trade process, focus less on finding a high bid and more on acquiring mature teammates.

But then I spot someone who doesn't belong here, someone with curls that frame her face and a grin the size of the moon. She's recording the scene like she was in on the whole thing, and I wouldn't put it past Rivera and the rest, especially because they think that the social media manager and I are a thing.

And if so, I can't snub her or her work. Not especially when she seems to be enjoying it, even if it's at my expense.

Sighing, I put up a big show of grabbing the gift and unfurling it before the camera. A pair of the most absurd socks —long, stark white except for the two tiny alligator feet at the knees—makes the whole place erupt in laughter.

Where normally I'd be bristling at being made fun of, I can't help but staring at Rose as she guffaws, her face bright with how hard it is to get air in, and how much her eyes twinkle when she looks at me.

And that's how I finally realize that I'm toast.

# CHAPTER 23
# ROSE

probably sound like a hyena but I can't stop laughing. The look on Logan's face is epic—deep annoyance, yet no surprise that his teammates have targeted him for the next silly prank. I wonder if this makes him want to leave even more, or the opposite.

And that's a sobering thought.

Not about Logan leaving. Rather, about him staying.

I guess that's a possibility, especially since he didn't jump to sign with any of the offers. But I don't know what it would take for him to stay when he's already made up his mind. I certainly can't ask him to consider it for my sake.

He keeps looking at me, not at Lucky or the others. I can't help but wonder if we're going to get to do the *SPORTY* campaign together after all.

As my laughter ebbs away, my grip is steadier in recording the guys chanting *wear them* at Logan. I'd pay decent cash to see him put on the silly socks, but there's no way he will. In fact, he wraps the long socks around his left hand and—

Starts walking over.

I take a step back like that's enough to blend me in with my surroundings, except that I do have a phone camera pointed at his face. That doesn't make me inconspicuous at all.

"What?" I ask when he doesn't stop.

My back bumps into a wall and suddenly I'm trapped. Logan braces himself against the wall with one arm, which brings him way too close. Closer than we've ever been.

My breath hitches. This would be so much easier if he smelled bad. Clearly he worked out since we last talked. That should be enough to make him reek of sweat and body odor, and yeah, I definitely detect the sweat. But there's also something that is fogging up my brain and weakening my knees. Suddenly I'm real glad that I have a whole wall behind me to prop me up.

I stiffen as he touches me—wait. Not him. The socks. There's enough space between us that I can look down. The balled up socks are pressed against my belly, right against my exposed skin.

Slowly, he leans down to my ear. "If you like them so much, *you* wear them." His voice is raspy and soft, nonetheless deep.

Annoying. Now I have goosebumps all over.

The *wear them* chants morph into wolf whistling and hooting. Logan pulls away to look down into my eyes. My flaming face goes from could-boil-an-egg to fire-itself when I realize what he's doing next.

Carefully, without touching my skin with his, he slides one end of the balled up socks into the waistband of my leggings.

Air rushes out of my lungs.

Before I can even formulate what to say, he pulls all the way off and turns his back on me. "Okay, that's enough, assholes. We have a game to play," he barks, clapping his hands.

Squeezing my phone against my chest, I keep my head down and make a whole dash out of the clubhouse before anyone starts divesting himself of clothes. I take one last peek at the door, and find Logan's eyes on me until the last second.

They were blazing. I don't know if from anger or, or…

Nah. Definitely anger.

Obviously I'm not the mastermind of the prank, we all know that's a Lucky Rivera special. But I overheard him and Cade talking about it when I was returning from Audrey's office, and they were sneaking out of the canteen. One thing led to another, and I agreed to record the whole thing for social media.

I touch my face with the back of my hands. Yep, fire itself.

"Hey, Rose." I screech to a stop in front of Hope. She's drying her hands with paper towels, clearly returning from the restroom. "What brings you around here?"

"Ah." I clear my throat. "Your boyfriend and his bestie let me know they were pulling the socks prank on Logan, so I came to record it."

"Aw dang it, I missed it." Her frown clears away as quick as it forms, replaced by a smile. "So, you and Logan, huh?"

I give a strained laugh. "Wild, right?"

"Not really." She wiggles her eyebrows. "We all saw the sparks that time at Cade's place."

"Sparks," I repeat amid more of those awkward chuckles.

"I'm really happy for you. Logan's genuinely a good guy, despite that bad boy persona of his."

"He really is," this I say with a lot more confidence, because it's true. He's far from perfect and annoys me too easily, but he's a gentleman.

And he smells really damn good.

"Well I, uh… gotta go. To edit this. See you after the game."

"Yep." Hope waves at me and jumps back into the alligator's den.

I breathe funny while I basically run for my life. It's not like the guy is chasing me down, but I still feel the need to put as much space between us as I can.

*

I'm freaking exhausted. It must've shown bad enough for Dave to send me home early while the game was still going. He'll cover the rest and even told me to go to the doctor tomorrow if I still look like gum someone stepped on. Geez.

I imagine myself walking into a doctor's office and saying, "The reason I'm here is because my growing guilt over using a guy to advance my career, and lying to friends, coworkers, and the whole internet about it is making me sick. What can you prescribe for that?"

It's close to midnight and I'm sure the game will be ending soon. While the guys duke it out in the stadium downtown, I sit in my room in front of my dresser applying all the products my hair needs to be happy. My lips are turned into a sad little arch as I work curl cream from my roots to my ends, which stretched out can reach the small of my back.

My chest expands and empties as I let out a big sigh. The Orlando Wild app pings with a notification that the team has won, three to one. Not bad. Maybe not enough for Logan to rethink his trade.

"Para, Rosalina," I say in the language of my parents, with the same inflection Mom's voice got that threatened with la chancla. I will throw a shoe at my own face if I continue.

It's not like he doesn't know what I'm doing. He agreed to participate of his own volition. I at least shouldn't feel guilty about that. And perhaps I could tell Hope the truth. There's no concern that she'll run and tell the internet or anything. Rather, I don't want to disappoint her for having lied.

"Ugh."

I work a bit faster on my hair, switching to gel and scrunching. My phone pings again and I intend to ignore it, but something about the blur on the screen catches my attention.

Leaning over the screen, I all but get a heart attack when it turns out to not be a text, but a phone call. From Logan. For the first time in my life—what with only having exchanged numbers a few days ago. And right after a game?

The more I think about it, the stranger this feels.

My hands are goopy with products, though. I rush to the bathroom to wash them off and of course, when I return to my dresser the phone screen is completely black. Did I hallucinate Logan Kim calling me?

But then my phone goes off again, and this time I answer right away. "Logan? Hi? What's up?" My voice comes out squeaky and choppy.

"Hey." Meanwhile, his is all velvet as usual. "I was looking for you but your boss said you went home because you weren't feeling well. Everything okay?"

My heart drops to the floor. I hate that he chooses this moment to show concern for me, when I'm drowning in worry and guilt.

"I—I'm okay. Just a bit tired." I swallow hard and look at the Rose in the mirror, asking her for some extra strength. "Is, um… Is that what you were calling for?"

"Originally, no," he responds with his shocking honesty. "Something else has come up. Something that's pretty damn bad, not gonna lie."

I gasp. "Did your fans caught on to the fact that we're lying?" I rush to my window and peek out of the blinds, as though the backyard wasn't right behind me and it was a busy street instead. "Are they coming for me now? Do I need witness protection services?"

Logan snorts and something like a laugh comes out of him, except I can't be sure it's really that because he stops it right away. "No, it's a different kind of bad. Worse, I'd say."

"Logan Kim, you're about to give me a heart attack."

"It's my parents." He sighs. "They just called me saying they're coming to town tomorrow to meet my new girlfriend."

Silence.

Silence except for my hair dripping on the hardwood floor.

Calmly, I walk into the bathroom again to get some paper towels. I drop them on the floor and wipe it with my foot as I speak. "Let me see if I get this straight. Your parents are coming to meet *me*. Tomorrow."

"Right. I can buy you a plane ticket to go wherever you want tomorrow. Mikonos, Banff, the Maldives, Cape Town, Bangkok, you name it." He sounds like he means it, too.

"So you don't want me to meet your parents? What's wrong with me? Is it because I'm not a Victoria's Secret model?" I grouch.

"What? No. You are the one who doesn't want to meet *them*, trust me."

"Are you kidding me?" I pause talking because my jaw drops. "I would love to meet TJ Kim and Freja Lindberg. I'm sure my boss would murder me if I didn't get some pictures and videos of them to use on our socials."

"Rose, I—Listen, it would be so much better if you let me provide you with an excuse to leave town than spend a whole night pretending to be my girlfriend in front of my eagle-eyed parents."

"Is that a pun because your brother is an Eagle?" I tease.

It takes him a surprisingly long time to speak again. "If you'd rather not go far, how about an all-expenses-paid stay at one of the spa resorts? Just for you. Or you can bring a plus one."

"Why do you sound like you want to be that plus one?"

"Because I do. Desperately," he rasps out, and my hormones titter in glee until he adds, "but they'll figure out a way to find me because that's just how they are. I'm trying to spare you from them setting their talons on you."

"Talons?" I whistle. "I'm starting to get the impression that you don't like your parents very much."

"I don't," he says bluntly. "I *really* don't."

"Then…" I bite my lip and dare to glance at the Rose in the mirror. Her eyes are way too bright and she doesn't stop me from saying, "I can't leave you all alone to face them."

"But—"

"Text me the address, Logan. I'll see you tomorrow." And I end the call.

# CHAPTER 24
# LOGAN

"You're early," I say the second I open the door.

"And you're, uh… underdressed," Rose fires back, the bite steadily dropping from her voice as her eyes drift lower.

Deadpanned I say, "Yeah, because you're twenty minutes early."

And I know because I had it all timed. Rather than showering at the Wild facilities, I rushed home all sweaty and stinky to tidy up first and then shower before her arrival to start the operation. But I was barely done lathering up when the doorbell rang. And kept ringing. And ringing some more.

Now here she is, outside my apartment door carrying a suitcase and eating me up with her eyes.

I'm very aware that I didn't have a chance to properly dry myself, that my hair is dripping down my naked back and chest, and that all I managed to put on was a pair of black sweatpants—and that's it, nothing else. If she had any decency she'd look away though.

Rose doesn't. In fact, she's doing a second pass now, lifting her eyes slowly over my thighs to fixate on the waistband of my sweatpants.

Leaning against the doorframe, I fold my arms and ask, "Need more time? Want me to turn around?"

But this is Rosalina Mena we're talking about, she's absolutely nonplussed about being caught staring. "Actually, yes. I'm curious about your back tattoos."

I almost laugh but she's dead serious.

Shrugging, I turn around—not because I'm eager to comply, but because I'd really like to towel myself and change to dry clothes. She can stare all she wants as I head to my room.

"Ohh," she whispers behind me in tune with her steps falling on my floor. She closes the door behind her. "I didn't know you liked animals so much."

I pause at my bedroom door and glance back. "What?"

"Your tats…" She wheels the suitcase all the way to the living room, pointing at me. "A massive phoenix on your chest, plus the huge tiger and horse entwined on your back."

Ah. I'm so used to my tattoos that I even forget they're there until someone reminds me, or I catch a glimpse in the mirror. Then everything comes full force—every single reason why I needed them in the first place.

"They're just symbolism," I say carefully, not trying to incite the curiosity of this journalist who would eat me alive if I let her.

"Is that so?" I can tell by the way her eyebrow rises that she knows there's more to the brief answer, and maybe it's my guarded body language what keeps her from outright asking. Maybe she does have some decency after all.

"Anyway, are you moving in or what?" I look pointedly at her suitcase.

"This? I just figured that if your parents are coming here

first, they might be weirded out if they don't see anything femi-nine at your place. And honestly, I think I had the right idea."

Placing her hands on her hips, she takes a good look around at the stark decor. All the walls are white, while every piece of furniture I own is black. There are no trinkets and the only splashes of color are the spines of countless books on the shelves around the TV.

"This place looks very… spartan." She presses her lips and returns her eyes to me. Or rather, to my phoenix chest tattoo. "Ironic for a guy who is covered in colors."

I sigh. "Don't tell me you brought a bunch of pink shit."

"Um, excuse me." She puts a hand on her chest, offended. "Haven't you noticed that my color is lavender?"

I have, actually. Her entire cubicle at work is decked with light purple, and she tends to wear the color often—like right now. She's in light purple leggings and an off white crop top, oblivious or uncaring to the fact that right now her hips look luscious enough to bite.

"Knock yourself out, then," I say with a thick voice, finally disappearing into my bedroom and shutting the door behind me.

Swallowing, I hesitate for a moment. Should I lock the door or would that actually be weirder? Like implying that I was expecting her to come in and… I don't know, debauch me with her eyes while I get changed, if not more.

"Stop this shit. Just because she browsed it doesn't mean she wants to buy," I whisper to myself. I'm sure she'd peek at any other reasonably attractive guy in circumstances like this.

I mean, if the roles were reversed I'd probably have been way less cool than her.

After smacking my face so I can get my mind out of the gutter, I head over to the bathroom to finish what I was trying to do. For not the first time this week alone, I contemplate whether shaving my head and face would give me less hassle, but I still apply products to my hair and beard with painstaking care.

I catch muffled sounds from outside as I step back into my bedroom. It's bizarre to have anyone in my space. I don't even bring hookups home, yet here I am, buckass naked while my coworker plays house in my living room.

"Better hurry before this feels even weirder," I mumble.

I'm not sure what she'll wear but I know I can't go wrong with black. Is it lazy? Sure, but I'm not angling for a modeling gig tonight. All I'm after is for the night to be short—not even uneventful. That's an impossible wish.

This time I make sure to put on underwear before donning black slacks. I pair them with a silky black button shirt, rolling the sleeves up to my elbows and leaving enough buttons open that the tattoos are visible. The more reminders my parents get that I'm the imperfect child, the black sheep of the family, the undesirable one they actually can't wait to get rid of, the faster the night will end.

Finishing the look with the douchiest black loafers in my closet just feels like the cherry on top.

Before leaving my room, I grab an Omega watch that isn't the most expensive in the market, but is black and indestructible. *Like my soul,* I think sardonically.

Outside, Rose's suitcase lays splayed open on the living room floor, mostly empty at this point. She's by my bookshelves, stretching on her tippy toes to place a purple vase with fake lavender flowers on the top shelf. Pretty sure she'd be offended should I ask if she needs help, so I let her stretch as much as she wants…

And instead, stare at her ass.

Yeah, those leggings should be illegal.

I tilt my head to get a better angle.

Of course, that's when she finishes and turns around. Her eyes widen at catching me in the act.

"I believe in equality," I explain calmly. "If you can check me out as much as you want, then so can I. Turn around again."

Rose splutters. Color blooms on her cheeks. "You're kidding, right?"

"Am I laughing?" I twirl a finger in the air. "Turn."

Unwilling to be called a coward, she *does* turn around, twisting just so to look at me over her shoulder. "Are you a butt man, Logan?"

I tilt my head to the other side, committing her curves to memory. Not terribly difficult when her leggings are so tight that I don't know how she put them on in the first place. "So I am discovering." I shrug and narrow my eyes. "Are you sure those leggings are legal?"

Blowing a raspberry, she faces forward again. "Thanks for lifting my self esteem, but I need your help to finish decorating your place so I can go get changed."

With considerable effort, I tear my eyes away from her to observe the changes. There's a fluffy blanket and a couple of cushions on my couch, all purple. A matching mug sits on the kitchen island, and a beige cardigan's strewn on the back of a barstool. She has replaced the kitchen towels with hers, and there's another vase with fake flowers on the sideboard table by the entrance.

While I'm noting all the little things, she approaches with a reusable shopping bag that she offers to me. "Put all this stuff in your bedroom and bathroom."

I take a peek at the bag and promptly glance up. "Are you sure?"

"We want to be convincing, right? Unless..." She tugs back at the bag. "Maybe you're not that chummy chummy with your girlfriends?"

I'm not. Like at all. It's why my girlfriends always left. They all wanted a level of intimacy I can't give. My more recent dates never even made it to girlfriend status, sparing me from having that conversation in the first place.

Rose is neither. But my mother is a hound and if she detects the slightest whiff that this isn't normal, she'll pounce. And probably on Rose.

I tug at the bag again until she lets go. "Fine."

"Great. Should I use your bathroom to change?"

"Even better, I have a whole spare bedroom and bath down that door." I point behind her.

"Thanks." Rose skips back to her suitcase and picks up the last item, another shopping bag that must've been crammed in there along with the other junk. "I should be quick, just need to do my makeup and change."

"Take your time, you're still early."

She glances back and smiles at the last second before disappearing behind the door.

"What the hell am I doing?" I ask myself, shaking my head.

Back in my bedroom, I circle my extra large king bed to the opposite night table, the one I use the least. I put the two bodice ripper romance tomes on it, along with some purple hair clips.

Up next, I set a purple toothbrush in the bathroom right next to my black one. They don't look terrible together. At least it's not pink.

Reaching into the bag again, I come up with the dicier items. Women's hygiene products.

I let out a long suffering sigh because now that I've seen this, I can't unsee it. I will forever know that Rosalina Mena prefers this brand of shampoo and conditioner, this hair cream and gel, *and* these tampons.

Going big with the deception here, huh?

Once I'm done, I ball up the bag and set out to wait in the living room. This can take anywhere from five minutes to five hours, and I wouldn't be surprised if my parents arrive before she's done. I dump the reusable bag in her suitcase and zip it up, wheeling it into my room and leaving it in a corner by the balcony door. The bodice ripper books catch my attention and I grab one to settle on the couch with.

I'm only into chapter two of the budding romance between a widower duke and his daughter's governess, when the guest bedroom door opens. I look up from the page, but the doorway is empty so I focus back on the book. The characters are about to accidentally encounter each other in the library in the middle of the night when I finally catch Rose from the corner of my eye.

The paperback slides from my hands.

"What the…"

"You don't like it?" Rose looks down at herself.

"That—" I shake my head hard and unglue my tongue from my palate. "That's not the issue."

"Then what?" Her pretty face scrunches up in a mixture of confusion and annoyance.

I run both hands through my damp hair. "I mean that this is going to force me to act like a boyfriend." She still doesn't get it and I grunt. "Otherwise you're going to get harassed all night."

"Oh."

*Oh*, she says, as if she hadn't turned into a walking heart attack in a black dress that hugs her body all the way down to her knees. It might even be considered somewhat demure because it shows no skin and is long sleeved—

I start choking.

"Now what?" Rose puts her hands on her hips again.

"T-Turn around," I command, still choking.

"Dude, you're gonna have to control yourself—"

"That's not—" I wave my hand. "Where the hell did the rest of your dress go?"

She clicks her tongue. "Nowhere, you silly goose. The dress is like this." It's missing a hell of a lot of fabric at her back, is what. She gathered her hair atop her head, which means the curve of her neck down to her spine and to the small of her back are exposed to… to…

My eyes and everyone else's.

How is it even holding up? Like, shouldn't the thing slide off her shoulders?

"Logan." Why is she looking at me funny? "You're a really bad host, you know that? You stare at my ass and don't even offer me a drink."

"Shit." I spring from the couch. "You're right, I'm not used to this."

"Aren't you?" Rose follows me to the kitchen. "That's surprising."

Ignoring the dig, I stop at the fridge and open it. "I have still and sparkling water, orange and apple juice, almond milk, and chocolate milk. No alcohol."

Another smile stretches her lips, now a deeper pink than her natural tone. "Does a kid live here?"

"Yes, me." I reach for a sparkling water for me and she motions at me to offer her another one. Opening the first bottle and handing it to her, I change the topic by saying, "Listen, Rose. There's something you should know about my parents."

"Are they serial killers? Is that why you're single, because they keep killing your girls?" she jokes.

I open my bottle and my voice lowers. "No, but it'd be a lot easier if they were. They'd just be in jail."

"Huh?"

"Don't trust people with dead eyes and fake smiles.

Remember that?" I ask before closing the fridge and leaning back against it. "Wanna know how I learned that?"

She can sense that I'm not playing around right now. Before I get too worked up about this whole situation again, I take a good swig from the bottle and force myself to take a few deep breaths.

Slowly, I lift my eyes to her curious ones. "My parents are narcissists. I don't mean the kind of people who stare at themselves in the mirror too much—I'm talking about the freaky ones. The ones who will make your life a living hell if you let them in."

Air rushes between her lips. "Logan—"

"Don't be interesting," I say vehemently. "Don't give them anything to latch on—not anything funny or clever, certainly not anything personal that they can use against you." I set my bottle behind me on the counter. "Don't talk back at them even if they're rude or they insult you. Be so boring as to make them sure that I'll break up with you soon and they'll never have to see you again. Please.

"It's for your own sake," I finish, realizing that as I spoke I got so much closer, until her hand that holds her water pushes against my stomach. Rose's head is tilted back as she meets my eyes, and even though she's not wearing heels, our height difference isn't so drastic that this is uncomfortable for her.

And she's not moving away.

"Are you trying to protect me?"

"Yes," I respond right away. "I'd protect the whole world from them if I could."

"Then..." Her big brown eyes roam all over my face, trying to read between lines to decipher the deepest parts of my psyche. And she does, because she asks, "Who is protecting you from them?"

I freeze.

And blink hard.

"Myself." And the prescription I'm loaded up on.

"What if you accepted help?" Her eyes fill up with warmth, genuine and unbridled. "From me, that is."

I open my mouth, but I still don't get enough air into my lungs. My throat works with a heavy swallow and I try to refute the offer, but no sound comes from my throat.

Instead, the doorbell goes off.

# CHAPTER 25
## ROSE

Part of me wonders if I'm hallucinating what I'm seeing, except the small contact of the back of my fingers against his rock solid stomach reminds me that no, this is very much real life.

Yet here he is, Logan Kim, the most intimidating guy in the Orlando Wild organization, whose plays make whole teams crumble irreparably, who is tatted up and a biker and stronger than an ox…

And there's no way I can mistake the flash of fear that passes over his eyes.

He turns his back on me and I wonder if it's to compose his expression, but he's looking into a monitor by the door and there's another sign of distress. His shoulders tense enough to wrinkle the back of his shirt. "There they are," he whispers.

Not going to lie, this is starting to feel horror movie-ish.

Slowly, I bring my hands to cover my mouth, muffling the violent gasp that I can feel coming. Something clicks in my mind.

I've always thought that Logan is this guy sitting on a pedestal so high that it makes him untouchable, but I'm starting to think that's always been an act. That he distanced himself from everyone else because of this—because he's carrying something ugly inside of him all on his own and he doesn't want to share it.

"Ready?" Logan asks, frowning at me when I don't respond. "Hey, I didn't mean to freak you out but we can still cancel all this—"

"There's no need—"

"Then why are you looking at me like that?" he asks while the doorbell goes off again.

My eyes widen. "Like what?"

"Like I'm a wounded puppy?" His lip twists in disgust.

My chest squeezes hard enough to physically hurt, making me brace with the kitchen island behind me.

Crap, he's right. I'm feeling the exact same tender thing that I would for an adorable cub with big round eyes that's limping. Logan doesn't need that. I have a feeling it'll piss him off even more than he already seems.

Moreover, *I* don't need that. I don't need to feel squat for him, *period*.

"Sorry, ignore me." I set my sparkling water down on the counter and pull down at my dress. "Let's do this."

Nodding, he waits until I'm next to him to open the front door.

Freja Lindberg and Taejoon Kim—aka TJ Kim—stand on the other side in the corridor, two small suitcases flanking them.

My mind, my senses, and my very being are working on overdrive. Freja and TJ are overwhelmingly beautiful by themselves, but together they have the same impossible effect of eating a candy that is so sweet you get an immediate cavity. I don't know if it's genetics or money, but they're both over fifty and look way better than I do. Suddenly I feel like I'm too frumpy to even stand near them.

Yet, I plaster on my brightest smile. "Hi! I'm Rose, it's so nice to meet you." I stretch my hand first to Freja.

"I'm the one who is excited to finally meet the woman who captured Logan's heart," she says with a twinkling smile fit for fairies. Ignoring my hand, she goes in for an air kiss that brings a strong waft of sweet perfume.

In contrast, TJ does accept a handshake and he too is all smiles. "A girlfriend, how charming. You must be really special if Logan is willing to use that label."

My expression doesn't falter even though I'm super confused. I'm sure Logan has had girlfriends before. There have been news articles comparing them to me already, and a fan favorite is the one pitting his former model girlfriend and me. I don't suffer from either extreme of the self esteem spectrum, but I can confirm that I have the kind of beauty that is okay for the pageant circuit, but not for high fashion or Hollywood—and the fans were very eloquent about it.

I turn slightly to Logan and freeze.

He looks like a beautiful statue, lips set firmly shut, devoid of any expression. If it wasn't for his sharp eyes, I'd have believed that his mind packed up its bags and went on a long trip on his bike. What's more, he's not saying anything at all to his parents.

"Shall we?" I motion into the apartment.

"Ah, yes. I'd love to change my shoes before we head out for dinner," Freja comments, wheeling her suitcase inside.

Logan and I step aside, taking opposite ends of the door as they pass. His mom pauses in the living room, zeroing in on the details I installed all around. The glance she tosses back over her shoulder is to assess me—not because she approves or rejects what she sees.

Meanwhile, her husband makes a direct line for the room I used to change my clothes and fix up my makeup, and I'm glad

I had the presence of mind to bundle all that into my purse before stepping out.

"What did your dad mean?" I ask in a low voice once Logan and I are alone again.

He runs a hand through his damp hair, the sleeve of the shirt stretching so tight over his bulging bicep that I worry for the fabric. "I've never introduced them to a girlfriend before."

"Why not?"

"They weren't the one." He shrugs.

"Well, neither am I, Logan." I give him a pointed stare, just in case he has forgotten that this is all pretend.

He takes a deep breath and expels it before saying, "I know." I try not to frown. He doesn't have to agree to it quite so quick. But then he adds, "Which is why I freaked out when *they* insisted on meeting you. I think they know it's not real and want to confirm it."

"Hmm." I fold my arms loosely as I ponder. "Maybe they're worried that I'm a gold digger or something."

"Or they want to use this against me somehow."

I lift my eyes up sharply. "Would they?"

"Absolutely," he responds with certainty in a sinister voice.

Then their door opens and out they come, and the only change is that Freja has discarded her silver sneakers for heels that would max out my credit card.

"Shall we?" TJ asks, placing his hand at the small of his wife's back. She leans into his side and looks up at him adoringly.

So far, all I've found to fault them with his how saccharine they are. But Logan's shoulders are still as tense as the wires that hold up the Golden Gate.

He leads the way for us out of the apartment and into the elevator, still not saying a word even though his parents engage in small talk. I try my best to follow the advice of not talking about myself—and definitely not about Logan—and turn into a veritable acrobat as I dodge their questions and turn them around.

I ask about their journey, which I discover was via private jet, and whether they were comfortable. I ask how long they're staying and whether they have plans in town, and they surprise me by saying they intend to visit the parks the next few days. I'd have thought that would be beneath a supermodel who has traveled all over the world, and also beneath a man whose country is way more modern than anything we have to offer around here.

Logan is happy to fall back and just casually chime with directions whenever we have to turn or keep heading straight, and as his parents shift their conversation between them, I slow down to match my steps with my alleged boyfriend.

"You doing okay?" I whisper.

He blinks slowly and admits, "No. Waiting for the explosion any second."

*It can't be that bad*, I think glancing at his parents.

Or can it?

"So…" I trail off, trying to think of anything to distract him with. Something comes to mind as I watch them. "I think we need to make a bit more of an effort to look like a couple."

Logan angles his face to look at me. "What do you mean?"

"Look at them." I point at his parents with my lips. "They're all handsy with each other. Won't they think something's up if we keep a six foot distance from each other all the time?"

His eyes narrow on his dad's hand still at the small of his mom's back. "They're just putting on a show. That's not real."

"Neither are we." I smile, nudging his ribs with my elbow.

Logan turns back to the front, and for a long moment I'm sure he's going to ignore me. But then he mutters, "I told you, you're the one making the calls here. Do what you want."

That shouldn't make me excited. My pulse shouldn't spike

this much—but it sure as hell does. If this whole Logan having a girlfriend thing is a big deal, I'm going to play the part of the most in love girlfriend there ever was.

We reach the restaurant, one of those fancy ones that are tucked away from the main roads downtown, and that I could never in a million years consider eating at. A host leads us to a table somewhere in the middle, and enough people to turn to watch our party that I realize this is when we need to start putting a show.

I sidle up to Logan's side, molding myself with surprising ease to his hard body. He stops in mid step, glancing down at me with some surprise. I hold his eyes in mine as I circle my arm around his waist, and he inhales sharply.

"Now you do the same," I command in a volume only for his ears.

He frowns. "But your damn back is basically naked."

"Does a little skin intimidate the great Logan Kim?"

He rolls those clever eyes of his and next thing I know, his hand is on the small of my back and I'm the one who's dying.

Maybe I shouldn't have teased him. I certainly wasn't prepared for the torrent of sensation expanding like wildfire through my skin, all the way down to my toes and up to my cheeks.

The thing is that Logan's hand is huge—it spans the width of my waist easily. And it's so hot that it feels like a brand, a surprisingly soft one for someone whose skin is calloused by a lifetime of playing sports.

Logan pulls my chair for me and a genuine smile blooms in my face. I don't remember the last time a guy showed me this bit of consideration. Too bad that it's just an act.

Following along with that train of thought, I wait for him to take the chair beside mine to scoot closer. This time he doesn't wait for a cue and reaches his arm over to embrace me. I lean into his side and because my left arm is squished between us, I have no choice but to drop my hand on his thigh. It's that or cut off my blood flow.

The muscles beneath my hand tense. I look at Logan to confirm if this is not okay—I'll cut off blood flow for sure if that's the case. But he's already looking down at me and our noses brush. I gasp, all thought fleeing from my mind.

Worse, I completely stop breathing as he leans lower, his eyes shifting to my lips for a second. My heart hammers against my chest hard enough that I'm sure he can feel it against his ribs. But at the last second he veers away from my lips and whispers into my ear.

"Comfortable?"

Shutting my eyes tight, I breathe in the masculine pine scent that clings to him and swallow hard. "Oh, yes. Very."

Oh. My. Word. My voice comes out all throaty and thick and it's so clear that he's affecting me that it's not even funny.

"Me too," he says before pulling away, forcing me to focus back on reality even though my head is swimming.

What completely snaps me out of the haze is the way that TJ and Freja look at us. There is no amusement in their expressions, or even curiosity, or secondhand embarrassment. I would think those would be normal reactions that parents would have about their adult kids being lovey dovey with their partners. But these two are neutral, except for their eyes.

Completely dead.

A chill crawls up my spine. Maybe Logan senses it, because he holds me slightly tighter.

Freja flips a switch. A smile comes to her and she leans over the table, speaking with a subtle lilting accent I assume comes from her Swedish mother tongue. "I am just dying to know how you made my son fall for you. He's remarkably closed off, you see."

"That's true." TJ bobs his head. "At times I wonder where he got it from when the rest of us are such extroverts."

It's subtle, to the point where I wouldn't have noticed if Logan hadn't warned me off them so intensely, but all they seem to do is throw digs at him. Reflexively, my hand tightens over his hard thigh.

"That's just part of his charm," I say easily, turning to him like he just plucked the moon from the sky and hung it over this restaurant table for me. "It's what made me fall for him."

Logan's lips twitch but other than that, there's no further reaction.

"So does that mean that you're the one who seduced him?" Freja asks. This time she's unable to disguise the needle thin sharpness from her voice.

Logan catches on right away and speaks for the first time. "There's been no seducing here. I'm the one who's been courting her."

I press my lips tight. That's too bold of a lie for my sake.

"Is that so?" Freja covers her mouth as she laughs.

"Good evening ladies and gentlemen," a waitress says with the utmost politeness, showing a wine bottle that she holds partially wrapped in white cloth. "May I offer you a sampling of today's wine? It pairs deliciously with the house specialty."

TJ diverts his attention to the waitress and asks her for details on the wine, but I can't pay any attention when Freja is still looking at me like I'm the most interesting thing she's ever seen.

They test the wine with great theater, swirling their cups expertly, smelling it, and discussing the richness of its body or whatever. Logan and I stay out of it because neither of us can drink—him because he has a game tomorrow, and me because I have to drive home once the night is over.

Unfortunately, once the nice wine lady leaves, TJ and Freja's attention turns back to me.

I squirm until Logan's hand suddenly starts rubbing my

arm up and down, gently but with enough pressure to remind me he's in on this act with me.

"It's just so striking to see you two," TJ says, eyes crinkling with a smile that actually doesn't make his eyes shine. "I never thought I'd see the day when Logan truly cares for someone else. You must be one of a kind if he's even sharing this special occasion with you."

"Special occasion?" I ask politely.

"It's his birthday." TJ glances at his son.

Logan doesn't react, which tells me nothing about whether this is true or not. But a girlfriend should know that, and I don't appreciate how both of his parents watch me like hawks.

"Of course," I say smoothly and snuggle even closer. "I have a big gift waiting for him after dinner."

His father chuckles. "Lucky you, Logan. Seems like you found a good one."

"Right?" Freja says her husband, lightly tapping his chest with the back of her hand. "It's just a shame that this is happening now when Lewis was so excited to have you back with the Eagles."

Logan's body, normally hard like a rock, positively turns to steel after that. A muscle in his jaw ticks. It doesn't take a rocket scientist to know that whatever this is, it's a touchy subject.

I run her words through my head again. Why would it be a shame for Logan to hypothetically be finding someone who loves him right now? Shouldn't that make them feel happy for him, relieved that their son isn't on his own anymore?

TJ asks me, "Perhaps you'd be willing to relocate with Logan to New York? I'm sure that would be a major step up for you too."

My eye twitches slightly. Is he implying that my life in Orlando is subpar or something?

Or is he trying to make plans for me the way they seem to do for Logan?

I open my mouth and the latter cuts me off. "Rose, didn't you say you wanted to use the restroom before dinner?"

I pinch his thigh for taking away my moment of glory, when I'd just been about to tell his parents where to shove it. His muscles jolt at the pain, but other than that he shows no reaction. Rather, he's giving me a look that says *run.*

"Right, thanks for the reminder, babe." I throw the last word in there for kicks and giggles. "If you'll excuse me…"

It takes surprising effort to extricate myself from him and once I do, the air conditioning in the place feels so much colder. I grab the strap of my purse that I absentmindedly hung on the back of my chair when we arrived, and make my way around the tables and the decor.

The floor plan is divided by partial panels that provide a semblance of privacy between the tables, but still allow for visibility to the staff on their feet. I make my way to the back and stop, peering around the corner.

Freja isn't following me, which is good. I hang my purse crossbody style and crouch lower so the panels hide me, retracing my way back to our table until I'm behind a potted plant, close enough that I can overhear.

"—Is this really what you came for, then?" Logan is saying in his deep, rumbly voice. "To convince me to go back to New York?"

"Of course not, we came to meet your new girlfriend," Freja retorts.

"It just so happens that we also wanted to talk about this, but we knew you'd ignore us if we gave you a heads up," TJ says.

"We wouldn't have to go to such lengths if you just talked with us, Logan," his mother chimes in perfect tune with his father.

My brow furrows. There's a blatant lie lurking in their words. It makes me feel like Logan hit the nail right on the head—that their visit isn't about me and I'm just the excuse. They're too smooth at glazing over it, trying to make Logan feel foolish for suspecting them, while also blaming him for their own behavior.

"Stop gaslighting me," Logan spits back. "If this is how the dinner is going to go, I'm going to take Rose and go somewhere else."

"Logan, don't be rude," his mother admonishes. "It's already enough that you lowered yourself to date someone like her, but to act so immature on top of that? We didn't raise you that way."

I freeze.

"Excuse me?" Logan's voice turns into a dangerous rumble. "What the hell did you just say?"

"Language, young man." His father's turns more into the crack of a whip. "I won't have you talking to us that way."

"But it's fine to imply that Rose is somehow beneath me?"

"Somehow?" Freja lets out an elegant little snort. "She *is* beneath us. You can just tell at a glance from how she—"

Something inside of me snaps. Before I can stop myself, I rise to my feet and it puts me above the edge of the decoration barrier. All three turn to me like deer caught in the headlights.

Tilting my head at Freja, I ask, "Is it because of the color of my skin? Or my Latin American accent? Or let me guess, it's because my dress cost fifty bucks, right?"

For the first time since our very brief acquaintance, Freja looks genuinely caught off guard. In contrast, TJ's face hardens. "This is why. She's been trying to manipulate you all night with every interaction, and now she's openly trying to pit you against your own parents. Where are your standards, Logan?"

"My standards?" Calmly, Logan pushes away from his

table and stands up. "I would choose Rose a million times over you."

His father's face, normally very fair for someone who spent a lifetime under the sun, suddenly turns crimson. "You would—"

Raising his voice, Logan cuts him off right away. "I will leave your suitcases with the concierge. I'm sure you can find a room at any of the resorts." Then he walks around to me. "Let's go, Rose."

Logan offers me his hand and I take it, lacing my fingers between his and not looking back for a second.

# CHAPTER 26
# LOGAN

ose stomps ahead of me, her hands balled up at her sides. Her purse has some black leather tassels that jiggle far too happily with every step—jarring against her body language.

She's absolutely fuming and I don't blame her. What my parents said is despicable, just like they are.

And that's my problem—I'm freaking exhausted. I knew they were going to muck this night up at some point, but I wish they had just shat on me and only on me.

I wish I had figured a better plan to keep Rosalina away from them, but telling them that she and I are only dating for publicity would've got them yapping even harder. And the next one to find out would've been their golden son, and then Lewis would have told the whole world.

The one who would've got the short end of that stick is Rose because that's just how shitty the world is to women, whereas I'd have been labeled a team player, a business man or whatever.

I run both hands through my hair and tug, mulling over

what I could've done differently. But the core of it is that I shouldn't have gotten involved with Rose at all. I should've just let her figure out how to do her job without me. I need to learn my damn lesson and understand that the best thing I can do for other people is not get involved—to be alone—and that way no one else has to be subjected to my horrible family.

"Why are you standing all the way there?"

I lift my head. Rose watches me from the corner across the street, eyebrows tight and eyes still flashing thunder. She motions at me to follow her.

Swallowing hard, I check the street both ways and cross to join her. I squeeze my jaws tight, trying to not let her figure out that I'm freaking out, that breathing is starting to get harder and that my vision's blurring.

The last damn thing I want is to have a panic attack in front of her.

Her angry eyes roam over my face. I use all my willpower to appear calm even as I struggle to breathe properly. "Follow me closely," she says through gritted teeth, and I manage to jerk my face in a nod.

I focus on her hair. That's it.

I know I should be more mindful of our surroundings because downtown at night can get dicey in areas, and I need to make sure she at least gets home physically safe. But all I can manage is to put one foot in front of another, breathe, and look at the one curl that cascades over the rest and bounces the most while she walks.

Every so often, she glances over her shoulder to make sure I'm following. I got the message, though, and I make sure the distance between us is reasonable.

Somehow that little curl is enough to keep me from the edge.

I finally snap out of it when she stops us at a red light and I have no choice but to stand beside her and take in my surroundings. We have approached the part of downtown with the most traffic, pedestrian and vehicular alike. Some guy on Rose's other side is eying her funny and I make a point of staring at him until he realizes that she's not alone.

After clearing my throat several times, I ask her, "Where are we going?"

"To eat," she responds in what is basically a grunt.

"You're angry… yet you can eat?" Every word comes out sluggish, almost like I'm drunk. If she notices it, she doesn't remark on it.

Rather, her brow darkens even further. "Yes. Can't you?"

"I can." I stuff my hands in my pockets.

The light turns green and I follow her for another block until a food truck appears in the distance. I recognize the flag that decorates the signage at the top—there are plenty of Venezuelan players in the majors that I recognize it. In fact, last year's MVP was the mega slugger Miguel Machado—Venezuelan. And so is Rose.

We approach the line and she asks, "You eat about three times what I eat, right?"

I travel back in time to the night we ate at my Korean spot and that math checks out. It's kind of funny that she noticed. "Yeah," I say, trailing the word off.

"Any allergies or intolerances?"

The fact that she's asking such a polite question while her pretty face is still scrunched up in severe anger does something to my chest. Something snaps, something that had me as tightly wound as a spring, and suddenly I can breathe easier, my shoulders relax and so does my jaw.

"Well?" she presses.

I blink hard. Run my tongue across my lips. What the hell just happened?

"None. I could eat an elephant," I respond with a voice that doesn't sound mine.

"Great." It almost sounds sarcastic. She points to the side. "I'll order the food and you find us a table."

"Rose, I—" I reach for my pocket with jerky movements. "I should get the food. It's the least I should—"

She stops me by just raising her palm. "Trust me, you're getting a fair bargain. The hardest part is finding where to sit."

"Fine."

I leave her to queue up and head over to the oversee the expanse of plastic tables and chairs. This food truck must be really popular because the place is packed, forcing me to peek into how far along people are into their meals to guesstimate how much longer they might take.

"Logan Kim?"

My head whips to the source of the question. A guy gets up from his seat nearby, grinning up at me in that way that fans have when they spot one of their favorite players. I unfurl my arms to adopt the more friendly postures I had to learn after fans kept complaining online that I was a jerk. I still am, I just try to mask it better.

"Hey, yeah," I say in a calm voice, hopefully denoting openness.

"Whoa. Guys, this is the best catcher in the world right now," he says to his friends congregated around two tables that are stuck together.

I'm not the best catcher in the world, just the top All-Star catcher right now. But there's no need to correct an enthusiastic fan who also seems a bit tipsy.

"For real?" one of the friends asks, completely surprised. Clearly not a baseball fan.

Another one, a woman, also gets up. "Wow, can we get a selfie?"

"Uh, sure," I say.

Next thing, I'm surrounded by a bunch of strangers as one of them angles a cellphone camera to snap a few selfies. I do my best to smile but I'm completely overwhelmed. The bodies of a bunch of strangers sticking to me isn't my idea of fun after a rollercoaster of a night.

Suddenly, like drawn by a magnet, my sight travels the distance to spot Rose as she approaches. She tilts her head at me and I don't know how, but I can read her mind from clear across the tables—and she's asking me if I'm okay.

I hesitate. I don't want to put her on the spot again, but I am *not* okay. I am so not freaking okay. I was on the mend until these people surrounded me and now I'm regressing, my lungs constricting, my jaw tightening.

So I take a leap of faith and I answer back with a minuscule shake of my head.

Rose immediately picks up the pace. When she's close enough, she calls out, "Babe, are there no tables?"

There's the *babe* again. Instead of cringing, I fling it right back. "Sorry, babe." To the fans surrounding me, I say, "Excuse me, I have to get back to my girlfriend."

The woman from earlier who didn't seem to recognize me gasps. "Wait, I have definitely seen you somewhere."

"Oh, hi." Rose gives a little wave. "I'm the baseballer's girlfriend."

I swallow hard. If only.

No, I can't go down that path.

What the hell is happening to me?

"That's right! I saw you on TikTok." The woman snaps her fingers.

Slowly, with careful movements, I extricate myself from the mass of people—but right as I think I'm free, a hand stops me.

"Take our table," the original guy says to me, and he's the one who stops me. "We were almost done anyway."

"I couldn't—" He cuts me off.

"No seriously, we're good." The dude grins. "We're actually running late to hit the club."

"Then uh, thanks."

After much shuffling, which includes them collecting all the debris on the tables and pulling them apart again, Rose and I finally take seats across from each other. She dumps her purse on her lap and scoots closer. "Thank you for your face," she says out of the blue.

"Huh?"

"It's what got us the table."

I lean back on the flimsy plastic chair and somehow manage to say, "You're welcome, *babe*."

Her eyes narrow slightly but for a long moment, she doesn't say anything. All she does is stare at me like this is how she makes a living, forcing me to be more self conscious about my facial expression than usual.

But no matter how well I mask, there's no erasing the shitty night we've gone through. Or that it's all my fault.

"I'm sorry—" I start saying, my chest deflating after releasing the apology that I had bottled up.

But she interrupts with, "Why didn't you tell me?"

"I did tell you." I scratch my head. "My parents are horrible people and I didn't want you to—"

"Not that." She waves her hand. "About your birthday. Is it really today?"

I jump a little like I just got zapped by electricity. "I—Yes. It is."

Rose leans over the table, eyes bulging. "Are you freaking…" She trails off, switching to a string of Spanish I can't dream to comprehend. After shaking her head hard, she returns to using the one language we have in common. "Don't you think your girlfriend should know when your birthday is?"

"Is that really what matters out of everything that was said tonight?"

"Yes!" She's vehement about it too. "Who cares about the other crap? This is the one thing that really mattered today and I didn't even know." She drops her face in her hands. "I should've looked you up on Wikipedia."

Speaking of, I could probably be the picture on the Wikipedia entry for *confusion*. "Rose, it's not a big deal. I don't care about my birthday."

"Well, I do. Birthdays are a big deal to me." She presses her lips tight.

Right then, a guy wearing a T-shirt that matches the decoration of the food truck approaches, his arms loaded up with what looks like baskets and baskets of food. He seems jittery, like he's permanently in a hurry. Tossing a quick greeting at us, he starts placing the plastic baskets on the little table. Rose and I have to make room for him to fit everything. A moment later he returns with two plastic cups filled with an iced brown drink that I don't recognize. It's thicker than tea and has no gas bubbles.

I don't know where to even start. Each basket has a different dish that I don't recognize, and I know that different cuisines have different eating protocols. I cave and ask, "How do I eat?"

"This one you'll need fork and knife for," she points at the big thing that looks like a sandwich but clearly isn't. "The rest you eat with your hands, or if you don't want to get them greasy you can use a napkin like I do."

She picks up a stuffed round thing and wraps it in a bunch of napkins before taking an enormous bite out of it. Her cheeks bulge like a squirrel's as she eats and it's…

Adorable.

I forcefully clear my throat and go for the plastic fork and knife in the basket of the sandwich-look-alike. Cutting up a piece reveals more food inside than any sandwich I've seen in my life, and when I put the morsel in my mouth I'm punched by way more flavors than I expected. And they're all over-whelmingly so delicious that I am healed.

A moan tears out of my throat.

Rose pauses from munching. After a moment she smirks and speaks with her mouth full, "Good, isn't it?"

"Amazing," I return, also with my mouth full.

There's no need for conversation after that. I appreciate that Rose doesn't judge me for scarfing down food like a ravenous beast, and that she's actually doing the same. What seemed like a lot of food dwindles down to nothing, and all I have left is to sip from the sweet, lemony brown drink to wash down all the fried food. This is way better than the overpriced steak we were going to eat back at the fancy place, and I don't care if I pay consequences for eating fried stuff tomorrow. I'll consider this my cheat day for the month.

Sighing, I lean back to stretch my stomach and she does the same, except she massages hers. "Do you have room for dessert?" she asks.

I almost choke. Somehow I manage not to. "Uh, not really."

"Well, make room."

My eyebrows rise. "Bossy."

"Any issues with that?" she asks in a deadpan.

"None," I answer in all honesty.

"Good, I don't like to pretend that I'm nicer than I really am."

That tears a grin out of me—despite the absolute garbage of a night. "That's at least not something you have to pretend with me."

"It's weird," Rose says softly, those searching eyes of hers digging into mine. "I've always known that. You're a no nonsense kind of guy. Yet I couldn't understand why every so often you shut down and hide behind a mask. Until now."

Well, shit. That makes all the amusement I was feeling evaporate in record time.

"Are you going to let me apologize now?" I fold my arms tight enough that the muscles bulge, and they catch her attention for a second.

It doesn't break her, though. She shakes her head. "You're not the one who should apologize. You're not your parents." She has no idea how that single sentence is making my head reel. "Unfortunately I have the feeling that they never will."

"You're not wrong," I say slowly, my voice choked up.

"I'm the one who's sorry." She huffs, her lips twisting in annoyance like they did on the walk over.

"What the hell for?" It takes a lot of effort to not scream in outrage, but that would get too many eyes on us.

"I should have defended you."

It's almost offensive how the people of a nearby table burst out laughing, a car honks down the road, and some dog barks on the park across the food truck. The voices of the truck workers reach over the noise of the customers as they yell food orders at each other. In the distance, someone's blaring reggaeton from their speakers.

That's all too ordinary of a backdrop against the wildest words I've ever heard in my life.

"I'm sorry, what?" I turn my head slightly to hear better.

"I can't stop thinking about how I only stood up for myself and *you*"—here she grits her teeth—"also defended me. But not yourself. What the hell, Logan?"

I am stunned. This is the second time she completely robs me of the ability of speech, and I don't recall anyone else doing that in my life.

"Why…" She smacks a delicate fist on the plastic table, making the empty baskets jump. "Why did I only realize that after we left?"

"Wait, wait." I run a hand down my face, wishing I could scratch myself all over because I'm so uncomfortable in my own skin. "Is this what you were stewing about this whole time?"

"Yes," she hisses. "I'm a terrible person. All I did was think about myself and—"

I bark a laugh.

Eyes turn to me.

"You're shitting me, right?" I know I've finally lost it because I'm still laughing, and because now she's the one who can't speak. "You really think a terrible person would even realize that? They'd suck *on purpose*, just like my parents."

"But—"

"Rose. You defended yourself because you were being wronged, and I did the same because I wasn't the one who was getting thinly veiled racist insults thrown my way."

"You were also being mistreated. Don't think I didn't notice how everything that came out of their mouths was to put you down one way or another."

"That's just how it is. I'm used to it."

"But you shouldn't be." Rosalina leans forward. "That's not right and you don't deserve it. Yes, you're more irritating than a thigh rub burn sometimes—"

"A *what*?"

She continues, "But beneath that lone wolf act of yours, you're a good guy. You do not deserve that, do you hear me?"

"What the hell is a thigh rub burn?"

She gives me an incredulous look. "That's what happens when your thighs are chubby and they rub against each other until the skin burns. Do you understand the main point I'm trying to make?"

"And your thighs burn?" I ask, resting my elbow on the table and my chin on my hand, my mind latching onto the dimensions of Rose's thighs.

"Logan." She gives me a look. I give her one right back.

She sighs. "Yes, they do. I'm wearing spandex right now to prevent rub burns."

Good thing I like some cushion.

I sigh, trying to get my mind out of the gutter it's sunk into all by itself. "And yeah, I get what you're saying. But you're wrong."

"No, I'm not," she says stubbornly.

"You are. You don't know me." I shrug. "That masking you so cleverly noticed? I do it all the time. I had to be coached by my agent and our PR team on how to conduct myself in public because otherwise I act like a jerk—and that's what I really am." Sardonically, I add, "The apple doesn't fall far from the tree."

Spreading both hands over the surface of the table, she leans as close as she physically can and murmurs in a kind of menacing tone, "Literally nothing I've seen since I've known you leads me to think *apple, tree.*"

"Here's the cake," a random voice says.

Rose and I turn to the same busy worker from before, and he's coming in with the biggest slice of tres leches cake I've ever seen, a candle on top and all.

I whip my eyes toward Rose. She's avoiding mine, or is simply busy with stacking baskets to make space. I do the same and we clear the table quickly. The guy places the cake between us, and I notice the two plastic spoons on the plate just as he reaches over with a lighter and lights up the candle. Collecting the empty baskets, he beats it back to the truck.

Slowly, I lift my eyes to Rose's stubborn face. "Happy birthday, Logan."

I don't understand why the stubbornness. It's not like I'd ever reject cake.

"Thank you." I rub my chest, where my heart is thumping in a painful way. She signals at me to blow the candle and I do, and even though I'm not hungry at all I dig into the tres leches.

She doesn't lecture me again after that, but I can practically feel her mind whirring as we walk back to my apartment so she can get her car.

The good news is that I don't waste a single second thinking about my parents the rest of the night. The bad news is that now I can't stop thinking about Rosalina Mena.

# CHAPTER 27
## ROSE

It seems like my roommates are asleep by the time I get home at one in the morning. I remove my sandals and tiptoe my way to the back, passing Hope's room to reach mine. I'm super careful closing my bedroom door because everyone here is a light sleeper.

But unlike the quiet in the house and the residence, I'm freaking buzzing.

I lock myself up in my bathroom with my phone. Checking it for the first time since getting on my car to drive home, I find a text from Logan that simply says, *I'll leave your stuff at your cubicle tomorrow.* Nothing else. Zero acknowledgment about anything else.

"This freaking guy," I grumble, tapping away from my text message app and to the contact list.

I find Mom's and press call. She's the only one who can talk my mind into making sense so I can get any sleep. Otherwise I'm going to ruminate about Logan Kim the entire night and hate myself at work tomorrow.

"What's wrong?" Mom asks upon taking the call, her voice slurring.

We have an evergreen agreement that we can call each other at any time and barring something truly incapacitating—like a surgery—we pick up right away, if only to check whether the topic is an emergency and agree on a callback. It's both the privilege and downside of being a family that only consists of a Mom and daughter duo.

"Not an emergency," I start with to bring her heart rate down. "But my head's an absolute mess and I can't function."

"Espérate." I can hear her bed creak as she sits up. "Okay, I'm all ears now but you'll owe me brunch after this."

"Deal." The Rose in my bathroom mirror and I take a deep breath. "I just really, really wanted to tell you how thankful I am that you're my mother."

"That is an acceptable reason to call me at one in the morning, but I fail to see why it's making your head into a mess."

I set my phone on loud speaker, modulating the volume so that Hope can't hear it next door, and as I talk I set out to open brand new makeup removing products. I have to use my stock, after staging my opened products in Logan's bathroom in case his parents snooped around. I don't regret making the effort, even if I do regret other aspects of the night.

Mainly how I didn't hug him goodnight. And that man sure needs a freaking hug.

"I met a friend's parents tonight," I say and before I can add anything further, my mom chimes in.

"A guy friend?"

"I—yes. And before you ask, not my boyfriend. Just a friend." If at all. I'm not sure that he'd consider me one.

"Uh huh." I won't acknowledge the skepticism in her voice.

"That's not the point. What I'm trying to say is that his parents are just hateful people, which really puts into perspective how lucky I am that you raised me."

"Should I be worried?" I hear her bed sheets rustle. "I

know you're an adult, mijita, but I don't want you hanging out with bad people."

"That's the thing," I whisper-exclaim, throwing my hands in the air and almost sending the cotton pad soaked in micellar water flying. "He is absolutely amazing. Kind of cranky if you don't bother to look deep, but actually a genuinely good person whose parents happen to be garbage, and who obviously messed him up."

Amusement laces her voice. "Seems like you care about this guy."

"*Mom.*"

"If you don't, why are you calling me at one in the morning to talk about him?"

Shots fired. Target hit. I double over from the pain in my chest, holding myself up by my hand on the vanity. "Maybe I do care about him but…"

"But?"

Squeezing my eyes shut, I take a deep breath and finally admit that this is what I really wanted to do all along: spill all the beans. Audrey knows the work part of the situation, but not everything else. Not the personal stuff.

I tell Mom everything… from the very first time Logan saved my life by making a wild catch that went viral, to the opportunity that opened up for me professionally, and how I roped him into helping me for nothing in return, other than the service I provided tonight of getting fans off him.

I do gloss over some details, for example me feeling up his thigh or how electricity shot down to my toes when our noses brushed. I definitely provide no commentary on how outrageously good looking he is, or the fact that he smells even better—good enough to drink.

Instead, I emphasize how the deal includes no kissing and restricted PDA that can only happen on my terms, and how he has respected all of that. And me.

Gosh, the way he defended me to his parents made my knees weak. If it hadn't been because he grabbed my hand right after that, I might've melted on the spot.

"What's the guy's full name?" Mom asks.

"Logan Kim," I respond in a daze after recounting the past couple of month's worth of shenanigans.

There's some tapping, which I'm sure is from Mom keying in his name into a browser. While I wait for the inevitable reaction, I work on removing my jewelry.

And there it is. "Oh my freaking goodness. This guy is a Greek god."

"Even better in person." I sigh.

"Husband him up. Right now."

"Mom!" I whisper-hiss. "That's not what's going on here."

"Why not? And don't give me any of that work assignment crap—you're both pretty deep in it if he's introducing you to his family."

"He didn't want to, trust—"

"But Rosalina, that guy *wants* you. And what's more, you want him." I freeze, watching as my face in the mirror reddens more and more. After the pause has stretched enough, Mom adds, "You've just never talked about a guy this way, chiquita. I think you have feelings for him and that's why your head's a mess."

"That's not true." I have difficulty swallowing down the lump in my throat. "I don't even like hot guys."

"Really?"

"Yeah." My chest rises and falls in tune with my rapid breathing, my voice growing more high pitched as I continue. "I like normal guys who don't give me an inferiority complex and don't keep me on my toes, guys who'd never cheat on me, and who are *not* professional baseball players."

"Is this Logan fellow a cheater?"

"No!"

"Then why does that speech sound so specific?"

"Because I... I..." A groan is all I can articulate for a second. "I already dated a baseball player and it sucked."

"You did *what*?" Mom sounds just the same as if she was trying to clarify whether I put the dark clothes in the laundry along with the white, and not as if I just admitted to having kept a hefty secret from her.

But this is what I wanted, to unload everything I had stuck in my chest, so I tell her that story too. I gloss over the part about how I gave myself to a guy who didn't deserve me because this is a Latina mother after all, but the gist is clear. I was duped by a guy who kept me a secret while he fooled around.

"Rosalina!" She also whisper-shouts this. "Why didn't you tell me this before?"

"I was too embarrassed, and then this thing with Logan happened and—ugh." I melt against the wall, sliding down until I'm sitting on the floor. "I deserve la chancla."

"No, that guy does! And the wooden one like the kind my mom used on me, none of this rubber crap they sell now and call flippy floppies."

I bite my lips and don't correct her. Flippy floppies is definitely the superior name.

"But what I don't understand is this," Mom says, "you yourself admit that this new guy, Logan, is a pretty good one. He sounds dreamy to me. So why are you comparing him to that Ben Williams asshole who now has a target on his face?" I have no doubt that should Mom ever spot Ben in the wild, she will land her footwear right in the middle of his mug.

"B-Because this is fake." I bring my knees up to hug them. "It's kinda like Ben not making our relationship public. This one is public but it's fake. Once again, the real thing escapes me."

"Then make it freaking real," she whispers with urgency. "Grab that man by the—"

"Mom," I gasp.

"—Face and plant a big, noisy kiss on that mouth of his."

"I can't do that, are you kidding me? That would be sexual harassment—it'd get me fired."

"Good point, get his consent first."

I give a dry chuckle. "Therein lies the problem. He barely tolerates me, forget being interested enough to let me kiss him."

"I know you're an adult," she repeats way more sardonically than earlier, "but your mother is right on this. You wait and see."

# CHAPTER 28
# LOGAN

feel shockingly good for someone who got very little sleep last night.

After getting up, I comb through my apartment collecting everything purple and packing it into a black overnight bag. The only things I leave behind are the books because I'm intrigued. I want to see how things go for the duke and the governess, and whether the rest are just as hooky.

There's a twenty-four-hour pharmacy in my neighborhood and I stop by to get a few things. Once that task is completed, I make the drive to the Orlando Wild facilities in record time, basically arriving at the same time as Jose and Harry, the groundskeepers. I dig into my bag to find two bottles of orange juice, which I know they both like. It's not my first time meeting them at the front doors.

The thing is that I didn't want anyone to see me sauntering into the admin area, beelining for Rose's cube the way I am. That's too… boyfriend-y. And I'm not in the mood to be teased.

Predictably, the marketing office is empty. I park myself on her chair and note that it doesn't squeak. I'm glad she has a sturdy one that won't leave her on the floor all of a sudden.

Unzipping the bag, I extract the two things I left at the top —a small chocolate box and a blank purple card. I pluck the latter and look around her desk for a pen. It takes little effort, since she has a mug stuffed with pens and pencils. I grab a random one and start writing.

I pause because it feels weird to write in purple ink.

She won't mind, though, not when literally this whole tiny space is decked in that color.

"At least she's easy to please," I muse to myself.

*Rose,*

*I'm sorry about the mess last night. Your things are in the black bag under your desk. Hope the chocolates make up for things a bit.*

*Logan.*

I stare at the note. I can't help but cringing at how cutesy my handwriting looks with this pen. And of course cheap chocolates from the drugstore don't compensate for shit. She should sue me for the emotional distress my parents put her through last night. Or at least send me an invoice for the dinner.

Hastily, I fold over the note and tuck it under the chocolate box. It's unwrapped, so she won't think I'm hitting on her or something. That would definitely send her running for the hills. Who in their right mind would want to go out with such a messed up guy?

I tuck the bag under her desk so it can't easily be seen by anyone passing by, and beat it all the way to the locker room. I'm going to do a light workout until people start arriving, and hopefully that'll reset my brain until I'm forced to be social.

*

A couple of hours later, I sit at the back of the room behind the rest of my teammates for a meeting with the manager and coaching staff. But where I expect Rob Beau to kick it off with the highlights and lowlights of the last series, as usual, he catches me off guard with a different topic.

"Gentlemen and lady," he says, tipping his hat toward Hope, who stands near the end of the staff line. "As you are well aware, trades are already happening all across the league."

I'm calm. Beau wouldn't break the news that I'm seeking one when I haven't told anyone myself.

Well, anyone other than our social media manager, who is surprisingly tight lipped for someone whose living is made off broadcasting stuff online.

"And if you take a look around, you'll notice that some of your teammates are missing."

There's definitely not thirty nine guys sitting in front of me. We're missing Stewart, left outfield, one rookie and one call-up from the minors. As the rest of the guys take stock of their surroundings, the realization starts to hit them.

"Ah, shit! He didn't even give me a heads up," one of Stewart's buddies says.

"Who's next? Starr?" another wonders. "Because if he goes, we're toast."

"No, we're real toast if Kim bounces," a third adds.

That makes a few of them turn back to make sure I'm still here. Thomason, one of the young pitchers, visibly sighs in relief.

The conversation snuffs out as Beau's voice rings again. "We have traded Stewart and Gonzalez, plus a draft pick, and sent Harrison back to the minors in order to make what is no doubt the best acquisition of the season."

My eyes widen slightly. That's high praise from the most level headed and strict manager I've ever worked with. Every guy in this room is constantly on a quest to get a crumb of

Beau's interest—forget scoring such compliments from him. That's basically a unicorn.

So who the hell did we acquire? Babe Ruth himself?

Beau nods toward the end of the line, and the last staff member reaches for the door to open it. We all—and that includes myself—crane our necks to get the first glimpse of this mythical acquisition.

Someone at the front drops back on his ass. Another drops an early *what in the actual* and someone else whistles.

Since I'm all the way at the back, I get on my feet and try to angle myself for better view, but everybody's doing the same damn thing and soon, I have even less visibility than before. All I know is that everyone is losing their collective shit and that freaks me out. I don't know that many players who can cause a reaction like this, but one of them is definitely my asshole brother.

Except that out of all the seasons he's had the chance to do this just to spite me, he never has. So why would he trade over here now? And especially when Cade Starr is proving himself to be the dark horse of the season, enough to rival Lewis.

It can't be him.

*Please*, I go as far as praying, *don't let it be him*.

One by one, the guys start taking back their seats until I'm the last one standing and—

What the shit.

The new guy makes eye contact with me, what with me sticking out like a sore thumb.

I raise my eyebrows, because this is legitimately the last person I expected to see coming to this organization. Slowly, I retake my seat as well.

"Everyone, let's welcome Miguel Machado, the newest member of the Orlando Wild family." Beau finishes that concise little speech with a clap of his hands, and is quickly joined by the staff.

The players are slower to catch on, and the one who kicks us off is Lucky Rivera pumping his fist in the air. "World Series, let's go baby!"

And that sends the room into absolute mayhem.

Hats and shirts go flying in the air, and the screaming is so deafening that I have to plug my ears with my fingers.

This completely derails the meeting and no one really pays attention as Socci and McDonald try to talk about the previous series. It's only when McDonald switches to some highlights from Machado in his previous team that people start settling down.

Leaning to the side, I pluck my phone from my back pocket and text Kaplan the news. It's the kind of big shit that he should know about because this potentially changes things. It'd be absurd to leave the team that has one of the best pitchers right now, and now also has the freaking MVP of the league— who is the top hitter all across the board.

My pulse spikes at the realization that maybe I don't have to leave. Maybe it doesn't make sense anymore. And if so, maybe that means that I can… I drop my phone on the table and shake my head.

Why am I thinking about Rose now? This has nothing to do with her.

When the meeting ends, I join the crowd in exiting the room, dragging my feet to allow myself more time to think. I can definitely ride out the rest of this season here and reevaluate my priorities afterward. Rivera wasn't entirely wrong in assuming that acquiring Machado makes us a strong contender now. I'd be a fool if I change teams now and then the Orlando Wild wins the whole damn show.

A hand falls on my shoulder, stopping me on my tracks. I lift my eyes from the floor to Beau's face.

What's with the twinkle in his eyes?

"Hopefully this makes you reconsider, hmm?" He pats my shoulder and leaves ahead of me.

I stand in the now empty room and narrow my eyes at his retreating back. Did he… Nah. There's no way he'd severely set the team's budget back to acquire Machado just to get me to stay.

Would he?

"Wait." My brow furrows. "This damn old man would."

My phone buzzes and absentmindedly, I take it out again. The words on the screen barely register and I have to reread them several times.

KAPLAN

Shit. This is a game changer

"No shit," I respond aloud.

Tucking my phone away, I finally get my legs in motion to head back out to the locker room.

As expected, a crowd has gathered around the latest circus attraction. Some of the guys at the back notice my approach and let me through, and I weave my way to the front to see if this is the good kind of crowd—the eager beavers—or if this is the bad kind—a mosh pit waiting to happen.

But I don't have to babysit anyone. In the middle are none other than the newest Wild player holding up a jersey with his last name in the back, standing in front of a locker that has newly been adorned with the same information, and our social media manager interviewing him with a professional camera.

My eyes zero in on Rose. From where I stand, the camera obstructs most of her face, but there's no mistaking the giggles escaping her lips. Like she's freaking delighted to be in the presence of Machado.

Something unprecedented happens then—the full force of it catching me by surprise. I grit my teeth so I don't say shit. Tighten my fists so I don't move a muscle. And I hope with all my damn might that none of these hawk-eyed assholes realize that I'm standing here, losing my mind because Rose is smiling at another guy.

And most of all, so that *she* doesn't notice that I want all of her smiles to myself even though I don't deserve them—don't deserve her.

# CHAPTER 29
# ROSE

"What are your thoughts about the newest addition to the Orlando Wild roster?" I ask Cade, angling the camera at his face. About half of the team is running drills across the green in the background.

"It's really exciting," he says with that Texas twang that makes the vowels sound rounder somehow. "The fact is that our team was already strong enough to pike the interest of the league's MVP. Now having him on board makes us a powerhouse."

My shoulders shrink, trying to contain the giddy energy that threatens to come out. Cade starts struggling with holding back a smile—I don't know if because he's also as pumped or if it's because I'm contagious—and I pause the recording to let out a squeal.

"Oh my gosh, Cade!" I make a series of little jumps. "This is huge! *Huge*, I'm telling you!"

He laughs and removes his hat to comb his brown hair back. "It really is, I still can't quite believe it myself."

"Are you all done?" Lucky asks from behind me. "It's my turn to be charming in front of the camera."

"Admit it, you have no interest in talking about Machado. You just want to grow your own social media followers," Cade tosses back.

"*Obviously*." Lucky snorts. "I'm two thousand away from a million on Instagram. I just need a little push."

"Just one million?" While he steps aside, Cade blows a raspberry in open mockery. "Talk to me when you have a million and a half, son."

"Son?" Lucky's outrage makes me laugh. "May I remind you that you're three years younger than me, you literal child?"

"You guys are ridiculous. Normal people like me barely have two thousand followers," I explain amid chuckles.

"That is only because you set your profile to private after you started dating Logan." Lucky points at me with narrowed eyes. "If you make it public you'll easily reach half a mill in a matter of days."

And that's precisely why I don't, because I'm not really Logan's girlfriend.

If that comes to light, or when we have our official breakup, I'm going to get tons of hate from his overeager fans. It'll make handling the team socials a pain in the bootie, and I'd rather not have to deal with all that on my own profiles.

Then again, with any luck I'll already be set to replace our retiring team broadcaster by that point.

I clear my throat. "How do you know I set it to private?"

"Because I tried to follow you and you completely ignored me."

His bestie pokes the wound even more by asking, "Why weren't you following her before, then?"

"What do you want me to do? Build a time machine and go back in time to follow my teammate's girlfriend on social media?"

"So, Lucky," I call his attention away from the silly argument. "Give me your take for our followers. If you make it really juicy, it might earn you those two-kay followers you want. Let's go."

"Listen, princesa…" I can tell by the mischievous glint in his eye that he's going to do a Lucky-thing next. Sure enough, he untucks his T-shirt and begins lifting it. "What's really juicy here is—"

"Are you going to keep fooling around or practice?"

We all freeze at the sinister voice approaching from behind me.

The first one to recover is Lucky, and that glint hasn't vanished from his eyes as he turns them to me. "Oh, no. Looks like the big bad boyfriend is jealous."

My lips curve into a wane smile. So many falsehoods in that sentence, the main one being that Logan is bad.

When he catches up, I say, "They're not fooling around. I'm capturing interviews about the big news."

But if he hears me, Logan pretends not to. He grabs the back of Lucky's T-shirt with one hand, and does the same to Cade with the other one. "Let's go, clowns."

"But—" Lucky waves his hands toward me. "My two thousand followers!"

Logan always wears a tight, purple undershirt under his team jersey, but even through the fabric I can see how tight his arm muscles are as he hauls the two clowns—er, the other players away. I shake my head. He's such a dad.

But in a different way from Miguel Machado. He's a daddy.

As in, he has a daughter. I think it's so cute how one of the considerations for Miguel to come over to the Orlando Wild was so that his daughter can be surrounded by more Spanish speakers. I'm so going to use that angle for a series about our players and their families, and what playing for the Orlando

Wild means to their loved ones. In the meantime, I need more testimonials about the team's enthusiasm for this trade.

Practice right now doesn't include live balls, so I don't need to be super mindful about my position on the field. I skip over to the water coolers where three other players are camping out between their sets. As I approach, though, I start making sense of a conversation that I absolutely can't share on social media.

"—Kidding me, right?" One of them grunts. "Like I know that he's supposed to be one of us now and all that jazz, but I can't brainwash myself that quickly."

"Totally, man. We were literally up against him for the season opener. It's just weird."

"And besides that, look at him." All three do. Even I turn. I don't see anything special other than Miguel Machado wearing an Orlando Wild uniform and running drills along with Mike Brown, our third base. "What a stinking show off."

Grunts and affirmations follow.

I pretend like I'm fiddling with my camera, waiting for them to rejoin the drills. My lower lip presses upward.

Call me naive, but it hadn't occurred to me that anyone on the team would feel this way. Most of them have shown genuine excitement over what this could mean for the season, and a hundred percent have manifested clear shock that this is even happening.

But of course there will be guys who are jealous. The skills gap will become that much more obvious for some of them, even though it's not like Logan and company were chump change before.

"Hmm…" I tap my chin. What can be done so that those three accept Miguel?

A figure breaks out from the drills, getting my attention.

Crap. I'm developing a Logan radar now.

He walks over to the coolers while removing his hat and wiping the sweat off his forehead with the back of his arm.

Right as he places his cap back on his head, I set out to review the footage on my camera once more. There's no denying how my heart picks up speed the closer he gets, or how I can now detect the subtle piney scent that clings to his skin even from afar.

From the corner of my eye, I observe as how he grabs a bottle. It must be empty because he uncaps it and starts to fill it back up. In silence. And without acknowledging my presence.

Come to think, he's been acting like this all day. Pretty big contrast for a guy who left a card and chocolates at my desk when I wasn't looking.

I click back to the video I caught earlier in the locker room with Miguel, where he told me about his daughter and how happy he is to become a Wild player. I'm sure the news are already blowing up the baseball internet, and I cannot wait to contribute to it with this video.

"Do you like him or what?"

My head whips up. "What?"

Logan turns around and leans back against the table. His eyes are out on the field, but the hand holding the drink points at me. "Machado. Are you his fan or his fangirl?"

"Is there a difference?" I'm so confused right now.

"Yeah. A huge one."

"I definitely don't identify as a fanboy. Do you?" I tease back, grinning.

For the first time all day, Logan turns his serious, deep set eyes on me.

My breath hitches and I'm really glad for all the noise in the field. Hopefully he didn't notice how just a glance from him made me, well, fangirl on the inside.

"Absolutely the hell not." His vehement answer makes me grin.

"Well, neither do I." I tip my head toward the new player at a distance. "But as a baseball fan, I think that this is the absolute best move our management has ever done. I can't help feeling on top of the world right now."

Logan tips his head back, opening his mouth to squirt water into it. I try not to stare at the trickle that runs down his chin to his neck, over his Adam's apple. And I fail miserably.

"Hey, Logan…" I catch myself right in time before asking him how dare he be so freaking hot all the time. After shaking my head and readjusting my brain, I tackle a different topic. "I heard some of the guys talking smack about Miguel—"

"Miguel?" He looks at me.

"Yeah, you know? Machado." I wave a hand. "Turns out that not everyone is as thrilled to have him on board as I am."

"You don't say," he mumbles.

"Wait." I frown. "Don't tell me you're also one of the jealous haters?"

The long pause that ensues is unnatural. His voice comes out way too measured when he says, "No, I am not."

I groan and roll my eyes. "Logan! You're the unofficial captain of the team. You're supposed to set a good example for the rest."

"I said I'm not."

"And I'm a legitimate princess of a far flung kingdom." I open my eyes wide.

Logan shrugs one powerful shoulder. "What do I have to be jealous about?"

"Exactly. *Nothing*." I slice the air with my hand. "It's true that you don't average as many homeruns as Miguel"—Here his eyes narrow—"But you're the most valuable catcher. Your strategic approach to the game is the envy of every other team. And that big brain of yours has to know that this is a—wait a damn moment."

"What?" He turns to stone, other than his brow that furrows a little.

I check our surroundings and lean closer to whisper,

covering my mouth from onlookers. "Are you annoyed because you're trading away and now the Wild might be stronger than your new team?"

"No." Logan turns to drink some more water. With the bottle obscuring his mouth, he mumbles, "I may not move at all now."

This time I don't bother to hide the way I gasp.

Logan turns back to me, his eyes roaming all over my face. "Does that make you fangirl?"

"Are you kidding me?" I grab his arm—but that feels like too much contact for two virtual strangers, so I drop it. I wish I could wrap my arms around him instead, though, and all I can do is cover my grin with my hands. "That is the best freaking news ever! Is it confirmed? Are you sure? Or are you just thinking about it? Do you—"

"Stop," he commands, suddenly digging his index finger under my chin and forcing my mouth to close. I do, but only because that brief touch shuts my brain down. "Breathe. I'm not sure, I'm just thinking about it in light of these news."

*Oh, please. Stay*, I beg with my eyes. *Stay so this farce between us can continue, so I can feel what having a good boyfriend is like for a little longer.*

I don't say any of that. Instead, what comes out of my mouth at last is "then we'll be invincible."

"Maybe." Pulling away, Logan twists to return the plastic bottle to the table and picks himself up to leave.

"Wait." I bite my lips. What I don't want is for him to leave quite yet, and I scramble to figure out a way. Then I remember my earlier point. "About the guys talking smack, shouldn't something be done?"

"Like what?" he asks, looking at me over his shoulder.

"I don't know, like…" My brain is scrambled right now and I just spitball. "Maybe you should do some kind of welcome thing for Miguel? I'm sure the guys will fall in line once they see that you approve of him." As he keeps staring at my face in silence, I ask, "Do I have something on my face?"

The corner of his lips twitches. "No, I was just thinking that you're starting to sound like a WAG."

I open my mouth. Close it again. End up asking, "So you'll do it, then?"

"If you help me organize it." With that, he takes off in a light jog, his low pony tail swinging behind him.

My eyes drift lower to his actual tail, the two perfect mounds of muscle working with every step.

"Damn it," I grouch as I ogle him. "Stop getting ideas about this man, Rosalina. Just because he has a perfect butt and might be staying, it doesn't mean you can do anything about it."

But so help me, I'll act like a WAG until the very last moment. I retreat back to my cubicle to eat my chocolates and think about how to welcome Miguel Machado into the team.

# CHAPTER 30
# LOGAN

Never have I regretted being a biker more than this moment, when I have a woman I'm attracted to as my backpack.

Somehow I behave well until the moment I stop at a light near our destination, and I catch the driver beside me watching Rose like he's Roger Rabbit and she's Jessica Rabbit. It's like I'm damn chopped liver.

My hands move of their own accords and fall on her knees. The part I'm fully conscious of is that I slide them down to the back of her knees and tug her even closer, her entire front molding perfectly to my back until we're basically glued.

And all throughout, I stare at the asshole.

He finally realizes that Rose isn't backpack all by herself and all but jumps in his seat when he catches sight of me. Dude is probably a college kid and is smart enough to realize that I give off I-will-screw-you-up aura with my black helmet, my black T-shirt that shows off my tats, my black cargo pants, and boots. Not to mention the black gloves that would hide my fingerprints from around his neck.

He gets saved because the light turns green and I take off.

See, these two issues wouldn't occur if I was man enough to drive us in a car with a roof over us.

First, that no one would see how mouthwateringly hot Rosalina Mena is in her high waisted jean shorts. Second, that I wouldn't be feeling every one of her curves pressed up against me. My sanity's slipping away the more we drive.

To my relief, we finally reach the neighborhood where the party is. Once again, Mike Brown and his narc wife ended up offering their sprawling home. It simply has the biggest pool and backyard out of everyone on the team, and now that the weather is almost like summer, the best way to welcome Miguel Machado into the team is by having a BBQ and pool party.

Credit to Rose for the idea. I'm absolutely dreading this whole thing.

Pool party means swimsuits. Which in turn means Rose in a swimsuit. I'm going to really have to exercise my acting skills if I don't want her to see how much that sight is going to mess me up. The backpacking is definitely not helping.

I pull into the residential street and even though I slow down, for some reason she tightens her arms around my stomach. Maybe she's nervous about also having to put up a front before so many people, because unlike the previous party, this one includes all the families. It's gonna be a nightmare.

"You okay?" I ask over my shoulder as the manicured lawns of other rich people pass us by.

"What? Yeah. Totally fine." Her helmet bumps into mine as she nods.

I almost tell her that if she hugs me any harder she's gonna stay imprinted on my body, but I keep quiet. Probably not a good idea to bring up the subject of, well, our bodies.

I no longer know if I'm really relieved when I find us a spot a few houses away from Browns. The whole street is packed with cars of all makes and price tags, so we'll have to do a bit of walking. And that's great, because I have to do something first.

After setting the kick stand in place, I lift my left leg and twist over to get off from the right. Rose quickly catches herself by grabbing my seat with her hands, and before she can panic even more, I grab her by the waist to stabilize her.

"Ready?" I ask.

Her hands shift to my shoulders and she holds tight, enough that I feel it in every fiber of my being. She repeats the same motion with her left leg until she sits facing me. "Ready," she confirms with more determination than necessary.

Good thing she can't see how that makes me smile through my helmet. I lift her from the bike, lowering her carefully until her feet touch the ground. This is what she asked me to do when we started the ride, because even while sober she doesn't feel comfortable with hopping off the bike all on her own, and I definitely don't want her to get hurt.

Plus, I get to put my hands on her with permission. Win-win.

But now I let them slide off and step away. The hot breeze makes me more aware of the sweat trickling down my back. Her light purple T-shirt is glued to her chest and stomach, wrinkled too. And that reminds me.

"Give me the backpack," I say, extending a gloved hand to her.

She stops fiddling with the strap of her helmet. "You do know how to use the word please, right?"

I do. It has come to mind a few times during this bike ride, but not precisely for family-friendly reasons.

"Please," I add, my voice growing raspy.

Finally I get the backpack, and I set it over the bike seat. It's a small-ish camping backpack that fits a surprising amount of stuff, but it's pretty stuffed between her things and mine. I have to dig all the way to the bottom to find the rolled up garment I need.

Right when I turn to her is when Rose finally figures out the helmet strap under her chin. She gives out a little "ah hah!" before removing it. The curls piled at the top of her head spring to freedom and I have to press my lips tight not to laugh. It's the cutest damn thing I've seen in my life.

Clearing my throat, I offer her the prize. "Here."

She watches the thing while tucking the helmet between her arm and her side. "What's that?"

"It's my team shirt." I unfurl it and spread it open, the back facing her. "This is what WAGs wear at these things."

Her eyes roam over the lettering at the back like it's her first time seeing KIM 2. "Marking territory, of course."

Damn freaking straight.

I don't say anything though. Even as far gone as I am, I know that I have no legitimate claim over her.

"Hold this." She gives me her helmet and before I can even process what's happening, she's tugging her purple T-shirt off her shorts.

"Whoa, what are you doing?"

"Changing." Her voice is muffled as the T-shirt goes over her face and off her head.

And I stop breathing. My jaw opens—fortunately, the helmet strap is there to catch it. Pretty sure the one whose face now looks like a cartoon with heart eyes and a wagging tongue is mine.

*This is a pool party*, a helpful voice reminds me in my head. Of course she was wearing her swimsuit under her clothes.

The top is strapless, twisting in the middle at the front in a way that accentuates her attributes. Her um, generous attributes. I work my tongue trying to swallow, but I can't. Something's wedged in my throat.

Meanwhile, she's completely oblivious to the crisis I'm in.

Her soft bright skin gleams under the sun as she works her arms into the sleeves of my team jersey. She leaves it open, grabbing the ends at the front to tie them at her waist.

Of all the conspiracy theories I never believed, the one that I now know is true is human combustion. I can feel my body temperature go from normal to damn volcanic in a matter of seconds. And now I'm sweating all over.

With jerky movements, I turn my back on her to zip up the backpack and load it on my back, trying to take as long as possible to compose myself.

*I'm a grown-ass man*, I tell myself. *I can control myself. I am not my hormones.*

"Aren't you hot?" she asks all of a sudden.

If it wasn't for my elite athleticism, I'd have stumbled on my own two feet. "What do you mean?" I ask all choked up.

She points at her face while we walk up the street. "Or does your helmet have air conditioning?"

"Oh." I unclasp my helmet in a second and pull the thing off. Rivers of sweat threaten my eyes and I wipe them with the back of my arm.

"There, that's better, isn't it?" She chuckles.

No, it isn't because now I can't face her. I'm too wired to trust that I'll be able to mask how much I want her.

As the Browns's house appears, we automatically reach to grab hands and I realize that I'm still wearing my gloves. After doing away with them and tucking them in my pocket, I clasp Rose's hand in mine again and we make our way to the back-yard, where all the noise is coming from.

I hang back as she greets every living creature that appears in front of us, from babies, to a dog, to more WAGs, and some of the players. I offer nods to everyone, which is as far as I can manage when my eyes keep going to my last name emblazoned on Rose's back. That's some heady shit.

We reach the dreaded scenario at last: the pool. Maybe not

so dreaded because surely dipping in the water will cool down my torch.

I'm still staring at the water as Rose and Hope find each other. "Oh my word, finally someone normal," Hope says in greeting.

"Hey, what about me?" Starr protests.

His girlfriend retorts with, "You're the strangest of them all, Cowboy."

"I'm sure Logan has him beat." Rose laughs.

I slide a side eye at her. She's not wrong, but she also doesn't need to laugh so hard.

"Anyway, is there anywhere we can put our things so we can change? We're so sweaty and gross," Rose says.

She's not gross though. That sheen of sweat on her skin is doing me in.

"Right here. Scoot over, Cade." The guy grunts but sits up so that his girlfriend can sit between his legs, freeing the other pool chair for us.

"Perfect." Rose turns to me, still grabbing my hand. "Logan, unload."

I mumble, "Yes, ma'am." Releasing her, I take the backpack off and dump it on the damp chair.

With a tug, the knot at the front of the jersey comes off and she removes it, tossing it over the backpack. I watch as she unbuttons her shorts. Of course, that's what was going to happen next. Of course. And somehow I'm transfixed as she reveals a matching bikini bottom, which as far as it goes, isn't even the most revealing kind.

And yet I'm still roaring on the inside.

I manage a heavy swallow.

"Cat got his tongue," Hope whispers none too softly, considering that there are squealing kids on the shallow end of the pool, pop music blares from speakers somewhere, and dozens of voices surround us.

"No," Starr says with laughter in his voice. "I think he just swallowed it."

Their observations—wholly accurate as they are—remind me that I need to freaking behave. I grit my jaw and bend down to undo the straps of my boots. I need that dip in the pool right yesterday. It's getting urgent.

"Need help with sunblock?" Hope asks.

"No," says Rose. "We were riding the bike so I put it on at home."

Damn it. I'd have liked to lather her up—

*No, stop this shit, you jerk.*

I chuck my boots under the pool chair, my socks balled up inside of them. Then I make quick work of peeling off my shirt and removing my cargo pants. I'm also wearing my swimming trunks already, and I barely stop to say, "Going for a swim. Later."

I don't even care where my clothes fall, or that the poolside concrete is hot enough to burn. I speed walk toward the shower for a quick rinse. The water feels absolutely freezing against my skin, which is good. I need that. In fact, an ice bath would be way better.

"Wait for me!"

I rake my hair away from my face and sure enough, that's Rose jogging over to me.

"Stop!" I raise my palm up. She all but screeches to a halt. "Walk slowly."

"What, why?" Lowering her head, she looks all around her. "Is it slippery?"

"No." I clear my throat and jerk my chin at her. "Your, uh —your chest."

We stare at each other, her blinking really hard. She wraps her arms around herself slowly. "I guess this may not have been the best choice of swimsuit."

I grunt. It's a heart attack waiting to happen, that's what it is.

I step away from the shower and motion at her to take it. And because I have zero trust in that top, I stand guard in case any perv is waiting to see if the shower will induce a wardrobe malfunction. No one's paying attention to us, though.

Unfortunately, now Rose is wet when she stands next to me again. I'm sure I'll never be able to function in front of her again.

"Shall we?" she asks, pointing at the deep end that is clearer of people. "Let's see who can make the biggest splash!" Her sentence ends in a squeal as she launches herself into the water.

Thirteen out of ten splash. When she emerges wiping water off her face, I note that her top is still in place. If that didn't send it flying, nothing will. My lungs start working again.

I pump my legs a few times and land the biggest cannonball in history. This pool is way deeper than I expected and it takes a moment to pull myself up. Rose's body underwater brands itself into my mind before I break the surface. Ironically, my hair tie was defeated by the cannonball and now my hair is everywhere.

"That was amazing," she's giggling. "I think you splashed even the roof of the house."

"We had a massive pool when I was a kid. It was the only place where no one in the house bothered me," I volunteer, shocking myself.

"Really?" Her head tilts, the tips of her wet hair sending droplets down her face. "Wasn't that dangerous for a kid?"

Oh, yeah. But it was the least dangerous thing in that house.

The fact that I'm even able to string a sentence now means that the water is helping. Except that the ripples seem to push her closer, and if we collide I don't know what I'll do.

But then a little voice talks. "Can you teach me how to do that?"

Both Rose and I turn to find a girl standing by the edge of the pool. I give her around ten years old, and a fifteen out of ten for the floatie around her that has a giant flamingo head.

"Teach you what, sweetie?" Rose asks in a very different voice from what she uses for me. This one is all kind and calm.

"Not you, him." The kid points at me. "I want to make a big splash like that."

"Do you know how to swim?" I comb my wet hair back from my face.

She raises her chin defiantly. "Yes, I do."

"And would your parents give the same answer?" I ask, and this time she falters.

Rose wades over to the edge, keeping her eyes on me. She mouths *smart* at me before addressing the kid. "Who are your parents, sweetie? We should talk with them before Logan can give you the tutorial."

My eyebrow twitches. Rose is trying to haul herself out of the water, too far from the ladder but too proud to admit how her arms tremble.

Tucking my tongue against my cheek, I reach for her waist again. Despite the water, it's still a shock to touch her bare skin. It's even more of a shock when I lift her and gain a front row view of her perfect butt.

"Marty! Marty." A new voice joins, and I watch as Miguel Machado breaks through a group of people to come over. His eyes are set on the kid. "I told you not to get out of my sight."

The girl stomps her bare foot and her expression turns into grumpiness personified. "But I want to swim. I don't want to talk with boring adults."

Rose now sits by the pool next to the girl, but her attention turns to me as I pull myself out of the water. I kneel to stabilize myself before sitting down half facing the pool, half facing everyone else.

And Rose's eyes are still on me, everywhere at once. Blatantly.

Okay, so… I affect her some. Good to know.

Or not. Maybe it's worse to know.

It takes herculean effort to shift my attention from her to my new teammate.

"We're going to swim after the conversation ends." Machado kneels in front of the girl, the massive gold chain and crucifix around his neck swinging with the motion. He grabs the kid's shoulders and looks into her eyes all serious. "Did I also not say to keep out of the deep end?"

"You did." The girl scrunches her face.

"She wants to learn how to cannonball like Logan," Rose supplies, grinning as the kid turns her glare on her.

I tense as Machado glances at Rose. But then something interesting happens. His eyes stay on her face, and there are no funny sparks even as he grins in return, like maybe he's nowhere as interested in her as I am.

On the one hand that makes him a fool. On the other hand it means he can stick around.

"Thanks for ratting her out."

"I hate you," the girl hisses at Rose.

I snort, and this pulls their attention to me.

"Hey, Kim," Machado says before pointing his lips at the girl. "This is my daughter, Martina. She prefers to be called Marty."

"Machado." I tip my head at him and then at his daughter. "Machado."

The girl narrows her eyes. "Isn't Kim a girl's name?"

Rose chokes.

Machado's light brown eyes grow dangerously wide. "Marty, that's ru—"

I interrupt him and say to the kid, "My name is Logan Kim, and that's a common Korean last name."

"Oh." Her expression changes, not because she's realizing her mistake but because something has clicked with her. "I ate at a Korean restaurant once. It was yummy."

I can clearly see Rose trying to suppress a laugh behind Machado's kid.

Meanwhile, her dad cringes. "I'm sorry, Kim. Marty never means ill, she's just very direct. Like, *very*."

Rose loses the battle to her giggles, but somehow manages to speak at the same time. "Just so you know, so is Logan."

My lips twitch.

"Good to know." The man slides a slight look of concern at me, before focusing on his child again. "Let's go, Marty. I'm sure Miss Rosalina and Mr. Logan have other things to do."

The girl accepts her dad's hand, yet doesn't wipe the grumpy expression from her small face. "When you say let's go it means to go swim and not to keep talking, right?"

"Yes, yes." Machado sighs and pulls to his full height. He's a pretty tall dude and has to bend slightly so not to stretch his daughter's arm too wide. I don't know why but that's the thing that makes me stop being wary about him. He seems like a pretty decent person.

"You're good with kids."

I turn to Rose. "I wasn't exceptionally nice."

"No, but you knew exactly how to deal with her." A corner of her lips stretches into a lopsided smirk. "How about you teach *me* that cannonball?"

I contemplate it all of one second. The busier we are, the less time I'll spend in the dangerous quarters of my head. So I nod and pull myself up to my feet, offering my hand to her. "Let's go, I'll teach you how to make a big splash." And that makes Rose laugh.

# CHAPTER 31
## ROSE

"Whew, close your mouth, girl."

I snap it shut and tear my eyes away from Logan. "Erm, is it obvious that I'm drooling over the man?"

"So obvious." Hope grins before taking a massive bite out of her burger.

"Oh, no," I whisper.

"What's wrong with that?" she asks with her mouth full. "He's your boyfriend."

I'm jealous of her sensible swimsuit, a navy two piece with thick straps over her shoulders that don't have her constantly checking herself. I try as discreetly as possible to pull my top up by pinched fingers.

I'm also viscerally jealous of how Hope can say that, because she can stare at her hunky boyfriend to her heart's content without fearing consequences.

If Logan catches me eating him up, he'll know that I have a thing for him. Or more than a thing.

Yes, I'm really attracted to him physically. Who wouldn't be? The guy is a masterpiece of chiseled muscles, a ridiculously perfect bubble butt, legs that never skip the gym, luscious hair that reaches his shoulders, and a five o'clock shadow that deserves awards. And then there's all the tattoos, most of which I had seen one way or another before, except that now I discovered one that peeks from under his swimming trunks at his thighs.

And the swimming trunks. The criminal piece of fabric that clings to his body under the weight of the water.

I had to latch myself onto Hope after we decided to get out of the pool because looking at him got too painful. Has anyone told him that his lips alone are enough to make a girl fantasize? And that's before peeping at anything under his neck.

"It's just…" I worry my bottom lip. "I'm trying not to freak him out."

"How?" she asks, swallowing.

I look at the burger on a paper plate balanced on my lap. "Well, you know him. He's kind of aloof and, like, after the whole thing with Ben I don't really want to be the one who wants the guy more, does that make sense?"

"Hmm." Hope reaches for the iced tea bottle at her feet and takes a healthy swig before talking. The sun is setting behind her, and the automatic lights around the pool start to turn on. "Well, Logan's not that aloof. He's pretty friendly, actually."

I look at her like she grew another head. Fortunately, she's more focused on her food than on how that lands.

I guess I'm also jealous of the relationship Hope and Logan have. It's true that he's a lot more relaxed around her than anyone else, including the rest of the team or myself. He basically treats me the same way he does Cade or Lucky—which is to say, not that friendly.

Hope has no way of knowing how my heart is squeezing when she continues talking. "And as for the other topic, I don't think you have anything to worry about."

"What?" I completely forgot what the other topic even was.

"Trust me, Rose. He's so into you, it's funny."

"Huh?" I lean forward abruptly, eyes bulging.

"You didn't see how he was looking at you earlier?" No reaction comes from me, so she adds, "When you were taking off your shorts. He kept doing this." She sets her plate down to open and close her fists hard enough that her muscles bulge. "Cade said he was surprised the dude didn't crack a tooth with how hard he was clenching his jaw."

"Clenching his… what?" I shake my head, still confused.

"You were this close"—She pinches her index and thumb close enough to touch—"To him picking you up and taking you somewhere to do unspeakable things during a family function."

As if on cue, a gaggle of toddlers runs by us, the leader holding a hot dog up high like it's a trophy.

I turn back to Hope. "You must've been hallucinating. There's no way that Logan—" I catch myself because he's supposed to be my boyfriend. Of course he's supposed to want me. So I correct myself. "That he would be that obvious in public."

"So is that the issue?" Hope checks our surroundings and lowers her voice. "Is he not affectionate enough, like whatshisface?"

Logan and Ben don't even belong in the same sentence together.

And that's the issue. Without having any feelings for me or ever having been intimate, Logan has already shown me much more affection than Ben ever did.

Logan probably thinks I don't notice the little things he does, like earlier when we were driving over and some guy in traffic was looking at me in a lewd way. It wasn't like Logan could do much in that circumstance, but reminding the stranger that I wasn't alone was enough to get him to look away.

I wonder if he could feel my heart hammering against his back, or if he had any idea that I wanted him to keep his hands around my thighs—pull me even closer if possible.

I wonder if he knows I almost cried when he gave me his shirt. That in this sham we're in, I've felt more like a WAG than I did in any intimate moment with Ben Williams.

"He is affectionate," I say with a sigh. "Just not so much in —in public," I lie, when actually Logan is the perfect boyfriend in public and a stranger in private.

"Give him some time. He's surprisingly shy—just don't tell him I said so."

"I won't." I smile weakly.

How right she is, dang her. Logan is a force of nature to most people, certainly a thorn on the side to Cade, but that's because they haven't caught a glimpse of all the hurt and loneliness hidden inside of him.

I did, back at the birthday dinner with his awful parents. I wish he'd let me in—for real. I wish this giant crush I'm harboring had a purpose other than to torture me.

Drawn by him, my eyes find him among the guys once more and I jolt, because Logan's looking straight at me.

He motions with his head in the universal *shall we?* way, and I nod. I am so ready to get back home, shower, condition my hair, and crawl in bed with a romance book I can live vicariously through.

"I think we're going to head out now," I tell Hope, watching as Logan extricates himself from Lucky's and Cade's hold, breaking from the group.

"This early?" she asks while chewing the last of her burger.

"Yeah, I'm sure Logan needs his beauty sleep before the trip tomorrow." I smile in a sad way, legitimately bothered that

I don't get to tag along with the team to the next away series, and that I won't see him for three days.

At least not in person. I'll sure look at the screen version instead.

"Fine, I guess I'll go nag the cowboy. See you at home later?"

"Yup." I also didn't have much left of my burger and polish off the rest as Hope and Logan meet halfway. She says something quick to him that makes him nod. Unlike a professional baseball player, I'm really bad at reading lips and I can't tell what he responds back with, and then they continue their separate ways.

My pulse climbs quick and nimble like a spider as he approaches. After hours of careful observation, I can confirm that his swimming trunks have dried up by the fact that they're no longer clinging to him.

"Ready?" he asks as he reaches the pool chairs that Hope and I commandeered for the better part of the day.

My response is a hum, since I'm still munching away. Logan reaches for the backpack and sets it on the free chair, opening it to pull out our clothes. I wipe my hands with a napkin before accepting my shorts and top—the baseball one, not my lavender one from Old Navy. He pulls out his black cargo pants and I watch, riveted, as his pecs jump with the motions of putting on his pants.

I drown down a groan with a sip of Dr. Pepper.

Now he's putting on that tight muscle T-shirt he wore on the way over. A sliver over his pants catches my attention and I nearly choke on my drink. That's a tanline right across the ridge of the V that goes down his pants. He deserves jail for showing me that.

As his T-shirt clears his head, I scramble to toss my towel away from my shoulders and start to get dressed as quick as possible. I wish I was brave enough to peek at him, see if he's watching me the way Hope described—but I don't dare. I need to get on his bike ASAP where he will look away from me for half an hour and I can stew in my own misery.

After putting on our shoes and grabbing our helmets, I grab his free hand with mine and tug him for a quick round of farewells. The whole disaster of the dinner with Logan's parents taught me to take heed of his advice about people, and even though I politely bid my thanks for the day to Amber Brown, I don't stick around long enough to enter any sort of yikes territory with her.

I'm much warmer saying good night to Miguel and his daughter, who is the spitting image of him, but tiny female version and way grumpier. Lucky, Cade and Hope get hugs from me and nods from my boyfriend.

Er, my pretend boyfriend.

That mental slip speeds me up and I all but drag Logan out of the property. When I'm sure we're out of sight, I drop his hand like it burns.

He sighs. Probably relieved to finally be free.

Logan puts on his helmet and as he fastens the chin strap, I observe his bulging bicep. Most of it is taken by a big red rose that must've been a pain to get tattooed on. "Logan?" I ask.

"Hmm?"

"I'm curious about something." He turns to me, which is kind of eerie when he's wearing his helmet, visor down. "Did it hurt to get so many tattoos?"

"Yes," he responds candidly.

My eyebrows rise. "Then why did you do it?"

"Because…" He trails off and I think he'll leave me hanging until he finally finishes the sentence. "I needed to pretend I'm different from them."

My brow furrows because at first I don't get it.

Pretend? From who?

But then he pulls ahead, opening one of the pockets of his

pants to extract the key as he reaches the bike. He slots it in and digs into the same pocket to produce his gloves, and I watch him put them on, his forearm muscles shifting as he works his hands in.

And that's when I realize that he needed to busy himself because he said too much.

Which means this is about his family. That's the one topic I unfortunately lucked into learning about that others don't know.

"You don't need to pretend," I say in a quiet voice that still snaps his attention to me, making my chest squeeze so hard that I almost gasp for air. Instead, I add, "You're very different from them."

I put my helmet on and feel around for the strap. One of them got sucked in and I hook my finger around it to pull it back out.

Logan takes a few steps toward me and I freeze as he reaches for my hands—no, not my hands. He actually pulls them away. Instead, his gloved fingers, which are so large they should be clumsy, easily find the straps and clasp them under my chin.

He taps the top of my helmet and says, "No, I'm not. I'm just as bad." Before I can protest, he makes a project of removing his backpack and hooking the straps over my shoulders.

Sliding my arms into the straps, I say, "No, you're not. An evil person wouldn't care if my helmet is tied properly."

"That's not why I was doing it. You were probably going to take two business days to tie it."

I harrumph because, yes, that's true. But also because I know it's a deflection. "How about earlier when you fended that creepy guy in traffic off me?"

Logan stops in the middle of raising his leg to ride his bike, and almost loses his balance. At the last second, he just drops his leg onto the seat. "You saw that?"

"Yes, I did." I fold my arms. "That was very nice of you."

"Nice?" He snorts with a little *ha!* "I didn't do it out of being nice."

"Then why?"

"What if I had ulterior motives?" he asks while completing the motion of sliding over his bike. Damn it, he even looks gorgeous from the back with that impossibly wide back and tiny waist.

I shake my head hard and approach to climb on. Hands on his delicious shoulders, foot on the peg, and hoisting myself up until I find the opposite peg. I lower myself down behind him and he does the thing again, the one that sends my pulse from normal to Speedy Gonzalez: he grabs the backs of my knees and slides me forward until I fall on him. I wasn't prepared for it and my hands land on his thighs, right against his hips.

"What ulterior motives?" I squeak out, lifting my hands quickly to hug his waist.

His chest expands with a big intake of air that he releases slowly. He turns the key and the engine roars to life beneath us. Twisting, he turns over his shoulder to look at me. Or at my helmet, I guess.

"Rose." My name comes out like a growl that can rival the engine. "When you're on my bike, you're *my* backpack. And I don't let anyone covet what's mine."

I suck in air.

Then the jerk kicks the stand back and accelerates hard enough that my body pulls back, forcing me to grab tight onto him.

Okay, I'm sure he can definitely feel my heart about to burst from my chest and tear into his. That's definitely what the traitor muscle wants to do, but I can't let it.

Logan said *when I'm on his bike*, as if I was an extension of his property.

That's not it either. I want to be loved hard and openly. I don't want to be a guy's possession. That feels too close to what I was to Ben—just a conquest, not a real person with her own feelings and needs.

Neither of us speak at any of the stoplights or stop signs, and the half an hour drive feels like it's been an entire hour by the time he pulls into my residence. I key in the code to open the gate and since we're going a lot slower now, I only grab onto his waist until he stops in front of the townhouse I share with Audrey and Hope. The lights are on inside, which means it's early enough and Audrey's still awake.

We do the whole operation of getting off the bike smoothly, like we've done this a million times. But unlike earlier, Logan doesn't release my waist right away.

I reach for my visor and lift it. "What?"

He tilts his head slightly and his hands tighten, making me jolt a bit.

I lift his visor too, hoping that looking into his eyes will help me understand what's happening. It doesn't work that way, though. I know it's dark and the light from the streetlamp is weak, but why do his eyes look like that? All dark and intense— unprovoked.

"What, Logan?" I ask again, my voice less certain.

"A really nice guy wouldn't be thinking the things that are going through my head right now."

My eyes widen. My heart kicks hard. "What things?"

His hands splay wider, covering more territory of my waist and the top of my hips. "How I would make you mine if you let me."

I gasp—and choke.

"Unthinkable, huh?" He shakes his head and slowly eases off my waist, his hands sliding across my stomach until he lets go. "That's not part of the deal and I know that. But I can't help thinking… and wanting…" He takes a step back, eyes lowering down my frame. "To kiss you. And more."

I hope it's dark enough that he can't see the goosebumps breaking all over my skin. I wrap my arms around myself. Out of breath without any reason, I ask, "Is that it?"

His eyes snap back to mine.

"You just want me physically?" I clarify.

After a beat, he says, "Yeah."

"Right." The word comes out very firm for someone whose chin is trembling and is about to burst into tears at any second. "That is definitely not part of the deal. No kissing. Certainly nothing more than that. I'm never going to be someone else's little play thing ever again."

"And that makes me the worst piece of shit, doesn't it?" he says slowly, quietly. "Because I know that. I saw how much that asswipe Williams hurt you, and here I am, lusting over you all the same." His shoulders shake with a sardonic laugh. "How does that make me freaking *nice*, Rose?"

I bob my head, getting the point—understanding that he also doesn't care about me.

That like many guys before him, he can't—doesn't want to —see past my body or my face.

But at least Logan is much more transparent about it.

I snap my visor closed so he can't see the tears that are starting to fall. "Well, thanks for the honesty. Good night, Logan." I'm proud of myself that my voice doesn't waver and neither do my steps. I walk into the house and that's when I realize that I'm carrying his backpack.

I sink to my knees, fully shaking as I take out all my things and dump them on the floor. Somehow I manage to open the front door and place his backpack right outside.

He's watching me from exactly the same spot I left him at, and he doesn't move a muscle even as I close door again.

# CHAPTER 32
# LOGAN

"How does it feel like to work together with your romantic partner under such an intense scrutiny?" the columnist asks us, and I make sure to keep my expression the same. Like I'm considering his question carefully and not like I want to turn around, walk out of the premises, keep going until I'm no longer in Orlando, and don't stop even as I reach the Caribbean.

Rosalina is better trained for this, and she has no issue with responding right away. "It works out really well on a professional level. Logan's focus on the game is unbeatable. I think if aliens suddenly land on the field in the middle of a game he would still play without making a single error." Here she gives out an adorable little chuckle and even looks at me like she finds me genuinely endearing.

I can't help but stare at her, wondering if she shouldn't have become an actress instead.

Then she continues, returning her attention to the *SPORTY* Magazine dude. "The scrutiny part has been harder to deal with. I even had to make my social media accounts private. But if anyone so much as looks at me funny in real life, Logan's immediately on it."

"So Logan, you're the protective kind of boyfriend?" The reporter grins.

Right now we're in a conference room by the clubhouse, and Rose sits on a chair next to mine. My arm is on the back of her chair—her idea to show we're comfortable in each other's space, not mine—and I observe her expression as she waits for my answer. A remnant of her earlier amusement remains, but it seems to ebb the more the seconds stretch.

The answer comes with vehement force, though. "Yes. I will protect Rose from everything."

Including myself.

I did the right thing by warning her off. She needed to understand that I'm not the right guy for her. That as much as I piss and moan about my bizarre family, I *was* raised by them. That she's better off without any of my bullshit in her life. I would just drag her down with me and for what? So I can touch her and kiss her like I'm dreaming about every night? That's not a good tradeoff for her.

The camera guy recording the interview makes a face like he thinks I'm as sweet as a puppy, and boy is he wrong. He has no idea that I'm on a constant war between my need for Rosalina Mena, and the traumas that make up who I am. That would actually be a way more interesting story for this damn magazine.

Someone knocks on the crystal door behind us and Audrey Winters from PR pokes her head in. "Sorry to interrupt, just wanted to give you a heads up that the photographer is all set up and ready to start."

"Excellent," the reporter says, shutting his notepad. "Let's get that going, and if I come up with any further questions I will ask you between shots. Does that work?"

"Of course. Thank you," Rose responds all polite.

I get up first to pull the chair away from her, and I hang at the back of the group, the PR rep taking the helm.

Rose walks just ahead of me and my last name and number at her back taunt me. I know that her wearing my jersey is a crucial part of the ruse, a social signal that she's mine, but it feels almost cruel now. I wish I could just rip off the shirt from her and burn it to ashes. That nothing of me haunted her any longer.

I rub my chest. It feels hard to breathe and I force my lungs to expand, trying to catch the vital oxygen I need for my brain to keep functioning. It would be way too juicy for this magazine to catch me in the middle of an attack.

The air outside restores me much quicker, though. The green was freshly mowed and watered this morning, and the smell permeates the air. A sunbeam hits directly into the dugout and I turn my face to it, hoping the warmth chases away the cold claw in my chest.

Heavy steps approach and then a camera shutter goes off. I crack an eye open and find the photographer aiming his massive professional camera at me. Here we go, I guess.

"Hi Logan, Rosalina, my name is Reynaldo and I'll be your photographer today." He first shakes my hand and then Rose's. "Were you briefed already on the kind of photoshoot this is?"

"Yes," Rose chimes in with a smile. "We'll reenact one of our videos that went viral, the one where I was recorded interviewing Logan."

"That's right, but also…" Reynaldo smirks a little. "We'll have to offer some fan service."

I do my best to stifle a sigh, but every single person around me can read my mind, or so I guess from their shared amusement. Even Rose.

Motioning at myself, I ask in a deadpan, "What should I remove?"

"Your agent made us include a clause to keep your pants

on, does that help?" Winters asks, doing her best not to laugh at me.

"She gets to keep everything on, right?" I ask Winters while pointing at Rose.

"Yes. She's not the athlete we're showcasing here," Reynaldo explains. "Though, we definitely would like a few shots of you two just being a normal couple."

I catch myself in time before snorting. There is nothing normal or couple-like between us.

"Like what?" Rose tilts her head at the photographer.

Dude waves his hand in a no-biggie kind of way. "You know, a little flirting, light kissing, that kinda stuff. Nothing terrible that kids can't see."

Kissing?

I look at her from the corner of my eye. Her smile has frozen and sure enough, she slides the exact same look back at me.

"Kissing…" She trails off.

"Shall we get started?" Reynaldo signals at me. "Logan, first I'd like to get some action shots of you in full gear practicing with your teammates. Then when you work up a sweat we can move on to the shirtless takes."

I nod, disinterested but cooperating because I don't want any backlash for my partner-in-lie.

"In the meantime, I want you to act like you're recording him for your videos," he instructs to Rose. "I'll stand at a distance and capture you both. Does that sound good?"

"Of course!" Rose is all rainbows and sunshine about this, confirming why I have to play nice. This is all for her benefit and not mine.

We end up using the minutes it takes to put on all my catcher gear to start the whole thing. Rose starts a conversation with me about what we're going to eat after the photoshoot and I play along as the photographer starts snapping pics. I guess this must count for the flirting part, but with literal lenses pointed at me, I can't ask her what we're going to do about the kissing part.

Too soon I jog out to the field. The rest of the guys are in the middle of fielding practice, so I head over to the bullpen where it should be quieter. This forces the practice to pause for safety—no one wants fly balls conking someone's head, and especially not *SPORTY* people's heads when they're the team's biggest sponsor. But the entire team and staff know that today is going to be disruptive with this whole thing and that the sooner we get through it, the sooner we can all get back to real practice. So the pitching coach immediately finds me one of the rookies to throw balls at me so I can pretend like I'm doing what I get paid for.

"Throw slow, I need to watch out for the guests," I tell the rookie before crouching into position.

Meanwhile, Rose is off to the side, her cellphone up as she pretends to record me. And then there's Reynaldo and his two assistants pointing reflectors at us for the pictures. It's ridiculous.

And yet, that's the easiest part of the whole thing. Where it starts to get dicey is when Reynaldo notices that some weak pitching isn't enough to make me break a sweat, and that I'll need makeup assistance.

Practice goes to shit after that, because I'm taken to the dugout to divest of my catcher gear—and my top—so that a makeup artist can oil me up. The catcalling is pretty deafening.

"Hey, you missed a spot!" one of the guys instructs at the poor woman who is rubbing baby oil on my chest with surgical gloves on her hands.

She takes it seriously and observes my chest to find whatever spot that jerk refers to. As she rubs even harder, I'd give her props for being a professional if it wasn't because her entire face is flaming red.

I lift my eyes from her, ignoring my heckling teammates, and I can't find Rose right away. I tense, wondering if she abandoned me to these wolves, finally sick of this entire mess.

But then I find her standing next to Reynaldo, watching as the makeup artist runs her hands over my stomach.

Rose's brown eyes are dark as she watches every motion. It's too far to hear what the photographer says to her but I'm a pro at reading lips. He's telling her not to be jealous, that Carly—I assume that's the makeup artist—is a professional and she's not really groping her man—Rose's.

First, Rose is not jealous. Like me, she's probably just wondering why I couldn't oil myself up. Second, I'm not her man. At this point, Rose would probably like to toss me over a bridge on I-4.

"Turn, please," Clary or whoever instructs. Sighing, I obey and rub my face.

It takes a while to finish my back and my arms. Afterward, I walk out of the dugout wearing my team jersey open at the front, and as the light hits my bare skin I have to admit that it does look like a sheen of sweat, and not like I'm trying to audition to be a nightclub dancer.

"Hey Logan," Lucky Rivera calls out and I make the mistake of making eye contact. "You know what I've always thought about you?"

"No," I growl.

He answers himself anyway. "That you're a pretty sleek guy."

To my surprise, the first person to join in his guffaws isn't his best bud who already went through this humiliation, but Miguel Machado. That sends the rest of the team into peals of laughter, like this ridiculous dad joke is the funniest thing they've ever heard.

I slice my thumb across the air in front of my neck. "You're all dead, you hear me?"

But they don't, they keep ribbing off me even as I join the photographer. Somehow, Rose's mood seems to improve as I approach, like the thunder on my face amuses her.

"Ready for part two?" she asks me.

I shake my head, unable to utter a word.

"Rose and I were discussing about the next stage," Reynaldo says to me while motioning at his assistants to move. "Let's head over to the water coolers so you can pour some water on your face."

My eyebrow twitches. "Okay…"

I follow, resigned to my fate. Rather than keeping pace with the rest, Rose hangs back next to me and I can feel her eyes on me—somewhere. There's a lot to look at right now.

"About the kissing pics…" She clears her throat and faces out to the front once I'm looking at her. "I was thinking about-to-kiss might do the trick just the same."

"Fine."

"Fine," she repeats. "I'll talk with Reynaldo about it while he snaps thirst traps off you." She breaks into a little jog to put some distance between us, like she can't stand to breathe the same air as me for a second longer.

My shoulders slump.

Sure enough, Rose chats Reynaldo up about her little plan while I pose for some saucier pics that consist of me squirting water into my mouth, trickles traveling down my chest and belly, and more shots of me sleeking my damp hair back. The reporter joins in to ask if we have issues with PDA, and Rose smoothly explains that part of her job is keeping media family friendly, and all that.

So here I am, holding very still while Reynaldo takes pictures of every angle as Rose and I don't kiss, but look like we're about to.

Rose's back is against the cushioned barrier between the field and the stands, face angled up and slightly tilted to the side. Her lips are parted just a notch, plump and a tad damp like they're ready for a taste. Her hands rest against my chest—under the open shirt—where she can no doubt feel just how violently my heart beats inside.

Those dark eyes that drive me wild lift from my mouth to my eyes. I have to grit my teeth to remind myself that this isn't real. That I'm not actually about to crash my lips on hers.

It's just really damn hard when our breaths keep mingling, when I have one arm propped against the wall so I can keep her cornered, when my other hand is on the curve of her waist over her leggings. My thumb has a mind of its own and sneaks under her shirt, tied at the front again, finding bare skin right away.

I'm not strong enough to stop it from stroking, even as Rose tenses and her eyes widen.

"Logan…" I don't know if her whisper is an admonishment or a plea. Instead of pushing me away, she grabs harder onto my chest.

"I told you, didn't I?" I whisper back, turning my face until our noses bump. "I can barely control myself around you anymore, Rose."

"Can you guys get closer?" Reynaldo asks a second later.

Rose gasps as I pull her right against me. Her nose bumps into my lips and it's torture to just not kiss it. It's even worse to have her pressed against me and be unable to do anything else. But if that's a metaphor of the situation I'm in, I wouldn't know one if it hit me in the face.

Here she is, the woman I want, right in my arms. And when Reynaldo declares that the photoshoot is over, I must cut her loose and keep her at arm's length forever. That's the best I can do for her, and I hope one day she understands that.

# CHAPTER 33
## ROSE

ésame, a voice says in my head, sounding suspiciously like Oscar D'León.

I desperately want Logan to lean down the rest of the way—that measly fraction of an inch—and press his lips against mine. I can't take another moment of being in his arms, pressed against his hot chest while I drink in his breath.

Oh. My Word. I hadn't realized that Logan had chest hair.

It feels so silly to only notice it now. He's clearly a guy with healthy testosterone levels who can grow a solid beard on his perfect face. Maybe it was the chest tattoos what created an optical illusion, or the fact that I've kept the PDA so restricted that this is my first time touching his chest. Heck, it's our first time being this close from the front. Not even during the pool party last week did I get so handsy.

Speaking of, my traitorous hands splay wider over his taught skin, the pads of my fingers memorizing the texture of that surprising chest hair. I wish I could explore further. I wish I had the right to.

I make the mistake of lifting my eyes to his and every muscle of my body tenses. What I see in his gaze is pure, unfiltered desire. Like if I let him, he'd pick me up in his arms and cart me somewhere dark and secluded, and it doesn't take a rocket scientist to know what would happen next.

But that's the issue. I can't do that. I can't be someone's secret affair anymore.

Last week Logan made it very clear that nothing more is ever on the table with him, and the reminder is like a bucket of ice cold water.

"Whew," Reynaldo says all of a sudden. "You were right, Rose. The about-to-kiss pose is even more tense than a real kiss. This is definitely going to move issues."

I lean my head back a little and give out an awkward laugh. "That's great! But, erm, are we done? I'm starting to cramp."

"Yes! I think I have enough shots for this issue. But if you two are open to a couple photoshoot let me know." He winks at us.

I'm still laughing that alien laugh when I push Logan away from me like he's burning me. And he is. One more second of this and he's going to stay branded in my skin forever.

Maybe it's a good thing that nothing will happen between us. I'm afraid that loving Logan Kim would be all too consuming.

He eases off the wall and retreats along with my not so gentle shove, but his hand grabs onto my waist more firmly, like he's debating not letting me go at all. With shallow breathing, I manage to extricate myself to follow after the *SPORTY* crew and Audrey escorting them out of the field.

Like it's an itch I must cure ASAP, I glance back and catch Logan leaning back against the padded wall on the same spot, watching me go as he buttons up his shirt.

Facing forward, I pick up the pace and pretend like I don't notice the catcalling of the players as we leave them behind. I don't even know how I manage to stay calm as I say my farewells to the visitors without giving away that inside I'm a jittery mess.

Once I'm alone in the corridor, I speed walk my way into the women's restroom near the cafeteria. I check that the stalls are empty and proceed to have my little menty breakie.

"Oh my word, oh my word," I repeat to myself as I pace back and forth, my eyes watering violently.

One thing is being attracted to Logan—he's impossibly freaking beautiful, no matter how much I used to deny it at first —but another is this.

I can't possibly have fallen for him. There's no way my feelings are that deep.

"Ugh." I squeeze the fabric of my shirt—his, actually, the one he gave me a week ago—over my chest, as if somehow that could counter the pain of betraying myself.

Because that's exactly how this feels, like I'm letting myself down for being in the same spot that I promised myself I wouldn't ever be in again.

I'm in love with a baseball player. Again. And not just any player... the worst one of all. The one who wants me but not enough.

Swallowing hard, I lean against the sink, watching myself in the mirror. "Didn't you promise never to shed tears over a baseball player again?" I ask myself with a shaky, choked up voice.

Opening the faucet, I splash enough water on my face to wash them all away. It takes a million paper towels to dry my face and blot my soaked top. When I look semi normal, I finally make my way to my office where I will grab my desk cardigan and use it to replace this shirt. I don't want to be reminded of *him* for the rest of the day if I can help it.

Of course, there's not a moment's rest because my boss hounds me the second I walk into the marketing office. "There she is, our best actress."

And I don't know if they're mocking me or what, but everyone else pops over from their cubicles—clapping.

"That was an amazing performance," one of them giggles.

"Totally believable! The chemistry was scorching." Another gives me a double thumbs up.

"At this rate I wouldn't be surprised if the guy catches actual feelings for you."

I flinch at that, and Dave notices.

"How about we go into the meeting room for a quick chat?" He extends his arm out for me to join him down the hallway. I do, wearing a tight smile as my coworkers keep teasing me.

"Y'all are gonna sell that magazine like hotcakes."

"Right? I'm sure that will make *SPORTY* increase their sponsorship investment into the Wild."

"Christmas bonuses, here we go!"

The chatter finally stops when Dave and I walk into the conference room and he shuts the crystal door behind us. I take the seat with my back facing the office, and Dave jogs over to take the spot across the table from me.

"As you can see, this is going way better than we expected," he starts saying, lacing his fingers together. "It really is because of your commitment to the plan, and how consistently you developed it through our social media channels."

"Thank you," I mumble, squirming. These compliments feel like a too scratchy shirt.

"If you're aware of this, why do you look like you just came from a funeral?"

Lowering my face, I lift one hand to rub at the ache forming on my temples. "I…" I obviously can't confirm that one of the jokes came true—not that Logan's in love with me, but the other way around. Or why that leaves such a bitter taste in my mouth. But I can admit to one thing. "I'm starting to feel like a fake."

It hits me right here and now how true that is.

That's another reason why these feelings make no sense. The relationship between Logan and I, if it can even be called that way, started under false pretense. For me to benefit from, actually.

"How so?" There is abject confusion in my boss's voice.

"This is all a stunt, isn't it?" I lower my hand and his eyes narrow. My face is probably still puffy from crying earlier. "One where I stand to benefit the most. I don't think I'd feel so crappy about it if the benefits were more even."

He tilts his head. "The benefits are more so for the brand than for you. What do you mean?"

"Um, wasn't this all so I could replace Steve Boateng when he retires?"

Dave's eyes bulge. "Wait, who said that?"

Now I'm the one whose jaw drops and eyes turn cartoonish. "You did!"

"No, no. I said this would definitely show your commitment to the organization, which can open doors—"

"Dave!" I throw my hands in the air. "That's the sole reason I've been doing all these wild things for! You know I dream about that position—" A sob interrupts me.

I smack both hands against my mouth. Dave's expression is a mix of horror and shock.

"But Rosalina…" He swallows hard. "Promising something like that would've got me in trouble with HR. You'll have to apply to it like everybody else."

My voice is watery as I ask, "So what the hell have I been doing all this for?"

He opens and closes his mouth. And again. And when I'm sure he'll finally say something, his attention drifts to the side and I feel the conference room door open.

"Rose, you left your phone in the dugout."

Shit, it's Logan.

My reflexes fail me and instead of hiding, I turn to him.

Sure enough, that's my phone in its lavender case in his hand. But what strikes me the most is how he takes one look at my face and… his expression transforms, first into surprise and then into fury.

"What did you do to her?" he asks Dave in a menacing way.

"Nothing!" Dave squeaks out. "I, myself, don't understand what's happening."

I wipe my face with my arm and push away from the table. I hate that my chin trembles as I look down at my boss "Dave, I don't feel well today so I'm going to go home early, okay?"

He nods rapidly. "Yes, yes. Let's continue our conversation when you feel better."

"Okay," I mumble, turning around. Logan is like a wall blocking the door, every line of him tense as he looks at me. I extend my trembling hand and it takes him a second to place my phone on it. "Thanks. If you'll excuse me…"

Logan's hands tighten into fists but he steps aside. I walk by, pretending like the scent of pine and sunblock and sweat doesn't follow me as I leave him behind.

# CHAPTER 34
# LOGAN

never thought the time would come when I'd have to ask, but… are you okay, Kim?"

I tear my eyes away from Rose while she records both Starr and Machado on the topic of the day: *if you could play any other position, what would you pick?* She's basically asked every guy in the clubhouse but me, clearly still icing me out.

Expelling a big breath, I ask, "What do you mean, Rivera?"

He folds his arms, turning to face me as he sits next to me. "At first I thought you were extra cranky because we're about to start the series against your brother. But then I noticed how you and Rose aren't talking and all you do is stare at her from afar. What's up with that, bro?"

My jaw tightens. I would understand if someone noticed that Rose and I are strained—it's clear as day—but the thing about my brother? And shit, why does it have to be this goof who noticed?

"How did you catch on?" I wince a bit. "About my brother, I mean."

"Easy, you look like you got a big turd stuck in your colon

sideways every time you look at him." He nods as if he had just imparted some sage words and not used a pretty graphic allegory.

"You know what? I prefer the version of you that pulls childish pranks on people than the observant one."

Rivera smirks a little. "And I really enjoy when you underestimate me." The amusement eases off his face and for once, the seriousness he adopts makes him look his actual age. "I know there's no power in this world that can force you to talk but just answer me this: is whatever you got going on at risk of affecting this game?"

"No." His eyes narrow as he studies me, and I add, "I'm damn good at compartmentalizing."

"I know that. It scares me sometimes." Sighing, he loosens his arms and runs a hand down his face. "And if it does start to affect the game?"

I swallow hard and he notices. "If so, I'll ask Beau to sub me out."

It's obvious that he wants to say something more, but at the last minute he changes his mind and gets up. Right when I think he's finally out of my hair, he retraces back a few steps and pats my shoulder. Hard.

"Also, just apologize to Rose."

Apologize? What the hell for?

For having the hots for her even though I'm a jumbo sized red flag?

I twist my face and bat his paw away. "It's not that simple."

"I bet it's actually not as complicated as that clever brain of yours is making it out to be." He points at my face. "Stop overthinking and apologize, that's all."

"Go away before I find the electric mosquito swatter."

He looks ready to chew me off some more, but then crew members of the New York Eagles stadium instruct us to get going. I feel a million years old as I get back up to my feet, and not like a professional athlete that is already warmed up and ready to go.

I follow along with my teammates trickling into the tunnel out to the away team dugout, trying my best not to be aware of Rose standing by watching. She says good luck over and over as the guys pass her by, and I pretend like I'm wiping the sweat off my face with my long sleeved undershirt so she doesn't feel obligated to acknowledge me. The going excuse is the mandate from HR for the couples on the team to act professional at all times, and no one had suspected anything was amiss until now. I keep forgetting that Lucky Rivera is a smarter jackass than he lets on.

I'm already decked in my catcher gear so I step out onto the green for the national anthem. The second I do, the booing is deafening enough that I have no doubt it can be heard throughout all The Bronx.

It snaps me awake. Finally my brain grabs every complicated thought about my fake girlfriend and locks it in a wooden chest.

Now I'm fully present in the moment, and I look on at the stadium where I started my professional career, packed to the brim with fans who still can't get over my betrayal years later.

I remove my mask and raise it in a mocking salute that gets me even more booing. It doesn't stop even when their Eagles take to the field, like it's much more important to shit on me than to cape for their actual team. Normal bird mentality.

I can spot my brother jogging over easier than anyone else. We look uncannily similar for brothers that aren't twins, the exact same frame and near identical faces. His nose has a tiny bump on the bridge that I don't have, his eyes are naturally wider, and mouth thinner. But that's my square jaw on his face and the same set to our eyebrows. He keeps his face fully shaved and his hair short in a similar style to our dad's.

But the biggest difference is that his eyes are dead. Looking at Lewis is the same as staring into a Victorian doll's glass eyes. I sigh, annoyed that he, of course, has to take the spot on the Eagles line that faces me.

"Look who we have here, my beloved little brother." He shows that empty smile of his.

I put my mask again and don't respond.

Unfortunately, Lewis turns his attention to the guy next to me, who happens to be our starting pitcher. "Cade Starr? I'm Lewis Kim, it's so great to meet the pitcher who is making waves in the league right now."

Starr ignores him too. Instead, he covers his mouth with his glove and asks me, "Doesn't he know we've already met?"

I also cover my mouth with my glove. "That's his way of saying you've been insignificant to him so far."

"Should I be flattered or pissed?" But the cowboy sounds neither—he's amused.

"Whatever makes you pitch some cannons tonight," I respond.

We quiet down for the national anthem, sang by the woman who opens for every Eagles game since before I was a rookie, and in the blink of an eye the game is starting.

I can feel Lewis's laser beams trained on me as I crouch for the opening pitch. "Play ball!" the umpire calls.

I signal for Starr to throw whatever he wants—fastball, curve, cutter or even the slider he's been practicing when he thinks I'm not watching, I don't care. But it has to come in right here, I tell him with my glove positioned in the middle of my chest.

Bold? Maybe.

Foolish? Certainly.

But if it works, the Eagles are going to get raging angry at missing a pitch down the middle, and that's what I'm betting on.

Besides, if it goes awry we now have Miguel Machado in

centerfield, where most of the Eagles bat toward. And the guy is as much of a homerun machine as he is at catching hits or would-be-homers.

Starr winds up, his throwing arm pretty compact behind him and— "Strike!"

My mouth twitches. I'm tempted to buy him a pizza for this alone.

The second pitch goes in a similar fashion and by the third, the Eagles's leadoff is so annoyed that he swings as wide as a pee wee playing for the first time. More booing ensues and I am healed. Whatever funk I was in, it's in the past.

The best part is that I don't have to deal with my brother directly during the game since he's not a two-way player. His designated hitter comes in next, a guy who often competes against Machado for the All-Star homerun derbies. Convention would dictate that I make more cautious plays against him, but that's not what makes me the catcher I am.

I, Logan Kim, am a little shit.

I call for an inside pitch, the least fave position for sluggers who like to swing big. Starr throws a nice cutter that stumps most batters, but this Eagle guy connects.

The ball hits the bat wrong. Instead of going forward, it shoots back at me like a bullet.

I can see it in slow motion, like watching a movie on TV. Rather than dodging it and risking it hitting somewhere worse, I stay put and brace. The ball hits on the inside of my left thigh. The speed makes the ball change course like I'm a human pinball machine, but my thigh changes the angle. The ball spins back and I catch it with my bare hand behind my right thigh.

"Strike!"

The stadium roars—or is that booing? I don't give a shit.

Wincing, I stand up and toss the ball back at a gaping Starr.

I can't tell what our basemen are screaming over the noise. But I do hear the batter's voice clearly.

"What the hell just happened?"

"A strike, is what," I respond, taking my stance again.

Great, I'm gonna have a bruise the size of a boulder but at least I can keep playing. I'll just have to ice the shit out of it between innings so I can run bases.

We hold them off to no runs during the first inning, but their cleanup would've put them on the board if it hadn't been for a spectacular catch from Machado that no doubt will make the highlight reels.

"Take off your pants, Logan," Hope says the second I walk into the dugout.

Starr gasps. "Darlin', you should only be saying that to me."

"Let's go." I jerk my head toward the clubhouse, conscious of a million cameras probably pointed my way.

She also ignores her boyfriend and follows me into the tunnel. As I walk, I work my belt buckle under my chest pad because I really will have to remove my pants. I'm unzipping them as Hope and I emerge into the clubhouse and I'm faced with an astonishing scene.

My brother, inside our team's clubhouse, and Rosalina Mena in front of him.

They both turn to us as we walk in. And both of them zero in on my hands lowering the zipper of my pants.

# CHAPTER 35
## ROSE

What the hell is happening?

First, a player from the opposite team barges into our clubhouse, and the guy bears a shocking resemblance to Logan that tells me this must be the infamous brother.

Then out come Hope and Logan, and Logan is undoing his pants right behind her. Which can only mean one thing—Logan is injured. The replay kinda made it look like that wild ball might've hit him near the… well, dangly bits. That must be hurting a lot.

I need to get this strange guy out so Hope can do her work.

"Excuse me," I call out louder because he ignored me the first time. "I asked you to please leave before I call security."

"Security?" Lewis Kim turns ice cold eyes back to me, making my shoulders tense. "Please, what are they going to do to me? I'm an Eagle."

"What are they going to do?" I ask back sarcastically. "They're going to escort you out of here, and then I'll personally file a complaint against your team that will get you suspended. How about that?"

"Rose," Logan warns, now right behind me.

"Ohh…" Lewis elongates the exclamation. "So this is the famous girlfriend."

"What are you doing here, Lewis?" Logan's voice is a low growl, danger lurking beneath. A shiver racks my spine.

Lewis puts his hands in the pockets of his uniform pants and rocks on his heels. "That looked like a pretty bad hit so I was worried about you. Are you sure you'll still be able to give me nephews and nieces?"

Logan takes a step closer that puts him almost beside me, and everything in his body language screams that he's about to do something unlike him. "What I'm going to give you is—"

My mind whirrs. There is absolutely no way I'll let Logan risk a suspension for roughhousing this jerkface, especially because in theory Lewis has done nothing to deserve it.

"Out!" I bark and push at Lewis Kim's chest. "You're trespassing and—"

Suddenly there's an impact against my sternum.

Air whooshes out of my lungs and I hurl backward.

Except that I don't go far because I slam into a steel bar—no, not a steel bar. An arm. It twirls me around until I bump into Logan's padded chest. I gasp into it, my arms curled protectively against my throbbing chest.

"Oops, sorry," Lewis says behind me. "I just wanted to show you that shoving others isn't nice. Did I go too far?"

That's when I get it. I get every warning that Logan has ever given me.

Lewis just shoved me hard enough to bruise. Who knows what else he could do as an oopsie. This guy is freaking unhinged.

"Hope," Logan says above my head just as he pulls me away from him by my arms. "Take Rose and get away."

"No," I wheeze. My heart beats faster than I can catch breath. "Logan, don't—"

Hope yanks me away from Logan and wraps her arms around me from behind, tight enough to hurt and also to make me understand that she won't let me go anywhere. Logan glances over his shoulder and when he's satisfied with Hope's work, he nods at her. Then he tosses his mask on the floor and rushes at his brother.

"No! Logan!"

"Mierda," Hope whispers in my ear.

Logan shoves Lewis so hard that he crashes against the doors. They swing wide and the Eagles pitcher loses his footing, crashing on the floor in the corridor. Voices outside quiet down.

"You wanted to teach her a lesson? I'll be the one teaching you something, asshole," Logan growls. All I can see is his back to us but somehow Lewis's disbelieving expression is clear between Logan's legs. "Don't you dare touch my woman again."

Hope and I turn to statues.

I turn my face toward her in robotic increments. "What did he just…"

"Oh my," Hope breathes out, a smile forming on her lips.

But then Lewis scoffs. "Your woman?" He shifts to sit up and I can no longer see his face, only how he brushes his hands off. "My sources tell me she's not really your girlfriend, that all of this is a publicity stunt and yet—" He cuts himself off to stand back up. "Don't tell me she's the real reason why you refuse to move back to the Eagles?"

Hope's arms relax a tad. "What did he just say?"

"I—No, it's not…" But I don't even know how to explain when I'm still reeling. How does Lewis knows all of this?

"Is that it?" Logan asks so low that I can barely hear. "Is that why you're causing this scene? You think this will somehow convince me to form a battery with you again?"

"What can I say, you're the only one who can make the

calls that draw out my full potential." Lewis takes a step closer. "Don't you get it? I'm paying you a compliment, little brother."

"I don't need shit from you, get out of my face." Logan pushes Lewis away from him again, less forcefully this time.

"The sources you claimed to have," I cut in with a loud, firm voice that forces all the attention back on me. "Who are they?"

In looking back at me, Logan creates enough space for me to meet Lewis's creepy eyes again. He smirks at his brother. "Looks like you got yourself a smart girlfriend this time around—if that's what she really is." But Logan blocks me again, getting in the way so that Lewis can't come back in. "Aww, c'mon, Logan. Your lady friend and I are having a conversation."

"Go back to your nest, you damn—"

"It's Kaplan," Lewis says over Logan. "Your agent also wants you to do the right thing and come back to play for me, little bro. We're just concerned that you're spiraling, and all for some random woman who is probably after your fortune."

"Screw off, you freaking weirdo. Logan is lucky to have Rose!" Hope shouts at him, making me flinch at the volume, even if the sentiment is touching. I tap her arms and she finally lets go.

"Security," Logan calls out as some steps approach. "Take this straggler back to his clubhouse and keep him there."

"Mr. Kim, you're not supposed to be here," a stranger's voice comes from the corridor.

"I'm coming, I'm coming. Was just checking that my little brother is okay." Lewis's feet shift away from Logan, and the latter finally closes the door.

That's when I notice two things. One, that Logan is breathing much harder than when he came in after the inning. And two, that we're not alone—and I don't mean because of Hope.

"What the hell just happened?" Cade asks behind us and the question makes Logan hang his head.

"A small accident," I respond right away, looking pointedly at my roommate. "Right, Hope?"

"Right," she says right away. "Y'all should go back out to the dugout."

"McDonald, find something to secure the door with," Rob Beau, the team's manager says and my shoulders slump. "Garcia, can you assess Kim quickly? I need to know if he can play the next inning."

Logan bends forward to pick up his mask. "I'm fine."

There is no way in hell he's fine. I'm about to say as much when someone beats me to the punch.

"Are you?" Lucky surprises me by asking, but his eyes are narrowed in a weird way. "Moving to the Eagles, I mean."

A ripple of whispers travels through the men flooding the clubhouse.

Logan tightens his jaw before speaking. "I am not." That settles a deep silence among everybody, except for the sounds trickling into the tunnel from the stadium. "I was thinking about it but not anymore. And once this game is over I'm canning my damn agent and maybe even suing his ass," he finishes in a growl.

My jaw drops. "Wait, you are? I mean, aren't? I mean—" I shake my head hard.

"Whew." Lucky lets out a laugh. "That's good."

"Yeah, man. You're absolutely insufferable but no one wants you to leave," Cade adds. A bunch of yeahs punctuate his sentence.

Logan's face twitches like he can't decide which expression best suits the occasion. Like actually, he just can't figure out how he feels.

"Okay, you guys. The clock is ticking and Hope needs to

look at Logan," I say, waving my arms to herd them out of the clubhouse.

"Can't I stay back to inspect the work?" Cade whines.

"No," I respond, pushing at him to activate his feet, and since Cade isn't a grade-A ass he complies.

"Is it always this dramatic here?" Miguel asks me.

But Lucky palms his back and says, "You'll get used to it."

The last one to exit is Beau, and for some reason he's chuckling. He glances between Logan and me a couple of times before following the rest of his team out to the dugout.

When there's supposed to be peace at last, my legs buckle from under me and I slide to the floor.

"Shit, Rose." Logan jumps to his feet from the bench, but his pants are down at his knees, caught by his kneepads, so he can't really go far.

Beside him, Hope has a Bengay spray in her hand and she tosses it at Logan before running over. "Talk to me, Rosie. What's wrong? Did that jackass really hurt you?" She kneels in front of me all worried and in a much bigger panic than when she had to take care of Logan's potential injury.

I prop myself up by my hands, shaking my head hard. "No, I'm fine. I suddenly… Logan, why are your boxers nude color? You look naked."

Hope presses her lips tight. "Is that why you almost fainted? You thought your boyfriend was naked?"

"I—no, um…"

Logan pulls up his pants enough that he can walk over without tripping, and then to my shock he lowers to sit right beside me against the wall. He sighs. "It's so they don't show through the white pants that are too damn thin."

"That makes sense. No need to flash people." I bob my head as if that was the most important part of this whole night's events.

Hope extends her hand out to Logan. "Spray yourself. I'm

gonna go tell Beau that you're just mildly bruised and check on the time."

"Thanks," Logan whispers.

As I watch Hope go, intense booing from the crowd filters into the clubhouse, which means we must've stolen a base or scored.

A bump on my shoulder gets my attention again, and it's from Logan shifting to pull his pants back down. I try not to stare, but it's really weird to see skin color boxers on a guy.

He folds his left leg, exposing a massive bruise on the inner thigh that I wouldn't define as *mild*. I watch as he sprays himself, and the medicine makes my nose itch. I sniff and he looks up right away.

"Are you crying?"

"No." I frown. "The spray is making me want to sneeze."

"Sorry. I'll stop."

"Are you kidding?" I grab his hand holding the can and pull it back over his thigh. "Keep going."

"But—"

"Logan Kim, I will douse that whole can on you myself if I must."

He sighs but keeps going, and after a while he asks, "Are you okay?"

"Me?" I blink hard. "I'm not the one who got pelted by a ball going at a million miles per hour."

"No, but you got Lewis Kim'ed and that's way worse."

I fully turn to stare at his profile and he pretends like his sole focus remains on the spray.

I think I know what that avoidance means now. Logan doesn't want me to peek into his eyes or I might get a glimpse of what's really going through his head. It must not be pleasant.

"I get you now."

He tenses and lifts his face. "What?"

My lips curl into a sad little smile that captures his attention, and it's what makes his finger stop pressing on the spray bottle nozzle. "I understand why you warned me off," I whisper.

Logan turns his face away and I watch the powerful muscles of his neck as they bulge out. His throat works a heavy swallow. "I told you, I'm screwed up. You don't need that drama in your life, especially not after your ex—"

Leaning on my right hand, I twist to hold his jaw and turn his face just a bit. I press my lips on his cheek, right on the bare skin over the sharp line of his stubble. Goodness, he smells so good that I can't help lingering. When I pull away, I put a little more pressure on his jaw so that he doesn't turn away yet, and run my fingers over the soft stubble.

"You are so not like your relatives, you silly man." I smile. "And thank goodness for that."

Logan's eyes widen. "I—"

"Sorry to interrupt, lovebirds," Hope says, poking her head out of the tunnel beside me. "There's like thirty seconds to the next inning and Logan's catching services are necessary."

"Right!" I squeak, dropping my hand. "You better go."

It almost seems like Logan wants to protest, but with a grunt, he grabs onto his pants and gets up. I watch from the floor as he bends forward to pull up the garment. He glances at me as he tucks his shirt into his pants, which strikes me as a scene that should be illegal, but leaves after Hope without saying another word.

I grab the Bengay can and shake it a bit. It seems like he didn't empty it on himself. Pulling my team polo up, I free my chest to spray before the bruise starts forming on my chest.

# CHAPTER 36
## LOGAN

I never thought I'd say this but coming out on the other side of the Eagles series feels more monumental than winning the World Series, and yet it doesn't solve anything. My brother is still a piece of shit who has now aired all my dirty laundry, my team knows it, and I can't ever face Rosalina Mena again—and it's not because she saw my embarrassing game boxers.

Oh, and my ex agent keeps calling me like some kind of ex girlfriend who still wants a piece of me.

I'm trying to jog on the treadmill at the Orlando Wild gym and Kaplan keeps blowing up my phone. For the nth time, I click the red button instead of picking up the call.

"Dude, why don't you block him?" Rivera asks on my right, panting as he runs uphill.

On my left, Starr suggests, "Or turn off your phone, at least. The buzzing is so annoying."

My upper lip trembles like a wolf about to start snarling. "It's way more fun for him to know I'm expressly rejecting every call."

"Oof."

"Cold."

From the treadmill on Starr's left, Machado chimes in, "What are you gonna do now that you need a new agent? Because I can recommend mine, she's awesome and really ambitious."

"I can recommend mine too," Starr says, also panting like a dog in his thirty fifth minute of running. "He's a cranky son of a gun, but he has ethics."

"I don't recommend mine," Rivera adds with a laugh. "The old grump's retiring any time soon, so I'll be on the market for a new one too."

Kaplan calls again. This time I let it ring for a good moment longer, click on the green button and when the faint sound of his tinny voice comes up, I hang up.

"Remind me never to incite your petty side." Rivera clicks his tongue.

Petty? I snort. That falls short. I'm litigious, baby.

The reason Kaplan is calling non-stop is because he violated the non-disclosure clause of our contract and my lawyer has already reached out to him. I'm not just on the hunt for a new agent, but also for everything Kaplan owns or cares about. That's what he gets after babbling my shit to the worst possible person.

I wonder if it would've made a difference at all if I'd been clearer with Kaplan about why I'm not close with my relatives, or if he would've betrayed me anyway. I've never wanted to run that risk with him or anyone in my life, but even that is all jumbled up.

Rose knows everything. Or almost everything. She doesn't know about the scars that my tattoos cover up or about the claustrophobia and the panic attacks. But she knows more about my parents and my brother than I ever even told Kaplan. And even though she's thankfully not involved with me *and* there's no contract binding us, she still hasn't betrayed my confidence.

Kaplan has no excuse. I shouldn't have had to tell him my whole sob story for him to uphold our contract.

"I'm still curious about something, though," the pitcher mumbles, side-eying me. "You confirmed that you were planning a trade but now you're staying. What about Rose, though?"

I tense and ask through gritted teeth, "What about her?"

"Is you dating her really a publicity stunt?"

Shit. I can feel all their eyes on me. Maybe even the whole gym's attention.

It's rest day before a home series and at least half of the team is taking it easy, training at home or joining in late. But for three days I've been the center of attention and I hate it. I can't wait for someone else to do something ridiculous soon and hog all the limelight.

I huff hard enough for the lone strand of hair sticking to my face to fly. "Yeah…"

"*What?*"

"No way!"

"But you two look like, so in love." Machado scrunches up his face in confusion. "Even my daughter asked me why can't I have what you two have."

I cringe. "We don't have anything. It's all an act."

"My ass," Starr declares boldly. "I recognize those slobbery looks on y'all's faces because that's the way I look at Hope myself."

"Can confirm." Rivera nods. "You look just as done for when you glance at Rose as Cade does with Hope."

"I do not." I frown at them in turns, but they're just amused. "Seriously, I don't. There's nothing going on."

"Let's test it then." Machado points to the opposite side.

We all turn right as Rose struts into the place with a smile that's bigger and more blinding than the billboards at Times Square. My feet stumble and I have to catch myself by grabbing the handrails before I lose all my dental work. The jerks around me notice right away and start snickering like this is middle school.

"Good morning, Wildlings." Rose puts her hands on her hips and I notice that she's wearing some short leggings. Or shorts. I don't know what they are, but they're tight, above her knee, and show off her amazing hips. "I've been sent down by my boss to take some thirst traps. Who volunteers?"

"Me!" One of the guys by the weights rack raises his hand.

"No, me!"

"Pick me!"

"You guys, Kim has dibs," Rivera says over the commotion.

But then one of our teammates fires back with, "No, he doesn't. He's not really Rosie's boyfriend."

And her smile falters.

I punch the button to slow my treadmill the hell down until I'm able to step off. I push that rogue strand of hair behind my ear and stalk toward the nearest machine, which is the pullup bar. The best part is how my back is to Rose so I don't have to see her get flirted with by the vultures. Gnashing my teeth, I grab onto the handles, cross my legs at my ankles, and go to town.

We haven't talked ever since she kissed my cheek and I had to go off to play a game. Neither of us has reached out to the other. There have been no chance encounters in the facilities. And now that the ruse is up with the team, I take it as my cue to go back to how things were before the publicity stunt.

We're perfect strangers.

It makes my chest all weird, like I'm missing a lung or something.

Yeah, I understand what's happening. I'm not a clown like

Rivera or Starr. I have a thing for Rose, one that's deep enough that I can't stop thinking about her. A thing that's as loud as the roar of a lion.

But then I remember how my parents talked about her. And how Lewis pushed her around like it was no big deal—like scaring her was fun. And then I remember the look of shock and anger and hurt in her face, and the fact that she tried to hide the bruise on her chest. Then that roar turns into a pitiful little mewl.

I can't put her through that again. And if I'm not going to grow a pair and ask her out, I have no right to feel as jealous as I am.

"Hey, Lucky. Is it okay if I get a shot of your butt?" Rose asks nearby and I swear I could rip this bar off the machine and slam it on Rivera's head.

"Shouldn't you be getting some good shots from Kim?" he asks instead, preserving the integrity of his skull. "We may know what's what, princesa, but the public doesn't know yet."

"Uh…"

"Also, look at him." Starr pauses before saying, "His clothes are so skimpy, he's the perfect thirst trap right now."

"You know, I hadn't noticed but it's true. That's a really skimpy tank top. You should definitely snap that, it'll go viral," is Machado's contribution.

*Skimpy?*

Are these—and here I interrupt my train of thought to grimace—are these fools trying to help me or humiliate me even more?

"I'm—" about to tell them to screw all the way off to the sun when Rose speaks.

"Is it okay?"

I pause in the middle of a pullup and glance back at her. "What?"

"If I take some footage of you?" she asks me, her expression devoid of any hint of excitement.

"Fine," I grunt, returning my focus to my workout.

"Make sure to get his lats," Rivera instructs. "What with him showcasing them and all that."

I'm wearing one of those tanks that are basically open on the sides. I like them because they help me cool down faster, especially in this muggy Central Florida summer from hell.

"Thanks, Lucky. Any other must-have angles?" Rose sounds amused.

The alluded hums from his throat. "The arms, I guess. Women like those."

"Just get the whole man in frame," says Starr. "Women like all *that*."

"Are you objectifying me?" I ask with a grunt that sounds pained.

"Not gonna lie, maybe a little," he responds without shame.

With a huff, I hop off the machine. By this point my face is drenched in sweat and I lift my tank top to wipe it off. The stooges—all three of them, now including Machado—start wolf whistling and I turn to glare them down. Except that makes it all worse.

Because Rose has her camera trained on me the whole time. And the camera lowers to my midriff. Which is bare right now.

"Now that's just too much." Rivera is in stitches as he waves his hands in the air. "That's just gonna melt the internet."

"Hmm." Machado runs his hands over his stomach. "I think I need to go on a diet."

"Dude, no." Starr smacks Machado's chest with the back of his hand. "We need all the power you already have."

"That kinda muscle would probably give me more power," Machado muses.

Since my laser beams have turned completely ineffective on that new terrible trio, I turn my attention to Rose again. She's still recording me, all right, her camera fully trained on the goods.

But so are her eyes. Like, they're not fixed on the footage but on the real thing.

"Should I just take it off?" I mutter, and I think my question gets lost among the ruckus of the guys, but then her eyes lift to mine.

And she bites her lip like she's mulling it over.

Okay, I mean it when I said I'm not a clown. I know that she finds me attractive. I know I could play that up—try to get her interested. But that would be a copout and it would still lead to the same outcome.

That she's better off without me.

Finally, she shakes her head. "No, I think that really would break the internet."

Nodding, I drop my shirt. "Are we done here?"

"What? Already?" Rivera complains.

"Actually…" Rose hesitates. And she never does that. My eyebrows pinch as she takes a cautious step toward me. "Can we talk after work?"

I have trouble unsticking my lips but somehow I manage. "Me?"

"Yeah, I—" She clears her throat. "There's something I need to tell you."

My heart does a thing. Like it attempts a cartwheel but sinks, because her expression has turned all weird and I don't think it's because my abs are still affecting her. So I nod and after returning the gesture, she transforms back into happy-go-lucky-Rose.

"C'mon, you guys, show me your abs," she jokes to the other three.

I swivel around right away before any of them can see the

volcanic annoyance on my face. I don't even know what the conversation topic will be, but the fact that it has to do with me and how it sours her entire demeanor rankles.

Meanwhile, she's all smiles and sunshine for the others.

Chopped damn liver, I am, and the sooner I come to terms with it the better.

# CHAPTER 37
## ROSE

"So what are we going to do about this?" I look from my boss to his boss and back, waiting for a reaction that doesn't come. "There has to be something. Do we talk with HR? Put out a statement?"

Dave's expression is the definition of confusion. "But Rosalina, I thought we were here to talk about you?"

I—Yes. Originally the topic of the meeting was to talk about whether it even makes sense for Logan and I to continue fake dating for social media engagement, and also about what this means for my career now that it's clear that my expectations weren't aligned with Dave's.

But then this happened.

I point at my laptop screen showing a frozen frame from the viral Logan Kim video of the moment. It must've been captured by someone from the New York Eagles stadium staff, or perhaps a teammate. The star of the show is Lewis Kim in the middle, and only peeks of Logan can be seen through the open door where Lewis came ejected from.

The whole thing is maybe thirty seconds long, cut to shed the worst possible light on Logan. None of Lewis's abusive behavior is shown on screen. Instead it's just about the moment Logan shoves him out and Lewis crashes on his ass.

The comments are mixed. Some hardcore fans recognize that it's unthinkable for a player from one team to invade the clubhouse of their series rival, and they're calling for sanctions on Lewis.

But the bulk of the commenters are condemning Logan. People are calling him violent, unstable, unprofessional, and many worse things. They're calling for his suspension, some even for a full-on ban, even though this was a private incident that didn't happen during play.

All the goodwill that Logan and I earned is being squandered, and there are even people asking for someone to check in on me in case Logan is also violent toward me. And the worst of the bunch are even wondering if perhaps I enjoy it anyway.

I don't care about that. I just can't believe how quick they are to judge Logan, when the real threat to other human beings is his creep of a brother. The hand shaped bruise in my sternum can attest to that.

"Not all the comments are negative," Tom says while he scrolls through them from his own phone. "Certainly the Wild fans are proud of how Logan defended our clubhouse."

"Yeah, but those are like five percent of all the comments," I argue.

"But it's publicity anyway and at the end of the day, that's what we want," Dave says with a shrug. "People are talking about him and therefore the team, so basically our job here is done."

"He's getting slandered." I widen my eyes. "And going by what a creep Lewis Kim is, I wouldn't even be surprised if he planned the whole scene and we just played along like puppets. And you're telling me we're not going to do anything to protect Logan?"

Both men give me funny looks that I don't understand. They should be just as furious as me.

Dave checks his boss's expression before turning to me again. "Rosalina, I have a questions for you, if you don't mind."

"Yes?" I frown and fold my arms, annoyed.

"How come you've never gotten this incensed when any of the other players get trash talked online?"

I blink.

Dave's mouth curls dangerously. Worse still, Tom's expression also turns amused.

"Well, well." Dave elbows his boss, since they're sitting on the same side of the table. "It looks like maybe the stunt wasn't a stunt all along."

I gasp. And choke.

"Just so you know, I recognize your excellent contributions to the marketing team and I have no problem with you dating a player." Tom's voice is grave, yet his cheeks keep twitching. "Just make sure that the other players don't feel the favoritism."

"Ugh." I push away from my chair and stalk to the door.

"Wait," Dave calls out. "Aren't we going to talk about you?"

"I can't." I scowl at them. "I'm too annoyed right now. I'll reschedule this meeting for whenever I can be more professional and not get myself sent to HR."

I leave them to have a really good laugh at my expense, knowing full well that my face is probably as red as beets and that I can't deny the allegation.

Technically, the stunt was just that. Logan and I never dated for real. But I do have some serious feelings for him. It's why I'm trying to protect him. And if that doesn't work— thanks to my middle schooler bosses not giving the issue any importance—then the least I can do is warn Logan. Even if I had vowed to never be alone with him again for my own sake.

I sit to fume in my cubicle for an hour where I achieve exactly zero productivity. Every five minutes I open the text message app to re-read the last communication between Logan and I, half dreading and half hoping for him to cancel at the last minute.

**ME**

Let's meet in the parking lot after everyone else leaves

**FAKE BABE**

Roger that

That's it. Nothing else. And a big gap between my text today and the last time we talked. Almost two weeks.

But Logan doesn't cancel, and with every passing second my heart rate increases more and more. Players on rest day tend to leave around five, like a normal nine-to-five job, and I wait until half past to start making my way to the exit. By the time I spot him waiting by his bike, in the middle of a nearly deserted parking lot, I can confirm that my heartbeat is one or two points away from a medical emergency.

I slide back into the lobby before he can spot me and force myself to take a few deep breaths. "You got this," I tell myself, nodding. "It's just a work-related conversation. You're not declaring your feelings for the man, here."

I turn and almost kill myself from fright.

For a second I think it's Logan standing right behind me but no, it's just a damn potted plant.

I need to be way less keyed up for this. Puffing my chest, I finally make my way out of the building and head over to him.

What was it that Lucky called it earlier? Skimpy? Because Logan's in another of those outfits that are like catnip—a black muscle T-shirt that clings so tight to his body that I can even make out the shape of his belly button, black cargo pants with a little black pouch tied around his left thigh, and black combat boots. I'm sure he'd look great in other colors but goodness, the all black ensemble makes my knees buckle.

Somehow I manage to stand upright in front of him. "Hi."

"Hey." He tips his chin. I wish I could tell him to unfold his arms so all those muscles, the veins and the tats weren't so in my face. It makes me want to lick them.

Clearing my throat, I start speaking. "Thank you for meeting me here. Er…"

He cocks one eyebrow but patiently waits for me to gather my wits, now that they've scattered all across the place at the sight of his incredible arms. But then I remember that the topic isn't a fun one, and that I'm not supposed to have *any* fun with this man.

"Right, I'm just gonna cut to the chase." I adopt his same posture, hoping it helps me brace myself. "You might have already seen this on your social media feeds, but you've gone viral again and this time it's not good."

"Is that so," he says flatly, not as a question, and it doesn't let me glean if he was already aware or not.

"Yes, someone recorded the altercation between you and your brother. The clip they published makes you look like the complete villain because there's no further context. I'm…" I swallow hard but press on. "I'm thinking the whole thing might've been orchestrated. By your brother."

For a second, all Logan does is hum from his throat like I'm just telling him about something that happened to the friend of a friend of a cousin.

"That wouldn't surprise me."

I frown. "Then why are you so calm?"

He shrugs those powerful shoulders of his. "Not my first rodeo with him."

"So—" I splutter. "You're fine with being dragged through the mud? With everybody talking shit about you like you're some two-bit villain? With your reputation going down the drain overnight? Is that fine with you, Logan?" I'm only conscious of how my voice has risen when I stop yapping to catch my breath.

Even worse, he just stares at me calmly. His hair is damp from a shower and still drips on his muscle shirt, and I'd much rather look at that than into his all-seeing eyes.

"What's it to you?" he asks in a quiet voice.

"Huh?" In contrast, mine is squeaky.

"Why do you care about what people say about me when even I don't?"

I—I—

Mierda.

He finally loosens his arms and puts his hands in his pockets. Then takes one step closer. I try to breathe deeper so I can get oxygen to my brain, desperately needing it to work, but that just brings that manly piney scent that clings to his skin into my lungs.

"Why do you care, Rose?" he repeats, looking down at me.

"I just—I just think it's unfair, that's all."

"So you'd react the same way if this was happening to, say… Machado?"

I lift my chin. "Of course." And that's not entirely a lie. The current crop of Orlando Wild players is made out of pretty standup guys.

But it's true that I don't care about all of them the same way.

Logan's eyes roam around my face, looking for a hint of that truth. My mind screams at my legs to run, to take me away from the danger I've put myself in. They stay rooted on the asphalt, though. The traitors know the feeling of being wrapped around Logan—on his bike, that is—and would rather do that again than run.

Wordlessly, Logan lifts his hand and carefully, as if the

motion could hurt me, he slides a finger into one of my curls and tugs gently. And I feel it right down to my toes.

"You care about me," he whispers, returning his hand back to his pocket. "Why?"

The one-word question snaps me out of the haze.

Taking a deep breath like I'm breaking out through the surface of pool water, I retreat by one big step and tighten my arms around me. "Beats me because I clearly shouldn't," I admit bitterly.

"Right." His expression changes. A wrinkle appears between his eyebrows and he reels back a little. "It's best if you don't get tangled with a bad apple."

"That's not it," I snap, annoyed out of my mind. "I already told you, you're nothing like your relatives. But even then you're not right for me." He stays quiet and I'm not even sure he understands why, so I add, "I don't want a repeat of Ben Williams—a guy who just wants me for my body and doesn't care about the rest of me. And I *know* that you're not like him at all, but that's all I am to you anyway. You are attracted to me, I can tell from the way you look at me and you can't deny it—"

He cuts in. "I don't."

I suck in air through my teeth but continue, "But you yourself said that you just want my body, and that's not at all what I envision for myself anymore. So yeah, I care about you, but from that night on it's only going to be as a friend."

"Friend?" Logan laughs the word out and punctuates it with a scoff, and this is the most emotion he's shown in this conversation. "I can't ever be your friend, Rose."

"Why the hell not?" I complain.

"I want you too damn much for that. I would be a stinking liar if I even tried to treat you as a friend."

My mouth opens.

"Damn it," he mumbles, running his hands through his damp hair and pulling at it as he looks away.

"Don't..." My voice trembles and I breach the distance again. He braces himself, rightfully so, because I smack his chest. "Don't you dare freaking say that. You can only want all of me, Logan Kim. Not just a piece. And if you can't do that, then stop. Just stop!"

Logan makes a sound like I'm hurting him, even though we both know it's my hand what's smarting.

But then his hands are around my waist and he pulls me against him just like he did one week ago at the photoshoot. My purse strap slides off my shoulder and it clatters on the ground, but none of us move.

"I told you, you're the one who calls the shots but I..." he whispers, lowering his forehead to mine. He takes a deep breath that makes his nostrils flutter, and sighs. "I really need to kiss you right now before I lose my mind."

My hands close against his chest and pound softly. "Is that all you want from me? Just a kiss? After everything I just said?"

His voice comes out like gravel. "I don't deserve all of you, Rose."

The words echo in my head. Something lurks beneath them that makes me even more upset than before.

"But I deserve more," I say.

Logan freezes and I take advantage of that to push him away.

My whole body trembles with anger and with want, but somehow it still functions. I still breathe. I still manage to pick up my purse and glare at him, and even take a few steps away until my willpower falters.

I turn over my shoulder. Like that night after the pool party, he stands exactly where I left him, but now that he's not wearing his helmet the desire is openly on display on his face.

His dark eyes are like fire as they take me in, and they beckon me to return to his arms, to kiss him. To surrender.

I want him, too—more, even. I would take all of Logan Kim gladly. His crankiness, his silences, his smiles, his frowns, his hopes and fears. I want him mind, body, and soul. And the fact that he doesn't want me the same way is a gaping wound the size of a chasm between who I was before him and after.

If it hadn't been for my ex, I would run to Logan's arms right now and set myself up for an even bigger heartache.

My chin trembles and the vision of him distorts with oncoming tears.

Logan notices and his eyes widen, one of his hands reaching in the air toward me before he drops it.

That tiny gesture makes my resolve crumble a bit because deep down I know he cares about me, just not enough.

Wiping my face with the back of my hands, I decide to call one last shot. "If a single kiss is all I can get from you, then I'm going to take it for my own sake, and after that we'll go back to being strangers. Not friends. Not exes. Two people who have nothing to do with each other. Are you fine with that?"

Logan hesitates for a second, but then he tightens his jaws, his fists and every muscle. "Yes, that's fine."

"*Fine*," I spit out, a loaded word between us. Tossing my purse wherever it falls, I launch myself at Logan and crash into him.

He stumbles back against the impact but catches me as our lips collide. His arms come around me and one hand settles at the back of my neck, grabbing it possessively. I land with my chest pressed up against his, his thighs around my legs, my hands cradling his jaw not so gently, savoring the feel of his stubble against the palms of my hands.

There is nothing sweet about this kiss. The need for him that I had bottled up for weeks—months even—drives me to possess every inch of his mouth.

Logan isn't a subtle kind of guy either, and his lips press against mine, forcing my mouth open for his invasion. A raw moan tears from my throat once his tongue finds mine, gliding and molding so perfectly that it doesn't feel like we're kissing for the first time. I run my fingers through his hair and close my fist around the silky strands, pulling slightly like I saw him do earlier.

Logan growls—straight up makes a sound I've only heard from an animal.

His mouth closes until his lips are the only thing in contact with mine. "Damn it, Rose. I—"

I don't want to hear anything else, and I rise on my tiptoes to interrupt him by trapping his lower lip between my teeth. I scrape it softly and say, "I'm in charge, am I not? And I didn't say this kiss is over yet."

Because when I do, this thing between us will officially end.

Logan makes that desperate, guttural sound again and steals my mouth. I try to press closer and he does the same. I try to memorize the texture of his lips, of his tongue, the taste of his skin, the tension in his scalp, the way he curves his body over me, the scorching heat between us, the sound of our breathing and our lips sliding and sucking. I try to convey in a single violent kiss that I want him, that I love him—or that I could love him if he let me. That he's enough. That I'm not afraid of him. That we could do this everyday for the rest of our lives.

But I'm not going to beg him. I'm done with that.

Gasping, moaning, whining—all of the above—I tear myself away from Logan so forcefully that even his arms can't hold me anymore.

Slowly, I raise my eyes to his face. It's red, like I've never seen it before. And Logan is panting harder than after a full day of training, his wide chest rising and falling frenetically, hands still suspended in the air, his fingers curling slowly once he realizes it's over. We're done. This is it.

I only realize I'm crying when I bend down to grab my purse again and tears fall on the asphalt. The cards are on the table and I no longer give a frick if he sees how much I care—how much this hurts.

"Don't talk to me again unless you're ready for all of me," I say between gasping breaths.

And then I run to my car, sobbing like a damn princess in a cruel fairytale, and because Logan is a damn gentleman he doesn't follow.

# CHAPTER 38
# LOGAN

"Are you okay?"

I snap my mouth shut and stare at Cade Starr, the author of the question.

We're on the mound right before game one in the series against the Denver Riders, fronted by one asswipe called Ben Williams. I enjoyed defeating him in the opening games of the season so he would understand that the sole reason he even grew an inch as a baseball pitcher was because of me.

But now I have a more personal interest in squashing his ego, knowing all the damage he inflicted on Rose. And while she and I are… nothing, anymore, I don't want her to see Williams's victorious face on her screen.

I roll my shoulders and speak behind my glove. "Why do you ask?"

Starr also covers half his face with his glove, but I can see him cock an eyebrow. "You're so on edge I practically get paper cuts from just being too close."

I groan. "Starr, that brain of yours is made for pitching balls, not for putting together fancy sentences."

"I'll have you know it's also made to keep Hope safe and happy. Wait—" His eyes widen. "That's it, isn't it? You had a fight with Rose."

"I did not." It wasn't a fight. We made out and she still sent me packing after that. Not the same. "Besides, we're not really dating."

"What's stopping you?"

Sighing, I sweep my free arm around. "You really want to talk about this in front of fifty thousand people?"

The jerk takes an exaggerated look as if only noticing just now that we're in the middle of a pro ball stadium in downtown Orlando.

The Wild and the Riders are being dubbed as rivals by media, ever since the opening game of the season where we faced our former starting pitcher with our ex relief pitcher in his place. And that was even before we stole their star slugger, Miguel Machado, the league's MVP. Now that we're deep in the season and boast a wild—pun intended—record, we're actually selling more tickets than ever.

And this place is packed to the brim.

"Well if not now, when? After we lose the game because you're obviously off?"

I bark a harsh laugh. "When the hell did you become an expert about me?"

"Since I have to see your ugly mug up close every damn day, you prick."

"First of all, my mug is not ugly," I grouch, which only makes his eyes crinkle with a smile. "Second, if I was really as off as you say, Beau would've benched me."

"He can't see what I see." Starr shrugs.

"What do you think you see?" I ask in a mocking way.

"A guy who is screwing things up with a girl who is perfect for him."

That lands like a bucket of cold water and it feels like an entire age goes by without me being able to process a breath into my lungs.

Finally I shake my head. "How the hell is this supposed to walk me off the edge before the game?"

"Oh, so you admit it? Because that's the first step, trust me."

"I'm done entertaining this topic." I clear my throat but it's not enough to relieve the sandpaper like feeling. I'm so damn glad that the one who is mic'ed up tonight is Machado and not either of us. "The Riders have shaken up their roster pretty deep since we last faced them. You need to be careful with inside pitches when—"

"Logan," he says in a much too serious way, which momentarily derails my train of thought. We don't really do the whole first name basis thing even after the BBQ at his place. "I want you to know that I trust you even on your bad days, but I'm just worried about the dark circles under your eyes today. That's all."

Boos are starting to sound all around because we're taking long in starting the game. They don't even filter into my brain.

"If you do then—" I punctuate every following word by jabbing his chest with my finger. "Stop trying to get in my head."

"Aye, captain."

"Careful with the inside pitches, use your control."

"What else?"

"Stop looking at me with pity."

His eyes crinkle again. "I only accept briberies for pizza."

"Field properly. If you make an error I will personally dismember you."

"Much encouraging, very leadership," he says in mockery.

Sarcastically, I add, "And don't break a nail."

"Oof, don't jinx me, man." Starr shudders.

"Focus," I command.

"No, *you* focus."

"Ugh." I give up and turn around to head back home.

The umpire has some words for me for delaying the start but it's not like we're out of regulations, so I ignore him.

That sets a pretty shitty tone for the start of the game. The umpire makes a bad call that makes us walk the Riders's lead-off, and I'd have left it alone if it wasn't because the guy steals a base and we tag him, but instead of calling the out it's deemed as safe.

"Really?" I take off my mask and stare down at the umpire. He doesn't like it because he's a full head shorter.

His face reddens. "Don't give me lip, Kim. You don't want this going even worse for you."

Lip? He calls that lip?

Well, shit. Clearly this guy can't make a right call to save his life.

I grit my teeth and put my mask back on, crouching to resume play. But the second guy also gets on base, which helps the leadoff steal third. I'm not gonna let them score shit, though. I don't give a rat's furry behind that their third batter has a round point-three batting average and one of the highest RBIs in the Riders lineup. The best way I can get us out of this unnecessary pinch is to get this guy out quickly, and the only way I can do that is by letting him hit.

So I signal Starr for an outside curve that the batter can get easily bat toward the centerfield, where Machado will pick it off like it's child's play.

It works perfect. The ball makes a clanging sound as it hits the bat and it's ejected in a fancy trajectory that makes the crowd roar, but as predicted Machado catches it easily and throws to second. That's an out for the first base runner. Fernandez in second base gets with the program and launches the ball toward me like a cannon.

The beauty of my baseball brain is that I can see everything in slow motion. I see the exact point where the ball takes on an undesired inflection and I know I can't catch it with one foot on the home plate. Without removing my eyes from the ball, I can see the leadoff batter barreling toward me from third base. I have maybe a microsecond to catch the ball and stretch a limb—any limb—to tag the plate.

The ball hits my glove. I'm off to the left, in the way of the runner. I don't have enough time to turn *and* run. So I leap—like a damn gymnast. I fly in the air like I'm about to do a cartwheel.

And then a freight train T-bones me.

The flight isn't controlled anymore. Pain explodes on my ribs, but I haven't lost sight of the plate. I will land on that damn house shaped thing even if I break myself.

"Oof!" Air swishes out of my lungs as I crash on the packed dirt, with two hundred pounds extra on top of me. There's roaring in my ears and for a second I'm weirded out that this Riders asshole is screaming in my ear.

But then the noise starts making sense. The roaring isn't coming from the runner but from the crowd. It's wilder than anything I've ever heard in my career so far.

"Out!" the umpire calls.

"What?" The rage finally propels the runner to get off me.

And I can't move.

"Shit," I whisper.

Now there's a different kind of roaring. I blink hard, sweat trickling into my eyes and distorting the most bizarre view a catcher can see through the grill of his mask.

And that is of my pitcher, my infielders, and my outfielders running at the same time. Toward me.

And of even more players pouring into the diamond. From both sides.

The umpires start blowing their whistles, but that's as effective as trying to bat with a pencil when something like a hundred men are losing their shit on the field.

"Kim! Kim!" I recognize the voice. It's the head of our med team. Feet appear around my field of vision and people start crouching around me.

"Logan," Hope's voice cuts through the others. "Talk to us. What do you feel?"

"Winded," I say in a wheeze. "Ribs hurt."

"Can you move?"

"I haven't tried," I admit.

"Try now."

I grit my teeth against the pain. Now the worst spot isn't my ribs where the Rider's jerk drove himself into, but my right shoulder. I landed with my right arm extended over me, the ball inside my bare hand tagging the home plate. I almost smile with perverse satisfaction. Turns out I did kinda break myself but still succeeded.

Groaning, I push against my glove to lift myself up. Yeah, it hurts like freaking shit but I can move. My legs bend under me and I manage to sit up. I get a bit lightheaded from just that, but I don't say a peep. There's no way I'm getting subbed out in the first damn inning.

"Look into the light, Kim," the physician says and I comply for all of one second, until a different voice cuts in.

"What a show you're putting, Kim." I move the doctor's hand away so I can turn and look up at Williams. Somehow he has escaped the rioting mass of testosterone to come here, and he's looking down like he's on a high horse and this is his chance to step on me. "I assume you want a really good reward from Rose after this, huh? But—"

I warn, "Watch it—"

"What can I say?" He gives out a mocking laugh. "She's not the best I've ever had."

I try to launch myself at him but several hands stop me.

One of the Wild players close enough to hear breaks out of the mosh pit—Machado.

"Williams," he says with menace, pushing at his former teammate. "Shut the hell up before Kim pulps you."

"Is that so?" Williams slides a slimy smirk that I can't possibly believe ever interested Rose. "I just wanted to give Kim a heads up that my leftovers aren't that great, but I guess he's okay with settling."

*Nothing can stop me now.*

They try. Someone even rips my elbow pad off.

But the pain is gone and I'm all muscle—muscle and rage.

The roar comes from my chest—from my soul. I'm just aware of two things: one, that I drop everything in my hands and two, that I slam my right fist in Williams's nose, and it makes a sound like a ball hitting a bat right in the percussion point. Before the motion takes him too far, I ram my other fist in his gut.

"Kim!"

"Logan, stop!"

I'm about to throw myself at him when hands grab me. More hands. Too many for me to move. I try but there are chains around my stomach—not chains, arms. Tanned. With a little scar that I recognize. It's Rivera. Someone's screaming something in my ear. I shake my head, trying to make sense of it but the words don't filter through. My feet leave the ground for a second. There are bodies around me. Sweat drips down my face. I can't see very well. It's getting hard to breathe. I'm only aware of being dragged away. The pain is coming back and I can't fight Rivera off.

"Move it! Move it!" The words penetrate because whoever it is keeps repeating them over and over.

And so I move it. I manage to get my feet going. I can't breathe. The lights disappear from over me and darkness swallows me in. The tunnel—we're going to the clubhouse.

I keep going. I let them keep taking me. I gasp for air but I can't—I can't breathe. My hands try to grab at everything and anything all at once, but the air escapes me. Colors swim in my vision—voices in my ears. And between all that it finally clicks.

I'm having a panic attack.

# CHAPTER 39
## ROSE

The crowd roars. So much for baseball being a gentlemen's sport, huh? You'd think this is a hockey match instead.

My jaw drops and my heart races like a horse. I don't know what Ben did to provoke Logan—did he try to literally kick him while he was down?—but I'm sure he deserved it and yet… this is no bueno. So no freaking bueno.

"Stop it, you fool!" I scream with all my power, my voice breaking at the end. "You're gonna get suspended!"

But Miguel was the guy who took off after his ex teammate and thank goodness for him, he slides his arms under Ben's and prevents him from pouncing back at Logan. Except that Logan's trying to go for another blow, and Lucky has to bracket Logan's arms with his to keep him off.

"Yeah! Hit him again!" a man shouts from the crowd.

I—I agree. A weird laugh bubbles up my throat.

That was… amazing.

Seeing Logan punch Ben in the face is a dream come true. I pinch my cheek but yep, I feel pain so this is all real. My um, fake boyfriend just socked my real ex, who is now dripping red from his nose down his baby blue uniform.

I put a hand on my chest, feeling the wild thumping of my heart against it. "Logan Kim, what are you doing to me?" This freaking man is a threat to my sanity. It's not that I'm a fan of violence, but my delusional hormones found that so... so sexy. I shake my head hard, trying to think straight. "Violence is never good, Rose," I tell myself.

But damn it, I know in every fiber of my being that Logan would never resort to violence with anyone who doesn't deserve it. In fact, when Logan pushed his brother hard enough to make him fall on his ass, was after Lewis hurt *me*. So Ben must've done something to deserve this.

And it's the fact that Logan can dish it that has my knees weak. Like it has woken up all my cavewoman hormones.

He's being dragged away by several teammates but he's using his own legs, which means that even if the risky out hurt him, it's not a life or career threatening. I hope.

I stop recording from the stands and finally take off. My lungs work extra hard getting oxygen to my racing brain, which in turn tries to compete with my legs, as if the power of wishing to be next to Logan could get me there faster.

I sort through some fans trying to get a closer view of the biggest fight of the season so far, through security, through the maze of corridors for employees. I have to grab onto my camera so it stops bouncing against my stomach painfully. The corridor leading to the clubhouse is packed with staff—from operations, to some marketing colleagues, and even the GM.

"Excuse me," I whisper, squeezing my arms between people and trying to make way as gently as I can. "Sorry about that. Coming through. Careful with that arm—excuse me."

Shockingly, they do let me through. I make my way into the clubhouse and the scene there is not at all what I expect.

Rather than angry men still raring for a fight, there's an eerie silence around the whole team, coaching staff, and support. They all stand in an odd kind of circle around something.

I find the nearest player, Mike Brown, our third baseman. "Mike, what's happening?" I ask in as low a voice as I can muster.

He does a double take that ends with his eyebrows twisting in worry. "It's Kim. He collapsed."

The air leaves my lungs.

My limbs turn to ice and I can't move them.

"B-But I—I saw him w-walk, he—he—" My teeth chitter like I'm naked in sub zero temperature.

Mike presses his lips together and shakes his head.

I claw at his arm. "What the hell does that mean? So help me if—"

"No, no. I think he's going to be okay, it's just... I'm debating whether it's best if you don't see him."

"Take me to him. *Now*," I order through gritted teeth.

Finally, Mike nods and grabs my arm. He parts the crowd, towing me to the front before letting me go.

As he steps away, I can finally see what he was debating whether to hide or not.

Logan sits on the floor, his knees up and face buried between them. His arms are braced so tight around his legs that he's probably cutting off blood flow. His shoulders rise and fall too fast for his breathing to be any healthy.

"Slower, man," Miguel instructs, kneeling right next to Logan with a hand on his shoulder. "That's it. In through your nose, out through your mouth."

"Wh—What is happening?" my voice is a trembly squeak.

"Panic attack," Lucky responds, his face a solemn mask.

I gasp softly, my eyes returning to the hunched over figure of the larger-than-life man who leads this team, who is capable of jumping into action in the most unbelievable circumstances, who has saved my life, defended me, teased me, annoyed me, kissed me. The man who walks through life with his head held high every day.

And right now it's bowed to whatever monster Ben Williams unleashed in his mind.

"Logan," I sob his name. I crash on my knees before him, not really knowing what to do but doing something. I meet Miguel's eyes with my desperate ones. "What can I do?"

"Touch him. Talk to him. Whatever it takes to ground him," he says.

I slide to the opposite side, stretching my arm around Logan's back to rub circles on it, and bury my face in the space between his arm and face. "Logan," I whisper into his ear. "Come back to us, babe. Come back to me."

His breath hitches and I wait, but no other reaction comes. I set my other arm over his, holding his knees up, and start whispering nonsense about how good he smells, about my knees smarting, about the fact that he most likely broke Ben's nose, and that I must be a savage because I liked that. Miguel murmurs more encouragements for breathing deeper and it almost seems to be working.

Until suddenly, Logan starts tilting—toward me. His arms slacken and he melts against me. I brace myself as his weight threatens to topple me over, but then suddenly someone is behind me.

"I got you," Hope says in my ear, holding me from behind.

Logan fully collapses against me, unconscious. My heart beats like a rabbit as I try to shield him from all the attention, guiding his face against my neck. "Um, doctor?" I ask.

"We got him," the head of the medical team says at last. He takes Miguel's place and approaches with an oxygen mask.

I recognize that it means I'll have to let Logan go. Squeezing my arms around him one last time, I let the doctor and his team take him from me.

It takes four grown men to drag an unconscious Logan Kim on a stretcher. They pause to slide an oxygen mask around his head and I don't know—I don't know. It strikes me as too drastic.

I try to reason with myself. He's just fainted because of breathing irregularly. He's not dying. No one is really taking him away from me. He's not going anywhere. He's going to be fine. This isn't a big deal.

I drop my face in my hands, sobbing.

"It's okay, Rosie," Hope says, now rubbing my back. "It's nothing major."

"Isn't it?" I lift my face and spot Cade. He removes his cap to wipe the sweat off his forehead. "What kind of stress is he under that he collapsed like this?"

He shakes his head. "I don't know. I would've never imagined that *the* Logan Kim could pass out like this. It's surreal."

"Don't you dare badmouth him," I threaten through gritted teeth. "He's your teammate. He deserves your compassion, not your judgement."

Cade raises his hands. "I'm not judging. I'm just worried out of my damn mind about him, but I don't know what I can do."

Murmurs of agreement rise among the team. My shoulders droop a little.

"Come with me, Rose. I'll give you a drink with electrolytes." Hope tries to help me up.

"But, Logan—" I glance toward the hallway that leads to the gym and clinic.

"He's in great hands," a different voice says. Rob Beau, the manager for the team, crouches before me. "We're going to take good care of Logan no matter what, okay?"

"Okay," I parrot back, nodding even as my chin trembles.

I let Hope guide me to the trainers's office, and she sits me down on a chair to rummage through some cabinets. "Be right back, I'm gonna get you some ice for this drink."

Her words barely register, the adrenaline has left my body. I slouch back on the chair, my eyes lost among the restlessness I can see in the clubhouse through the door. There's noise now, the guys talking over each other. I can only make out a few random words like *what now*, *suspension*, *time out*. Someone's clapping and it gets the guys heading in the same direction—toward the tunnel.

Hope makes her way through them, hands busy with a half empty sports drink bottle and a reusable one on the other. "Here, this is sweet and will restore you right away." She hands me the reusable bottle.

I take it with trembling hands and look up at her. "You were there on the field. How the—How did this even happen?"

"I'm not sure myself." Hope's face pinches with the first sign of worry she's shown. "One second we're there checking for injuries, the next Ben Williams opened his mouth and made Logan lose his ever loving mind."

I almost choke on a sip. "Ben? What could he possibly say that…"

"It, um…" Hope wrings the sports drink bottle. "It was about you."

I slam my bottle on the desk beside me and jump to my feet, towering over my shorter friend. "What did that piece of crap say?"

She presses her lips and shakes her head. "I don't want to say it."

"I probably got it recorded," someone else says. We both turn to find Miguel poking through the threshold. He taps the black device on his chest. "I've been mic'ed up all night."

"Bless you." I side step around Hope, heading for the exit.

"Damn it, Machado," Hope whines. "You're just adding fuel to the fire."

"Hey, hurry up!" someone calls out from the distance.

"One second," Miguel says to the caller before returning to us. "Listen, the truth is that Kim is probably getting a suspension because he struck first, but I think that asshole Williams should get suspended for what he said too. So I know it's gonna suck hearing it, but someone needs to do something."

Hope and I exchange a glance.

"Wait," I mumble. "Do you have beef against Ben too?"

"Do I?" Miguel snorts. "He's one of the reasons I left my old team. I didn't want to keep dealing with his toxic ass."

A corner of my lips lifts. "You're officially on my good books, Miguel Machado." Cracking my knuckles, I set out to the broadcast team, who must have the recording that will bring about Ben Williams's downfall, and maybe that will help Logan.

# CHAPTER 40
## LOGAN

come to my senses with a jolt. Stabbing pain on my left flank immobilizes me and I swallow down a curse. Bright lights above me dance like they're mocking me.

"What the…" I murmur, trying to sit up.

"Welcome back, Kim."

Rather than trying to get up again, I just lay where I am and turn to the source of the voice. The head of the medical team is nearby along with McDonald and Socci, and a bunch of other staff members. I blink hard, trying to clear my vision but it doesn't work. The dancing lights aren't the ceiling fixtures, they're the beginning of a migraine. Good thing I'm in the clinic, huh?

"What happened?" I ask. That's when I notice that my voice is muffled by something. I paw around my face and feel the oxygen mask strapped around my head.

"You had a panic attack that made you pass out," dude says with all the chill in the world, like he didn't just voice my own worst nightmare.

"I—*what*?"

"Yeah, the guys took you off the field but we couldn't get

you under control in the clubhouse." He's scrolling through his iPad next to my bed, no doubt reviewing my chart. "I think we might have to change your medication and get you in therapy again."

That's—That all is fine, I don't care. It wouldn't be the first time I relapse. Something else is more pressing, though. Grunting, I brace my hands on the edges of the thin bed to lift my torso until I'm sitting. My side and my head pound just as strongly, but asynchronously. I peel off the oxygen mask and remove it, leveling a look at the doctor.

"Was I alone?" His eyebrows scrunch in confusion. I clear the grogginess off my throat and clarify, "When the panic attack happened. Was I by myself?"

"Ah." He nods like he now understands with that big brain of his. "No, the team was there."

"The team was…" I run a hand down my face.

"We have a really good crop of guys this year, to be honest. I'm really proud of the way they wanted to support you," Socci says, smiling from ear to ear.

McDonald nods. "Machado surprised me, actually. I wasn't expecting him to take control of the situation the way he did."

"Sure made my job easy," the doctor says with a chuckle. "I really thought for a second that the social media girl was gonna get you through it, but I guess it had already been too long with irregular breathing. How are you feeling now?"

"Rose?" My eyes go as wide as they possibly can. "She was there too?"

"Oh yeah. Wouldn't let you go. We practically had to pry you off her to bring you here."

"I thought the whole thing between you two was for show?" Socci's eyebrows rise.

"I don't think it is." McDonald smirks at him.

Slowly, because my side is absolutely killing me, I bring my hands up so I can bury my face in them.

Maybe it shouldn't matter to me if she saw me at my weakest. I've already taken myself out of the race. This might also be a blessing in disguise—she'll finally understand that warning her off came from an honest place. This will make her move on and forget that I exist.

"Glad you're awake," a newcomer says. Beau's entrance into the clinic filters in some of the noise in the clubhouse and I can clearly hear someone asking "how's Kim?"

"Wait, the game is still on? I have to—" I swing my legs over the bed to get up.

"Nuh uh. You're not going anywhere." The doctor stops me with a hand on my shoulder—my bare shoulder. I look down at myself and find that I'm shirtless and there's a massive ice pack strapped around my torso, directly over the area that hurts the most on my side.

"I'm placing you in the injured list," Beau says, and if the revelations of the past few minutes weren't already absolutely shitty, this is worse. "I don't know which list yet, we needed you to wake up so we can run some tests."

"I can't go on the injured list. What about the series? What if this throws the whole season?"

Beau doesn't mock the obvious dislike in my voice over this decision. He also doesn't shoot me down as he could, because who the hell am I to question the manager? Instead, he says something even more lethal.

"This team isn't as weak as to crumble without you."

"But…" I splutter and a new ache squeezes my chest hard enough that I almost double over. My mind races with colliding thoughts, setting off sparks that threaten to burn down my flimsy sense of worth. "But I thought you needed me on the team."

"Oh, I do. *We* do." He motions around. "The team knows that losing you is a big blow, so they're playing even harder. I think this will force them to evolve even faster, and by the time you return to the roster we might be unstoppable."

Behind Beau, the other men glance at each other like they can't quite comprehend what he's talking about.

I do. He and I are the same type of people who can manipulate situations, even accounting for the variable behaviors of people.

The difference between us is that—first, the obvious fact that he's a sixty something Black man with a wife and kids around my age. And second, that he's genuinely at ease with himself. There are no edges or shadows to Rob Beau. He's a steady, dependable rock. Of the diamond kind.

He's everything I wish I was, and the respect I have for him is why I finally suck it the hell up. If Beau says this, then it is what it is.

I slump a little. "Is the game over?"

"No, bottom of the fifth. We're leading by two."

I was out that long? My eyes widen slightly, but more light aggravates my head and I wince.

"We'll leave you to rest for a bit while we get the X-ray machine ready," the doctor says.

Beau pats my shoulder before signaling to the other coaches to follow him, and everyone clears the holding room so they can go do their jobs.

Alone, I stare at the floor for a while.

"Damn it." The façade I carefully maintained for years finally crumbled. Now everybody knows that I'm an impostor and that I'm actually a walking shitshow. I try not to wince as I lean on my bad side so I can lay back down, and throw my arm over my face to block out the light.

The door opens again. Sighing, I drop my arm. "Already coming to take me for X-rays?" A caveman grunt comes out of me as I pull myself back to sitting.

"No," a feminine voice responds.

I lift my face. My eyes grow wide. "Rose?"

She leans against the closed door, her hands behind her but watching me like a hawk. Her attention stays glued on the ice pack. "How are you feeling?"

Subhuman. Worse than garbage.

Actually, like a garbage truck ran me over and left me in the middle of the road. And that's just on the inside—in the throbbing in my chest.

"I've been better," I respond in a low voice, trying for diplomacy. I let my eyes fall to her sneakers and stay there.

"Yeah, I imagine it can't feel too good being rammed by a runner at full speed."

I run my right hand through my hair. "Did you see the whole thing or only the part where I freaked the hell out and humiliated myself in front of the entire team?"

With a huff, she picks herself up and stomps over. I lean back as if that could add any real distance between us, but Rose stops a step away from me. Or maybe less. If I close my legs I could trap her between them.

"I need you to listen to me carefully," she says with a not so veiled threat underneath. "What happened—that episode you suffered—it did not diminish the opinion anyone on the team has of you, do you hear me? If anything, the guys seem to be divided between worrying about you and guilt."

"Guilt?" My forehead scrunches up, upper lip rising in the ultimate *huh?* expression.

"Yeah, like Cade for example. He seems to think that he could've prevented it somehow. That he failed you."

"What the hell?" I snort. "He did not—he doesn't even know—"

"Exactly," she cuts me off sharply. "He had no idea what you've been going through all by yourself. I sure as hell don't either, right? You made sure of that."

I snap my mouth closed tight.

She's not done, though. "You purposely put your real self behind closed doors—scratch that, inside a damn vault. And if you don't let us in, how can we possibly help you?"

"I don't need—"

Rose grabs my face in her hands, smooshing my cheeks until it's hard to form words. "You do need help, Logan. You need us. And we want to be there for you, but you have to let us in." The last part she says through gritted teeth.

I shake my head slightly, trying to free myself but she doesn't let off. I grab her wrists and try to tug gently. But she still won't let go.

I don't know what that means. I don't know if it's a metaphor of some sort, of how she refuses to drop me. I can't stand the damn hope itself making my heart gallop violently in my sore ribcage.

At least she eases enough that I can talk again. "It's better off this way. You don't want to get… contaminated by my mess."

"Contaminated?" Rosalina scoffs and rolls her eyes so big, it's a wonder she doesn't get dizzy. "You seem to think I deserve to be put on a pedestal or something, when you know probably better than anyone here just how messy I really am. Why's that, Logan?"

"Why's what?" I swallow hard.

"Why did you punch my ex?" Rose waits but I can't speak. Or more like I don't trust myself to speak. Her hands slide away from my face, going over my ears until her fingers find my hair. Her fingers close around strands of hair at my nape, holding me in place. "What did he do to deserve that?"

I can't imagine that she'd be defending Ben Williams in any circumstance. It makes me suspect that she knows and is fishing for confirmation. Fessing up would be like flying too close to the sun, though.

"He was mocking Starr."

"Liar. He said I'm not the best he's ever had and to enjoy his leftovers, didn't he?"

"How the hell do you know that?"

"Miguel was mic'ed up." Her lips curl in as menacing a smile as someone as beautiful and sweet as her could possibly get. "I went up to the broadcasting room and it turned out the whole damn team heard that. So now everyone knows I was with Ben and that apparently I'm a bad lay."

Volcanic heat rises up my belly and to my chest. I try to get up. "I'll murder that son of a—"

"And there it is again." She lowers her forehead to mine, pulling at my hair just a tad and keeping me prisoner on this hospital bed. "How come you care so much about me that you're willing to fight for my honor all old school, but you can't say it to my face?"

And there it is.

The last ruse is finally up.

I grit my teeth hard and squeeze the edge of the mattress with my hands. "You know why."

"No, I truly don't. It's why I'm asking you, and I deserve to know why."

I close my eyes, not being able to stand the prying intensity in her eyes anymore.

"You know why," I repeat, growling. "You deserve the world, Rose. You deserve safety and love and stability, and I can't provide any of those. I can't be the man you deserve. I'm too broken and all you see is fake—I'm barely holding it together. I'm medicated. I'm deathly terrified of turning into my father or my mother or my brother. I don't know how to be a good person, I didn't have a single good example to learn from growing up. I—"

I gasp, my words stopping because my lungs are struggling for air again.

And then Rose tilts my head back, forcing me to open my eyes to see her and not the shadows in my head.

"You are a good person, Logan. You're not perfect, but you know that and you work on it." Those words slam me harder than the Riders's runner. "You didn't send me packing when I asked you for help with my job. You open doors, protect me from strangers and from exes, and even from your own relatives. You make sure I get home safe and you feed me." She breaks off for an incredulous laugh and shakes her head down at me. "All you've done is prove over and over that you're a good man—the right man. For me. I wish you could just see it the way *I* see it and stop getting in the way between us.

"We could be great, Logan," she whispers, her nose lightly nuzzling mine. "We could love each other. But you have to let it happen."

I choke on nothing, and then her hands ease off and she pulls away.

Rose gives me a solemn look. "I'll be waiting for you, Logan." And with that, she calmly walks out of the clinic without a backward glance.

If she had, she would've seen the devastation in my face because what she just said—all of it? It has destroyed every notion of who I am. Who I was before her.

# CHAPTER 41
# ROSE

pace like a caged lioness who wants to fight for her lion. If said lion was a delusional man who can't seem to understand that his place is next to her.

But at least I've now done everything I could, or almost. I'm in the operations area with my boss, his boss, the whole broadcasting team, PR, and the head manager. The game is finally over—which we won, *ha!*—and we can all finally leave our posts behind to gather together.

"In theory, it doesn't matter if we try to clear Logan's name or not," says the head of operations, showing how out of touch with reality he is. "He's going to be in the injured list and can serve his suspension during that timeframe."

"It's about the principle," I spit back through gritted teeth. "Logan was provoked, so the incident wouldn't have happened otherwise. And also—" My voice grows harder than flint. "Are we going to dismiss the slander that jerk threw my way just because I'm not a player?"

"Of course not," Tom, my boss's boss, responds right away. "There are rules about sportsmanship conduct and this falls squarely into that."

I throw my hands in the air. "Thank you."

"Also," he smiles at me in amusement, and then turns his focus on the head of operations. "What kind of spineless cowards would we look like if we don't do anything? All of marketing's hard work will go down the drain."

Murmurs arise around the meeting room but the one who snuffs them is Beau, the team manager. "Tactically speaking, we need to force a suspension on Ben Williams for our own benefit. The Riders would be out of superstars, giving us a series win."

To my surprise, Audrey speaks then, "And depending on how long the suspension is, it may affect their season and make them slide down in the rankings even further."

"Correct." Beau bobs his head. "So I agree with Miss Mena here. We must submit the recording to the league and request an immediate suspension for unsportsmanlike conduct."

"Would you be okay with that?" Dave asks me, turning all the attention our way. "Because one thing is everybody here present knowing what Williams said. You know we have your back. But once we submit the evidence to the league, everyone and their mom will find out."

"Who cares?" I shrug, twisting my lip. "Everybody already knows that I date players. No one can talk even more crap about me than they already have. I don't care, as long as this clears Logan and the team from culpability."

"What a team player," Julien Chen, director of broadcasting, says with a nod my way.

I press my lips tight. This guy's recognition is all I've ever dreamed of, and I had no idea I'd get it in such weird terms.

But no one's treating me like a floozy. In fact, it seems like they read Ben's words as a big fat lie to provoke Logan, and it worked on him but not on them. Like maybe they respect me too well to read into it.

And it's not like Logan doesn't respect me and believed the horrid things that came out of Ben's mouth. Instead, he was outraged on my behalf.

Like I am right now, after the cable from the league came with a fat fine and suspension for Logan.

He tried to defend me and now I'm doing the same. Because we're in love with each other, damn it. Why can't he realize it?

"Very well." The head of operations relaxes in his chair. "Do I have everyone's approval here to make this claim to the league?"

I lift my chin and am the first to answer. "Yes."

"Aye," Audrey says, representing PR since her boss is on vacation.

"Please," Beau says, and one by one the rest of the department heads agree and the meeting is adjourned.

I sidle up with Audrey, waiting for the meeting room to clear out and whisper toward her, "I need a roommates meeting at home. With booze."

"You got it." She reaches for her phone in her back pocket and taps at it at the speed of light. "Hope's already on the way home. I just gave her a heads up to get us prepped."

*

And prep she did. By the time Audrey and I walk into our shared townhouse, Hope has set up a margarita pitcher on the coffee table with an assortment of snacks that aren't precisely healthy for one in the morning. It's exactly what I need.

"Be right back, I'm going to get comfortable," I say to them, seeing that Hope is already in her baggiest, rattiest T-shirt and shorts. Audrey and I join her sans makeup, manes in messy buns, and equally unflattering attires.

Hope greets us with full cups and well into a bag of snacks

from Trader Joe's. "Cheers—to men being hopeless buffoons," she says, lifting her cup.

"Cheers!" I exclaim with the same feigned enthusiasm I had to adopt on stage in beauty pageants. Taking a hearty sip, I join her on the corner of my couch and Audrey takes her armchair. "I'm starting to question why I even bother with them." I reach for a bag of dried cheese bites.

"I would tell you to be like me and swear off men, but I think you're already too invested in a certain catcher." Audrey looks at me over the rim of her cup.

I slouch back. "It's like I didn't learn my lesson after Ben-cheater-Williams. Why am I like this?"

"Logan and Trash Williams can't possibly be compared," Hope says while chewing at the same time, her hand buried in the snack bag.

Audrey giggles. "Trash Williams, I like that."

"You're right. Logan is a trillion times better." That makes my annoyance return full force, though. "But there's a big, big problem with him."

"What's that?"

"He can't seem to realize it," I all but bark before stuffing my mouth with crunchy cheese bites and chewing violently. "I know that we started out under a ruse—"

"By the way," Hope cuts in. "I still can't believe you didn't tell me."

"I'm sorry." My shoulders slump—my *soul* slumps. "Only a few departments knew and we wanted it to look organic and—ugh. That's no excuse, you're my friend and I lied to you. I'm so sorry."

"It's okay—"

"No, it's not okay. You've been an amazing friend and I'll—"

"You haven't stopped being an amazing friend yourself so I—"

"—Do whatever I can to regain your trust so—"

"You don't have to—"

"Just hug it out so we can get back on topic," Audrey chimes in, impatient.

It's not a bad idea, though. I set my margarita down and throw myself at Hope. She pats my back awkwardly because even though she's warmer than Audrey, I wouldn't necessarily say that Hope is touchy-feely in general.

"There, there. I forgive you." She chuckles over my head. "You were saying?"

Grunting, I release her and return to my corner. I bend my legs and tuck them inside my oversized T-shirt. "As I was saying, I have very real feelings for Logan, and I'm pretty sure they're mutual."

"No shit."

"Yeah, that right hook kinda confirmed it."

"The problem is…" They both lean toward me. "He has put me on some pedestal and fully believes that he's not worthy."

"What?" Hope frowns.

In contrast, Audrey leans back. "Oh, that's good. Nothing better than a man who knows his place."

"Audrey!" Hope admonishes her before turning to me. "But that makes no sense. The Logan I know—"

I interrupt. "According to him, the Logan we've known has been a fake."

That makes Hope close her mouth for a moment. "Based on the events tonight, we clearly don't know him enough. But he's a pretty good guy—I mean, I still can't get over how he maneuvered Cade and I together because he knew we were right for each other, even if that made him look like the villain for a hot second."

"That was pretty silly but noble of him, I concur," Audrey says.

"Exactly." I snap my fingers. "Logan is silly and noble, and self-sacrificing and protective and all of the things I've ever dreamed of—*and more*, to be honest. But I can't force him to see that, and I don't know how to love someone who doesn't love himself."

"Love?" Audrey's eyes bulge. "You're in love with him?"

I reach for my cup and down the rest of the contents in one go. Sighing, I admit, "So help me, but I am. I'm in love with the fool."

"Oof." Hope pours me another cup. "Then, what are you going to do?"

"I told him I'm going to wait for him to snap out of it."

Audrey tilts her blonde head. "What if he takes ten years?"

"Hopefully he doesn't. Now that I've found him, I'd rather not spend a long time waiting on my own." I give out an awkward laugh and drink some more.

"I give him a week," Hope says drily.

"Three days tops," challenges Audrey.

"Hundred bucks?"

"You're on."

I sigh, ignoring the betting going on. "Am I doing the right thing?"

"Yes," Hope says unequivocally. "You're going after what you want with no reservations. No matter what happens, you won't have any regrets."

Audrey shrugs. "If he makes you happy then yes. Don't pass him up."

"Thank you, girls," I whisper, cradling my cup of margarita tenderly.

Hope presses her toes against my side. "We're here for you."

"Couldn't we be there for you from our respective beds?" Audrey asks casually.

"No, we're drowning all my sorrows together."

"All right." She tosses back the rest of her drink. "Guess we'll Uber to work tomorrow, then." And we spend the rest of the night complaining about shortsighted men.

# CHAPTER 42
# LOGAN

As if tonight couldn't get more bizarre, I find myself eating pizza from Cade Starr's favorite place in the parking lot of the ballpark. We sit on the walkway, two extra large boxes with extra meaty pies between us. We even went off the rails and got sodas to wash down the grease.

And by we I mean Cade Starr, Lucky Rivera, and Miguel Machado. What a weird combo.

Chewing through a giant, cheesy bite, I ask the latter, "Don't you have a kid at home to get to?"

The newest member of the team swallows his mouthful to respond, "The nanny already put her in bed. She's not missing me right now."

"Ah." I guess well cared for kids would go to bed early. I wouldn't know. My parents didn't give a shit about what I did when we weren't in public.

"You're right," Rivera says to Starr, observing his own slice carefully. "This really is superior pizza. There's just something about it."

"I'm thinking of investing in the place so that it never closes," says the cowboy, which strikes me as something very *him*, for some reason.

Since when am I familiar enough with anyone that I can even think that way?

Actually, since when am I close enough to anyone that they'd stay around me when I feel like absolute garbage? And even feed me?

"What are you all doing here?" I ask at last, even though we've been sitting here for like half an hour.

They waited for me to get my tests done, and even had the food waiting beside my bike—which by the way, I won't be able to ride for a while, so Rivera offered to take me home.

It turns out I have bruised ribs, a strained shoulder, and a mild concussion. The combination wouldn't make me a safe bike rider for myself or anyone else.

I also got a suspension and fine, the cherry on top.

Turning the baby blues on me, Starr says, "We told you, we wanted to know what the verdict was."

My eyebrows come together. "And I already told you, so why are you still wasting your time here instead of going home?"

"Because the pizza won't eat itself," Rivera says, taking another bite.

"And also because we didn't think you should be alone," Machado finishes off.

That raises my hackles and I drop my half-eaten slice on the box. "What? Do you think I'd harm myself or something? You don't know me, you—"

"Of course I don't," he says with surprising calm, considering I was just about to snap his neck. "And that's not what I meant. I just thought it'd be really shitty to leave you alone after the really shitty night you've had."

"Very eloquently put, brother," Rivera says, but pronouncing the last word the Boricua way—*brodel*.

"I have to say…" Starr brushes the flour off his hands before reaching for his plastic cup filled with soda. "Your face gave me a weird feeling that something was gonna go south tonight, but I didn't think it would go so epically south, you know?"

"Since when do you know my face so well?" I ask in a deadpan.

He stops the cup halfway and gives me an incredulous look. "Dude, I'm your other half. I see your freaking mug everyday. You have like one smile and seven different types of frowns, and tonight your expression was neither of them."

"I thought Kim's other half was Rose?" Machado teases.

The cowboy looks at him. "Other *platonic* half, I meant."

I sigh. It sincerely hadn't occurred to me that just as I've been analyzing Starr's every move and mood, he might've been doing the same. Or that I've been more transparent than I thought.

"I hate this," I admit quietly.

"Hate what?" Rivera prods.

"I hate that everybody knows I don't have my shit together."

"Bah." Rivera waves his pizza, sending a slice of pepperoni flying in the air. "None of us do. We just pretend in different ways."

"Yep," Starr confirms.

"Uh huh." Machado nods.

"Wait." Starr smacks the slugger on his chest with the back of his greasy hand. "You're a dad. Don't all parents have their shit together?"

"Hell no. What makes you think so?" Machado snorts. "Because bing a single dad isn't for the faint of heart."

"I wouldn't know. I grew up in an orphanage." Starr shrugs.

Machado's jaw drops. "Oh, damn. I'm sorry."

"I also can confirm that not all parents have their shit together," I say, for only the second time in my life volunteering this information. "In fact, mine completely screwed me over. It's why I get the panic attacks and all that shit."

"Wait, what happened?" Starr frowns.

Meanwhile, Machado holds his hands up. "Listen, dude. You don't have to share if you don't—"

"Screw that. If you don't talk to us right now I'm running you over with your own bike," Rivera says, kicking my legs that are extended beside his.

I make a deliberate pause to take a fortifying swig of soda. "I guess I could say this in many different ways but the gist of it is that my family is abusive and neglectful." I set my cup down and reach for what's left of my pizza slice.

"Did you just casually drop a bomb like that?" one of them asks.

"Yeah…" I trail off and take another bite.

"Well, shit. I didn't see that one coming," Starr admits.

"I did." We turn to Rivera. "That shit your brother pulled last week clued me in. That was some psycho behavior."

"He's never got officially diagnosed, but my old therapist believed that Lewis is a sociopath, actually." What do you know? It feels freaking great to get that off my chest. It's like I've been protecting Lewis all these years by keeping it quiet, instead of talking. And that spurs me on to add, "And both of my parents are narcissists—and not of the kind that just like their own reflection in the mirror. The manipulative kind."

"So the great TJ Kim is evil?" Machado asks to clarify.

"Yup."

Starr watches me closely. "Do I understand correctly that the whole thing with your brother messed you up and you didn't say a word about it to anyone, and then Williams came in and basically poked a sleeping bear?"

I don't respond.

"You ass, you could've trusted us."

I grunt. "I'm not used to trusting. My biggest nightmare was me not being able to hold it together in front of other people, and that just happened tonight. That's the only reason I'm even saying shit—that and I'm drunk on gluten and sugar."

"So now that your worst nightmare already happened and you didn't die, are you going to start trusting us at last?" Rivera narrows his eyes at me when I don't answer right away. "Don't make me punch you in your pretty face, you little shit."

"It's not that easy." The words come out of my throat loaded with irritation. "It's not a switch I can turn on and off as I please. I don't even know if I have one, and that's the big issue because…"

"Rose?" Machado asks sharply.

I groan. "Shit. Don't tell me you're another clever fox I have to watch out for."

"Oh, thanks. No one's called me clever before." He smirks. "In fact, my own kid thinks I'm dull as a rock."

"Wait, I don't consider myself clueless, but how does this relate to Rose?" the Boricua asks.

Machado clears his throat. "I might've overheard them a little at the clinic."

"You are on borrowed time, Machado," I say through gritted teeth. That's about as much mojo as I'm able to put into the threat at this point.

"It wasn't much, something about how you don't seem to understand that you're enough for her." He raises a leg and rests his arm on it before tipping his chin at me. "So is it actually because of your trust issues?"

"I trust her." I growl.

"Then what's the hold up, man?"

"Why in the freaking hell would I want to put her through this?" I motion toward my head, which they now know is a royal mess. "She could have any guy in the world. A doctor. A teacher—I don't know, someone who isn't a powder keg. Why would she settle for me?"

"Because she wants to, period." We all turn to Starr. "As your resident guy who is going steady with a woman who teaches him something new every day"—Here he interrupts himself to chuckle dryly—"I can confirm that women make their own decisions regardless of your opinion, and the sooner you adapt to that, the happier you'll be."

"Checks out." Rivera nods.

"Yeah, that's true." Machado rubs his jaw. "Ask me how I know."

I reel back. "You're saying that I should go along with Rose even if I'd be a terrible addition to her life?"

"But she chose you for a reason, you gigantic, steaming pile of turds." Starr opens his eyes wide. "Ever stopped to think with that busy brain of yours that maybe her decision isn't flawed?"

"But—"

He raises his paw. "Shut up for a second and hear me out. We now know that the princess made a bad call in dating Williams." We all give various forms of acknowledgment to that. "Now tell me, are you like Williams?"

"Hell freaking no."

"Which already means you're an improvement."

I give him a deadpanned look. "Wow, rousing endorsement there."

"Next question," Starr continues, ignoring my jab. "Has she openly manifested her interest in you?"

"Yes, but—"

"I'm not done." He leans toward me. "Are you aware of how cool she is?"

"Cool?" I frown. "She's more than cool. She's the golden hour bathing you with warmth and light and—"

"That's good," Rivera stretches the word. "You're waxing poetic already."

That makes me shut my mouth.

"Do you think she's smart?" the cowboy continues grilling me.

I respond through gritted teeth. "She's freaking brilliant."

"So, isn't she capable of making her own decisions?"

"Of course she is." I drop my head to expel an exasperated sigh. My hair falls forward and I use my one clean hand to brush it back. "I just don't want to hurt her."

"Well then, just don't."

I stare. "Easy to say for anyone who doesn't have a toxic waste of a family or an unstable mind."

"Your mind isn't unstable," Machado chimes in, derailing my train of thought. "It just has different coping mechanisms, and they're going to work better once you stop ignoring them."

"How the hell do you know about this stuff?" I bark.

"Yeah. How did you even know how to walk him through the panic attack?" Rivera asks too.

Machado shrugs. "It's from reading so many parenting books."

"Are you parenting me right now?" I scrunch up my face.

"Anyway, I have one more question." We refocus on the Texan. He's done eating and leans back against the concrete as he stares at me. "Do you want Rose or not?"

I tighten my jaw and swallow hard. "With every fiber of my being."

"Then stop being afraid of happiness and go for her."

"I don't know how," I admit reluctantly, tired of having this dialogue with myself and at last exteriorizing it. "I don't know how to show up for her or be good to her."

Rivera interjects with "but do you want to?"

I give a jerky nod.

"How about you tell her all of this…" Machado glances

from one of us to the other. "In a letter? Like I get that it'd be hard to say this for someone who seems more used to expressing himself in grunts and hand signals—"

Rivera laughs. "You got him to a T."

"But maybe it's easier if you take your time to think it through and put it on paper," Machado finishes.

"Damn, now that's an idea." Starr gives Machado the finger guns. "Women love a grand gesture."

"We can help you." Rivera pats his chest. "I've been known to write a romantic poem or two in my youth."

"Your youth?" His best bud barks a laugh that echoes in the quiet of the night. "What are you now, a grandpa?"

"Fine," I say, and their amusement dies down. "I'll write a letter." I chug at the rest of my soda and sigh like it's a beer instead. I take a deep, painful breath and add, "And I hate to admit it, but I'll need help to not sound like a tool."

"Let's do this." Rivera reaches for the lid to close the box nearest to him.

"Right now?" Machado blinks.

"Damn straight. Love waits for no sleep," declares the king of the stooges.

After some logistics and a short but uncomfortable commute, I find myself on a different floor—this time my living room, surrounded by my teammates as we brainstorm on the best way I can convey my feelings for Rosalina Mena. Old school.

# CHAPTER 43
## ROSE

"Nngh." The incoherent cavewoman sound comes from my throat, cheek smooshed over my purple keyboard at the office. The air conditioning feels extra cold so I'm hunched over, arms around my torso trying to preserve body heat.

Or I'm just hungover and unrested. Maybe staying all night drinking and snacking and talking crap about men wasn't my brightest idea.

Hope and Audrey felt equally garbage-y this morning and we grabbed an Uber together, but I don't know how they're going to peel me off this desk to get me home again at the end of the day. Or how I'm going to muster the energy to be remotely productive until then. I wonder if it's too late to call in sick, but that would require moving as well and I am so not looking forward to that.

"Rosalina, do you have the—whoa." My boss stops just outside my cubicle and stares at me like I have transformed into a trashcan raccoon. "What the heck happened to you?"

"Men," is all I respond.

"Ah." He puts his hands in his pockets. "All men or a specific one?"

"A bit of all, a lot of one."

"My sympathies. I still need the transcript from the behind the scenes interview yesterday after the game, sorry." He's trying hard not to grin, the jerk.

Groaning, I use all my willpower to tear myself away from my makeshift pillow. No doubt I have key marks on my cheek. "You'll have it between one and ten million business days."

"Great, thanks." He palms the threshold of my cubicle and keeps it moving to go talk with someone else.

My only decent idea of the day so far has been pouring myself a gigantic mug of coffee. I cradle the monstrosity in my hands and breathe in the steam. I know that some of the emptiness I feel is due to the hangover and the lack of sleep, but most of it is the Logan Kim-sized hole in my chest. And dude is massive. It's shocking how he was able to worm his way to my heart even without trying, and that doesn't speak well about me. So much for steering clear of men, and particularly of baseball players.

"Bah." I take a sip of coffee and frown at my screen. Somehow, I'll have to find a way to move past this again. Except there's a massive difference.

When Ben Williams cheated on me, I swore off men who appear to be nice guys but are actually slimy.

If Logan doesn't give us a chance, that's it for me. I'm staying single and heartbroken the rest of my life, because there's no getting better than him. And the heartbreak wouldn't be for me, but for him not realizing his own worth.

"I'm so d-damn c-cold here," I mutter, my teeth clattering but it's not because of the cold, it's because my eyes are raining again.

Okay, maybe I'm a bit heartbroken for myself too.

"Rose?"

Quickly, I wipe my face with the back of my cardigan sleeves and swivel on the chair to face Hope. It's not just her, though. Audrey's also there. I only take a second to admire the deep dark circles under both of their eyes that match mine, until I realize that this gathering is weird.

Frowning, I ask, "What are y'all doing here together?"

They glance at each other. Audrey nods at Hope, and the latter puffs her chest and stands up straighter. "We have something for you."

"Tell me it's more caffeine or something greasy."

"Um, this can't be eaten," Hope says with a tiny Mona Lisa smile. "Or I guess it could be, but it would probably upset your stomach and it wouldn't taste very good. Besides, it might offend whoever is sending it and—"

Audrey nudges her with an arm none too gently. "Stop babbling and just give it to her."

"Okay, okay." Hope reaches for the back pocket of her joggers, taking out whatever the mysterious item is, and offers it to me.

I stare at it. My brain is slow this morning and all I can discern for a hot second is that this thing is white and rectangular. But then I see some scribble at the top and something about it snags my attention. Squinting, I make out purple ink first. And then my name.

*To Rosalina Mena.*

Full name even. No nickname. And the handwriting…

"Hold on." Saying those two words sends my pulse to uncharted territory. Where I was inert a moment ago, I'm now jittery as I open my drawer and rummage through the mess, until I find what I'm looking for.

A card, also in the purple ink I recognize from one of my gel pens. I open it and look at the handwriting—small, incredibly neat and even, and thick. Bold, like he is about everything but himself.

Which means this envelop comes from Logan.

Gasping, I swipe it from Hope's hand as if she was about to take backsies, and hug it to my chest to prevent her from doing so.

She starts chuckling. "Sheesh, it's all yours, woman."

"Besides, it's a federal crime to tamper with other people's mail," Audrey says dryly, even though that only applies to official correspondence in one's mailbox. "Well, aren't you gonna open it?"

"Right now?" I ask, breathless.

"Yeah, we're dying with curiosity."

"Okay. I will. One second." I take a deep breath, my mind racing through the million possibilities printed on this note.

A cease and desist? A bill for all the emotional hardship I put him through? An invitation to screw off? Or… or…

My hands tremble when I turn over the envelop and open it. I extract a folded up piece of paper, my eyes widening the more of it is revealed. The paper is creamy in color and to the texture, except for watercolor-like borders in my favorite color. And it has a delicate scent, probably because there is a whole stalk of real lavender taped to it.

My roomies and I gasp, and they tumble into my tiny cubicle to take a closer look too.

"Wow," Hope whispers.

"That's unexpected." Audrey blinks fast.

"Guys." I look up at them, feeling hot tears trickle down my cold face. "I can't stop shaking. What if I tear the paper?"

"Can we help?" Hope asks and I nod. She's careful and a lot calmer as she takes the note from me and unfolds it, and the sheet is a lot longer than a normal letter sized one. The flower is stuck to the back of the paper, where there's no writing, and she turns it over so that the writing faces out to me. She pins the top corners against her belly. "How's this?"

"Perfect," I respond with a shaky voice.

Audrey smiles at our roomie. "You're the real MVP right now."

Hope bows her head. "Thank you, far too kind." She tips her chin at me. "Now read and tell us what it says."

I nod and wipe at my eyes again, because the blurriness makes it impossible to focus. But then I do.

*Dear Rose,*

*You've probably noticed but I'm not that great with words, especially not the important ones. And you have the curious power of making my tongue turn to lead more often than you realize.*

*So I… I asked for help. I've spent all night writing this letter with the help of my teammates, but I assure you all the words are mine. They just plied them with tweezers out of my brain. So… here we go.*

*I find it interesting that we all call you by the name of a flower you don't seem to care about that much, at least if I go by the fact that you smell like lavender. I've never told you this but after I packed up the trinkets you left in my apartment to fool my parents, I started buying the same hand soap you use. I told myself that it was better quality than mine, when really I just wanted to feel your scent on my skin even if you weren't around. Maybe that should've clued me in a little—or at least creeped me out, to be honest—but I admit I may not be as smart as I pride myself to be.*

*Do you know what the meaning of lavender is? There's serenity, grace, calmness, but my favorite one is devotion. That one stuck to me because I could easily see myself being devoted to you. Just you. I can see us living under the same roof, making bulgogi stuffed arepas, fighting over the remote and giving up in favor of reading books and cuddling instead. I can see us driving to work together, your arms around my waist, my heart racing because you're with me, riding along life together. And when I close my eyes I just see you, your smile, your bright eyes, those curls that make me unable to look anywhere else.*

*I don't see the broken glass, the tears or the lies, the cruel laughter or the scars. I don't see any of the things that have trapped me in a small box of my own making. I don't see the pain I viscerally hate but can't get rid of.*

*I just see love. I see you.*

*I don't know what version of myself is there next to you. I doubt it's the current me, the Logan Kim that is still broken and afraid. That's not who I want you to be with, you deserve so much more—and not because I'm putting you on a pedestal. If I work on myself, if I get better, then maybe I could have a right to be with you. But you seem to want me as I am, and I also can't deny you anything you want. That I definitely don't have a right for, as you've taught me time and again.*

*Remember when I told you that you call the shots? I'm used to being the one who makes the calls, but not this time. You decide where you want to take us yesterday, today, and tomorrow. So if you still want me—if you can give me another opportunity, even after I made such an error that I should be sent back to the pee wees—then write me back. Please.*

*I'll be the one waiting for you now.*

*Love,*

*Logan*

An ugly sob tears from my throat. I try to stuff it with my hands against my mouth, but it's too late. I'm pretty sure everyone in the office heard it, going by how quiet it is all of a sudden.

"What is it? Is it something bad?" Hope asks.

"Give that to me." Audrey extends her hand out and since I'm a goner, Hope passes the letter along. The blonde is a lot faster taking in the words than I was, and the worry eases off her face. "Oh."

"Gimme." Hope opens and closes her hand until Audrey passes along the letter. The process repeats again and Hope lifts his eyes to mine when she's done. "Are you going to respond?"

The lump in my throat doesn't let me speak, and I nod frantically.

"Okay, paper." Hope looks around my cubicle, spotting the million purple pens on the mug, along with my assorted junk. But no paper. "Shit, why did he have to do this in such an old fashioned way? Doesn't he know we live on the digital era now?"

"I'll get some paper from the copier," Audrey says and slides through the small threshold out of the cubicle.

Hope folds her arms, smiling from ear to ear. "What are you going to reply?"

"I don't know." My chin trembles. "But I really need some tissues."

"On it." As she leaves for that new errand, Audrey returns with a whole stack of paper.

"Where did Hope go?" she asks.

"Tissues."

"Ah, yes." After a pause she also asks, "What are you going to write?"

I sniffle through a smile. "Words."

"Hmph."

Chuckling, I reach for my favorite pen and take the top sheet on the stack. I hunch over as I write my response, not letting them see. When I'm done, I fold it over until it's a small square and I tuck it in the back of my jean pocket.

"Wait, we wanted to see." Audrey's expression turns grumpy.

I bite my lips. "I want him to be the first to see it. I'll tell you later, okay?"

"Fine."

"So you'll deliver it yourself?" Hope asks as she hands over a wad of tissues from the restroom.

"Yes, where is he? Home? I need to get an Uber, I need to —" I blow my nose into a tissue and use two more to dry my face. Maybe I should stop to wash it, but I don't want to waste a single second. "Where is he?"

Hope answers, "He's here, he—"

"But he's hurt! He's supposed to be resting," I whisper-yell.

"Don't worry, he just came by to the clinic." Hope steps out of the cubicle, pulling at Audrey to clear the way for me.

I take a deep breath and go. They follow me, clearing our path every time someone wants to stop for a chat, fully understanding that I'm a woman on a mission.

And that the mission is getting her man.

Adrenaline courses through my veins as we make our way into the clubhouse. Instead of finding it empty like I expected, the whole freaking team is clustered here and in the way between me and my man.

"Attention," I bark like I'm a drill sergeant, and it serves to freak out the nearest guys. I clear my throat and speak again even louder. "Make way right now."

"Yes, before she barrels through you," Hope adds from behind me in an equally booming noise. Meanwhile, Audrey snickers.

Josh Thomason, one of the relief pitchers, is the first one to deliberately move out of the way, and one by one the other guys fall in line until there's almost a clear path to the clinic.

Except that there's someone who is in the way and not moving. It's Logan—he was the eye of the hurricane and the rest of the team was just congregated around him.

His eyes widen slightly at my approach. I keep my head high, my shoulders back and my step way firmer than I actually feel. Inside, I'm a roost of butterflies threatening to spill all around the clubhouse.

I stop close enough that if I stretch out a hand I could touch him, and I can see the muscle ticking in his jaw, the heavy swallow that makes his Adam's apple bob, and the dark shadows around his eyes. Like maybe he also didn't sleep a wink last night.

Without saying a word, I reach into my back pocket and

produce my response. His eyes zero in on it right away. His arm muscles tighten like he's preventing himself from reaching for it.

So I offer it to him. And I point at it with my lips for good measure.

Slowly, maybe because of the pain in his ribs, he takes the note and unfolds it. Unlike his very carefully redacted letter, mine is messy, quick, and ridiculous. It's a final test to see if he's willing to put the work, because saying it is not enough, and I won't settle for empty promises ever again. Actions are what matter.

Lifting his eyes to mine, he folds the paper again and hides it in his pocket. Then he's in motion, walking around me toward the door.

My heart thumps painfully. Maybe I took it too far. He's a proud man after all.

But Logan stops at his locker and pulls it open. He braces against it with one arm, searching in the space with his free hand. I know what he's looking for. He re-gifted it to me in a fit of annoyance that sent my pulse skyrocketing, and I returned it to his locker via a certain prankster.

"Ha!" Logan's little victory travels to my ears in the intense silence in the clubhouse, and I'm aware of the eyes watching the show.

I grab my hands tight as I follow along as well. Logan sits down carefully, holding a small bundle in one hand, his face pinching a little as he tries to bend forward.

"Wait," I exclaim, immediately getting his attention. "You're hurt and I didn't really think it through. That's enough—I get the point."

"No." Logan narrows his eyes and cocks an eyebrow. "The instructions are clear. I must do this."

I run a hand down my face. "Logan, I was kind of kidding."

A corner of his lips lifts. "And kind of not, so just hold tight."

"What's happening?" one of the guys whispers far too loudly.

"I don't know, but I guess we're about to find out," someone else responds.

And find out we do—at a snail pace. Logan toes off his sneakers and steels his expression to lift one foot over the opposite knee, removing his sock before unfurling the bundle in his hand.

Lucky gasps. "No way."

I suck both of my lips in because I want to scream, cry, and laugh—especially the latter.

Logan stretches the extremely long sock—mostly white, except at the top where there's a tiny alligator leg painted on it. The grand reveal sets off a wave of chuckles and murmurs while Logan works the sock up, pushing up his pant leg to his knee so the full practical joke is revealed, and then he starts the process with the other sock.

I cover my mouth but I'm sure it's clear that I'm about to explode with joy. Logan works painstakingly with the other sock until he's fully decked, and he stands up in his full tiny-gator-legged glory to face me.

"Well?" He places his hands on his hips.

I let out a gurgling laughter and take off, slowing down at the last minute so I don't crash against him. Instead, I wrap him in a gentle embrace, resting my cheek against his heart that's beating wildly.

And then his arms come around me and the place erupts in deafening cheering.

I cringe a little at the explosive noise, but Logan buries his face in my hair and molds himself around me, and I forget the rest.

"Is that a yes?" he murmurs in my ear.

I rub my face against his chest while I lift it. Our noses brush and I grin. "It's a hell freaking yes, babe."

"Babe?" His right hand comes up to make a screen for the side of my face that the crowd can see, and his lips touch mine if only to speak softly. "I could get used to that."

Impatient, I stand on my tiptoes and kiss him, finally—*finally*—making the great Logan Kim mine.

And the response letter that did it?

> *Dear Logan,*
>
> *You know I've been burned by guys who speak a pretty game. So show me, please. Show me that you'll do what it takes for yourself and for us.*
>
> *Wear the socks that Lucky gave you for a whole day, and then I'll know your fears aren't bigger than us.*
>
> *Waiting to be yours,*
> *Rose who smells like lavender*

I grin into his lips.

# CHAPTER 44
# LOGAN

"Rose?"

Her name spills from my mouth the second I wake up.

My chest rises and falls rapidly and I'm covered in sweat, the bed sheets tangled around me uncomfortably. I feel around my bed until I find my phone tucked under a pillow. With groggy eyes, I light it up to find that the call got disconnected, but it's logged.

We spent hours on the phone last night and at some point must've fallen asleep. That's what's real—not the nightmare that woke me up bathed in cold sweat, where my past and my present got tangled, but instead Rose was the victim.

I rub my face with my hands. I'm never going to let that happen. I'll do whatever it takes to keep Rose safe, even what I never dared to do before. It's not like I had much to lose before, but there was nothing worth doing it for—certainly not myself. I was just waiting until I found what I've been searching for all along.

Belonging. I belong here in the Orlando Wild, and with Rosalina Mena. I don't belong to my parents or my brother, no matter how much our blood links us. I can't subject Rose to them, and so they need to be cut out of my life.

"Like pruning flowers," I murmur with a smirk, looking at my blue bell and rose tattoos running down my arms.

This was the answer all along, and I think I knew it. I just wasn't brave enough—didn't have a reason to be.

My therapist will be both proud and horrified that it took me this long to figure it out.

Groaning, I pull myself up on the power of my left arm alone. My right shoulder is still angry, but not more than my ribs. Gnarly bruises spot my left side but my stomach is clear. I run my hand across my abs, wondering if this is a good spot to tattoo some lavender bunches on me now.

It takes considerably more effort than usual to get out of bed and hop in the shower, but I manage. I take my sweet time grooming my beard to perfection because I want to see Rose today, even if it's on FaceTime only. She's at work and I am… not, what with being put on strict rest for at least a week.

"Shit, I haven't even asked her out on a date." I frown in the mirror. Sure, we've gone out several times, but there was always that cautiousness wedged in between. What would it be like to just be us? No pretense, no deadlines, only honesty between us?

I better find out ASAP.

Picking up my phone, I find her contact at the top of my text messages and ask if she has lunch plans. She responds right away.

MY ROSE

Shouldn't you be resting?

ME

I can rest better while looking at your face

MY ROSE

Oh

Okay

I like that

My face stretches into a grin. The worst part of it is that I mean it—it wasn't just an empty line to flirt with her. Between being cooped up in my apartment with internet, a TV with cutting edge sound system, and a million books, I'd rather be with her. There's no need to pretend like that's not the case any longer.

After much protesting on her side, instead of buying lunch for us and coming to my place, we agree that I'll go to the facilities. What eased her is that I have a couple of team meetings to attend, even if I'm on the injured list, so it's not like I'm going out of my way just to see her.

Let's face it, though, that's exactly what I'm doing. I'm actually not mandated to attend the team meetings in person for a week.

I hop on my Maserati and don't even put the top down. I only remember that I could've done that when I'm already parking at the ballpark, like the fact that my mind now feels fully free means that I don't have to compensate for that by driving in the open wind. I doubt that my claustrophobia is fully cured, but I sure as hell feel different.

My watch says that I'm way too early to whisk Rose away for lunch, but I figure I can at least drop by her cubicle for a little make out session. At the entrance I veer left into the admin offices, where I normally veer right toward the team area. The closer I get, the more my pulse climbs in anticipation, but when I get to the marketing area, the place is deserted and I stop at the entrance cursing my timing.

"She's in the big meeting room with everyone else."

I glance over my shoulder. Audrey Winters stands a few paces away, a stack of manila folders in her arms. I won't even ask her how she knows who I'm looking for because at this point there is a giant, neon sign hanging over my head that says *I'm wild over Rosalina Mena.*

Instead, I motion at her folders. "Need help?"

"I'm good, but thanks for offering." For some reason, she starts smirking. "I can see why Rose chose you."

"Sorry?"

"You're a good one, Logan. I trust that you'll stay good to her?" She tilts her head, a challenge clear in her expression. I get the feeling that she's capable of inflicting great harm on anyone who hurts her friends.

"Always," I respond, solemn and with my whole damn chest.

"Good." She nods at me, and continues going. I watch her retreat, long blonde hair swinging behind her. Where Hope is straightforward and headstrong, and Rose is clever and sweet, this one is confusing. She reminds me of the me before Rose.

Or maybe I'm just so damn in love that I'm starting to see funny things that I didn't notice before.

Shrugging my good shoulder, I change direction to the big meeting room and thanks to the fact that all the walls around the admin area are made of glass, I spot Rose easily. It's the curls—I've started to be able to pick her out in a crowd of thousands at a packed ballpark.

I hide my grin behind my hand as I lean against the wall outside in the corridor. But Rose also notices my presence and it stops her mid sentence. That stupor leads to other heads turning my way.

I raise my hand for a wave.

Rose pushes her chair back and scrambles around the large meeting table. With everyone watching, she opens the door and pokes her head out. Her voice sounds breathless when she speaks, "Logan! You're early."

"I wanted to see you."

"But…" She glances back.

"I can keep just seeing you from over here. Or I could go if that bothers you." I resist the urge to cringe, realizing only now how annoying I must be coming across.

"No, it's just—" She bites her lip.

"Oh, for goodness's sake. Let him in," says Dave Rogers, Rose's boss. "It's not everyday that we can get a player's input while we brainstorm."

A moment later, I find myself sitting next to Rose and watching her in her element. I offer a couple of thoughts about whether the guys on the team would or wouldn't like some potential sponsorship products, but for the most part I spend an hour witnessing Rose kick serious ass.

I can tell that the team respects her because even managers several rungs above her listen intently when she speaks, and how could they not? She's freaking brilliant, hardworking, confident, and so damn beautiful it hurts to look at her directly. Yet I can't stop. Even if she burns my retinas, I won't.

"What?" she whispers at me once we're walking out of the meeting room together, her smaller hand in mine, her other one holding onto my arm.

I lean toward her. "I'm just in awe of you."

Her eyes widen, cheeks growing hot like I've just performed a magic trick.

Some of her coworkers snicker as they glance back at us, but they leave us alone in the corridor and no one gives us any further crap. I shift my hold on her, bringing my arm around her waist to pull her against me.

She runs her hands over my chest, awakening my skin. "Why?" She asks, placing her chin at the top of my sternum.

"Just you." I look at her button nose and finally do what

I've always wanted to—I give it a tiny peck. "Your very existence is a miracle to me."

"I could say the same." Her lips smile and her eyes light up. "You're who I've always been waiting for, Logan."

I kiss her.

Rose melts against me with a feminine sigh that makes my blood roar. I grab onto the back of her neck, barely grazing her curls so I don't damage them, and this way I can tilt her head so she can offer me her mouth fully. And I savor it slowly, like we have all the time in the world. Like no one's watching, even though we're very much in public.

I slide my free hand down her back, reaching the top of her curves and keep going. Her perfect butt cheek fits in my hand like it was made for it, and I palm it with gusto, squeezing.

"Logan," Rose gasps.

"Do you not like that?" I nibble at her trembling bottom lip with my teeth and the tip of my tongue.

"I more than like it," she chuckles all throaty. "I'm just afraid that if we keep going someone's going to call HR on us."

"Screw HR," I mutter, traveling my lips down her throat to where her scent is stronger.

Her hands fist around the fabric of my T-shirt as I find the spot where her pulse throbs harder, and I kiss it like it's her mouth. With mine open, with tongue—so I can really brand the taste of her skin in my brain forever. A guttural moan tears out of her throat and my hand presses her even closer against me, not releasing her butt for a second.

"Damn, I really wanted to do this last night."

"Oh yeah?"

"To start with," I tease.

I feel her turn her face slightly, her breath fanning over my ear. She whispers, "And I wanted to do this." Then she lightly bites the shell of my ear, and it sends such a powerful shock down my body that I freeze. She takes advantage of it to free her arms from between us, running her hands down my chest, my belly. I wait, my heart pounding against her chest as her hands find the waistband of my jeans, but rather than traveling lower, she lifts my T-shirt and touches my stomach. "And this."

"You're an abs girl?" I ask, panting like the dog I am.

"I'm a your skin girl."

"Ah. Touch away."

"I have to get back to work, though." But even if that's true, she sure cops a good feel under my T-shirt.

Smirking, I lean back so I can look in her eyes again. "Do you now?"

"Uh huh." She nods all serious, her hands now grabbing my pecs almost possessively.

"Hmm…" I pretend to think. "What if I join you and sit on your chair and you work from my lap?"

"Extremely tempting, but surely too compromising for the office."

"And this isn't?" I look down at my T-shirt, lifted up to my chest that she's still feeling around.

"You're right." She sighs. "I'll unhand you when you release my butt."

"Your first."

"No, you first." Her lips twitch.

We end up releasing each other at about the same time, but I can't fully cut off contact quite yet, so I offer my hand. And she grabs it tight.

After that, we resume our leisure pace through the corridors, as if our blood wasn't drumming at the pace of each other's hearts.

"What do you have to do now?" I ask.

"Edit some videos of the guys. You?"

"Crash the team meeting."

She turns to me. "Crash it? I thought you had to attend."

"It was an excuse so I could come fondle your ass."

Rose blows a raspberry, but after a second she says, "Dang it, I should've fondled yours too."

That makes me bark a laugh. It sounds rusty, like it was chained in the depths of my chest for decades.

And maybe it was, I haven't felt joy like this ever before.

After a shorter kiss, but no less scorching, we finally part ways until lunch. I watch her head over to her office in her little cardigan and the light purple leggings she once wore to give a quick makeover to my apartment, and I promise to myself that one day I'll map the exact dimensions of her body with my hands.

Rose stops and turns back, finding me still rooted in the same spot while I check her out. It brings a smile to her face and she blows me a kiss delicately. I'm a catcher, though, so I pretend to catch it like it's a fastball and put it in my pocket for later. Chuckling, she finally disappears around the corner.

My mouth trembles with another smile that threatens to spill. It takes the whole walk down to the team area to school my features into something resembling professionalism.

By this time, the team is either about to finish the morning workout, or already in the auditorium for Beau's highlights and lowlights of yesterday's game. Since today is the last game in the series with the Riders, and after more careful review the whole shitshow of two days ago caused their leadoff batter *and* starting pitcher to get suspended—ha!—I assume it's going to be a spicy one.

I come in through the back door and find literally every single guy with their hands up like this is kindergarten and they were just asked what's two plus two.

"Huh?" I mutter to myself.

A few heads swivel to me and someone says, "Oh, shit."

More people turn and Beau stops right in the middle of

whatever he's saying. That's when I see the massive screen behind him projecting some words. It takes me a hot second to process them, but they say:

*Raise your hand if you want to make Logan Kim the franchise's first official captain.*

My jaw drops.

A chair scrapes against the floor and one of the players sitting around the middle stands up. It turns out to be Lucky Rivera. He waves a hand, motioning at me to step out. "Can you just go out and pretend like you didn't see this?"

Beside him, Cade Starr starts lowering his hand and says, "Damn it, there goes the surprise."

The first one to start laughing is Miguel Machado and it's an infectious laugh, the kind that belongs to a sitcom or something and sends the whole room into a fit.

Meanwhile, I manage to snap my mouth shut and with a nod, I walk right back out. But there's no stopping it anymore, I grin like a whole ass clown.

# CHAPTER 45
## ROSE

"Of all the things we could've done on our first date, this is what you really wanted?"

"Yup." I grin radiantly at Logan and snuggle carefully into his left side. It was best that I sat here so that he could put his arm around me—like he has it right now—without aggravating his strained shoulder, but also so that I can protect his bruised side from anyone accidentally bumping into it.

He's trying to school his expression but keeps failing. His eyebrows twitch with the desire to furrow, yet his lips want to smile. It's interesting to see that I can cause so many emotions on someone, but especially on this particular guy.

"So just to clarify," he says in his deep voice, only for me, while his hand casually feels the contour of my shoulder under the sleeve of the Orlando Wild jersey with his name and number. "We could've gone to any of the amusement parks, or a Michelin starred restaurant, or the beach, or even another city altogether—and what you *really* wanted was to watch a Wild baseball game with me?"

"That's correcto, mi amor." I reach over with a kernel of popcorn and bring it to his mouth.

Logan's eyes narrow but he opens his mouth and I drop the popcorn in it. Except that the sneaky man captures my finger.

"Logan…"

"Hmm?"

He's not biting hard at all, just enough to keep my finger prisoner. But then he closes his lips around it and I feel his tongue lick at the salt on the pad of my finger.

I gasp and glance around. "Oh my word, what if someone's watching?"

He grabs my whole hand and brings it against his lips, placing an otherwise sweet kiss on the palm. "Let them."

"What if we get on the kiss cam?" I ask, pretending to be grumpy about the idea.

"Then we give them a show."

I shake my head and return to eating my popcorn. "Looking forward to it."

His body vibrates with a silent chuckle.

A few fans turn to look at us none too discreetly and I can't blame them. It must be bizarre to see Logan on this side of the park instead of on the diamond, making the mastermind calls he's famous for. But it's been a week since he got bulldozed and everyone knows he's only coming back to play in a month at the earliest. With a low key injury like his, he'd normally be watching the home games from the dugout or even the broadcasting area, but I hijacked him instead for our first official girlfriend and boyfriend date.

Yeah, we decided to not screw around and just put labels on it already. It's not like this is our literal first date.

"So, how does it feel like to be watching the game from here?" I ask him, munching on popcorn with little elegance.

He sticks his hand in the bucket and grabs a handful.

Before biting into it, he says, "Weird. Like I assume this is how it'll feel like whenever I'm retired."

"Have you thought about what you'll do when that time comes?" I pick up the gigantic cup of soda we bought for the two of us and offer it to him.

His eyes stay on the play as he sips from the drink. Miguel is stepping up to the plate for his at bat, and the whole place is electric with the collective knowledge that something amazing is about to happen.

While Logan isn't buzzing, he's attentive, his mind clearly calculating outcomes and possibilities. I almost think he might've forgotten my question until he speaks. "I'll join the coaching staff and climb my way up to manager one day."

"I can see that. That big brain of yours can't possibly go to waste."

"What about you?" He tears his eyes away a second before Miguel's bat connects and the ball flies like an explosive cannon. The crowd goes absolutely feral, people jumping to their feet all around us. And yet Logan doesn't care about that, he saw what he needed to see and his attention is now fully on me.

What a weirdo. And maybe I'm one too, because his antics make my tummy flutter.

"What about me?"

"Didn't we fake date for the sake of a promotion? What happened to that?"

My feel-good hormones wane and I slump. "Turns out that wasn't a done deal. I'll still have to apply when Steve Boateng retires."

"I'm pretty sure it's a done deal." He jerks his thumb at the fans that keep peeping at us. "Those people aren't just looking at me. You're the face of the team now as well, you know?"

"But—"

"No buts." He grabs my chin, turning my face toward him. "Also, the kiss cam is on us."

"What?" I nearly upturn the bucket with my surprise.

Freeing myself from the gentle hold on my chin, I swivel my face side to side like a fan until I spot the camera trained right on us, and our faces perfectly squared on the gigantic screen next to the scores.

"Logan Kim." I turn back to him. "Did you do this?"

"I did not," he assures me calmly. "However, I did mention to Lucky in passing that this is where we were gonna have our date. So I suspect that this is his latest prank."

"Lucky?" I raise my eyebrows.

"What can I say, they're starting to grow on me." He shrugs a little. "Are you gonna kiss me, woman?"

"What terrible hardship you inflict upon me," I say dramatically before leading him toward my lips, my hand on his jaw.

The cheering booms all around us again. Logan shifts so that he's facing me better and does the same trick as last week, hiding our connected mouths with his hand. But it must be pretty clear that this isn't a simple peck in the lips going by how he works his jaw to devour my mouth.

He's capable of soft and tender kisses—especially on my nose, he seems to like it a lot—but it's like he's trying to mark his territory in front of fifty thousand people, plus everyone else on TV. I hope my mom's not watching the game right now or she'd be a little alarmed at how frantically I'm trying to do the same.

I need everyone to know that this thing between Logan and I is the real deal, and not just because there have been rumors going around on social media that it isn't—*thanks, Lewis*—but because I don't plan to give him up for anything or anyone in this world.

Something like a moan echoes in his chest when he finally

pulls away, and I'm glad it's too loud for anyone outside of our cocoon to hear it, or for them to catch the way our lips smack once they separate.

"Rose. Rose." He squeezes his eyes tight and repeats my name one more time. "You drive me wild."

Dazed from that kiss, I mumble, "Does it help if I tell you that you do the same to me?"

"It does not." His eyes darken. "I want to treat you right, like a gentleman. But I'm not having very chivalrous thoughts right now."

"You're injured." I swallow hard, knowing exactly what he means.

"A damn bummer, at that."

"And are you okay with me calling that shot?" I ask, leaning back on his shoulder.

"Always." He drops a pretty chaste kiss on my lips that still manages to give me goosebumps.

Still staring at his swollen lips, I say, "Even if I'm not ready for it any time soon?"

"Rose." He reaches for my legs, sliding his hand behind my knees and lifting them until my legs swing over his powerful thigh, and I sit facing him. "I want you—all of you—as you decide to reveal yourself to me. I'm not going to force you to do anything you don't want, and I'm not going anywhere."

I turn the bucket of popcorn in my hands over my lap, worrying my lips. "And if what I want is marriage?"

I know it's too soon to even bring up the M word, but if the past year has taught me something, it's that I'm sick and tired of lying and of hiding what I really want.

Going for broke, I say, "Because it might not seem like it, but what I really want is that old school house with a white picket fence and a dog, and dancing in the kitchen until our kids get embarrassed by us."

Logan studies my face for what feels like the longest time, enough that I start to sweat.

But then he says, "You know, I'm actually not against that."

"Really?" I startle. "Even though your upbringing was… well…"

"Shitty?" Logan nods. "Yeah, that's why. I also want a family—a real one."

"Okay." I bite my lip but a smile is still poking through. "Good to know we're on the same page."

"What size is your ring finger?"

I bark a laugh. "Too soon, man!"

"When should I ask? In a year?" He turns back to watch the game but apparently is still pondering the topic. "Which type of gold do you like best? I assume you'll want a purple stone."

"Stop." I'm still giggling up a storm when I smack his knee, connecting with the bare skin beyond his shorts. Logan grabs my hand and keeps it there, lacing his fingers between mine.

The memory of us doing this for the first time hits me, but it was in the back of Cade's pickup and done as an experiment.

Now it's real, and I have no doubt that my hand will be in his for a long, long time. Maybe one day with a purple rock on it.

# CHAPTER 46
# LOGAN

"So, I've noticed something."

"Hmm?" I turn to Rose, since we're stopped at the world's longest red light just at the entrance of New Smyrna, where Rose's mother lives.

Our hands are linked but she has my arm extended almost over her, and with her free hand she traces the lines of my rose tattoos. She already has the full story of what my tats mean to me—though she has no idea that a Rosalina Mena tattoo is in development—but this is the first time she actively tries to map them. It raises goosebumps all over my skin and I do nothing about it. It's not like she doesn't know I have the hots for her.

"First, you usually drive a motorbike. Second, you drive with the top off. Is it a pattern or am I reading too much into it?"

I tense as her finger leaves the ink to trace a vein on the inside of my arm. Now we're moving toward electric shock territory, rather than just measly goosebumps.

"I love driving with the top off." I pointedly look at her—more specifically, at her chest proudly on display in a bikini top themed with the American flag. We're on our way to spend July 4<sup>th</sup> at the beach with her mom, and there's nothing more American than driving a convertible and wearing only bathing suits to celebrate this great nation. Yee and haw.

Especially because she's freaking gorgeous. All that brown skin gleaming under the sun, those curves, that softness and—

She cuts off my very dangerous train of thought but makes it worse, because she cocks an eyebrow and looks at my stomach. "Trust me, I'm really enjoying it too."

Ah, yes. I'm also shirtless.

I run my left hand over my abs and she bites her lip.

The only reason why neither of us lose our minds right here and now is because the light turns green. Sighing, I focus back on the road.

Rose clears her throat. "Anyway, that's not what I mean and you know it."

She lowers my arm to her lap, gifting me a scorching brush against her bare abdomen, and it takes me a hot second to find my wits again. I'm pretty sure I'm only able to sober up because she's asking about something kinda gnarly about my life, and I'm not going to hold it from her. I'm a full open book now.

"There's a reason," I start, allowing my brain some time to find the best way to explain this. I turn us into a street with old houses surrounded by palm trees. "When I was a kid, I used to hide in closets so I could escape the drama between my parents or from Lewis and his games. Until one day he discovered what I was up to and locked me up for a whole weekend."

She gasps.

"So, I'm claustrophobic." I shrug, stopping at yet another red light and facing her again. "I panic in small spaces or when I'm surrounded by a lot of people. Enclosed vehicles feel like closets to me, I can't stand them for long."

"Wait." Something clicks in her brain. "Does ginger ale make it better?"

I startle a little, but it shouldn't surprise me that she made that connection. "Fizzy drinks force my throat to open up when I'm in the very beginnings of an attack. Strong menthol candies work too."

"Making a mental note to always carry some Halls with me," she says, hugging my arm against her like it's a precious stuffed toy.

"You know how else you could help me in those cases?"

"How?" she asks right away.

"By sticking your tongue down my throat."

"Logan!"

I chuckle and the line of cars starts moving, so I set us in motion again. The GPS says that we're just two minutes from the building where her mom lives, two blocks away from the beach.

"Are you sure we shouldn't bring something?" I inquire to change the topic.

"Babe, no. My mom is going to have a whole feast ready. We'll go back to Orlando weighing fifty pounds more each."

"But not even a present?"

"Nah, she's pretty chill. What you need to brace yourself for is the inquisition."

We're rolling down the street so I can only glimpse at her for a second. "The what?"

Rose offers me a sneaky smile and refuses to say anything further on the topic. I'm still trying to pry some hints when we pull into the gated parking lot and retrieve our beach bags, and even as I follow her on the way to the beach. She cleverly ignores me by calling her mom on the phone to tell her we have arrived and are looking for her.

There's no need, though. I spot the hair right away. Turns out Rose gets her incredible curls from her mother.

"Mija!" The woman drops a pair of tongs on a little table by a grill, which is the center of a whole array of stuff—beach chairs, a massive umbrella, towels, floaters, two coolers.

Just how did she haul all this by herself?

I hang back as the two women take off and meet in a tight embrace that threatens with toppling them over. Where Rose is only in a bikini top and short jean shorts—emphasis on *short*—her mom is in some sort of flowy tunic, but also in 'Murica motif.

They kiss each other's cheeks with loud smacks. Mrs. Mena holds her daughter's face to inspect her, fixes up her daughter's hair, and declares, "Mija, you're too skinny. I'm glad I get to feed you."

My lips twitch. What she doesn't know is that I've been feeding Rose for about a month now, and she's very well nourished. The owners of our fave Korean restaurant and the Venezuelan food truck would agree.

"I brought another mouth to feed," Rose declares, stepping aside to motion at me. "Mom, meet my boyfriend, Logan Kim. Logan, meet my mom, Diana Mena."

I drop our bags in the sand and wipe my hand with my trunks before offering it to her. "Very happy to meet you, Mrs. Mena."

She glances at my hand and doesn't take it. Instead, she does a thorough scan from my hair—longer than most guys keep it—to the tattoos, and all the way down to my toes buried in the hot sand. When it's clear that she's not going to shake my hand, I lower it to my side.

Mrs. Mena turns to her daughter and blinks fast. "You just told me you got a good boyfriend, not that you won the lottery."

Rose barks a laugh.

Now grinning, Mrs. Mena approaches me and I raise my hand again. But she keeps going and instead gives me a hug.

It's one of those that force me to bend forward, and she even pats my back.

"Just call me Diana," she says, pulling away and holding me at arm's length. "And you also need some more food. I can see your ribs, boy!"

"Those aren't ribs, Ma. Those are muscles."

"Well, muscles also need food, right?" The woman chuckles. "Tell me, is there anything you don't eat?"

I answer right away, "No sugar or alcohol because I'm still in the middle of the season. Everything else is game."

"Got it. Sit tight, the hot dogs are almost done."

Rose motions at me to join her and she guides us under the umbrella. "Shouldn't we help?" I whisper.

"Trust me, feeding us is her love language. Best we let her enjoy it." Rose winks at me and pops her shorts button open.

I lose track of the conversation altogether, just watching avidly as she slides them down her thighs. As far as bikini bottoms go, this one is tame—high waisted and covering everything—but just the contour of her body gets my heart pumping.

I don't think salivating over her daughter in front of her would be the best introduction to Diana, so I force myself to just sit beside Rose and stare at her mother.

"So, Logan…" Diana says clearly over the noise from the families around us, the crashing waves, or the birds flying overhead.

"Here we go," Rose mumbles in my ear, again grabbing my arm and hugging it against her chest. No complaints from me.

"Yes?" I prompt her mom.

"I hear that you come from a baseball dynasty. Is that so?"

"I—Yes, I guess that's one way to put it."

"What do you plan to do after baseball?"

"Also baseball, but in the coaching staff," I say.

She looks over her shoulder. "Does that pay well?"

"Mom!"

"What?" Diana raises her hands. "I'm just trying to gauge if he can provide for you in the future."

Rose grunts. "I'll have a job too, you know?"

"That," I say, pointing at Rose. "But also yes, it pays well. And I have invested most of my professional salary, so Rose and you won't lack anything."

This makes her drop the hot dog she was assembling on the table. "Me?"

"Rose told me you two are very close." I scratch my head, wondering if I screwed up already.

"We are, but I thought Americans don't give a hoot about the in-laws."

I'm aware all of a sudden that at some point, my hand fell between Rose's thighs and I've been running my thumb up and down her skin. I stop before this catches Diana's attention, and make a plan to just put my arm around Rose when Diana's back is to us again.

"Well, my father is Korean and I grew up more closely to his side." After all, Korea is an easier trip from California than Sweden. "And uh, Koreans are very doting to their elders."

"Then, are you?" Her eyebrows rise.

I take a deep breath. "Not to my own elders, I guess."

Her eyes shift to her daughter, who says, "It's very complicated. Logan's family is…"

"They're abusive and I cut them off." They both look at me in shock for different reasons. Diana because no doubt she didn't expect this. But Rose probably because she didn't think I'd put it so bluntly. I try my best to appear nonchalant but make circles in the sand with my other hand.

Finally, Diana clicks her tongue. "Good for you. And you're more than welcome into my family, but not because of your money."

"Thanks?" I say when she adds no further color to that.

"That's it?" Rose's jaw drops. "No more invasive questions? He's approved already?"

Diana heads our way with two paper plates heaping with loaded hot dogs and a potato salad, wooden forks wedged into them. As we take them from her hands she says, "I didn't really need to. I know that he's a good one based on what you've told me about him."

My lips twitch a little but I say nothing.

"A good one?" Rose scoffs and reaches for a hot dog. "He's the best one. A completely wild catch. A bit shortsighted at times but eh, no one's really perfect."

I can feel the rare phenomenon of heat in my cheeks, and I busy myself with biting into my hot dog. Flavors punch me in the mouth and I realize this isn't your run-of-the-mill dog, but chorizo. Fortunately, even they pour their interest on their food, and for a solid half hour we do more chewing or drinking lemonade than talking.

After lunch, Diana laments that beaches here aren't as good as the ones in her home country, with truly crystal clear water and white sand. Oddly, she misses that back there people can play music on their radios as loud as they want, but I think that would overwhelm me. They agree to introduce me to some guy named Oscar, and it takes me a few beats to realize that they're talking about some singer and not a person, which makes them guffaw at my expense.

I don't mind it at all, though. Rose's mother is as easy going as described—talkative, buoyant, and friendly. Nothing that Rose has said indicates that this personality may change behind closed doors, the way I was conditioned by my parents, and I can feel myself relaxing the more time I spend in Diana's presence.

I've never thought this about someone else, but I'm so damn glad that Rose grew up with healthy, loving parents, and that the only big suffering they gave her was losing one early.

It's why Rose is the smart, fun, and empathic person that she is. It's why I love her.

*

Later, her mom has headed home for a moment to use the restroom and it's just Rose and I under the sun. She's tucked against me, her head on my healed shoulder while one hand lazily takes turns playing on my chest or my stomach. Then she finds one of the scars on my side, hidden from sight by the tattoos, but not to the touch. The scar is more of an indent than a relief, but she keeps running the tip of her finger softly over it.

"Will you tell me everything one day?" she whispers.

Lifting my head from the towel, I press a kiss on her forehead. "I can tell you everything right now if you want."

"No, later." She shakes her head, curls brushing my skin with the movement. "I'm happy right now and I think if you tell me, I'd book a flight to go beat up your parents."

"Fair." Shifting, I turn on my side so I can face her. She naturally tips her head back to look at me. "I can tell you something else instead."

"Hmm?" She hums the same way I did back to her earlier.

"That I love you," I say without much ceremony. "Maybe it's too soon, but I'm pretty sure this is what that is, and I thought you should know."

"Thank you for the news that I definitely needed." I still as her leg slides over mine, the friction setting off more sparks than the fireworks to come. A slow grin stretches her pink lips. "And also, I love you too, and I don't give a rat's ass that it might be early. We don't have to go at other people's pace."

"Agreed." I run my hand from her waist, over the strap of her bikini at her hip, and down her thigh. Then I hike it higher. "I quite like our pace. Not too slow and not too fast. Just right."

Rose swallows with difficulty and bites that thick lower lip that drives me wild. "Wait, what were we talking about again?"

I bark a laugh, just overcome by the effect we have on each other—pure joy, like I had never known it before. And if that's not right, I wouldn't know what right is.

# EPILOGUE

## DECEMBER

I walk into Logan's apartment and I immediately know something's up.

It's too quiet, to the point where the only sounds are the soft buzzing of the A/C and the fridge. He said he'd be home by the time I arrived and normally when this happens, he greets me with a smothering hug and a scorching kiss that weakens my knees.

"Logan?" My voice echoes right back at me, and I detect the edge of concern in it.

This one time, I walked in to find him in the middle of a full blown episode in the living room. Later, when I got the story from him, he said that he'd been stretching while listening to an audiobook that he didn't know should've had trigger warnings. And triggered he got.

But he's not there either.

I leave my purse on the kitchen counter and toe off my sneakers, treading on socks across the apartment toward his room, my senses on high alert. I open his bedroom door slowly, in case he's napping or something. But I peep and confirm that the bed is perfectly made, sans gorgeous man. Swinging the door wider, I wait for shower sounds but there's also silence from the bathroom.

Right as I'm about to pull up my phone to call him, there's an explosion.

I scream and whirl around. But it wasn't really an explosion, it was a bunch of party poppers going off at the same time—from the hands of my friends spilling from the guest bedroom.

"Congratulations!"

Logan emerges from between them, holding a cake with sparkly candles on it. I stare, mystified because it's not my birthday.

"What's happening?" I ask, my jaw hanging.

Behind him, Audrey and Hope unfurl a banner and the guys help to raise it up. The answer is clear then, because the banner says *Congratulations on Your New Broadcasting Job!*

"Oh!" I cover my mouth with my hands. "You guys—you didn't have to."

"But we wanted to." Lucky winks at me.

Miguel nods. "It's a big milestone."

"We're proud of you, princess," says Cade.

"For the record," Logan says with a deadpanned expression. "I told them to say that."

Chuckling, I circle around the cake and rise on my tiptoes to peck his cheek. But at the last second he turns his head and our lips meet instead. Sneaky man.

"Thank you. And I know you're proud of me too, you've only told me—oh, a trillion times."

He motions at the cake that literally has *I'm proud of you* spelled out in icing over it. I can't help but cackling like a hyena at that.

It's kind of bittersweet to leave my social media role behind. I won't get to ask fun, silly questions to the guys, or film thirst traps for the internet girlies. But I still get to travel with the team and interview them with more meaningful questions. I get to support the history and records team with new developments, and moreover, I get to show my face on camera. One day I'll be an anchorwoman for a sports channel and this is the start of my new dream.

And I get to do it right next to my dream man. How did I get so lucky?

It's hard to think that a year ago I was being cheated on by the guy I thought I wanted to be with, and that I've been able to leave that heartache well behind. I couldn't have done that without my friends or Logan.

We hang out in his living room, eating cake because it's the offseason and the guys are allowed to deviate from their strict diets. The one who seems happiest about this is Miguel, but instead of finishing his ginormous slice, he packs most of it away for his daughter like the teddy bear dad that he is.

Logan is the first one to grow impatient, and at first I don't get why he's fidgeting so much until I see him jerk his head at Lucky.

The Boricua's eyes light up with understanding. He claps his hands loud and reaches for his crutches by the couch. "Well, I think it's about time to head out."

"What? But it's only like six." Cade's eyebrows rise.

"Dude." Lucky looks at Logan and I, then back.

"Ohh. Right." Cade turns to Hope. "Yeah, we should go too. Didn't we say we're having pizza for dinner?"

Hope appears confused. "Did we?"

"Yep, we did. We decided on the way here."

Of his own volition, Miguel says, "Marty said she wanted some help with her homework after softball practice."

"What kind of help?" Audrey asks as she also gets up from

the carpet. "Because if it's math, you're not the right guy for the job."

"After you, sugar," Lucky says, adopting Cade's nickname for Audrey and hopping aside for her to pass first.

I watch, amused that the one who said she wanted nothing to do with men, ended up picking one of those guys, when I wouldn't have imagined that he would be the right fit for her.

After farewells—more enthusiastic from me than from Logan—I close the apartment door and turn. My boyfriend's not behind me but still sitting on the carpet in the living room, his back resting against the foot of the couch, head tipped back on the seat. He raises a hand and motions at me to join him.

Now that we're alone, I decide to stop acting demure altogether.

I skip over and instead of sitting beside him, I swing a leg and lower myself to his lap. My legs are curled around his and I lace my hands behind his neck. "Hola."

Logan's eyebrows rise, but his hands get with the program right away. He grabs my butt and pushes it—me—closer. "Hey," he returns in that deep voice of his that drives me wild.

"What's the plan for the rest of the evening then? I eat frost off you?" I ask, smiling sweetly.

He snorts, a smirk curving his delectable lips. "I have something else in mind before that."

"I'm all ears and nerve endings."

This makes the smirk transform into a full grin. His hands leave my butt to rise toward my back, and I'm only mildly disappointed that he didn't sneak them under my sweater.

"I have something for you," Logan murmurs. Rather than the saucy addition I expect, instead he presents one of his hands.

I stare at it.

More accurately, at the thing laying on it.

I look into Logan's eyes, deep and bright and full of all the love that also resides in mine. "I don't have a grand speech because I didn't want to recruit the guys for it this time."

"Understandable." I nod seriously. "It's a very private moment."

"Exactly. And also, I don't have fully altruistic reasons."

"Is that so?" I tilt my head.

"The simple fact is that I want you all for myself. I'm willing to share you with your mom and our friends, but I want the lion's share for myself. And I want the whole world to know that."

"Oh, so this is because my finger is going to be visible on camera?" I ask with a hum.

"That's right." His pretty face sours. "I need to be hired full time to beat guys off you."

I lean down and press my lips on his for a quick kiss. When I pull away, I don't go too far at all. "You do understands that this means I'll also put a ring on your finger and claim you in front of the whole world, right?"

"It's a fair trade," he whispers against my lips. "And I know we've only been dating for six months but—"

"It's right."

He repeats those two words as well. "And you can keep your last name too, I like it better than mine."

"Fine by me." I twirl strands of hair from his nape. "When are you thinking?"

"Whenever you want. We can take our time planning a grand affair, or have a smaller but quicker wedding."

"Smaller and quicker." I nod.

He bites his smile. "Destination wedding or here?"

"Here. We save the destination for the honey moon."

"Deal." Logan shakes his head. "Wait, is this a yes?"

I smack his shoulder. "It's a heck yes, Logan. Would I be making plans otherwise?"

He reaches forward and captures my mouth in a searing

kiss, pressing me against him by the small of my back, and making me squeal with delight. Without breaking apart, he feels around until he finds my left hand and slowly, still devouring my mouth, he slides the engagement ring on my finger.

The silver band with a soft purple rock fits perfectly, and I laugh into his mouth when I remember that he was planning for this precise design since we started dating.

That's what I get for dating a guy who lives in his brain, and now it's my life mission to get him out of it and teach him how to smell the roses. Or the lavender, now that he has tattooed it on his belly.

I slide my hands under his flannel shirt to feel precisely that, to remind myself with the heat of his skin that this is not a dream. Logan is real and what we have is the real deal, that he might've saved my life once but I'm the one who made the real wild catch.

**THE END**

*

***Turn to the next page to read a bonus scene from Logan's point of view!***

# BONUS SCENE

## LOGAN

"**H**ey, sexy. Are you here by yourself?"

I tear my eyes away from the blurb of the book in my hand, and get stricken by the vision in front of me. She's in skin-tight leather pants, matching boots, and a tiny leather jacket that's unzipped to reveal a hell of a lot of cleavage. There are two hot coffees in her hands, one clearly for me.

"I'm afraid I am," I respond smoothly. "My wife is with me."

"Is she the jealous type?" the woman asks with a sultry smile.

"Super jealous. You better watch out if you wanna keep your teeth."

She throws her head back and laughs. "Damn, I've trained you well."

A grin stretches my lips. "I haven't forgotten how you threatened that woman at our honeymoon."

"Please." Rolling her eyes, Rose passes along one of the

coffees to me. "She was trying to grope you. She was lucky I didn't send her to the hospital."

"Indeed." I smell my coffee from the little sipping vent at the lid. "Thanks, by the way."

"You got it, americano with oat milk for you, lavender latte for me." Delighted, she takes a big drag of the steam rising from her cup, before pointing at the book in my hands with her lips. "Anyway, found something good?"

I lift up the completely absurd cover to her. "Monster romance, can you believe this?"

Rose's jaw drops. "What even is monster romance?"

"I don't know, but I'm going to find out." I toss it into our cart. "What are you getting?"

"Do you even have to ask? I'm a historical romance girlie through and through."

I sigh. "I'm tired of reading about dukes and shit. I think I'm going to relate to the monsters better."

"I plead the fifth," she says, not without sweeping a strategic glance down at me. "Get some vampire romances too. Those are fun and you do like to bite."

A corner of my lips rises because this is very true. I didn't know that about myself until our honeymoon. "Fine, it might give me some new ideas."

"Trust me, you don't need new ideas."

"Excuse me," I tease back. "Are you flirting with a married man?"

"Yes, I am. It just so happens that it's my favorite pastime."

I set my cup of coffee on the bookshelf and carefully grab hers to do the same. Rosalina watches me, amused and anticipating. It wouldn't be the first time I hit on her in the romance section of the bookstore, tucked far away from the main entrance, and in a low traffic corner. Whoever designed this store was a freaking genius.

I walk her until her back comes up to the opposite shelf,

and brace myself against the rack of Amish romances. My finger slides down her throat and to her chest, and keeps going.

"Has anyone told you that you're really freaking hot?" I whisper.

"Yeah, a certain someone tells me daily." She runs her hands up my chest until she finds the zipper tab of my jacket, pulling down at it slowly to minimize the noise. It might be winter, but the Florida version of it, and my winter leather jacket is really damn hot, so underneath I'm wearing one of those tank tops with deep cutouts that make Rose salivate.

She grabs my sides and I know we're a go.

I capture her lips in mine and she moans, arching into me and surrendering right away. She's already had a taste of her coffee, and I run my tongue across her lips in a slow, languid swipe, until the flavor is engrained. Her lips part and I take the invitation with no hesitation.

While her tongue comes out to play, her hands grope at my sides with dedication. She lets them travel, one to my chest and one to my back—and that one scratches me slightly.

Now I'm the one groaning and it makes her chuckle. "You bite but I scratch, perfect match, huh?"

"Oh yeah," I say with a guttural voice. I slide my hand up from her chest to hold her neck and tip her head back. I feather hot, wet kisses across her jaw, working down the column of her throat and to her chest. And I keep going.

Now she clutches at my hair, which is how I know it's getting way too good for us to continue. I take a few swipes with my tongue, tasting the salt of her skin and feeling her tremble, before straightening to my full height for a more PG-rated kiss.

Of course, that's when I notice we're not alone.

I stop and turn to the employee supposed to be stacking books on the shelves. She's staring openly at us, mouth wide and face as red as a tomato. "Um, sorry," she squeaks.

"Oh my word." Rose hides her face in my chest and her voice comes out muffled as she says, "We should be the ones apologizing."

"No, no. Carry on. Um…" The woman does a double take. "But maybe keep the clothes on, okay?"

I nod calmly. "Will do, thanks." I wait until she's gone before turning to my wife. Or to the top of her head, more like. "She's gone. Do we continue or do we do what we came here for and *then* continue at home?"

"The latter. Definitely the latter." Clearing her throat, Rose pushes me away and I catch the glint of her engagement and wedding ring as she reaches for our coffees.

Sighing, I stare at her perfect ass for a second longer before retrieving my cup and going back to browsing. But neither of us are that much into it anymore. Instead of buying thirty books between the two of us, like we planned to do, we leave the store with just five in her backpack. She's *my* backpack on the way back home, and her hands are completely inappropriate during the drive.

I love it. But that's because I love her. I make sure to tell her as much for the rest of the evening, and plan to do so for the rest of our lives on this earth.

*

*Thank you for reading* **Wild Catch***! I hope you can take a brief moment to leave a review on Amazon.*

*Preorder* **Wild Hit***, the third and last book in the Wild Baseball Romance series featuring Audrey and her mystery man.*

*You can also read* **Wild Pitch***, the first book in the series that features Hope and Cade.*

*Turn to the next page to see my other works.*

# MORE FROM THE AUTHOR

## WILD BASEBALL ROMANCE

· Wild Pitch · Wild Catch · Wild Hit* ·

## *SPORTY* CHRISTMAS ROMANCE

· Mistlefoe ·

## ST. CLOUD HOCKEY SERIES

· Faceoff · Overtime · Shutout ·

## VOLLEYBALL ROMANCE NOVELLA

· Set Me Up** ·

*Coming soon.
**Newsletter exclusive.

# GLOSSARY OF SPANISH VOCABS

## Chapter 1

- Tú puedes: you can do it.

## Chapter 4

- Aquí: here.

## Chapter 5

- ¡Mala mía!: my bad!
- Ay bendito, casi te mato: oh blessed, I almost killed you.

## Chapter 6

- Tacos de flor de calabaza: pumpkin flower tacos (yes, flower—not flour).

## Chapter 7

- Mierda: crap/shit (see also Chapter 35, 37 and 39).

## Chapter 9

- Mi Mamá: my mom.
- ¡Sí, mija!: yes, my little daughter! (see also Chapter 46).
- Papito: 'daddy' but not in the weird way.

## Chapter 10

- Pendejo: dipshit (male).

## Chapter 11

- Princesa: princess (see also Chapter 29 and 36).

## Chapter 15

- Cojones: men's dangly bits (see also Chapter 36).

## Chapter 19

- Mamacita: hot mamma.

## Chapter 23

- Para, Rosalina: stop, Rosalina.
- La chancla: the flip flop every Latin American kid gets acquainted with at least once (see also Chapter 27).

## Chapter 26

- Tres leches: three milks cake.

## Chapter 27

- Espérate: wait.
- Mijita: my little daughter.
- Chiquita: little one.

## Chapter 33

- Bésame: kiss me.

## Chapter 39

- No bueno: not good in terrible grammar fashion.

## Chapter 45

- Correcto, mi amor: correct, my love.

## Epilogue

- Hola: hi.

# ACKNOWLEDGMENTS

This is officially my sixth book (under this name, IYKYK), and I *know* that I'm super repetitive with my acknowledgments, but what can I say? I'm steady as a rock and also, it's because these are all my rocks:

As always, I first have to thank the Lord. Contigo todo, sin ti nada.

To Tara Lush and Avery Keelan, who believe in me more than I do, and who have more patience than they think (otherwise they wouldn't be able to put up with all my yapping, lol).

To Enni at Yummy Book Covers who is an absolute delight to work with in every sense. Sorry for making your life more complicated with the similar titles (Wild Pitch to Wild Catch, seriously, Mari?!).

To my ARC team and to Lindsey. Y'all are my engine and without you I'm just a stalled car. (I tried to come up with a baseball allegory but the mechanical engineer in me reared its head instead).

To my cheerleaders: you're my safe space. I know that I can ask you random market research questions in the middle of the night and that you won't be weirded out. That's the real deal.

Last but not least, I want to thank my mom, my sister, and my dad up in heaven. Thank you for encouraging me to never give up. Los amo con todo.

# ABOUT THE AUTHOR

**Mari Loyal** was born and raised in Venezuela, a baseball country that only cared about another sport, football soccer, every four years. As such, she decided to make hockey her whole personality because she had to make a point of being different. These days she no longer suffers from Not Like Other Girls syndrome and is very happy to be in the sports romance fandom. She writes closed door romance with a Latin American flair and an abundance of cinnamon rolls heroes. She also enjoys eating cinnamon rolls (the confections), in her spare time.

**Find her:**

Website & Newsletter mariloyal.com

Instagram mariloyalauthor

Threads mariloyalauthor